Praise for

The Road to Paradise

"Don't miss Karen Barnett's new release *The Road to Paradise*. This novel combines endearing characters taking on big challenges, nail-biting moments hoping that the land developer doesn't win the day, the magnificent setting in the national park at Mount Rainier, and happiness that there will be more books like this one. Keep it up, Karen."

—LAURAINE SNELLING, best-selling author of the acclaimed
Red River of the North series and many other novels

"A story as invigorating, inspiring, and perilous as Mount Rainier itself! *The Road to Paradise* by Karen Barnett pulled me in with humor and fascinating characters and a delicious romance, then kept me up late as Ford and Margie strive to save the national park that seems determined to kill them. The author's experiences as a park ranger give this novel both authenticity and passion, and I can't wait for her next national parks book!"

—SARAH SUNDIN, award-winning author of *When Tides Turn*

"Karen Barnett has done it again: held me hostage from the first page and made me like it. This seasoned author takes us to new heights as we encounter stories behind the formation of our national parks. Great characters, precise and fascinating images, a plot that kept me turning pages. *The Road to Paradise* is a top-notch novel that will remind readers of why we love our national parks and make us want to visit every single one, envisioning where the characters found their faith, friendships, and love. But I don't plan to climb Mount Rainer . . . this author already did it for me!"

—JANE KIRKPATRICK, award-winning author of *This Road We Traveled*

"A true delight. With its expertly rendered setting of breathtaking beauty and danger, combined with charming characters and a swiftly moving plot, *The Road to Paradise* is a journey worth taking more than once!"

—JOCELYN GREEN, award-winning author of *The Mark of the King*

"The majesty of Mount Rainier shines in Karen Barnett's lush novel. The story is both gentle and inviting, with a warmth that meanders its way along every page and a setting that captivates. Barnett's broad brushstrokes pay homage to a magnificent landscape, yet her gentle sketches draw the reader's heart to the intricacies of God's creation—not only in nature itself, but in the human heart."

—JOANNE BISCHOF, author of *The Lady and the Lionheart*, RT Book Reviews 5 Star Top Pick!

"As fresh as the northwest woods, *The Road to Paradise* is just that, a reading adventure replete with romance, suspense, and poetic prose, all wrapped in a gorgeous vintage cover. Having lived and worked in the national parks, I found this novel to ring with authenticity and spirit. Karen Barnett does credit to one of America's most picturesque historic places. Well done!"

—LAURA FRANTZ, author of *A Moonbow Night*

The Road to PARADISE

BOOKS BY KAREN BARNETT

FICTION

Mistaken

The Golden Gate Chronicles

Out of the Ruins

Beyond the Ashes

Through the Shadows

The Road to PARADISE

A VINTAGE NATIONAL PARKS NOVEL

KAREN BARNETT

WATERBROOK

ROAD TO PARADISE

Scripture quotations are taken from the King James Version and the New King James Version®. Copyright © 1982 by Thomas Nelson Inc. Used by permission. All rights reserved.

This is a work of fiction. Apart from well-known people, events, and locales that figure into the narrative, all names, characters, places, and incidents are the products of the author's imagination or are used fictitiously.

Trade Paperback ISBN 978-0-7352-8954-3
eBook ISBN 978-0-7352-8955-0

Copyright © 2017 by Karen Barnett

Cover design and illustration by Mark D. Ford

Published in the United States by WaterBrook, an imprint of the Crown Publishing Group, a division of Penguin Random House LLC, New York.

WATERBROOK® and its deer colophon are registered trademarks of Penguin Random House LLC.

Library of Congress Cataloging-in-Publication Data
Names: Barnett, Karen, 1969- author.
Title: The road to paradise / Karen Barnett.
Description: First edition. | Colorado Springs, Colorado : WaterBrook, 2017. | Series: A vintage national parks novel
Identifiers: LCCN 2017004475 (print) | LCCN 2017011094 (ebook) | ISBN 9780735289543 (softcover) | ISBN 9780735289550 (e-book) | ISBN 9780735289550 (electronic)
Subjects: LCSH: Mount Rainier National Park (Wash.)—Fiction. | Man-woman relationships—Fiction. | Park rangers—Fiction. | BISAC: FICTION / Christian / Historical. | FICTION / Christian / Romance. | FICTION Christian / Suspense. | GSAFD: Christian fiction. | Love stories.
Classification: LCC PS3602.A77584 R63 2017 (print) | LCC PS3602.A77584 (ebook) | DDC 813/.6—dc23
LC record available at https://lccn.loc.gov/2017004475

Printed in the United States of America
2017—First Edition

10 9 8 7 6 5 4 3 2 1

In memory of Shelley Eddleman.
Thank you for sharing your love of books, tea,
gardens, and especially the Lord.
Your influence lives on through your students.

"You can never get a cup of tea large enough or
a book long enough to suit me."
—C. S. Lewis

Of all the fire-mountains which, like beacons, once blazed along the Pacific Coast, Mount Rainier is the noblest.

—John Muir, *Our National Parks* (1901)

ONE

June 1, 1927

Mount Rainier National Park
Ashford, Washington

*T**he promised view of the mountain peak waited, cloaked in mist
like a tissue-wrapped gift not ready to be unveiled.* Margie Lane
drew a small, leather-bound journal from her pocket and braced it against
her knee to jot down the words flooding her mind. The lush treetops in
the valley below inspired her. Twisting sideways in the automobile seat for
a better view, she tucked her skirt tight under her calves and then placed
pencil to paper.

As Superintendent Harry Brown guided the old truck around a bend
in the gravel road, Margie scrawled a jerky line across the linen page. She
bit her lip and tucked the book back into her pocket. Best wait to record
the thoughts tonight after she'd settled in.

The vista sent a shiver across her skin as she composed more lines for
her evening log, storing them in her memory. *Droplets hanging from each*

fir needle like so many diamonds. She frowned. Diamonds were her mother's business. *Beads of dew, each a tiny mirror reflecting the brilliance of the mountain sky.* She filled her lungs with the cold, moist air, heavy with the fragrance of ferns and trees. No jewels could compare to the majesty of God's creation.

As a child she'd dreamed of living and working in Mount Rainier National Park, a park her father had campaigned to create. In time she realized that the daughters of United States senators didn't run off to live in the woods. They endured a slow death at the hand of high-society parties and tedious political functions.

But one fact remained—Philip wouldn't think to look for her here. Margie brushed knuckles across her cheekbone, the skin still tender. Her throat tightened at the memory.

The superintendent glanced at her with a smile. "Enjoying the scenery, Miss Lane?"

She dropped her hand, her fingers landing on the simple pearl necklace she'd chosen to bring on this adventure. "It's breathtaking. How much farther?"

"Only about fifteen minutes. I'll take you to headquarters, and you can meet the rangers."

Margie's heart jumped. She'd longed to meet the stalwart men of the mountains since she'd first turned the pages of Thoreau, Emerson, and Muir. Surely the men of whom Superintendent Brown spoke—the caretakers of Longfellow's forest primeval—would approve of her desire to shake off the trappings of the material world and immerse herself in the simplicity of God's creation. They needn't know the rest. "How many rangers work at the park?"

He pushed back his hat and glanced at the sky. "The whole park? We have six permanent rangers and bring on seventeen or eighteen more during the summer months. You'll be working with Chief Ranger Brayden, getting things ready for the camping season."

The first man she'd need to impress. Hopefully she'd memorized enough botany and zoology books to suffice. Margie tightened the scarf around her shoulders as the cool spring air teased her neck beneath the edge of her cloche hat. "Has he worked long for the National Park Service?"

Superintendent Brown snorted. "Ford was born on this mountain, and he'll probably die on this mountain—like his father before him. The park service couldn't find a better man to look after this land."

"Ford?"

"He goes by Ford. Ashford Brayden is his rightful name. Can't think of anyone who calls him that, though."

"Didn't we just pass a town named Ashford?"

The superintendent nodded. "His parents were friendly with the Ashford family, the folks who homesteaded the area."

Margie sighed. Ranger Brayden—born on a mountain, untainted by human society. He sounded like the embodiment of Rousseau's noble savage. "I'm positive we'll get along splendidly."

Ford grunted as he swung the double-blade ax, sending yellow chips scattering. The spindly fir listed across the road at a steep angle, its root wad torn from the soggy ground during the storm. A massive cedar on the far side had broken the smaller tree's fall, and now it hung like a drunken man draped over a friend's shoulders. After a few more blows from the ax, the wood creaked. Ford jumped clear as the tree crashed the rest of the way to the muddy road. He wiped his grimy fist across his brow before slogging down the slope.

Steam rose from the warm back of the waiting Belgian. Athena stamped her hoof on the gravel-covered hardpan.

Walt Jennings wrapped a chain around the gnarled trunk. "That makes six trees we've cleared between here and Narada Falls today. I thought it'd take all day to open this stretch after last night's blow." He snapped the fasteners and straightened. "What's stoked the fire under you?"

Ford grasped the horse's bridle. "We could have campers this weekend. Those city folk get perturbed when their fancy automobiles can't make it up to Paradise."

"I enjoyed pulling that roadster out of the wash last week. That fellow was pretty hot under the collar seeing his flashy two-seater up to its fenders in mud."

Ford clucked to the mare. The animal snorted once before dragging the log to the far embankment. "Just means more work for us."

"We see more of those folks every year. Last summer their cars and tents were parked higgledy-piggledy all over the meadows."

Ford sighed. He understood Jennings's concern. Additional people and automobiles meant extra mess and noise. The society folks brought their city ways right to the mountain's flanks without ever considering the dangers. They desired a simple diversion, a taste of freedom before departing in a swirling cloud of exhaust.

Wilderness showed no mercy, no favoritism. He knew that fact too well.

As the log teetered on the edge of the road, Ford bent to unhook the chain. Giving the log a shove with his boot, he sent the timber crashing into the ravine, snapping a small sapling in its path. He glanced at the misty sky. The clouds were burning off, and the mountain threatened to make an appearance. He couldn't wait to get back to headquarters, prop his feet on the porch rail, and inhale a strong cup of coffee. Likely as not, Jennings would head to his cabin to read. That suited Ford just fine.

A quiet afternoon alone with his mountain? Nothing could be better.

Superintendent Brown parked the automobile near a cluster of quaint buildings, just six miles past the park entrance. Margie stepped off the running board and sighed as her new calfskin boots sank into the muck. They'd been far too clean anyway. Perhaps a few smudges of God's good earth would improve them. Hopefully it would improve her as well.

Best of all, staying out here in the wilderness would keep her safe.

The superintendent banged the car door shut. "Welcome to Longmire, or as we fondly refer to it—Quagmire. In the summertime, most folks like to continue on up the hill to Paradise, but we keep the headquarters here. The Paradise meadows are pretty enough in July and August, but we'd be buried to our necks in snow during the winter."

She glanced around the settlement. Whatever jokes the man might make, Longmire's charm couldn't be denied. The limbs of the towering hemlock and fir trees hung low over the squat wooden buildings, roofs were coated with dead needles, and curls of smoke rose from stone chimneys. The National Park Inn, with a wide porch running nearly the full length of the building, stood out in particular. "It's lovely."

"The Longmire family homesteaded here and built a mineral-springs resort. When the park was established in 1899, the administration made quite a few improvements to the area. Lately we've added a couple of new structures, but we hope to make more changes in the future. Big plans. You might mention that to your father." The stocky fellow hitched up his trousers and smoothed his green jacket.

"I'll do that."

"Of course, it's not at all like you're accustomed to, living in Tacoma and Washington, DC."

Margie tightened the belt of her wool cardigan as a tremor raced through her shoulders. Thanks to her father's connections, she stood on sacred ground. She didn't like to think what sorts of steps he'd taken to make it happen. "I'm certain I'll adapt, sir. I've anticipated this adventure my entire adult life."

The corners of his lips twitched, and he turned away with a slow shake of the head. "If you say so. Let's go inside. I'm sure Ranger Brayden will be delighted to meet you."

As if on cue, a tall figure appeared in the doorway. Ducking under the low frame, the man stepped onto the wooden porch. "Superintendent—I wasn't expecting you today. You brought a guest."

Margie froze midstep. The man facing her resembled nothing short of a Greek Adonis—his blond hair glinting in the filtered rays of light, eyes grayer than a bitter tempest. If her imagination had dreamed up such a visage, it couldn't have done a better job.

Superintendent Brown placed a hand behind Margie's back and gestured to the stairs.

The mud released her feet with only a minor squelch of protest, and Margie climbed the three stone steps to the porch, her heart pounding. Here was the man who would teach her the mysteries of the forest, the secrets of the mountain—her spiritual guide into the divine wilds.

The superintendent shook the ranger's extended hand. "Ford, I have someone for you to meet. This is Miss Margaret Lane, and she's going to join you fellows for a spell."

The ranger's eyes narrowed, lips thinning to a line above his rugged chin. "What do you mean?"

Margie pressed a smile to her face. "Ranger Brayden, it is such an honor to meet you."

The man dragged a hand through his hair, brows drawing low. He gave her a quick nod. "Nice to make your acquaintance, Miss." He turned back to the superintendent. "I don't understand. Joining us?"

Superintendent Brown cleared his throat. "Miss Lane, why don't you step inside and have a seat. Ranger Brayden and I will be with you in a moment."

Margie swallowed as she pulled her attention from the ranger's stern face, her stomach quivering. His reaction left little room for doubt: her presence was not welcome.

He stepped back and pushed open the door for her to enter.

She brushed past, the overwhelming odors of sweat and sawdust speeding her steps. A crackling blaze in the stone fireplace warmed the room, casting an amber glow across the dim interior. Two wooden rockers sat together like close companions, and a rag rug softened the plank floor. A ledger sat open on a table. One chair stood askew from the other five, as if Ranger Brayden had been seated before coming to greet them.

A narrow stairway led up to what must be a small loft. The ranger's office, perhaps? The building seemed cramped for park headquarters, but perhaps these men didn't spend much time indoors.

She wandered over to the hearth, running her fingers across the smooth gray stones. Volcanic andesite, probably hewn straight from the mountain, like Ranger Brayden himself. Doubt curled around her heart. Who was she to think she might belong here? Mama had argued against Margie's decision, and running home would only prove her right.

She lowered herself into one of the waiting rockers, the chair creaking as she sat. She'd do whatever it took to prove herself worthy of this position.

After all, going home was not an option.

"Harry, she won't last a day." Ford dug his fingers against the weathered porch rail.

"Lower your voice; she'll hear you."

Ford spun, grinding his heel into the floorboards. "I don't care what she hears. What were you thinking?"

Superintendent Brown raised his hands. "Give me a minute to explain." He pulled off his large hat, smacking the brim against his palm. "I know you're not going to approve, but frankly the brass don't care. We're struggling to make ends meet. The feds make the rules, but they don't like to pay the bills."

"What do bills have to do with this woman?" A twinge pulled at his neck, already sore from poring over the ledger books. He didn't need Harry to tell him they were in trouble.

Brown stepped close, glancing toward the doorway before returning his attention to Ford. "Her daddy's Senator Thomas Lane. When a wealthy tycoon with Washington connections asks you a favor—"

"And greases your palm?"

His boss scowled. "Let's say, a few donations crossed my desk. Not for my pocket—for new park facilities. We're stretched thin after putting up the new community center in the campground. And you still want that administration building by next year?"

Ford lifted his head, staring up at the moss-blanketed roof. The building wasn't that old, but it had been poorly planned. His father had dreamed of erecting a two-story log building with a wide porch designed to welcome weary travelers. If only they had the money. "What are we supposed to do with her?"

Brown folded his arms across his ample girth. "She's working for you, even if her father is paying the bills. She can make nice with the visitors, teach them about the flowers, the trees. The senator assures me she's very knowledgeable." He grunted, jerking his chin toward the small parking area. "She can give Jennings a hand with the naturalist programs. Let her give some talks, show people around. Quote poetry." He rolled his eyes. "Trust me—I heard plenty on the way up here."

Ford pinched the bridge of his nose. "How long? And where's she going to stay?" A young, dark-haired beauty living among his men? It sounded like a recipe for disaster.

"You've got empty quarters, and I'm betting she'll be ready to return to civilization in a few weeks. But Ford, don't do anything to hurry things along. We don't want her running home to Daddy in tears. Understand?"

As a Douglas squirrel chattered in a nearby tree, the sound rattled in Ford's head along with his boss's demands. "This scheme is doomed and you know it, Harry. I'm not the man for this job—entertaining little rich girls? I'm not cut from that sort of cloth." His mouth went dry. "It's bad enough we have to pander to the townsfolk who come out on the weekends—now they can demand work?"

"You want to keep your job? Continue living here in the park?" Brown's bushy eyebrows folded inward. "Find a way to make it work. Show her a good time." He snorted, a smirk pulling at the corners of his mouth. "Who knows? Maybe she can turn you into a gentleman."

Ford gritted his teeth. "Unlikely."

TWO

*F*ord hoisted the lady's trunk from the rear bumper of the superintendent's vehicle. The weight caught him off guard, and the box slid from his grip, dropping into the dirt. Muck splattered across his boots. "What have you got in this thing? Granite?"

Miss Lane blinked at him with deep brown eyes. With the hat framing her pale face, the woman resembled a cornered barn owl. "I wasn't sure what I would need, so I erred on the side of caution. Likely as not, I overpacked. I usually do, I'm afraid."

He reached around the box with both arms, grasping the leather handles before heaving it to his shoulder, smearing his uniform with mud. "I didn't know dresses weighed so much."

The woman laughed, her lips forming an impish smile. "Not dresses. Books. I brought *Forests of Mount Rainier National Park, The Glacier Playfields of the Mount Rainier National Park, Features of the Flora of—*"

"I see. Well, there's only so much you can learn from books." Ford turned and plodded down the path. She may be well read, but he guessed she couldn't tell the difference between a raccoon and a spotted skunk. Might be fun to find out.

She caught up a moment later, her short legs matching his stride. "That's why I was so eager to come and study with you."

"Study . . . with me? I'm no teacher."

"Not with *you,* exactly. But someone like you. One who speaks the language of creation—who can hear the whispers of the waterfalls, see the secrets hidden in the soulful eyes of the black bear . . ." she lifted her hand to gesture to the surrounding forest. "To sit at the feet of a master."

What kind of fairy world had Margaret Lane dropped out of? He looked her up and down. Clearly, she'd never been in close quarters with a bear. Ford turned away, the weight of the box crushing against his shoulder.

Ford's mother had passed when he was just a boy, and he'd spent precious little time with women since. He vaguely remembered her bedtime stories of forest sprites, but this was the first time he'd met anyone meeting their description.

The woman's skirt swished as she trotted at his side. "I'm determined not to waste a minute of this opportunity. I shall soak in the timeless wisdom of the forest primeval." She beamed. "And I shall endeavor to live up to your expectations, just like any other ranger."

Ford halted a few feet from the cabin door. "You are not a ranger. Is that what Harry told you?" The twinge in his spine grew talons.

She took a step back. "Not in so many words. But Superintendent Brown said I'd be working for you, so I assumed—"

"You assumed wrong. A person—a man—has to earn the right to that title. We don't just hand out . . ." Ford caught himself, Harry's warnings still ringing in his ears. "You're not a ranger. Just a—a naturalist. And here on trial, at that." Ford tromped up the cabin steps and dropped the box at the door. The sharp sound echoed through the stillness.

Margie stared at his back. *"A naturalist."* The word coursed out from her heart to her fingertips, like a flower unfurling in the morning light. She clutched the small leather bag containing her journal to her chest. She couldn't wait to record the day's events on its crisp pages. The first thing she'd do would be to inscribe her name on the inside cover. *Margaret Lane, Naturalist.*

She hurried up the steps, her foot slipping on the damp, lichen-crusted wood. Thankfully, the ranger's eyes were focused on the open door. She recovered and joined him in the doorway, peeking around his arm.

A musty scent hung in the still air, the chill of the room untouched by the filtered sunlight outside. A narrow bed and spindly three-legged table sat in one corner, while a bookshelf, desk, and a shabby bureau lined the opposite wall. Wooden shutters covered the lower reaches of the windows, casting shadows across the colorless room. Margie swallowed. If Mama could see this cabin, she'd demand the superintendent's immediate resignation. Good thing she'd never deign to visit.

He grabbed hold of the wooden trunk and dragged its muddy base across the floor. "These quarters haven't been used in a while. Sorry if it's not what you're accustomed to."

Margie took two steps and turned a slow circle. If she aired the room, swept the floor, spread her pink quilt on the sagging mattress—it would still be a hovel. But surely, Thoreau had known worse. "It's quite cozy. Rustic."

His brow lifted. "That's one way of putting it." He glanced at the fireplace. "I'll let you get settled in. Do you need me to light the fire for you?"

"I'm sure I can manage." How hard could it be? Even cave men could build fires. She scanned the room. "Where do you keep the wood?"

"There's a pile out behind headquarters. I'll have one of my men bring you some."

"And—and for cooking?" Margie's stomach twisted. In her urgency, she hadn't thought through all this adventure might entail. Was she to cook over an open fire like a pioneer? Her parents had always employed both a cook and a housekeeper.

"Mrs. Brown cooks for the men at the community kitchen, two doors down. Just listen for the dinner bell."

The stitch of tension in Margie's shoulders eased. "Ah, I see. Good. And when should I report for duty?"

The man scuffed the toe of his boot across the mud tracks as if seeing them for the first time. He pulled off his hat and ran a hand through his short hair, setting it on end. "Tomorrow morning, eight o'clock. We'll head up to Paradise, take a look around before any visitors arrive."

Chills crept up Margie's arms. She'd been to the Paradise Inn once as a child and had dreamed of little else since—a carpet of meadow flowers stretching up to the flanks of the peak, a mountain of impossible grandeur dominating the skyline. She sucked in a quick breath. How would she ever sleep tonight? "'The mountains are calling, and I must go.'"

His forehead furrowed. "What?"

She swallowed. Quotations had a way of springing to her lips before she could stop them. "So said John Muir, the great naturalist."

"Oh." He swiped a hand across his chin. "All right, then. Dress warmly, it's still snowed in."

"I'll be ready."

He gave her a sharp nod, shoved his hat back over his hair, and turned for the door. "Dinner's usually around six-thirty. You can meet the men."

"I'll be changed by then. Thank you."

He hovered in the doorway, mouth open. "We don't . . ." His Adam's apple bounced. "We don't dress for dinner. Nothing special, I mean. It's just supper."

Margie smiled. His awkward fumbling with words was endearing. "I understand." Did he think she was going to show up in an evening gown? She just wanted to put on something warmer than this thin dress. Margie shivered, drawing the sweater snug around her sides.

As the door closed behind the tall fellow, Margie glanced about the stark room, a far cry from her parents' grand home overlooking Commencement Bay. She'd grown up seeing Rainier framed by her bedroom window. Now she'd live on the mountain itself—who cared about the state of the housing? It was a dream come true, regardless of the real reason she came.

She folded back the wooden shutters and stared out at the hemlocks and firs, their supple limbs nearly brushing the glass. Pushing on the casing, she jarred the swollen frame upward. The sweet smell of damp forest flooded her nose, chasing away her doubts. The air might be chilled, but at least it was fragrant.

Margie turned and faced the room. A well-worn broom stood in the corner. She might have been raised with housemaids, but a broom didn't seem too difficult to decipher. After a little effort, she kicked up a choking cloud of dust and succeeded in driving most of it toward the door. The rest escaped through the cracks between the floorboards. An old handkerchief from her trunk proved useful for wiping down the desk and shelves.

Margie tucked her neatly pressed garments into the aging bureau, then hung a few items on pegs embedded in the log walls. Drawing her favorite quilt from the box, she buried her face in the soft folds, losing herself for a moment in the scent of home. She spread the quilt over the bed and topped it with a plump feather pillow.

The room already felt more welcoming. Margie dug into the depths of the box and retrieved handfuls of books. She stroked a finger down each well-loved spine before finding honored places for them on the lonely shelf. She set her three favorites—*Our Greatest Mountain, Flowers of the Sub-Alpine,* and *Wildlife Encounters of the West*—on the small desk, ready for an evening read. She added her Bible, caressing the leather cover before placing it on the wooden surface. At last, she retrieved her satchel, lifting out her journal and the pen and pencil set from Daddy. She placed it on the stack, like the cherry atop an ice-cream soda.

Margie studied her new home. Above her roof were tall, stately fir trees. Inside she had her quilt and books. What more could she need? And best of all, she was miles away from Philip Carmichael. She shivered at the thought. If deer could conceal themselves among the trees, so could she.

Scooping up the journal, she went outside and sat on the stoop. After flipping to the first open page, she sketched a tiny image of her new home and inscribed her favorite Bible verse underneath: "But they that wait upon the LORD shall renew their strength; they shall mount up with wings as eagles; they shall run, and not be weary; and they shall walk, and not faint."

Margie paused and listened to the sounds—wind toying with the evergreen boughs, a squirrel chittering a complaint, the faint buzzing of an insect—the heartbeat of the forest. She closed her journal, sighed, then stood. A playing card dropped from one of the pages, fluttering to the step. Scooping it up, she recognized the distinctive goldfinch pattern from a deck her father kept in his study. He knew how much she loved the design. Had he tucked it in her journal to boost her spirits? She ran a finger across the sweet yellow bird before flipping it over.

Philip's even handwriting across the front of the ace of hearts made her heart stutter.

"Margaret, I hold all the cards."

As Ford pushed away from the table, the red ink in the ledger books seemed to mock him. He hadn't signed on to be a ranger to worry about money. He closed his eyes, letting his thoughts drift back to hiking the Tatoosh Ridge with his dad four years ago, watching his father point out each of Rainier's rocky crags in the distance. *"It's God's mountain, son. We get the honor of watching over her and protecting her."*

No one had protected him, two years later.

That climb. A cold sweat tracked across Ford's skin at the memory, his throat closing. *I should have stopped him.* The mountain cared for no one. Not even its staunchest defender.

Ford clutched his half-empty cup and wandered over to the open door. The late-afternoon sun dropped to the edge of the treetops. High over Rampart Ridge, the white dome of Rainier glowed in the light, and the long shadows accented the texture of its crumpled glaciers.

His father's mountain.

Harry chose the wrong man to fill his dad's boots. Ford wasn't cut out to protect a mountain any more than he could safeguard the people who roamed its flanks.

Ford glanced across the meadow to the ramshackle cabin perched at the far end. His mood lightened as he remembered the woman's dismay at seeing the shack. He'd intended to have the old place pulled down this summer, since they'd built new housing on the other side of Longmire. Hopefully its lack of creature comforts would shorten her stay.

He leaned against the doorframe and sipped the lukewarm coffee as the early evening chill sent shivers across his arms. The last thing he needed was one more person to keep watch over.

THREE

*M*argie burrowed deeper under the covers, the icy air stealing her breath. The wool stockings did little to stave off the chill. She'd already pulled two sweaters over her nightgown, in addition to the wool blanket and quilt. If the stack of wood in the fireplace had cooperated, this wouldn't be a problem. Instead, her palms stung with splinters, and the hearth remained cold.

She blew against her fist, the warm air bringing momentary relief. The cabin might be frostier than an icebox, but at least Philip didn't know where she was. She wouldn't let his menacing words ruin this first night in her mountain hideaway.

A rattle in the darkness scattered Margie's thoughts. She lowered the quilt below her nose and peered into the gloom as weakness spread through her arms and legs. *Someone's in here.*

As if in response to her thought, some*thing* skittered across the floor.

A mouse. Tiny. Harmless. Margie yanked the covers over her head. She could probably survive a prowler of miniature proportions.

The claws scrabbled through the cabin, pausing every few seconds. The more she tried to ignore the disturbance, the harder her ears labored to locate its position. What if it came up on the bed? Did mice climb?

Jump? She hadn't bothered to study the smaller creatures inhabiting the park. Margie rolled to her side, hauling her knees close to her stomach. She'd read up on them tomorrow.

The scratching noise moved again. Was there more than one? She jerked upright. Perhaps if she made some racket, the creatures would leave.

"Go . . ." Margie's voice faltered. She cleared her throat. "Go away. This is my home now, and I'm trying to sleep." She clapped her hands together, the sharp sound cutting through the stillness.

The rustling halted.

The night air penetrated her wool sweater like frosty fingertips. Margie yanked the sweater tight around her arms, shoving her hands under its folds. "Thank you. Good night." Her voice echoed off the log walls.

She flopped back on the bed, gripping the patchwork as a shield against the darkness. *I'm talking to a rodent.* Wiggling her numb toes, she tried not to think of her warm bed at home. Tomorrow she'd find every crevice and stuff each one with rags to prevent nighttime visitors. That might prevent her from freezing, as well.

The skittering renewed, clawing at the corners of Margie's consciousness every time she drifted off. She groaned, folding the pillow around her ears. The padding did little to muffle the new sound—crunching. Mrs. Brown had insisted she take an extra cookie, even though Margie had already eaten enough to feed a whole logging camp. No wonder the mouse had come inside. Who could resist a good snickerdoodle? The men at dinner had carted off handfuls of them.

Margie pushed the blanket aside and swung her feet to the floor. Best retrieve the dessert and toss it outside. Maybe the animal would follow. She reached for the box of matches she'd left on the bedside table after her hopeless encounter with the fireplace. Pushing open the box with clumsy fingers, she fumbled with the small wooden sticks.

The crunching paused, replaced by the scraping of an item being dragged across the desk.

The cheeky little devil's absconding with the entire thing. Margie ripped the match across the rough surface, ignoring the irritating smell of the igniting sulfur. The light flared for a second before fading to a manageable level. She stood, holding the match in her trembling grip.

A pair of beady charcoal eyes stared across the desk at her. The monstrous creature sat on her journal, its girth nearly covering the book's length, her favorite fountain pen clutched between its front paws.

Margie shrieked as the flame died.

Ford jerked upright in the darkness. *A mountain lion?* His pulse quickened as he wiped the sleep from his eyes. He jumped from the bed, taking a moment to yank a pair of trousers over his wool union suit before shoving his bare feet into the waiting boots.

He grabbed the rifle from the pegs over the door and paused, listening. He didn't mind the big cats, but this one sounded too close for comfort. When the second shriek split the air, the sound ricocheted through his cabin. Not cougar—woman. His throat clenched. He'd rather face the cat.

Ford retrieved a flashlight from the shelf and raced for the door. Throwing it open, he clomped down the steps. The light split through the darkness as he swung it in a slow arc. Mrs. Brown? Or that new city girl? He opted for the latter.

He hurried to Miss Lane's door and hesitated. Quiet, whimpering cries reached his ears. Ford's stomach twisted, and cold sweat formed between his shoulder blades. He tucked the rifle under his arm and rapped on the door. "Miss Lane? You all right?"

A soft gasp was followed by a short, choking cough. "Yes, come in, please!"

He swallowed, glancing behind him. He turned the knob and pushed the door inward. "I thought I heard—"

"Over here—on the desk. The light, please!"

The beam washed across her figure as she hunkered beside the bed, her hand gesturing to the desk. He swung the flashlight about, pointing it in the direction she'd indicated. A stack of books lay on the desk beside a half-eaten cookie. He aimed the shaft of light up and down, searching the corners of the room, unsure what he was looking for.

She took a long breath. "It's gone." Miss Lane bent down, scooping up a pile of matches scattered across the wood floor. "Where's it gone?"

"What?" Ford frowned, turning the light back to the woman. "What could possibly be so frightening that you're screaming like a banshee?"

Miss Lane straightened, her face drawn. She folded both arms across her midsection and scowled. "It was the largest rodent known to man. Now, shut the door, you're letting all the cold air out."

Ford rubbed a finger across his eyes. He must still be asleep. "You mean *in*. I'm letting cold air in."

"It's colder in here, don't you think?" Little puffs of condensation rose from her mouth as she spoke.

Ford glanced at the fireplace. "Looks like your fire went out. You need to bank it better."

She pulled a quilt from the bed and wrapped it around her shoulders. "Actually . . ." she sighed, sitting down on the mattress with a thud. "I never got it lit. Maybe the wood was too green."

A smile pulled at his mouth. "You don't know how to light a fire?" Didn't everyone?

She struck a match and touched it to the wick of the oil lamp sitting on the small table. "I understand the basics. The wilderness survival manual explained it." She shrugged, replacing the glass chimney. "But we had a maid who always took care of the fires."

Ford hovered in the doorway. Enter a woman's room alone in the middle of the night? What would the men think? He leaned the rifle against the wall, leaving the door open wide. Jamming the flashlight in his pocket, he strode to the fireplace. "Toss me the matches, would you?"

She stood and carried them the handful of steps to his side. "Bless you."

Crouching down, he began to rearrange the logs. When they resembled a log cabin, he tucked some slivers and crumpled paper into the center and touched a match to the paper. As the flames crept upward, the heat prickled against his face.

Ford closed the matchbox and held it out to Miss Lane. "When that's good and hot, add some bigger pieces. But don't smother it."

Her icy fingers brushed against his as she took the container.

He frowned, fighting the urge to take her hand in his and rub some warmth into her skin. "You're cold. Come closer to the fire." He backed away so she could take his spot. Reaching for the desk chair, Ford noticed the fountain pen lying askew on the floorboards. He scooped it up and placed it on the desk next to her cockeyed pile of books. A line of crumbs trailed off the edge of the wooden surface. No wonder she was attracting rodents. The place was a mess.

He dragged the chair to the hearth. "Best not keep food sitting around like that."

Miss Lane covered her mouth with a hand as she yawned, the firelight silhouetting her slight frame. "I didn't intend to. But I also didn't realize you grew rodents out here the size of Massachusetts." She sank into the seat.

He frowned. If she couldn't handle a little deer mouse, she wasn't going to be staying long. "Part of the territory, I'm afraid. You're in their home now."

She pulled the quilt tight about her arms, the pink fabric matching the flush in her cheeks. "I understand. It won't happen again."

"Yes, it will." Ford slung the rifle over his shoulder. "But next time you won't scream and wake me up. Not unless it's a bear or a mountain lion."

She struggled to her feet, the quilt puddling at her heels. "That's—that's not likely, is it?" The flickering light exaggerated the shadows in the room.

Forcing himself to look away from the woman's nightclothes, he hurried to the doorway. "Out here? You never know who's going to come knocking." Ford pulled the door closed behind him, the image of her pale face making him smile. She'd be packed by morning. Maybe then things would return to normal.

FOUR

*F*ord gripped the coffee mug with both palms, willing the hot brew to give him some strength. The sound of Miss Lane's scream had triggered the familiar nightmares, images of his father's climbing accident haunting him until the wee hours of the morning. This time she'd encountered a mouse, but what if something worse happened? A single woman shouldn't be living alone here. He glanced around the long table at the four men shoveling scrambled eggs and pancakes into their mouths.

Jennings leaned forward, grasping a fork. "So, what's she like, this woman? I missed supper last night, didn't get a chance to say hello."

Ford grunted, staring over the rim of his cup. Morning conversation was best limited to the day's itinerary.

Carson smirked, fiddling with the silver park-service pin on his collar. "She's a tomato, that's what. Wouldn't mind having a girl like that to keep me warm." He reached for another strip of bacon.

The room silenced as Mrs. Brown marched in from the kitchen and plunked a steaming pot of oatmeal onto the table. "There'll be none of that kind of talk in my dining hall, Ranger Carson. Miss Lane is a lady and will be treated as such. About time you fellows learned a little culture. You're like a pack of wolves."

Carson licked grease from his fingers. "More like bears after a long winter."

Ford lowered the cup. "You heard her, Carson."

The man scowled. "I wouldn't think you'd be excited about this bird waltzing in and nicking one of our jobs."

"Miss Lane's here as a favor to the superintendent. She's not replacing anyone." Ford reached for a spoon. He might be the youngest man in the room, but since he'd served in his father's post for two years now, the others had grown accustomed to deferring to his authority. "And she's a bit nicer to look at than your ugly mug."

The door swung open. Miss Lane stepped inside, her cheeks pink, eyes downcast. "I apologize for being late. I'm afraid I overslept this morning. It won't happen again."

Ford pushed to his feet, the other rangers following his lead.

Mrs. Brown rushed to welcome the newcomer. "Don't worry, we're very casual in the mornings. You come whenever it suits you." She tilted her head toward Ford. "Though the boss may disagree."

"We won't be leaving for another twenty minutes or so anyway." Ford's breath wedged in his chest as he caught a clear view of her attire. "What kind of—" He swallowed, then gestured at her clothes. "What exactly are you wearing?"

Miss Lane closed the door behind her. She lifted her chin, brushing a gloved hand across her slim legs. "Not unlike what you are wearing, I believe, Ranger Brayden. Riding breeches." Her long forest-green coat did little to obscure the tan trousers and glossy boots.

"We've got a truck, Miss Lane. We're not going on a fox hunt."

She settled a hand on the tailored waist of her coat. "I saw a photograph of a lady ranger in Yellowstone. She wore a standard issue uniform, complete with badge and Stetson."

Carson chuckled. "This ain't Yellowstone."

Ford cleared his throat. "I don't think breeches will be necessary for your duties. You'd probably be more at ease wearing something less"—he tore his attention from her well-defined legs—"less unusual."

Jennings pulled out a seat for her. "It makes sense, if you ask me. You can't expect her to plow through the woods in a skirt, now can you?"

Miss Lane beamed. "I'm quite comfortable, thank you." She sat in the offered chair.

Ford pushed himself back into his seat, suddenly anything but comfortable.

The other men made swift work of their remaining bites and rushed to excuse themselves. Within minutes, the room had cleared, a strained silence lingering in the air. Ford itched to join them, but he'd told their visitor he'd escort her up to Paradise this morning.

Buttering a slice of toast and nibbling at its golden-brown edges, Miss Lane didn't seem to notice his discomfort. She hummed a familiar tune under her breath. A hymn?

Ford scraped his spoon across the bottom of the bowl for a last mouthful of oatmeal. "Yellowstone has lady rangers?"

The woman raised her head, eyes lighting up. "For several years now. And Yosemite, too."

Ford's dad had hired a young woman to work at the Nisqually gate back during the Great War, but only to issue entry permits. Rangers were expected to be big men who could fight fires, cut trails, fell timber, and apprehend poachers. How could a lady do any of that? "A few of the men's wives help out from time to time."

Miss Lane sipped her coffee. "I hope to do more than help out. I've dreamed of working here my whole life."

"All—what? Seventeen years of it?"

She straightened. "I'll have you know, I'm two decades, plus three years."

Two decades . . . Ford did the math and frowned. That made her only three years younger than him. Then again, it seemed he'd aged a lifetime in the past couple of years. "Why were you so set on working on the mountain?"

Her lips pressed together. "God led me to this place, Ranger Brayden. The beauty of His creation speaks of the Father's love. If I can get one person to see God at work in nature, my mission will be complete."

"One person?"

She set down the cup and folded her hands. "Yes."

He swiped a napkin over his mouth. "We'd better get to it then." With all the eccentrics visiting the mountain lately, she was sure to find someone to listen to her spiritual claptrap.

Any sensible fellow could see the majesty of the place—but a show of God's love? A single careless step on this mountain would teach you how little attention God paid to the humans who walked its slopes. His father was proof of that.

Margie choked down her toast as Ranger Brayden reached for his hat. He'd promised to take her up the road to Paradise today, and her spirits rose like the thermals. Hopefully the few bites of food would last her until the noontime meal.

She pushed back her chair and stood, retrieving the camel-brown hat she'd chosen to complement her forest-green jacket. She'd rather wear a Stetson like the men, but the cloche would have to do until she could prove her worth.

Mrs. Brown bustled into the room. "Everyone done already? I swear, these men eat faster than a flock of scrub jays. And about as neatly, too."

Margie paused. "Should we stay and help you clean up?"

The portly woman clucked her tongue. "Of course not, dearie. You two young folks go do what you're being paid to do. This is my lot in life. I'm too old to go traipsing through the wildflowers. Though I had my day." She laughed. "Me and my Harry used to walk those meadows hand in hand, back when we was youngsters. Don't tell him I told you." Her skirt swished as she bent over the crumb-strewn table. "Never dreamed I'd grow so old and creaky."

Ranger Brayden touched Margie's arm, jerking his head toward the door.

Margie set her plate back on the table. "Thank you for the wonderful breakfast, ma'am. It's most kind of you to feed us all."

The woman laughed. "You are a sweet thing. No one ever stops to thank me." She paused, a stack of dishes balanced in one arm. "You're going to be a good influence on these men; just wait and see."

Margie followed the ranger outside, pulling the door shut.

The man strode toward a dusty Model T truck. "If we're heading to Paradise, we shouldn't delay any longer. I know it's June, but there's still plenty of snow at that elevation. Are you going to be warm enough?"

Margie trotted to match his long gait. "Yes, I think so." She'd had the coat made out of the finest merino wool. "What will we be doing when we get there?"

"There won't be many visitors around, so I'll give you the tour. Show you around the Paradise Inn, the Guide House, and the ranger station. That sort of thing."

Margie's heart skipped, and she fought to keep her feet from doing the same. She waited as Ranger Brayden opened her door. Margie climbed inside and reached as though to tuck in the edges of her skirt, a lifetime habit. She settled her hands atop her knees as the door slammed shut.

The ranger took the spot behind the steering wheel, and the seat springs squeaked under his weight.

Margie tilted her head to examine the driver as he guided the vehicle onto the road. She'd told him her age, but she could only guess at his. Ranger Brayden's unlined face and thick hair suggested he was younger than many of his coworkers. And yet, Superintendent Brown had introduced him as chief ranger over the park. Either the man had started his career at an unimaginably young age, or he'd shot through the ranks. Or perhaps he was just a good example of Mendelian genetics. Without meeting his parents, she'd never know. Margie tucked her fingers into her coat pocket. "Do you spend much time at Paradise, or do you primarily serve at Longmire?"

He seemed to inspect her for a brief moment before returning his attention to the road. "I do a little of both. I go where the visitors are, so in the summer months that tends to be at Paradise. I make visits to our other stations too—Carbon River, White River, Mowich Lake, and some of the fire lookout towers. The rangers who work the more remote outposts live most of the year by themselves. I spend the winter months catching up on things at Longmire."

"And what happens to the Inn during the winter?"

"We have a live-in caretaker who keeps an eye on things. But the place can be buried to the roof peaks sometimes."

"Have you ever wintered there?" Margie closed her eyes for a moment, imagining a quiet, snow-covered scene.

"Not for the whole season. A little too desolate for my tastes."

Margie sat back, watching the scenery slip past. "Sounds like heaven to me."

He chuckled. "You might not say that after a few days of isolation. It's complete silence except for the roof timbers creaking under the weight of the drifts and the mice scurrying about in the darkness."

She buried her fingers in her pocket. It would take some time to live down her reaction last night. "The animal in my room was not a mouse. I checked my guidebook."

He cocked a brow. "What do you suppose it was, then?"

"I believe it was *Neotoma cinerea.*"

"Care to translate?"

The man rose to the post of chief ranger without understanding basic Latin names? "Bushy-tailed wood rat."

A grin spread across his face, a dimple showing in one cheek. "A pack rat, you mean?" He laughed, swiping a palm along his jaw. "No wonder you looked so alarmed. Those critters can get pretty big."

A smile tugged at her lips, but she tucked it away. "I tried to explain that to you. I checked my book this morning, and the author described what I witnessed as a wood rat. I remember the beast having a hairy tail, not those naked rat tails people typically describe."

"Welcome to forest life. Missing any jewelry?"

Margie touched the spot under her coat where her pearls normally resided, but she'd placed them into her trunk for safekeeping. "No, I'm not much for ornamentation. But I did find my fountain pen out of place. I think that may have been its intended target."

He nodded. "Best stash it in a drawer. Those pack rats are known to make return visits."

Margie wrinkled her nose, burying her fingers in the wool collar as a prickle ran down her arms. She'd hoped for intimate views of wildlife, but she hadn't anticipated her first encounter being Rodentia. She didn't care for the idea of a whiskery roommate. "Perhaps I can discover some way of discouraging him. Find his entrance and block it."

"Those cabins are built like sieves. They were slapped together in haste when the government moved in because the folks running the hot spring refused to house park staff. If you've got a pack rat nesting under that shack, you'll soon be smelling it." His nostrils flared as he spoke.

The thought turned her stomach. "So I just have to live with it?"

"We could put out a few traps and see what happens. But we'd probably trap the main culprit and a few of its cousins, only to have a new batch move in."

Margie sighed. "I suppose rodents are a part of God's creation too. I'll just need to learn to appreciate His lesser creatures, right Ranger Brayden?"

His brow furrowed. "Why don't you call me Ford? Everyone else does. The ranger title is more for the visitors than the staff."

Her breath caught. Did that mean she'd be staying? "All right."

"May I call you Margaret?"

"Oh, please don't."

His eyes widened. "I'm sorry. I just thought—"

"Only Philip—I mean . . . only a few people call me Margaret. My friends call me Margie." A quiver raced through her. What was she thinking, mentioning Philip's name? He had no place here. And she was determined to keep it that way.

"Margie." The ranger nodded. "I like it. Sensible."

She relaxed against the seat as the truck jostled over the icy road. The drifts grew in size as they ascended the winding switchbacks, until one last turn opened onto the white-covered meadows at Paradise. The cluster of alpine buildings appeared out of the mist, a welcoming haven even though they remained half-buried. The ranger parked the vehicle in a cleared area and stepped out.

Margie buttoned her coat under her chin and hurried to join him. Her boots sank deep in the powder as her breath rose in curls of fog from her mouth and nose. She gazed at the steeply pitched roof of the Inn, which looked like a priceless treasure wrapped in a cloak of cotton batting. The tall gambrel-roofed Guide House loomed behind it. "Seems odd to have this much snow in June. Is it normal?" The shoveled snowbanks along the edge of the roadway reached above Margie's head.

Ford rubbed his gloved hands together. "The meadows don't usually melt out until July. And even then, there are still patches here and there, and permanent snow fields not far beyond. Come on, let's head inside. We'll see if the caretaker has any hot coffee." He glanced to the left and right as if choosing the best route. Even though a mostly cleared path existed farther down the parking area, the ranger set out across a patch of virgin snow.

Margie took a deep breath and followed. With her first step, her boot crunched through the frozen crust and jammed down in the snowbank, sinking past her knee. With a grimace, she pulled it out. She tried to take lighter steps, but each time she placed her foot, it smashed through the icy covering into the mush below.

Her supervisor waited at least fifty feet ahead. "Need help?"

"Um, no. I'll be fine." She picked up the pace, using his already trampled path rather than breaking her own. Margie slogged her way through the final drifts until she reached a cleared walkway. Winded, she stomped the powder from her boots. Growing up in the lowlands, she was much more accustomed to rain than snow.

Ford held the door open with a flourish. "After you."

The icy air burned in her chest. "I'm coming."

⌒⌒

Ford entered the cavernous lobby of the Paradise Inn, the room's warmth gripping him like a bear hug. A crackling fire beckoned from the enormous stone fireplace on the far end of the building. He blinked several times as his vision adjusted from the snow's glare to the darker tones of the lodge.

The young woman paused beside him and leaned down, busily brushing slush from her breeches and the top edge of her riding boots with her gloved hands.

Something about her brought out Ford's mischievous side. Sure, he could have found an easier path to the door, but he wanted to see how she'd handle herself. She'd followed without whimper or complaint. For the daughter of a wealthy senator, Margie was made of tough stuff. "Snow's pretty deep, eh?"

She glanced up, cheeks pink from the cold. "As it should be. We're on a mountain, after all." Margie straightened, scraps of ice still clinging to her legs. Her eyes widened at the sight of the lobby. "This place is astounding."

"I thought you'd visited before." Ford unbuttoned his coat as he strode toward the fireplace.

She followed. "It's been some time. I was just a child, and the building wasn't complete. My father and I camped in the meadow with some friends. My mother wouldn't set foot up here."

"Perhaps she'll visit now that she won't have to camp." Ford surveyed the large hall. At least the park administration had demanded the construction match the location. The slope of the roof, the Alaskan yellow cedar columns, and the peeled log furniture fit in with the rugged nature of the mountain.

Margie drew off her gloves, extending trembling fingers toward the fiery blaze. She looked up, following the line of the exposed chimney to the wall to where the stones met the ceiling. "Perhaps."

Ford studied the woman. Her expression had darkened at mention of her mother, not unlike the way a shadow had crossed her face when she'd spoken a man's name back in the truck. What was it? Philip?

"Ford!" A gravelly voice echoed through the open space. Luke Johansson strode toward them from the dining room, his sleeves rolled to the elbow, dark pants covered in dust and grime.

Ford smiled at his friend's approach. "Spring must be here. Looks like you've been busy cleaning."

"Someone's got to knock down all the winter cobwebs, even though the dust makes me sneeze. It's good to see you. And you've brought us a guest." He yanked a large white handkerchief from his trouser pockets and wiped his red-tipped nose.

Ford touched Margie's elbow. "This is the caretaker—and my old friend—Luke Johansson. We used to ride patrols together on the park's east side, but now he works for the concessionaire, the Rainier National Park Company. He keeps this place in perfect condition." He turned to his friend. "Luke, may I introduce Miss Margie Lane? She's come to us from Superintendent Brown for . . . well, to . . . I mean to say she's the daughter of . . ." The words evaporated from his tongue.

"I'm a naturalist." Margie stepped forward as a quick smile spread across her dainty features. "It's an honor to meet you, Mr. Johansson."

Luke brightened. "Superintendent Brown mentioned you when he stopped in yesterday. He said you might be willing to do fireside talks here at the Inn. You'd be a welcome change. Old Ranger Edwards used to put the guests to sleep."

Ford frowned. The elderly ranger had been a close friend of his parents' and had worked on the mountain since long before it was a park. Ford had been disappointed to sign the man's retirement papers last year, but Edwards's arthritis had made the steep paths too difficult for him to navigate.

Margie clasped her hands together. "I can't wait to begin. My mind is overflowing with ideas." She stepped away from the fireplace, looking around the large room. "The rangers speak here in the lobby? It's a beautiful location."

"Here and in the campground." Ford leaned against the mantel. "We typically arrange a few rows of seating just beyond the hearth. We can bring the chairs close, since you're soft spoken."

Margie turned a slow circle with a light growing in her eyes. She lifted her voice so it echoed through the massive foyer.

"How the patient pine is climbing,
Year by year to gain the sky;
How the rill makes sweetest rhyming,
Where the deepest shadows lie.

"I am nearer the great Giver,
Where His handiwork is crude;
Friend am I of peak and river,
Comrade of old Solitude."

She paused, hands hovering in front of her chest, fingers extended as if guiding the poem's lines out into the open air.

"Not for me the city's riot!
Not for me the towers of Trade!

I would seek the house of Quiet,
That the Master Workman made!"

Ford's stomach tightened, her words wrapping around his heart like vines inching up the trunk of a tree. He gave his head a quick shake to dislodge the odd sensation.

Luke swung around to face Ford. "You should have told me she was stage trained. I can't wait to bring a crowd in here and let her work magic on them. We'll pack this place to the rafters."

Margie's cheeks reddened. "Herbert Bashford's 'The Song of the Forest Ranger' seemed appropriate for the moment."

Ford took a step back, and his heels bumped against the hearth. He'd never considered the possibility she might actually be good.

Luke grasped Margie's elbow and drew her to the side. "You're so petite. Where do you store such a magnificent voice—such stage presence?"

"I'm not certain what you mean. It's a well-designed room. Anyone would sound good in here."

"That's because you've never heard Ford try. He's miserable. His dad, however, that man could tell stories that would curl your hair."

Margie turned to Ford with a bright smile. "Your father is a ranger, too?"

"He was." Ford's throat tightened. "He died two years ago in a climbing accident."

The smile fled. "Oh. I'm sorry."

Ford nodded, glancing away. Two years. It never seemed to take much to reopen the wound—especially the reminder that he'd never live up to his father's reputation.

Luke cleared his throat. "I could start her this weekend."

Ford jerked his head up. "You don't open for another two weeks."

"Didn't Harry tell you? We're hosting a dinner for some important people from Olympia and Seattle—the governor and his wife, plus a few prominent businessmen and their families. Miss Lane will have them singing her praises by evening's end. This is an answer to prayer. Chef has already been up getting the kitchen ready."

Margie backed a few steps, her eyes widening. "The governor? Oh, I'm not sure."

"Yes, I'd heard about it." Ford pressed fingers against his brow, an ache settling behind his temples. "Harry said you wouldn't need any assistance beyond making sure the roads were passable."

"That was before you showed me this little gem. She must perform. There's no question."

Margie fiddled with the clasps on her coat. "Excuse me, Mr. Johansson, but I don't perform. I teach, and I might actually—"

Luke stopped her words with a touch to her shoulder. "Yes, yes. Of course, my dear. You teach, speak, recite . . . whatever. But the key is you're entertaining. Governor Hartley has never been a strong supporter of the park. We need to woo him over to our side."

"Luke, she just arrived," Ford protested. "And you want to put her in front of the politicians?"

The caretaker turned to Margie. "Could you be ready?"

She glanced between the two men. "Of course, if you think it appropriate. But you should know, my fa—"

"Luke." Ford pulled his Stetson from his head. "I don't know if this is wise."

"Unless you'd rather do it?" His friend folded his arms.

"You know better than to ask me that."

"We should be cleaned up in time." Luke scrubbed a handkerchief across his red nose. "Deliver her at six o'clock Saturday evening. No, wait—

come at five. You two can join our guests for the meal, as well. The governor's wife was excited to meet a real ranger, and now she'll have two. I've asked Henrik Berge and some of the other climbing guides to join us too. That should help entertain the ladies."

Ford's jaw tightened. *Henrik Berge.* He'd spent the past two years avoiding the guide at every opportunity. The last thing he desired was to sit across a table from the man responsible for his father's death.

Margie glanced down at her breeches. "Considering that these guests are dignitaries, perhaps I should dress for the occasion?"

"Yes, absolutely." Ford jammed his hat back on his head.

"Splendid idea." Luke's pale eyes gleamed bright as the snow outside. "If Mrs. Hartley wants rangers, Miss Lane should be in uniform."

Margie's jaw dropped. She shot a glance at Ford.

A bitter taste rose in his mouth. "Right. Whatever you think best, Luke."

FIVE

*A*s soon as Luke finished the lengthy tour of Paradise, Ford hurried back to the truck. The glow on the young woman's face only served to deepen the tension in his shoulders. His plans to discourage Margie fizzled under the weight of Luke's bottomless flattery. "You understand, this doesn't change anything."

"Of course."

"We can dress you up like a ranger, but it doesn't make you one." Ford fought for balance as his foot slid across a patch of slush. Why did this bother him so much?

"I'll play the part, to the best of my ability. What do you think they'll want to hear?"

"Ranger Edwards usually told stories. All sorts." A hole seemed to open in his chest. He'd miss the old man. No one else could have seen him through his father's death.

"Mr. Johansson said he wasn't much of a crowd pleaser, but who wouldn't love stories?"

Ford wrenched open the truck's door and gestured for Margie to climb in. "Sometimes they did go on a bit. But the man had a heart of gold."

She took time knocking the snow off her boots before gingerly step-ping into the vehicle. "Was he a friend of yours?" Her eyes settled on Ford, her inquisitive stare unsettling.

"Practically family." And about the last family he had. To prevent any more questions, he slammed the truck door with a little more force than necessary. He'd rather clear brush than escort a woman around the park. Perhaps he could pass her off to Jennings for a while. He was the park naturalist, after all. Opening his door, he clambered in.

"Ranger—" She paused, as if weighing her words. "Ford. I was think-ing—if you had other work you needed to attend to, perhaps I should start planning my speech. If this evening is as important as Mr. Johansson sug-gests, I'd like to put forth my best effort."

His spirits lifted. "Already?"

"Unless you had other duties for me. I'm at your service, of course."

He leaned back against the seat. Here he was trying to figure out how to avoid spending more time entertaining the young lady, and she cleared the path. "I had no specific plans for you this afternoon. If you're sure you'd be comfortable on your own, I could help Marcus with opening the Rampart Ridge Trail. We've had plenty of blowdown this winter."

She nodded. "I could assist, if you have need of me."

Ford put the truck into gear and eased down the road toward Long-mire. The image of the little thing wielding an eight-pound splitting maul sent a chuckle through him. "You handy with a crosscut saw, too?"

She smiled, ducking her head. "Perhaps not. But I'd like to pull my weight."

"Well, you don't look like you weigh much. Let's make a deal, shall we? You focus on keeping the visitors happy. The boys and I will take care of the heavy lifting."

"That sounds fair. What about church?"

"What do you mean?"

"I meant to ask yesterday. What do you do for Sunday services?"

"I think Harry and his wife take some folks down to Ashford. You can ask Mrs. Brown at breakfast."

Her head tilted as she studied him. "What about you?"

"No." Ford cleared his throat. This woman seemed to like keeping him on edge. His father used to lead services at the National Park Inn in Longmire. Ford had informed Harry that it was one part of his dad's job he refused to take on.

As they drove around the corner, a man jumped out of the bushes along the side of the road, waving his arms. Ford jammed on the brake. "What now?"

The man hurried over, face drawn. "I'm sure glad you came by. My car slid off the road, just down a ways. I was walking back to the Inn to get help. Name's Joe Craig."

Margie slid closer to Ford along the seat, leaning over to address the man out the window. "Was anyone hurt, Mr. Craig?"

He shook his head. "Nah. But the wife and kids are pretty shook up."

Ford gestured to the far side of the truck. "Climb in."

As the fellow clambered into the seat, Ford tried to ignore the warmth of the young woman's trousered leg pressed against his own. He put the truck in gear and followed the man's directions to where his family waited by the side of the road.

The vehicle sat with one of its front tires over an embankment. Ford whistled. "Another few inches and you might not have walked away."

"A deer ran out, and I swerved. The missus is pretty upset."

Ford backed up behind the unfortunate automobile and hopped out. "It'll only take a minute."

Margie hurried over to Mrs. Craig and her children. "Is everyone all right?"

The mother held her two children firmly by their hands. "I've never been so frightened in all my life. I don't know what Joe was thinking coming up here today. These washboard roads are only suitable for mountain goats."

Her sharp tone wrenched at what was left of Ford's good humor. He pulled the chain from the bed of the truck. The sooner he got these folks on their way, the better.

Margie's soft voice seemed to soothe the woman's fears. She drew the family off to the side, lifting the little girl up to her hip. The boy raced over to a patch of snow and proceeded to throw chunks of ice at the nearest tree.

Ford hooked the chain to the vehicle's frame.

The owner sighed. "That'll scratch. It's a brand new Cadillac. I thought my wife would take a better liking to it if I could show her how well it handled."

Ford snorted. "It didn't go over the bank, so I'd say it did pretty well."

"I'm not sure that's how she'll see it."

Climbing back into the truck, Ford threw the engine in reverse. He preferred to do this with Athena. The draft horse's steady strength and balance often proved a better match for this type of job. The shiny Cadillac teetered for a moment before easing back onto the roadway. He set the brake and joined Mr. Craig. "Looks like you didn't even blow a tire."

"That's a relief, let me tell you." He shook Ford's hand, a grin spreading across his face. "Maybe we'll salvage this day yet."

The rest of the group crossed the road to join them, with the little girl clutching Margie's fingers.

Margie smiled. "Are you done already? We were having a wonderful time." She bent down next to the child. "Can you show Ranger Brayden what you have?"

The girl's blond curls bounced as she opened her fist and displayed a yellow flower crushed in her palm.

He'd never had much luck talking with women; little girls were even more of a puzzle. "A flower, eh?"

"What kind is it, Mary?" Margie touched the child's chin.

She screwed up her face. "A . . . a glacier lily." Her eyes brightened as she remembered the name.

Her brother jerked his chin upward. "I was going to say that. And Miss Lane said she shouldn't have picked it, but since she already had, she could keep it. And I've got a fir cone!" He held out his prize.

Mrs. Craig laughed, the gentle trill a welcome change from her earlier complaints. "Very good, children. Now say thank you to the nice ranger for helping with our automobile."

Mary broke loose from Margie's grasp and threw her arms around Ford's leg. "Thank you, Mr. Ranger."

Margie waved as the visitors rolled back toward civilization. "What a sweet family. I'm so glad we got to meet them."

He shook his head. Perhaps Margie had a few talents after all. She did pretty well with those kids. "I just hope they stay on the road from now on."

"I'm sure they will." She smiled, her optimism spilling over.

"With that ice patch he spun out on, it's a miracle we weren't scraping them off the rocks down at Christine Falls. Another ten feet and this story could have had a different ending."

"God was watching out for them, I suppose."

"Or sheer luck." People were far too quick to attribute good outcomes to a higher power. He'd seen too much evidence to the contrary to buy into that sort of talk.

She picked her way through the snow-covered roadside to a clump of trees near the edge. "Isn't it fascinating how the composition of the forest changes from the higher elevations at Paradise as you move down toward Longmire? This roadway is like a lesson in forest science. Is that a Pacific silver fir?" Margie reached for a limb, sloping down toward her like a dripping ice-cream cone.

"No, don't—"

The wet snow and ice slumped from the tree, knocking the woman off balance and pitching her over the embankment.

"Margie!" Ford bolted to the edge. Harry had left her here for one day and already . . .

Margie slid to a halt fifteen feet later, loose ice and rock rattling down the hillside toward the river far below. She coughed, digging her toes against the rock face.

Ford scrambled down the slope, careful not to dislodge more ice. "Are you all right?" He grabbed her outstretched arm and hauled her up to a more stable perch.

"I—what happened?" She pressed a gloved hand to the side of her head, an angry red mark on her temple suggesting a bruise to come.

He forced himself to look away from the precipitous drop she'd somehow avoided. "You don't walk under trees when they're practically leaning with snowmelt. Don't you . . ." *know anything?* He bit off the words, his heart hammering in his chest. "Are you hurt?"

"I don't think so. I didn't expect it to come cascading off like that."

What else didn't she know? Predators, avalanches, rock slides, exposure—so many dangers. This is why the park service didn't hire women. Or at least, they didn't used to. He pushed up to his feet, brushing the ice from his knees and eyeing a path back to the road. "If you're going to make it out here, you'd better watch yourself."

Because I can't protect everybody.

Margie's legs still shook hours later as she maneuvered through the large cobbles littering the banks of the Nisqually River, a heavy knapsack balanced on her back. How could she have been so careless? Everything had happened in a blink, and seeing the steep ravine stretched below her had left her heart little more than a quivering lump. Maybe she wasn't cut out for this job.

The ranger had been quiet during the remainder of their drive. He'd also wasted no time dropping her off at the cabin, as if glad to be rid of her. He'd probably like nothing better than to see her packing.

Unfortunately, going home wasn't an option. Philip had never failed at anything in his life—he didn't allow it. And his cold eyes as he'd walked away told her she hadn't seen the last of him.

Margie scooped a stone off the bank and cast it into the river. She preferred giant rodents and slippery roads to facing any more of Philip's retribution. And being free of his suffocating control was like breathing for the first time.

Margie put away the dark memory. Right now, she needed to focus. The event at the Paradise Inn was less than a week away. With only a few remaining hours of daylight, she hoped the mountain would inspire some grand thoughts.

The rushing cascade roared in her ears, the ruckus matching her unsettled heart. After wobbling over a few more stones, she sat down on a large boulder overlooking the frothing water. Pulling the knapsack into her lap, she waited for the peace she usually sensed in nature.

A few days? It simply wasn't enough time to prepare for the biggest moment of her life. Mr. Johansson had been kind to offer her the opportunity to speak at the banquet, but whatever could she say to encourage the audience to see the significance of this place? Any sensible person could see it for himself. She untied the knotted drawstring and pulled out the stack of books, placing her Bible on top of the pile.

Lord, I need help. She flipped through the fragile pages, then stopped at Psalms. The book's poetry always spoke to her soul. Scanning the verses, her eyes lit on a reference to "wilderness." "He clave the rocks in the wilderness, and gave them drink as out of the great depths. He brought streams also out of the rock, and caused waters to run down like rivers." She sighed. He even made the rivers flow. What were her fears in the face of such majesty?

The Nisqually drew her attention. The water thundered past, as if rejoicing in its freedom. Two deer lingered at the forest's edge, lifting their noses to sniff at the air.

For years she'd buried her nose in books, learning as much as she could about nature and its mysteries. She'd walked the city parks, studying the insects and flowers. But to sit here at the foot of God's mountain? It was beyond a dream. It was a gift. And yet, the image of Ford's stern visage haunted her thoughts. Margie swallowed, tension gathering in her chest. For some reason, the idea of wearing a ranger Stetson no longer seemed quite as appealing. He obviously resented her presence, and the dour-faced man had the power to send her home.

She needed this place. As soon as she stepped foot in Longmire, its forests had wrapped around her like God's comforting arms, hiding her from the world. Now Mr. Johansson wanted to set her on display—in front of the governor and his wife, no less. She pressed a hand to her stomach. Who else might she recognize in the crowd? And how long until Philip knew she was here?

Margie closed the Bible, reached for another book, and opened it to a map of the park. Running her finger along the line representing the nearby river, she traced it up to its source—the Nisqually Glacier. Closing her eyes, she focused on the stream's song, imagining the course it had traveled. Water, locked for years within the glacial ice, now set loose to frolic down the mountainside. Free. *Just like me.*

Ford said Ranger Edwards told stories. Margie pulled out her journal and pencil. Every story needed a good beginning.

SIX

*M*argie turned in front of Mrs. Brown's looking glass, tugging at the waistband of the saggy trousers. "I don't think these will work."

Mrs. Brown drew back and pursed her lips. "I agree. You look like a scarecrow minus the stuffing." She tucked the uniform shirt tight around Margie's waist. "This might do, with a few adjustments." She reached for some pins.

"I feel like a child playing in my father's closet." Margie rolled the shirtsleeves up over her wrists. "I should wear my own clothing."

"We'll fix it up fine, honey. I'll put in a few darts." The portly woman folded a crease under Margie's arm and added some pins. "Of course there's no way Ranger Jennings will ever be able to wear it again." She chuckled. "Good thing we have one small fellow on staff. I can't imagine altering one of Ford's or Carson's shirts to fit you. We'd as soon start from scratch."

A tap sounded from the door.

Margie gasped, gripping the loose trousers to keep them from heading south.

"That'd be Ford." Mrs. Brown's mouth quirked upward at Margie's reaction before she turned toward the sound. "It's all right, you can come in."

"Are you sure? I can come back later." Ford's voice echoed from the hall. He sounded as if he much preferred to stay put.

Mrs. Brown strode to the door and pulled it open.

Ford's frame filled the space, but he kept his hands hidden like a guilty schoolboy. His eyes searched the room until they settled on Margie.

She wrapped an arm across her midsection at the sudden scrutiny. "It's a little large, but Mrs. Brown thinks she can alter the shirt. I'll wear my own breeches. Or perhaps a riding skirt." A wave of heat climbed Margie's neck as she studied the man's face. *He must regret ever laying eyes on me.* "Or . . . or I could just wear one of my dresses and explain to—"

"I brought you something." He pulled a grey Stetson out from behind him, the embossed leather band catching the light.

Margie's words turned to dust in her mouth. "For-for me?"

"A loan." He held the hat to his chest, his voice fading. "It belongs to my dad. Or rather, it did."

Mrs. Brown touched his arm. "You're a good man, Ford Brayden. Your father would be proud."

His eyes lowered. He thrust the item toward Margie. "For the dinner."

She swallowed against a lump rising in her throat. "Are you certain?"

"I'll reclaim it after."

"Of course." She closed her fingers over the solid brim, caressing the beaver felt. The mark of a hero, a caretaker of this bit of the Lord's garden. How could she ever be worthy of such an honor?

"Put it on, dearie. We're waiting." Mrs. Brown steered her toward the glass.

Margie stared into the mirror. Ford's face reflected above her shoulder, shadows deepening around his eyes. *How it must have hurt to lose his father. Everything in the park must trigger a memory.* She glanced down at the item in her hands—a physical link between father and son. She pressed it close, as if he'd handed her the heart of the mountain itself. How could she wear such a treasure? "I can't. It's too precious."

"It's not the crown jewels." With a loud exhale, Ford grabbed it and plopped it over her head. The hat sank past her eyes, the crown landing with a soft clunk on her skull.

Mrs. Brown's laugh broke the silence, followed by Ford's quiet chuckle.

Margie pushed the brim upward, peering out from the depths. Her hair puffed out underneath. At least no one would recognize her.

The older woman tipped it back over Margie's ears. "You look like a turtle with an oversized shell."

Margie frowned. "It matches the baggy clothing. Everyone will know I'm nothing but an impostor."

Ford pressed his lips into a firm line. "Give it here."

She handed him the Stetson, but the sudden movement caused the trousers to slip. Grappling with them, she twisted the waistband between her fingers. Standing in front of all those dignitaries dressed in such a manner would be a disgrace.

Ford pulled a bandanna from his pocket and folded it into the hat's liner.

Careful to keep one hand in control of her clothing, she edged closer. "What are you doing?"

"I saw my mother do this once. She wore Dad's Stetson a few times."

"I'm not sure anything will make that fit me."

"It only has to be for one evening, right?" His gruff tone seemed to have softened. He tucked the tails of the handkerchief out of sight. "May I?" He stepped close, lifting it above her head.

Her eyes locked on his shirt buttons as the room grew stuffy. The hat settled against her hair, nicely hugging just above both ears. Her heart jumped.

Ford nodded. "Much better."

She spun to face the mirror. "I look . . . I look—"

"Like a ranger?" Mrs. Brown adjusted the brim so it rested parallel to the floor. "You do, indeed."

Ford stepped back, his expression unreadable. "You'll fit right in."

Saturday afternoon, Ford paced around park headquarters, fiddling with his formal uniform jacket and shrugging his shoulders until the stiff garment felt more natural. Meeting with businessmen was one of his least favorite parts of the job, somewhere beneath refuse collection and privy cleaning. And having his newest employee asked to speak pricked like a splinter. Margie had been here less than a week, but she'd already set the place on its ear. The men were skulking around, looking for excuses to assist her instead of doing their jobs. Now this fancy dinner?

Ford ran a soft cloth over his collar pin and badge. Perhaps since she came from those circles, she'd know better how to handle the dignitaries. He stepped outside and stood for a long moment on the small porch. A shroud of mist kept the peak hidden. Unfortunate. Their important guests would expect the mountain to make an appearance, but Rainier cared little for those who walked its flanks. It didn't need their help any more than it desired their devotion.

The sound of footfalls drew his attention.

Like a deer, the young woman stole up the path, cautiously glancing from one side to the other. She held his father's hat clutched to her chest.

The altered uniform matched her curves in an uncomfortably tantalizing manner.

Ford trotted down the stone steps. "Expecting the pack rat to sneak up on you?"

She brightened. "I'm just admiring the flora. Do you think Mr. Johansson would like some ferns for the tables?"

"I'm sure Luke has that all planned out. You're responsible for the presentation, not the decor."

Margie glanced down, as if hesitant to meet his gaze. "I just thought some camouflage might be in order."

Luke had no business placing this naive young woman in front of a cluster of greedy businessmen like honey before a bear. "You don't have to do this, if you aren't feeling ready."

"Of course I do. I gave my word. I just hope it will meet with your approval."

An evening of poetry and fancy quotations? Unlikely. "I'm not the one you need to impress."

"I should have warned him—I might know some of the guests. It could prove awkward."

"Will your father be in attendance?"

"I haven't heard from him, but it's possible." A shadow crossed her face.

Ford led the way to the truck and swung open the door. "It will be fine. As you said, who's going to recognize you, dressed as you are?" He never should have gone along with this. The poor girl wasn't up to the task, not to mention that she looked a little silly wearing his father's hat. This evening would send her packing faster than the encounter with the rodents.

Margie scooped up a fir cone from underneath the truck. She held it in her open palm with a smile. "For luck."

And just like that, she sent him spiraling back into bewilderment. "There are millions of those lying around. How could they bring luck?"

She closed her fingers around the small object. "Every cone carries somewhere between twenty-five and fifty seeds, just waiting to spring to life. A new forest, right here in the palm of my hand." She tucked it into her breast pocket before slipping into the vehicle. She patted the pocket flap, looking up at him with her warm brown eyes. "Perhaps *luck* isn't the right word. Hope."

Ford latched the door, shaking his head. This woman saw meaning in every twig and blade of grass. He'd spent his entire life on this mountain, but had never seen the things she caught in a single glance. Perhaps the responsibility of caring for this place had blinded him to its magic.

Tomorrow might be a good day to hike up the ridge. He was long overdue for a little quiet time. Maybe he'd give the mountain a chance to reintroduce itself.

Margie sucked in a deep breath of the icy air at Paradise. *Philip doesn't care a scintilla about nature. He won't be here.* Ford led the way to a shoveled path. At least he didn't have her sinking to her knees through snowdrifts today.

She pulled the coat's collar up around her chin. That day had been a test. She'd spent enough time around powerful men to know when she was being scrutinized. The number of times he rolled his eyes while she spoke suggested he found her little more than an amusement.

Hopefully this evening's program wouldn't confirm his suspicions. Margie paused at the massive doors, her fingers jammed into her coat pocket for warmth. No matter the weather, she'd rather hightail it across the meadows than seek refuge inside the lodge. Perhaps she could be like a pika and burrow under the snow to find a protective haven.

A surge of warm air beckoned from across the threshold, but Margie still had to force herself through the doorway. She'd rehearsed her presentation countless times during the night. Now she only had to find the courage to open her mouth and speak.

The spacious lobby yawned open in front of her, the yellowed timbers stretching upward toward the peaked roof. Clusters of people gathered around the fireplace and lounged on the log furniture.

She straightened, willing the starched uniform jacket to instill her with strength. At least she looked the part. She caressed the hat's brim, imagining the man who'd worn it before.

Ford stepped up beside her, his tall frame like a sturdy tree.

"So many people." She swallowed. "I thought Mr. Johansson said this was a small party."

Luke Johansson rushed toward them, a fine picture in his gray suit. "Ford, Miss Lane—I'm so glad you're here. I can't wait to introduce you to some of our guests. We've expanded the festivities a little. Some big wheel from Tacoma found out about our event and offered to round up some additional supporters. We have over a hundred and fifty people now. Isn't that phenomenal? There are even reporters from three of the area newspapers. Tomorrow folks could be reading about our evening. Can you imagine?"

"Newspapers?" Her stomach dropped. If her name was mentioned in a Tacoma paper, Philip would be on her doorstep within the week.

"Don't be nervous. They're going to love you."

Of course they would. More fodder for the gossip columns. Perhaps if no one mentioned her family connections, the reporters wouldn't take an interest in her. She ran a hand across her jacket, checking the buttons. "Thank you, again, for inviting me, Mr. Johansson."

His grin lit the room. "Purely selfish motives, Miss Lane. I know you're going to charm the socks off these old curmudgeons. Parks are the nation's playgrounds, but we need the support of men of means in order to protect our vision. Otherwise timber and mining interests will be breathing down our necks forever."

She nodded. "As President Roosevelt said of the Grand Canyon, 'Leave it as it is. You cannot improve on it. The ages have been at work on it, and man can only mar it. What you can do is to keep it for your children, your children's children, and for all who come after you, as one of the great sights which every American if he can travel at all should see.'"

Mr. Johansson's booming laugh carried through the long hall. He grasped her hand and tucked it beneath his elbow. "And that's why I want you on our side, my dear." He glanced up at Ford. "Come along, Ford. Miss Lane will show you how it's done."

Margie traveled beside him like a leaf being swept along by the wind. She shook hands and nodded at the various people to whom the caretaker introduced her. Ford eventually sidled away, joining another uniformed park service administrator on the far side of the room. Obviously, he had little desire to make small talk with donors.

"Margaret!" A familiar voice bellowed from the dining room. "Is that my daughter I see under that monstrosity of a hat?"

Margie's heart jumped as she spotted her father. She released Mr. Johansson's arm and stepped into Papa's warm embrace. "I wondered if you'd be here."

"I wouldn't miss the chance to see my little girl." He stepped back, keeping a firm grip on her hands. "Though are you sure you're my daughter? No lace gowns for you now, eh?"

A warm flush crept up her neck. "It's just for this evening."

Mr. Johansson straightened. "We're honored that you chose to join us today, Senator." The man's smile widened as he glanced from father to daughter.

Margie's expectations sank into a clump at the pit of her stomach. So much for hiding her family connections.

Her father patted her arm, his voice lowering. "You should know, dear, I won't be the only familiar face tonight."

A chill stole over her. *No, not already.*

Papa tucked his chin. "Philip must have anticipated your plans. In fact"—he glanced over his shoulder, his voice quieting to a conspiratorial whisper—"he helped arrange the event."

A buzzing, like a nest of bald-faced hornets, took residence in Margie's ears. She took a quick step back, yanking the hat from her carefully arranged curls. "Why . . . why would he do such a thing? He doesn't care about wilderness."

Her father shook his head. "I don't believe it's the wilderness that draws him."

This couldn't be happening. The whole dinner was a sham. She rose up on tiptoe, searching the room.

Philip Carmichael leaned against one of the large pillars at the opposite end of the lobby, his blue silk suit strangely out of place in the rustic atmosphere. A faint smile touched his lips as he raised a near-empty glass toward her.

Margie had never realized one could feel chilled and flushed at the same time. Perspiration broke out across her skin, and the treasured uniform seemed nothing but a childish costume.

No mountain hideaway could protect her.

SEVEN

Ford jabbed the baked potato with his fork, casting a quick glance across the dining room. Luke had been smart enough to seat Henrik Berge and his fellow guides at a table in the opposite corner of the hall. The last person Ford wanted to deal with was Berge, though the middle-aged socialite beside him wasn't much better. A guest of the governor and his wife, the woman hadn't stopped talking for an hour. She'd scooted her chair toward his at least twice. At one point, she'd leaned so close, the beaded fringe hanging from her bodice snagged on his sleeve.

He'd tried shifting his seat the opposite direction, but that only pushed him closer to Margie. The naturalist was no help, having gone uncharacteristically quiet. Hadn't Luke insisted on dressing her as a ranger to distract the governor's party? Why was he doing all the entertaining?

Mrs. Chamber's piercing voice pulled his attention away from Margie. "The view of Kilimanjaro was stunning, absolutely breathtaking. It makes this peak look like a snowdrift. Have you ever been to Africa, Ranger Brayden?"

"I'm afraid not." He'd barely stepped foot out of Washington.

Senator Lane leaned forward, gesturing with his spoon. "I took Margie on safari when she was just six years old. Do you remember, sweetheart?"

Margie's fork stilled over her plate. "Um, yes. Vaguely."

"You really should go, Ranger." Mrs. Chambers toyed with the jewels on her gown's cascading neckline. "It would put these Northwest mountains into perspective for you. You've climbed it, I imagine?"

"Kilimanjaro?"

"No, silly." Her laugh drew the attention of nearby tables. "This one. You must have been up it dozens of times, right? Rescuing careless hikers, stray mountain sheep, et cetera?"

The unwanted memory swept over him anew, like stepping naked into a blizzard. "Um, yes. But not in—"

"You've probably scaled hundreds of mountains." She latched onto his upper arm. "Just look at this rugged physique." Her red lips pressed together as she caressed his bicep. She turned to the governor's wife. "Our husbands only ascend the capitol steps, isn't that right, Nina? Not quite the same."

Her husband? Ford tugged at his collar. *Poor man.*

The governor's wife pushed away her half-eaten trout. "Some would say every step to the capitol is a mountain of its own, Sylvia."

Ford scrabbled to get back into safe conversational territory. "I'm sure I'd be lost on Capitol Hill. Conquering a mountain is all about challenging yourself against the elements. Politics, on the other hand, is man against man."

"Well said," Governor Hartley chortled. "There are days when I wish all I had to conquer was a hunk of rock. How about you, Senator?"

"Hear, hear," Margie's father answered.

The governor wiped his mouth on the linen napkin. "Senator Lane, I just received the invitation to your gala reception at the Tacoma Hotel. Sounds like quite the party."

Mrs. Hartley nodded, "Yes, we're looking forward to it."

Senator Lane beamed. "Wonderful. I'm hoping I can woo my daughter away from her duties here for that evening. What say you, Margie?"

She frowned. "I don't know. I just started. It seems presumptuous to be asking for time off."

"It's a couple of weeks away yet. I'm sure they can spare you by then." He smiled at Ford. "Right, Ranger Brayden?"

Ford nodded. "Of course."

"In fact," the senator leaned forward, "you should join us, as well. See how these sorts of things are done in Tacoma." He gestured to the dining room. "Not that this isn't fancy enough for me."

Ford glanced up from the strange array of forks beside his plate. "I'm afraid our summer season is a hectic time of year for us, Senator. I don't believe I could get away."

Mrs. Chambers released Ford's arm, flicking her fingers against his elbow as she set him free. "Oh, you men. It's all about work with you, isn't it? You should come. There'll be dancing. I imagine you're quite a sight on the dance floor."

That was one way to put it. Ford slid his chair back and stood. "If you'll excuse me for a moment, I need to step out." Hopefully she wouldn't follow. Trifling with a politician's wife didn't seem like the type of good impression Luke had in mind.

He glanced over at Margie. Either the green jacket had cast an unpleasant shade to her skin or she needed a breath of air as well. "Miss Lane, we should prepare for your oration."

She jumped, her eyes lifting to meet his gaze. "Oh . . . yes." She glanced at her untouched plate and then around at their tablemates. "If you'll excuse me?"

The men rose as she stood. Her father leaned over to place a kiss on her cheek. "Good luck, sweetheart."

"Thank you, Papa." She clutched his sleeve for a moment.

Ford steered her out of the crowded dining room and into the still lobby. "You barely touched your food. Nervous?"

"A little." She touched her hair as if checking its placement. "I didn't realize how many people would be attending. I thought Mr. Johansson had planned a little dinner party, not a gala."

"Luke never does anything halfway. The impressive part is that the arrangements were made so quickly. This is a surprising turnout. Are you ready?"

"Of course. I'm fully prepared." She glanced about the lobby as if in search of someone. "I won't let you down."

"You don't have to worry about me. I'm just glad to not be up there tonight. Luke was correct in inviting you to speak. You're familiar with these people. You know what will impress them."

"Yes, I do know them. All too well."

The strain in Margie's voice made Ford uneasy. Was it really just nerves, or was there something more?

She looked back at him, a faint smile easing the tension around her eyes. "I just hope I can turn their hearts toward God's creation. If only for a few moments."

Ford nodded. Whatever was bothering her, at least it hadn't distracted her from the job at hand.

As her boss stepped away to assist with the seating, Margie took several deep breaths to slow her racing heart. Its percussion provided a perfect background to the hum of conversations echoing around the rustic lobby. She pressed damp palms against the long jacket as she scanned the room.

Philip lurked on the far edge of the crowd, like a storm refusing to break. Ignoring him during the presentation would prove a distinct challenge, but every time she glanced his way, her throat tightened a little further. Any more and she might lose her voice completely. Not only were her father and the governor in attendance, so was the supervisor of the Tacoma Eastern Railway and some of the most prominent businessmen from around the state. The odor of freshly minted dollar bills practically hung in the air.

She lifted her eyes, focusing instead on the gleaming yellow timbers supporting the massive roof. Richly colored native rugs hung from several of the crossbeams. *Lord, I don't know why I'm here, but I pray You'll use my humble offering to bring glory to Yourself.* She couldn't afford to be distracted—not by Philip, Ford, or anyone else.

"Are you ready, Miss Lane?" Mr. Johansson's voice rose above the murmuring crowd. "I'll introduce you, then you can work your magic."

"I've no magic." She raised her chin in an artificial display of confidence. "And when you make your opening remarks, I'd greatly appreciate it if you don't mention my family ties." Philip might have already discovered her whereabouts, but she still didn't wish to be the talk of the scandal sheets. The story of a senator's daughter playing park ranger would feed the gossipmongers for weeks.

The man rubbed the back of his neck. "But—"

"Please. I understand your intentions, but I'm determined to sink or swim on my own strength, not my father's." She straightened her forest-green tie.

"Fine. Whatever you wish." He folded his arms.

She took a seat next to Ford, locking her hands on her knees. She should have worn an evening gown. At least then she'd be meeting these people on their terms.

Mr. Johansson stood and called the crowd to attention. After several minutes of merriment and polite flattery of every important party in attendance, he finally gestured to Margie. "And now, I'd like to introduce to you our newest park naturalist. Miss Margaret Lane is a delightful young woman, and she offers a feminine perspective on what has long been a man's wilderness." He held out a hand. "Miss Lane?"

Margie took her place beside the crackling fire, the warmth penetrating the wool trouser legs and knee-high boots. She shifted from foot to foot as a few men lifted doubting brows. Philip stood in the far corner, both arms folded across his chest.

A quiver took up residence in Margie's stomach. Why had Philip taken an interest in this? Surely it wasn't for her benefit. His eye was always, ever, on himself. Or the bottom line.

She shifted her attention back to the gathering. "Mr. Johansson honors me by saying I bring a 'feminine perspective on a man's wilderness.' I would counter that there is nothing more feminine than nature—an unending cycle of birth and rebirth. God granted female creatures the awesome responsibility for bringing life into the world. When we look into Mother Nature, we see womanhood staring back."

Several women nodded, smiles spreading across their faces. One masculine whisper cut through the silence. "Fine words from someone masquerading as a fella."

Margie pressed her hand against her leg. "I'd like to tell you a story. The tale of a great mountain." She relaxed into the words as she spoke of the mountain's birth in fire, how God clothed her in glacial ice, how the elements had worn her down. How the mountain protected the creatures who called her home.

The audience listened in complete stillness. Every rustle and fidget died away until her words and the crackle of the fire were the only sounds permeating the room.

She stole a glance at Ford. He leaned forward, elbows on his knees, gray eyes locked on her.

His intense gaze flooded her with strength. She took a half step toward him, wishing for a breath free of the smell of the fireplace. Careful to maintain eye contact with all her listeners, she trained her mind on Ford. *Speak only to him.* "Allow me to focus this tale for you. A story within a story, some might say. The native peoples had their own legends. The Puyallup, Nisqually, Cowlitz, and the Yakama—they all looked to the mighty Rainier. Or as they called it, *Tahoma, Takhoma,* or *Tacobet.* Her lands were priceless and sacred.

"Tell me, when you stepped foot inside the park's gate, did you remove your shoes? Did you know you walked upon holy ground? Can you imagine if Governor Hartley arrived aware of this place's sanctity?" She nodded to the businessmen who dotted the crowd. "Would you see the mountain as a resource to be harnessed? Timber to be cut? Minerals to be stripped from the rocks? Precious water to be diverted to thirsty soils of the eastern orchards? Or would you think it a treasure too lovely to be threatened, too valuable to be defiled for human spoils?"

Several of the men glanced at each other. She'd found their soft underbelly and poked it with a stick.

"Even among the native people, there walked those obsessed with personal gain. One in particular turned his greedy eyes to Tahoma's crest, where he believed was hidden great wealth." Margie spun the story's web

thoughtfully, choosing each word with care. She told of the miser's difficult trek and the riches he found. As the audience leaned in, she delivered
the tale's lesson. "He didn't bother to give thanks for what he had taken.
Instead, his only thoughts were for himself. A storm swept up, chasing him
with thunder, lightning, and winds until—out of fear for his life—he
threw every bit of treasure away. Exhausted, he sank into the snow and fell
asleep.

"The man woke to green meadows and sunshine, his hair now long
and matted. He didn't know how much time had passed, but his soul felt
light and free like it did when he was a boy. He hurried home and discovered his lonely wife had grown old but lovely. She drew him into her arms
in welcome. The miser returned home a changed man. As the years went
by, he lived with a heart for others and never again longed for the mountain's riches. Instead, he rejoiced in the gifts the earth bestowed upon him."

She blinked, for a moment lost within her own storytelling. How
would these wealthy businessmen react to old legends? Margie placed a
palm against her chest, her heart's pounding evident through the rough
fabric. "When you leave this mountain, Tahoma, when you go home and
look upon its silvery beauty from afar, I hope you will make plans to return. Leave your billfolds at home."

A quiet chuckle rang through the audience, Margie allowed herself a
smile. *Probably not what Mr. Johansson had in mind.* "Come back to
have your spirit filled. To be touched by the artistry God has presented in
this place.

"I leave you with the words of American naturalist John Muir. 'Everybody needs beauty as well as bread, places to play in' "—she looked around
the room, meeting as many eyes as she could—" 'and pray in, where nature
may heal and cheer and give strength to body and soul alike.' "

Her final words rang out in the stillness, as if everyone held their collective breath. Had she pushed too hard? Likely as not, she'd offended every businessman in attendance and played right into Philip's hand.

Applause swept through the hall like a mighty earthquake rumbling the mountain. Her father jumped to his feet, a grin spreading across his face from one ear to the other. Mr. Johansson strode to the front, latching his arm around Margie's shoulders. "Didn't I tell you, folks?"

She glanced over at Ford. He stood with the others, his arms at his sides, expression unreadable.

Her attention was pulled to the rear of the lobby as Philip joined in the clapping, his hands beating a slower rhythm than those in the front. If only she could escape without speaking to the man. Perhaps now that he'd demonstrated his control, he'd leave her be.

Mr. Johansson addressed the crowd as Margie moved to sit. "I promised this fine lady I would avoid embarrassing her during my introduction, but I said nothing of afterward."

Margie stiffened. "No, please."

He grasped her arm, tugging her back to center stage. "Margaret Lane is none other than our Senator Thomas Lane's only daughter, educated at Bryn Mawr, and welcomed in many of the finest drawing rooms in Tacoma and Seattle. We're honored to have her join our staff—and our cause. I hope you enjoyed Miss Lane's presentation as much as I did."

Further applause followed his declaration, and Margie stepped free of his grip, her cheeks burning. Would she never cease to be an object of adoration because of her father? Had they heard nothing she'd said about the mountain? About God's provision and grace? About greed and avarice?

Her words were swept away as the businessmen and their wives clapped for the wealthy daughter of a politician.

Ford stood in silence as the crowd milled around. He glanced down at his empty hands. Had he forgotten to applaud? He'd fallen so deeply under the spell of Margie's voice, he'd become lost in the story. Could she truly have spoken of the land of his birth? The forests he'd played in since he was barely able to walk? She'd nearly convinced him the mountain was a trusted friend, rather than a beautiful, but savage, wilderness. He shook himself. If only he could live in her version of the world rather than reality.

Margie smiled, speaking to everyone who came forward to congratulate her. Thankfully, Mrs. Chambers joined the throng of admirers, her fascination with Ford long forgotten. The woman's perfume still clung to him, however. He'd have to hang his jacket out on the porch tonight. Hopefully it'd smell fresh as fir needles by the morning, or he'd have a thing or two to explain to the men.

A dark-haired man relaxed on one of the upholstered sofas in the rear of the room, an arm draped across the seat's back. He gestured at Ford with the cigarette dangling from between his fingers. "You must be proud of that young woman. I've never seen a lady ranger before."

The words dug into his skin like a thorn. "She's not actually a ranger."

The man took a long drag and then pulled the jade cigarette holder from between his lips. "Is it a privileged title?" A cloud of smoke escaped with his words.

Privileged? Ford scanned the man's expensive suit. Odd choice of words from someone who'd likely never shined his own shoes. "I wouldn't say that."

The gentleman jumped to his feet and strode to Ford's side. "Allow me to introduce myself. The name is Carmichael. I'm the manager of the Tacoma Hotel and a few other businesses here and there." After squeezing Ford's hand, he ran his palm along his suit lapel.

"It's a pleasure to meet you. I'm Ranger Brayden."

Carmichael cocked a finger at Ford's chest like he was aiming a pistol. "*Chief* Ranger, right?"

A chill trailed down Ford's back. Had Luke introduced him at some point? "Yes, you're correct."

"Just the person I'd hoped to see." Carmichael offered a haughty smile. "I've been discussing some ideas regarding the concessionaire, Rainier National Park Company, with your man, Johansson. I see a lot of promise here tonight, including your lovely Miss Lane." He turned to study the lodge. "But there's a lot of work to be done. This rustic look—is that really what tourists are seeking today? They don't just want scenery. They desire luxury. So many millionaires frittering their American dollars away in the Swiss Alps when they could be spending it here."

Ford glanced about the lobby. "The guests seem to appreciate the Inn. If they want something fancy, perhaps they should stay in your grand hotel in Tacoma."

"Then maybe they'll leave their dollars there, too. Your loss." Carmichael turned his attention toward the front of the room, his eyes resembling those of a long-tailed weasel. "Ah, there's the little princess now."

Margie chatted with some guests nearby, Ford's father's hat clutched protectively in front of her chest. Her skin had taken on the same ghostly pallor she'd had before the talk. Shouldn't she have relaxed by now?

As the other visitors departed, Carmichael strode in her direction, arms outstretched. "Margaret, my dear."

She backed just out of his reach. "Why are you here?"

Margie's guarded expression caused a prickle to travel down Ford's neck. Who was this man?

"You expected me to stay away? Once I heard where you'd run off to, I decided I needed to give this hideaway another look." Carmichael locked his eyes on Margie. "And I must say, I like what I see."

Ford fought the instinct to put himself between them. "Mr. Carmichael, perhaps I could introduce you to the superintendent. I'm sure you'd like to meet the person in charge. Or Senator Lane, perhaps?" He'd never been one for mingling, but every fiber in his being demanded he escort this fellow away from Margie.

Margie glanced at Ford. "He's met my father on many occasions, Ford."

Of course he had. The man's chummy behavior should have tipped him off.

Carmichael flicked cinders toward a nearby ashtray. "The senator and I are old friends. He gave me my start, you see. I owe him much." He nodded to Margie. "And I intend to repay him."

Margie touched Ford's wrist. "Will you excuse us?" Latching onto Carmichael's sleeve, she tugged him toward one of the secluded alcoves.

Carmichael cast a grin over his shoulder. "I believe the lady wants some privacy."

Ford shook off the sensation of a cold fog dropping over the room. A former love, perhaps? A family friend, at the least. Likely he intended to talk Margie into returning to civilization.

In the distance, her stiff gestures suggested the conversation wasn't going well.

Ford leaned on one of the cedar posts, torn between respecting the woman's privacy and his gut instinct suggesting she shouldn't be alone with that man.

Margie's whisper carried across the space. "Our association is over. I think I made myself clear."

Ford moved to leave. He'd lost all sense of respectability, spying like this. But when Carmichael grasped Margie's hands, he paused.

"You're not going to hold that incident against me, are you? We had words. It happens. But look at you. Is this what you really want?"

"You'd never understand."

The man shook his head, a stitch forming between his brows. "So you're interested in horticulture. I'll build you the biggest greenhouse conservatory on the Puget Sound."

She yanked her fingers free. "I don't wish to grow hothouse flowers, Philip. I want to understand the creation and through it, the Creator."

"Enough of your religious babble, Margaret. Look at what you've become." Carmichael picked up the Stetson from the table where she'd set it. His nose wrinkled as he held it out. "You're making a spectacle of yourself in public. It reflects poorly on your family."

She pulled the hat from his grip. "How is that any of your concern?"

"Your father hasn't informed you, then? I'm his new campaign manager. So his reputation is high on my list of concerns."

"Campaign manager?" Color drained from her face. "No, that's not possible."

The sight of Margie's clenched jaw set off alarm bells in Ford's head. Whatever this man had to say, Margie needed a friend at her side. If Carmichael reached for her again, Ford was going to intervene.

The hotelier folded both arms across his chest. "And after all . . . is it wrong to care about my fiancée's reputation?"

*M*argie backed several steps. "You already know my answer."

In the distance, over Philip's shoulder, she met Ford's eyes. Was that man everywhere? How would she explain this disgrace?

The Inn's timbered walls closed around her, her heart thudding against her ribs. Philip had a knack for sucking the oxygen out of a room. At one time, she'd mistaken the odd sensation for love. Now she knew better. "Philip, we're done. Please leave."

"Done? Never." His lips hitched up on one side, the shadow of a dimple appearing in his right cheek. "And you just asked us all back for a visit. Minus our wallets, remember? Of course, that wasn't what you really meant." He nodded his head at the milling crowd. "You'd prefer these fellows leave their dollars here for the upkeep of your precious park." He closed the distance she'd gained a moment before. "I can make that happen, you know."

She lowered her voice, determined not to let anyone overhear her reply. "You'd have nothing if it weren't for my father."

"I have a rare gift for talking men out of their excess, it's true. You want them to spend it here, and I want you. Everyone could be happy."

Bile crept up her throat. "I'd never be happy with you."

"Let me prove you wrong. You must forgive me for my outburst at our last encounter. You made me angry. It won't happen again." He reached as if to touch her cheek. "You know I don't typically behave in such a fashion. I have much more effective ways of expressing myself."

Philip never heard a word she said—only what he wanted. "Leave me alone." She knocked his hand away and brushed past him, suddenly desperate for fresh air. Hurrying to the exit, she pushed open the heavy doors. A cold wind blasted her skin, erasing any pretense that this might be a dream. The night sky revealed a star-studded heaven.

Instead of clinging to the cleared path, she stumbled through the snowbank and into the meadow, the icy damp seeping through her wool trousers. Margie's foot slid, and she dropped to one knee, her palms plunging through the frosty surface. "No, this isn't happening."

"Margie?" Ford's voice floated through the darkness.

She blew out a long, fog-laden breath and forced herself up to her feet. "Over here."

The ranger crunched closer, her long overcoat over his arm. "I saw you leave. You might want this." He lowered it around her shoulders, his fingers lingering on the collar. "Are you all right?"

She forced a smile. "Yes, thank you. I just—it was quite warm in the lodge."

He glanced at the building, light spilling through the windows onto the snow. "Was that man bothering you? Would you like me to speak with him?"

The ranger's kindness sent a ray of warmth through the night air. Why couldn't Philip be more like him? Perhaps he had been once, before he left for university. Or at least so she had thought. Father's new campaign advisor? It couldn't be true.

She pulled the coat tight around her neck, wrapping her hand in its folds. "No, it's fine. After this evening, I'm sure Philip Carmichael will turn his eyes elsewhere." She glanced down at her attire. "I mean—who wouldn't?"

The man's frown deepened. "Miss Lane . . . Margie,"—he paused, as if searching for words— "I thought you looked very smart up there." He ran a finger along the edge of her hat, his eyes reflecting the pale light of the snow.

Smart. Margie's spirits floundered. She never should have placed him in such an awkward position. "God was faithful. He provided me with the words I needed."

"You're the one who rose to the challenge. You can take pride in your own accomplishments."

A lump gathered in Margie's throat. She drove her hands into the coat pockets. "We should go back in. I'll say goodnight to my father, and then we can return to Longmire. Unless you have other business here?"

The ranger shook his head, shadows settling into deep grooves on his brow. "I'm at your service—whatever you need. Anything at all."

Three days after the banquet, Ford tossed a second grub hoe into the truck bed, alongside several saws and shovels. No telling what he and Carson would be up against once they set foot on the ridge trail. Winter blowdown was always a problem on that stretch. Even though city folk claimed to want the wilderness experience, they rarely liked muddying their fancy boots by traversing around fallen logs.

He took a deep breath; the fragrance of the trees was almost as energizing as a good cup of coffee. The chill in the air would burn off in a few hours, and the morning sunshine suggested a pleasant day ahead. Many more of these days and the woods would be overrun with people.

Perhaps the superintendent was right. Margie might prove useful to the park in the long run. In the two years since he'd taken on his father's job as chief, it had become increasingly clear that park administration was more about managing people than resources. She had a talent for dealing with visitors—at least most of them. The memory of her altercation with that Carmichael fellow still rankled. Hopefully they'd seen the last of him. Still, something about the look in the man's eye suggested he wasn't the type to walk away from a fight.

What had Margie done to earn Carmichael's devotion? Ford hadn't heard a word past "fiancée," but her reaction had been anything but loving.

Sure, she was an attractive little thing, but her odd ways made her seem an unlikely match for a fussy stuffed shirt like Carmichael. Did he really desire a woman who dressed in trousers and prattled on endlessly about flowers? Ford shook his head. No sensible man would put up with her whims for long.

Thankfully, today he'd have to listen to nothing but the wind in the trees and Carson's whining about the workload.

"Ranger Brayden—Ford—I'm so glad you haven't left yet." Margie hurried down the path.

The woman's blue skirt was a welcome change from her typical attire of late. Ford closed his fingers around the tailgate, the icy metal smooth against his palm. "Just waiting on Carson. He was finishing a second stack of flapjacks, much to Mrs. Brown's delight."

She glanced over her shoulder toward the community kitchen. "I just came from there. She was pouring him another cup of coffee, I believe." Margie pulled a large canvas pack from behind her back. "She was kind enough to pack some food for the trail. I told her it would just be us three, but she seems to have included enough food for every ranger in the park. Will there be another work crew joining us?"

The air rushed from Ford's chest. "Us?"

Margie stood on her toes and hoisted the bag into the truck bed. "Yes, I hope you don't mind. Ranger Carson invited me to come along. I imagine the river's quite swollen now with all the snowmelt." She glanced at the sky. "It looks like it'll be a fine day."

A distant slam of a door suggested Carson would soon follow. Leave it to the slick fellow to include the new recruit. He'd insist on showing Margie the sights while Ford did all the back-breaking work.

Ford snorted. "Yes. A fine day, indeed."

She beamed. "As Muir said, 'Another glorious day, the air as delicious to the lungs as nectar to the tongue.' I've been looking forward to seeing more of the park. I've brought a flower press along, so hopefully we'll find some good specimens." Margie settled a felt hat on her head. At least she wasn't still sporting his father's Stetson.

Carson sauntered up, both hands on his belly. "After a meal like that, I could curl up and hibernate with the bears." He raised his brows at Margie. "Course it's the wrong time a year, isn't it? They're just digging themselves out now. Maybe we'll see one today. Wouldn't that be a treat, little lady?"

Margie smiled, fastening the clasps on her coat. "Then I'm glad to be escorted by such seasoned rangers. I'm not sure I wish to face off with a famished *Ursus americanus* by myself."

Carson frowned. "*Ursu* . . . what?"

Ford slapped him on the shoulder. "Don't worry, Margie. If we meet a hungry bear, I imagine he'll be drawn to Carson's maple syrup breath. We'd be safe."

The second man wrinkled his nose. "Unless he prefers perfume. What have you been up to these days, man? Your coat smells like a French salon."

Ford rubbed the back of his neck. Three nights of fresh air hadn't shaken the woman's lingering presence. What had she done? Marked him like a she-wolf?

Margie stepped within a few inches, leaning close for a whiff. A smile turned up her pert lips. "Mmm. Rose and jasmine, I believe. Shalimar? Quite an expensive fragrance."

Carson cackled. "I knew it. That Sheba from Luke's shindig, weren't it? What happened? You slip away for some necking? I didn't think you had it in you."

A burning flush crept up his neck. "I'll have none of that kind of talk, Carson. Every woman in the place was drenched in perfume." Every woman but one, anyway. Thankfully Margie had more sense. She always smelled of fresh air and soap—like a body should. "The day is getting away from us while we stand here talking nonsense. The only thing I want to smell is wood shavings as we deal with those downed trees. Margie, you'll have to do your own sightseeing because Carson and I are going to have our hands full. But we'll point you in the direction of the ridge."

She answered him with a curt nod. "I didn't intend for you to babysit me. In fact, if you need assistance, I'm sure I could learn to use a few of those tools."

Carson swung his pack up into the truck bed and chuckled. "Miss, I think you'd best leave the labor to the men. You can go off and pick your flowers while we work up a sweat. Maybe that'll make Ford here smell less like a French poodle."

Ford ground his teeth as he swung open the passenger door for Margie. He'd see to it that Carson sweated today. In fact, he was going to be so sore, he'd regret ever signing on to the park service.

Margie trotted down the trail behind Ford and Carson. The men hadn't allowed her to carry a single tool while they bent under the weight like pack mules. She pulled off her hat, appreciating the sensation of the chilled breeze lifting her hair. Even with heavy loads, the two rangers pulled farther ahead with every step.

She bent down to examine a three-leaved plant, its white blossom rising to meet the morning sunshine. "*Trillium ovatum*. So pretty, yet so simple." She tightened her grip on the wooden flower press. Hadn't she read somewhere that picking a trillium bloom killed the whole plant? If only she'd purchased one of those Brownie cameras. Trading the press for her journal, she sketched the small plant into the pages. It would have to do.

A cloak of tranquility draped over the forest as the scratching of her pencil blended with the occasional bird song, trickling water, and the movement of the limbs above her head. Warmth spread through her chest. She could stay here forever—alone with her thoughts.

Alone? She glanced up the trail. Her companions had vanished into the woods. Margie pushed up to her feet, brushing the damp soil from the edge of her skirt. They'd been on the trail less than twenty minutes and already she'd been left behind. Men were so single-minded. All Ford could see were logs across the path. What would it take to get him to look outside himself and his duties? She shook her head. And Carson? Obviously his interests lay elsewhere, but it wasn't in the diminutive foliage struggling for existence at the feet of massive cousins. These fellows were raining all over her image of wilderness caretakers.

Margie shouldered her pack, clutching the journal and pencil to her chest. This forest primeval held so many mysteries, she'd surely need them again soon.

The pointed lobes of a purplish-brown flower caught her eye; its muted colors blended with the scattering of needles and other detritus. *Is that wild ginger?* Margie bit her lip and scanned the trail ahead. At this rate, she'd never reach the lookout. She yanked a ribbon out of her pack and affixed it to the nearest tree. She'd stop on the return journey. She couldn't have the two rangers worrying about her delay. Hurrying along the path, she forced her eyes forward. This forest was littered with temptation. She needed to hike at a good clip, or she'd never catch up.

Her thoughts careened back to Philip's sudden appearance at the Inn. His intrusion reminded her of their first meeting, back when they were children. She'd been wandering in the scruffy woodland behind their property and had found the scrawny boy throwing rocks into the stream to build a dam. Such an innocent beginning.

Before leaving the gathering at Paradise, she'd tried to ask her father about Philip's claims, but she couldn't maneuver him away from the governor. She hadn't heard from her father since that evening, and the uncertainty hung on her like the heavy pack. Perhaps he thought if Philip were busy with the campaign, he wouldn't bother her here? As much as she hated the idea, it had some merit.

The distant sound of sawing cut through her thoughts. Quickening her pace, she launched herself down the path. Philip was the last person she wanted on her mind right now.

The massive log reached well above Ford's shoulder, yet he pushed and hauled the saw through its diameter in a steady rhythm. The sweat-stained shirt adhered to his back, the damp fabric doing little to obscure the movement of each muscle as he worked.

Margie paused at the edge of the clearing, her breath catching in her throat. *Such a perfect form.* A hot prickle touched her cheeks, and she forced her eyes down. He wasn't some specimen to be gathered, even though the man certainly belonged in a museum. An art museum, if not natural history.

She fanned herself with the journal as she approached, locking her gaze on the fallen tree instead of her supervisor. Just off the trail, the root wad rose starkly against the disturbed soil. The idea of this behemoth being wrenched from the ground and crashing to the forest floor chased away her audacious train of thought. The sound must have been deafening.

The saw hung up, drawing all progress to an abrupt halt. A muttered curse sounded from the opposite side of the trunk as the blade rattled in place. Ford swept a forearm across his brow. "Hold up, Carson." He caught sight of Margie and straightened. "We were wondering if you'd met with disaster."

A sawdust-coated arm reached over the log, and Carson heaved himself into view. "What happened?"

"Too much to see, I'm afraid." Margie tucked the book under her arm. "It looks like you fellows are working hard."

Ford snorted. "We've barely begun. We should have brought Athena. I didn't figure on the downed tree being one of the patriarchs."

Margie ran her fingers over the cinnamon-colored bark. "Patriarchs?"

He smiled. "That's what my dad called 'em. Trees this size would have been growing long before we were a nation. Probably before the Puyallups or Nisquallies imagined up the legend you shared at Paradise."

Fresh sap perfumed the air like memorial incense. Margie filled her lungs with the sweet smell. "Imagine the stories it could tell."

"The forest builds on the bones of those who went before." He gestured to a nearby fir, growing from the top of a decomposing stump.

"Don't we all?" Margie opened her journal. "We learn from those who've gone ahead of us. That's why I love quotations and legends—and perhaps why you fondly remember the words of your father."

He ran a hand across his bicep as if it pained him. "I suppose."

She sketched the image of the small sapling, keeping her focus from wandering back to Ford's muscled arms. "I should probably make my way to the ridge, or you two will be done before me." Tucking the book under her elbow, she scrutinized the impediment in her path. "Should I go around?"

Carson threw one leg over the log's girth. "If Ford gives you a boost, I can lift you over, Miss."

"Oh, dear. Really?" Margie turned and looked at the root wad. "Wouldn't it be simpler—"

"Just put your foot here." Ford stooped down and laced his fingers into a mock stirrup.

"All right." The moment she placed her toe into his palms, he hoisted her skyward. Carson guided her to a seated position on the damp, moss-strewn surface. "It's a nice view up here, ain't—isn't it?" He straddled the log, a few inches closer than she'd have preferred. "If only we had a picnic or something."

Ford's brows drew down. "It's only ten o'clock, and I'm sure Miss Lane desires to move on to the lookout."

"Yes, yes, of course." She scooted away from Ranger Carson. "How do I . . ." She shifted her legs to the far side. "It's still a long way down."

"Don't you worry." The man shimmied down, landing with a thump. He pointed to a protruding limb. "Put your foot there, it'll get you part way. Then I'll catch you."

Margie cast one final glance at Ford before edging her toe toward the branch, hoping it would support her weight. Her skirts tangled on the rough bark. She was likely giving Carson an eyeful. Of all days not to wear trousers. She wedged her boot against the limb, bouncing against it slightly to test its strength.

That was a mistake. It snapped with a sickening, crunching sound. Margie dug her heels against the bark to slow her momentum. By the time she landed against Carson's chest, the hem of her skirt had traveled quite the opposite direction.

His grin deepened. "Now that's what I call a fine landing." He gripped her backside as he lowered her to the ground, gravity pressing her against him in a most unladylike fashion.

"You can let go now." She shoved his chest with both hands.

"What happened?" Ford's disembodied voice sounded over the barrier as Carson loosened his hold. "Margie, are you hurt?"

"I'm fine." Her tone ratcheted up a few notes above normal. "Ranger Carson managed to break my fall."

Carson chuckled. "And thankfully, she didn't break me."

A scrabbling sounded from the far side and Ford's head appeared. Carson stepped away, spreading his arms. "No harm done, boss."

Margie straightened her skirts. "I appreciate your help, gentlemen. But next time, I'll go around."

The chief ranger glanced up at the sun, as if gauging the hour. "By the time you return, we'll have this monster cleared away. You'll walk through the mud like a queen."

Carson rubbed his chin. "Not unless you put your sweet-smelling coat down."

Margie cleared her throat. "That won't be necessary, I'm sure. But I'd best be on my way."

Ford frowned. "Maybe it's not such a good idea for you to go alone."

"I'll be perfectly fine. I have specimens to collect. You've much work to do. If I don't return in a couple of hours, you can come track me down like the mighty mountain men you are."

Ford scrambled to a sitting position and looked down at her. "All right, but be cautious. If I have to come pluck you off a ledge, Senator Lane will have my badge."

She folded both arms across her chest. "I can assure you, I'm going nowhere near any cliffs. Not if I can help it."

NINE

*M*argie stood at the rocky overlook and let the powerful scene wash over her. Ridgeline after ridgeline of deep green rose to meet the jagged edges of the enormous peak, tucked into its rumpled blanket of white. Her heartbeat thudded in her chest from climbing the steep path to the viewpoint, but a breeze swept upward from the valley and chilled her flushed cheeks. Margie nestled her fingers under her elbows. Her mother would be incensed that she was out in public without gloves, but this didn't really count as such, did it?

The earthy fragrance hanging in the crisp air sent a rush of energy all the way to her toes. Another week or two of this June sunshine and the higher elevation trails would be snow-free, with meadow flowers lifting their eager faces to the burgeoning sunlight. She'd already gathered a good collection of forest plants to preserve, but she longed for the subalpine blooms. So far, she'd only seen a few of the early risers like the avalanche lily and the white pasqueflower. Winter ruled the subalpine year, with the three other seasons squeezed into a few short months. Margie gazed across the wooded valley toward the summit rising up in the afternoon splendor, appearing almost close enough to touch.

What would it be like to climb to the crest and look out over Rainier's entire domain? Women had made the ascent in the past—two hard days traversing crumpled glaciers, living under the constant threat of rockfall and avalanche. She shook her head. She'd rather spend her time reveling in the abundant life on Tahoma's flanks. Leave the mountain conquering to men. She had nothing to prove.

Margie sighed, leaned against one of the boulders and flipped open her journal. A view like this deserved a poem. She tapped the pencil against her lip a few times, hoping the words would spill forth.

In this sheltered spot, the wind was no longer a problem. She unfastened a few buttons below her neck and let the sun's rays chase away the gooseflesh. The stones behind her back radiated warmth, as if they'd been soaking up heat just for the purpose of providing her comfort. Margie closed her eyes, relaxing into the mountain's gift. *God's gift.* Opening her eyes, she lifted the pencil and sketched the scene before her, tracing the rise of the peak against the blue sky. Underneath she penned one of her favorite verses. "Every good gift and every perfect gift is from above, and cometh down from the Father of lights, with whom is no variableness, neither shadow of turning." The image of God as the perfect light brought a flutter to her soul.

Ford's lack of beliefs cast the only shadow over her good mood. Her pencil stilled as a new thought rushed through her mind. Perhaps God hadn't sent her here to escape Philip's control. Maybe it was to shine the light of His love on a man who'd lost his faith—or never had it to begin with.

How could someone live in the sight of such majesty and not understand the heart of the Creator? She laid her journal in her lap and let the peaceful scene quiet her soul. *Lord, as the men brought tools to clear the trail, may I be such an instrument in Your mighty hands. I know You can clear the path to Ford's heart.*

Ford used one sleeve to wipe the sweat dripping down his face, gluing sawdust to his skin in the process. The stinging smell of cut wood lingered in the air, as if the dying tree decided to protest with one final gasp. He and Carson had managed to slice a path through the giant log and roll the cut section free. Standing in the gap between the remaining lengths, Ford studied the trunk's exposed rings. In good years the tree would be able to lay down a thick layer of wood, while slim years showed as a mere etching. He traced a finger across the lines. If the human body held such markers, his past few lines would be thin, indeed.

Year after year the tree had withstood wind, rain, fires, and pests, but this week's deadly combination of saturated ground and high winds had been its downfall. One minute it stood tall and strong, the next it was crashing to the soil that had so long held it firm.

His father had his roots sunk deep in Rainier's soils, as well. The fact that an avalanche had casually swept him to his death without so much as an afterthought seemed the cruelest insult imaginable.

Ford stepped away from the log, adding his saw to the pile of equipment he and Carson had hauled in.

Carson tossed the last chunks of wood over the embankment, grunting with the effort. "What about the little gal? She should've returned by now, don't you think? Should I go after her?" He brushed his grubby hands against his trouser legs.

"No, I'll do it. Take some of this stuff to the truck. I'll get the rest on my way back." Carson's hiking pace was slower than molasses. Ford could be to the end of the trail before the shorter man made it halfway to the vehicle. And the brisk walk would clear his thoughts.

Carson shouldered two axes and the saw. "I'm going to sleep well tonight, that's for certain."

Ford set off in the opposite direction, striding up the ridge through the dripping forest. Margie should have easily hiked the round trip in the two hours they'd been working. He'd been a fool to allow her to traipse off by herself. The woman could string together a lovely line of prose, probably while painting a picture and quoting useless scientific facts, but she wouldn't know how to react in a crisis. Harry should never have allowed the senator to talk him into this ridiculous scheme—money or no. Perhaps Margie had learned her persuasive manner from her father.

The distant shriek of a camp robber jay nearly made him jump out of his boots. Ford shook his head. He was as twitchy as a squirrel under a bobcat's paw. He'd walked these woods since he was a tyke; certainly a fully grown woman could manage unhindered. Chances were, she was knee-deep in plants, categorizing her latest discovery without a thought to the time.

As he approached the lookout, he craned his neck to peer down the slope. A spot of color on the granite outcropping sent all humor leaking out of him.

Margie lay spread-eagled across the rocks, one arm across her face. Bare legs poked out beneath her skirt, her pale skin gleaming in the sunlight.

He stumbled forward, scrambling downhill as fast as his boots could travel. Loose stones sprang free, bouncing away at a rapid clip. "Margie?"

She jerked to a sitting position and swiveled to stare at him, shading her eyes with a wrist. "Yes?"

Ford lurched to a halt, stopping his forward momentum before it pitched him over the precipice. A few more pebbles clattered down the bank. "Wha-what are you doing? I thought . . ." He swallowed hard.

She pulled her skirt down over her knees and pushed up to her feet. Her stockings and shoes sat nearby. "I was just resting my eyes. I couldn't resist the feel of the sun-warmed granite against my tired leg muscles. Did you know the Chinese use heated stones placed against the abdomen to assist in digestion?"

Ford picked his way to her side. Leave it to Margie to find some obscure fact to explain her bizarre actions. "I thought you'd fallen."

"Again? I wouldn't make that mistake twice. I must have dozed off." She stretched, glancing up at the sun. "How late is it?"

He drew a deep breath, slowing his skidding heartbeat. "Late enough that I came after you."

"I'm sorry. I gathered quite a few foliage samples and then treated myself to lunch with a view." She gestured at the overlook. "Two pesky golden-mantled ground squirrels made off with most of my sandwich while I was writing in my journal." Her lips pressed into a frown. "I would have been more than happy to share, but it would have been polite to ask me first. I do believe they were working as a team."

Ford reached down to gather her pack and books, averting his eyes from her crumpled stockings. "You seem to attract rodents." The words stuck in his gullet. "I mean—"

"No,"—she held out a hand to stop his apology—"you are correct. I've had a string of bad luck with the lesser species since I arrived. Though I'm quite looking forward to making the acquaintance of . . ." She squinted and bit her lip. "What were they called?" She took one of the texts from Ford, flipping to a marked page. "The hoary marmot. I've done some reading, and it appears to be a fascinating creature."

Ford couldn't resist a smile "Whistling jacks? I suppose they are pretty entertaining." He glanced toward the mountain. "There are usually quite a few whistlers up at Indian Henry's Hunting Ground. Rock rabbits, too."

"Rock rabbits?" Her lips pursed as she flipped through more pages. "You mean pikas? Technically they're not rodents, but I'd still like to see one."

"Trust me, by the end of the summer you'll have seen plenty."

"Is that a promise?" The fervor in her eyes drew him.

The sudden flicker in his chest caught him off guard. Ford glanced back at the mountain to steady himself. The last thing he needed was to tangle his feelings with the likes of Margie Lane. If he wasn't careful, he'd be under her power just like that businessman fellow. And what good would he be then?

"We should get back to the truck." He cleared the cobwebs from his throat as he shoved the books into her pack. "Carson will be wondering what happened to both of us pretty soon."

"You're right, of course. Thank you for checking on me." She scooped up her shoes and stockings.

He turned away as she put herself to rights, even though the image of her shapely legs was forever imprinted on his brain.

Keep free from Margie's charms? He settled the knapsack on his shoulder. It just might be entirely too late for that.

TEN

June 23, 1927

*F*ord sank into the desk chair, setting his mug of coffee beside the tall stack of district reports. He'd spent days looking over the papers and trying to put the information into bite-sized pieces for the superintendent. He still hadn't filed last month's paperwork. Ford flipped through the fussy descriptions of each area's activities. Every man seemed set on impressing Ford by recording ridiculous amounts of data—weather statistics, wildlife counts, hours spent on patrol duties, trails cleared.

Ford skimmed past the numbers and tried to concentrate on what Harry would want to see. The people factor, he called it. The figures spelled it out. Visitation was up in all corners of the park, even with the snow lingering late into the season. The dispatches pointed to an increasing number of vehicles, more demand for campsites, clashes between people and wildlife, and plenty of traffic tickets written. All those facts meant one thing—Ford chained to his typewriter.

He stretched his arms over his head, missing the days of being a simple trail ranger. Now his job demanded endless meetings, reports, managing a staff spread over three hundred and fifty square miles, and the relentless task of hiring crews to maintain both the road and telephone network. Ford hadn't set foot on the trail since climbing the ridge with Carson and Margie two weeks ago.

He'd promised to take Margie to Indian Henry's Hunting Ground, but perhaps he should assign someone else to escort her. She could even ride one of the guided horse tours from the National Park Inn. It seemed a shame for her to miss out just because he was swamped with other duties. Ford swiped a palm across his weary eyes. Who was he kidding? He wanted to see the delight on her face as she first set foot in the magical place.

Ford jabbed at the typewriter keys, picking out one letter at a time. He glanced up at the window, sunshine illuminating the mountain's white dome. He'd gotten an early start in the hopes of finishing this distasteful job today, but the morning beckoned. It would be a crime to spend the day cooped up indoors.

A man keeps his promises. Ford glanced at the desk. Filing reports should be reserved for overcast days, of which this park had plenty. He swung his coat off the hook, jammed his arms in the sleeves, and hurried out before he had a chance to reconsider.

A polished midnight blue automobile sat in front of the National Park Inn, its hood topped by a silver ornament shaped like a springing greyhound. Ford stopped to admire the auto's lines, though why any man would drop hard-earned dollars on such a useless vehicle was beyond him. Even the tires were deluxe, the gleaming white rubber standing out against the dark ground. There'd be no way to keep them free of mud, especially here in the Northwest.

He hurried past, aiming for the new Community Building by the campground. Jennings and Margie had spent the last few days organizing plant identification cards for a display at the Paradise ranger station.

Jennings bent over the collection, fanned out across a long table. "Hey, boss. Checking up on me, or taking a new interest in the naturalist programs?"

Ford picked up one of the colored note cards, studying the flattened flower sample. "I was wondering how Miss Lane was fitting in. Are you finding work to keep her busy?"

A smile spread across the man's face. "Ford, she's a firecracker. She knows every plant and creature from here to Paradise. The visitors adore her." He fiddled with his tie. "Frankly, I'm not sure why you need me."

"She's here as a favor to Harry. You're in charge of programs. Just fit her in where you can."

Margie appeared from the kitchen area, her arms filled with mounted plant samples. "Ranger Jennings, about this saxifrage." She stopped midstep. "Oh, I didn't know you were here, Ford—Ranger Brayden. I was just updating some of the displays. I found a few identification errors."

"More?" Jennings turned to Ford and shrugged. "As I said, she's extremely knowledgeable."

"Book knowledge. But she's a little short of practical experience." Ford cleared his throat. "It's time to fix that. I was planning on patrolling up to Indian Henry's today. I've had reports of a bear harassing campers for handouts. I thought Margie might like to tag along."

Margie's nose wrinkled. "Ranger Carson was feeding a black bear at the Longmire camp last night to entertain the children. He had it begging on hind legs. Quite degrading, if you ask me."

"He thinks it's funny. But when they start knocking down tents, it stops being humorous." He glanced at Jennings. "Do you mind working on your own for the rest of the day?"

Jennings tipped his head, a twinkle lighting his green eyes. "Patrolling with the chief? Quite an honor, Miss Lane."

A prickle crept down Ford's back. Was he so obvious? "Unless you're busy."

She bit her lip, glancing down at the plant cards. "I probably shouldn't leave all this work for Ranger Jennings."

"Go." Jennings sighed and reached for the stack. "Someone should be out enjoying this fine weather."

Her brows drew together. "Why don't you come along? We could get some new specimens to replace some of these aging ones."

"No, I want to get these up to Paradise. It'll be a busy weekend."

Ford snapped him a quick nod. He liked Jennings, but this hike would be more pleasant with two. He held the door for Margie as they stepped out onto the porch. "Do you need anything before we go?"

She glanced down at her skirt. "Perhaps I should change into my trousers and sturdier boots. And I'd like to get my journal."

"I'll walk you to your cabin." Ford kept his hat under his arm as they walked. "I suppose I should have given you more warning."

"I'm a little surprised. Surely you'd prefer to patrol with one of the men."

"Sometimes it's nice to share things you love with someone new." The words flew from his mouth before he could reel them back. *I didn't just say that. What a sap.*

A smile danced across Margie's lips. "I know exactly what you mean." She reached for the doorknob, her hair bouncing as she tossed her head. "I'll be out in a twinkling."

A twinkling? He watched her disappear into the ramshackle cabin, unsettled by his flood of emotions. For years he'd preferred hiking alone, but now all he could think about was seeing Indian Henry's through Margie's eyes. What had changed? With her penchant for stopping, he'd probably be ready to hog-tie the woman and toss her over his shoulder by mile two. And yet he volunteered for this task.

She'd bewitched him. That's all there was to it. He scrubbed a hand across his face to hide any eagerness. No sense looking like a silly schoolboy.

Minutes later, she popped back outside. "Shall we?" Hefting a massive knapsack, Margie resembled an explorer ready to head out on a major scientific expedition.

He moved to take her pack. "This is a day hike, not an African safari. What do you have in there?"

She pressed the bag to her chest, stepping out of his reach. "Just a few books. A pair of binoculars. That sort of thing. I can carry it."

With a shrug, he headed up the path leading to the National Park Inn, the muddy path squelching under his boots. "I'll ask them to prepare us a box lunch. Since the trailhead is right across the road, we should be on our way in a few minutes." An awkward silence followed. Shouldn't she be prattling on about something? He glanced over his shoulder.

Margie stood stock-still ten paces back, staring at the small parking area.

"What's wrong?"

She pointed with a trembling finger. "How long has that vehicle been parked there?"

He glanced at the automobile. "I noticed it on my way over. I'm not sure if the owner spent the night or arrived this morning. Does it matter?"

Margie clutched at her load. "Not at all." Her voice wavered. "On second thought, this pack is rather heavy. I think I will leave a few books and grab a muffler instead. Why don't you go ahead? I'll meet you at the trailhead." She edged back toward the cabin.

"All right." He watched her disappear into the cottage. Removing some of the weight from her sack was wise, but the change in her demeanor was unmistakable. Ford turned and studied the unusual vehicle. Perhaps he should figure out why.

Margie's thoughts scattered as she pressed her door closed and huddled in the dark cabin. Philip's automobile was the last thing she'd expected to see this morning. She yanked open the pack and rifled through the supplies she'd stowed just moments before. If only she could step back in time a few minutes, just to be free of this wild fluttering in her chest. Having Ford show up at the Community Building had seemed an answer to prayer. Ever since the day at Rampart Ridge, she'd been hoping for an opportunity to talk to him about her faith.

"Sometimes it's nice to share things you love with someone new." The truth of his words echoed in her ears.

A whole day of hiking—the perfect time to tiptoe into the deep places of his heart and plant a few seeds of faith. After that? Her heart jumped. No, she couldn't allow herself to go there. This was about the man's soul, not his love life. And definitely not hers.

She hadn't planned on Philip Carmichael showing up uninvited.

She angled the shutters up an inch, peering toward the parking area. She couldn't let Philip cast a shadow of gloom over this day or chance him ruining their outing. Pulling the long red muffler from its hook, she wrapped the knitted garment twice around her neck, pulling it up over her chin. She exchanged the small toque for her cloche, drawing the felt hat down low over her eyes and ears. On this warm day, she might perish from heat exhaustion, but it was imperative she reach the trailhead unseen.

Once Philip realized he wouldn't find her at Longmire, he'd leave.

Certainly he wouldn't follow her into the woods—not in his Italian leather loafers.

Margie dumped the books out onto the bed, limiting herself to one plant and one animal guide, her journal, flower press, and the binoculars. She wedged the items in next to her first-aid kit and extra sweater. Strapping the canteen over the top, she shouldered the knapsack and took a deep breath. She checked her bundled reflection in her tiny hand mirror, ensuring that only the tip of her nose peeped out between the hat and scarf. By skirting around the far side of the Inn, she could arrive at the meeting spot before anyone had a chance to interfere.

After locking the door behind her, Margie scurried down the walkway, darting through the trees like a snowshoe hare. A hundred yards or so and she'd be under the protection of her beloved forest. She could hide in the sanctuary of its shadows until Ford arrived.

Where did he say he had to go?

She paused in her flight, heart pausing midbeat.

The National Park Inn.

Ford tucked the lunch into his pack, imagining a pleasant late-afternoon meal in the high meadows. Nothing worked up an appetite like hiking, and no one made a better sandwich than the chef at the Inn. Ford hoped Margie, accustomed to fancy restaurants, would still appreciate ham and cheese on bread, especially if the view provided the seasoning. He hoisted the pack onto his shoulder and turned to leave, sidestepping a well-dressed man in the lobby.

"Ranger Brayden, such a pleasure to see you on this fine morning. I thought you'd be out wrestling mountain lions or some such heroic activity."

Philip Carmichael's sly grin sent Ford's stomach sliding south. The gaudy vehicle—of course. "Mr. Carmichael, I'm surprised to see you back at the park so soon. I guess Miss Lane's presentation made a positive impression on you?"

The man laughed as he straightened his tie. "You could say that. I had breakfast with your superintendent, and now I'm on my way up to Paradise to speak with Mr. Johansson and some others from the Rainier National Park Company."

Ford's chest tightened. What sort of business did Carmichael have with Harry and Luke? "Sounds like a busy day."

Carmichael ran a gloved palm across his shirtfront. "A profitable day." He glanced about the lobby. "I thought perhaps I'd ask Margaret if she wished to join us at the Paradise Inn. She seems to have such a fondness for the place."

Ford shoved the pack further behind his arm. "I'm afraid Miss Lane is indisposed today. She's—she's out on the trail."

"I should have guessed. Ever since she read Thoreau as a child, nature has been her siren song." He shook his head, lines forming on either side of his mouth. "I once found her stripped to her shift, lying in a field of wildflowers. Now there's an image one doesn't soon forget."

"I can imagine." Though he was really trying not to.

"She quoted some nonsense about pondering the creation, but I realized the truth of the situation. Margaret is a flower—at heart, if nowhere else. Not one of these mountain weeds of course, but a rose destined to provide inexplicable beauty to the finest garden." Carmichael's gaze was unflinching. "And I intend for her to decorate mine."

Acid burned in Ford's throat. "I believe her interests lie elsewhere."

Carmichael's brows shot upward. "What would you know of her interests? Margaret and I have been close since we were children." He stepped closer, narrowing the distance between them. "She's developed a strange fixation on this place, but if it's a mountain she wants, a mountain she shall have. I can certainly afford it."

A laugh burst from Ford's chest. This man harbored grand delusions. "In case you're unaware, the mountain isn't for sale. National parks belong to everyone."

The businessman's eyes narrowed. "That's what you think."

*T*wenty minutes later, Margie strode down the path, the ferns catching at her legs as she brushed past. Why was Philip in Longmire? It had been bad enough seeing him at Paradise, but now he was practically on her doorstep.

"Where's the fire?" Ford's voice trailed some distance behind her. "I didn't realize you were *this* eager to get to Indian Henry's."

She slowed, glancing back as the ranger's long-legged stride brought him alongside in a matter of moments. It's not like he'd been taxed by the pace. Ford's easy grin melted the tension from her neck and shoulders. She needed to leave all her concerns about Philip behind. Ford had said nothing of encountering him at the Inn. Now with enough distance, perhaps she could pull this day away from the cliff-edge of disaster.

Margie forced a smile. "No fire, but I don't want to keep you out too long. I'm sure you have other work to do."

He buttoned his jacket as they walked side by side on the narrow trail. "Truth be told, I'm relieved to be away from the desk and those unending reports. It's duller than watching moss grow on the trees. Writing them isn't so bad, but I fear I'm all thumbs with a typewriter."

"The superintendent should provide you a secretary."

"We're expected to do for ourselves up here." He shot her a sideways glance. "I don't suppose you type, do you?"

She hoisted the pack a little higher. "I'm fair. Do you need help? I'd be happy to assist you." If Philip was still lurking about Longmire upon her return, it might be best to stay out of sight, anyway. "In your office?"

"Yes." A smile spread across his features. "Are you certain? If we worked together, maybe I could get caught up."

She couldn't resist studying his profile against the serene forest back-drop. Ford's bearing had changed the moment they started hiking, as if he'd cast off every last burden at the trailhead. His steps seemed light, and a boyish sparkle lit his eyes. His broad shoulders appeared uncommonly loose and relaxed. She could almost imagine running her fingers over the muscles of his arm, kneading away any remaining tension.

Warmth flooded Margie's veins. How he'd laugh if he knew her thoughts. No matter how her heart yearned, he was still her supervisor and was unlikely to view her other than as someone working for him. She touched her flushed cheeks. "You are taking time away to give me the grand tour, after all. The least I can do is type a few reports."

Margie focused on her feet just in time to manage a quick hop and skip over a greenish-yellow banana slug. She couldn't bear to crush the in-nocent creature under her boot, but bumping into Ford's arm had not been part of the plan.

Ford reached to steady her, the warmth of his touch obvious through her sleeve—or perhaps that was just her imagination. Margie veered to her own side of the trail, no longer trusting her runaway thoughts.

Ford cleared his throat, running the same hand over his jaw. "This outing is no sacrifice, trust me. I used to spend most of my time out in the woods. I never realized how much I'd miss it when I took over for Dad."

The place obviously teemed with memories. "You must live every day in his shadow."

"In some ways. Huge boots to fill." He shoved his hat back and stared up at the forest canopy.

"I believe you're blazing your own trail. The men respect you. You must be doing a fine job."

"I'm younger and less experienced than many of the crew. Harry took a big chance promoting me like he did. I'd worked enough years, but served only one season as a district ranger." He exhaled a long breath. "His decision was motivated by sentiment, and we all knew it."

Margie tucked her hand into her coat pocket, fighting the urge to take Ford's arm. "I've sensed no animosity or jealousy toward you from anyone. I don't believe they begrudge you your post."

"I hope you're right. I'd hate anyone talking nepotism—not that I'd blame them." He shrugged. "I almost turned down the job, but Harry convinced me that taking the position would ease the staff through the transition and their—their grief." He grimaced, glancing down.

Their grief. Margie lifted the brim of her cloche, letting the air cool her neck. Ford's father must have viewed the park staff as family, perhaps more than his own son even. Her father was much the same. His devotion to his constituents bordered on obsession.

And now her father had granted Philip control over his next campaign. The thought constricted her lungs like a spreading vine. He'd taken Philip under his wing years before, at Margie's request—one she'd long regretted.

Why was Philip at Longmire, anyway? She should have confronted him rather than allow the specter of his presence to cast a pall over the day. Margie drew a deep breath of the mountain air, like a tonic to her raw soul. Thirteen miles on the trail would surely chase away her worries.

With such a day under her belt, she might actually be able to face the likes of Philip Carmichael.

Ford glanced back as Margie paused and stooped over another fern, running the delicate fronds between her fingers. It looked just like the past three ferns she'd halted to examine. He chuckled, allowing the quietness of the day to settle into his chest. He'd needed this more than he'd realized. Normally when he headed out on the trail, he burned up the miles under his boot soles, intent on achieving some type of remarkable distance worthy of his time. This day was all about Margie.

Seeing her discover new plants was like watching a child opening gifts at Christmas. Or how he imagined it, anyway. He didn't have any nieces or nephews, so the holidays had turned into rather lonely affairs the past couple of years. A family of his own seemed like a far-fetched dream. What sort of woman would agree to live way out here?

Margie glanced up from the fern with a smile. "Sorry. I couldn't resist. Do you know what this is?"

He'd walked this path hundreds of times; had he ever bothered to look? He retraced his steps to stand at her side. "Tell me."

She rattled off a scientific name that tickled his ears like a feather. Her voice took on a musical lilt whenever she spoke Latin.

"Really? Is it rare?"

She stood, brushing loose soil from her trouser knees. "Probably not at this elevation, but I've never seen it in Seattle. Its rhizomes can be prepared as a tea useful for treating gout and rheumatism."

"Maybe we should bring some to Mrs. Brown."

"And if I'm wrong in my identification, we could end up brewing poison."

"I trust you." Without thinking, he plucked a loose twig from the sleeve of her coat. *Stop doing that.* The last thing he wanted was Margie thinking he was seeking excuses to touch her. Even if he was.

"That's sweet." A flush tinted her cheeks. "I'm not sure I'd trust myself, though." Margie returned to the trail, joining him as they inched toward their destination. She continued to rattle on about the uses of ferns, her words ringing through the morning air like birdsong.

Ford had spent his life in these woods, but he'd never seen it through the lenses with which Margie viewed the world. He surveyed the forest floor as if taking it in for the first time—all the little bits and bolts of life working together. Each had value alone yet also served as part of some mysterious whole. It was little wonder she saw God at work in everything. He swiped his hand across his eyes. Had his thoughts really jumped from romance to plants to religion?

They walked the next two miles in near silence. Ford took the lead, pacing through the woods until it opened out onto the Kautz Creek valley. He checked over his shoulder occasionally, but Margie plodded obediently behind him, no longer halting to examine the undergrowth.

He gestured at the river up ahead. "We'll cross here, and then it'll be a good, steep climb up to the meadows. Do you need to rest?"

"No, thank you."

She had good endurance, considering her short legs. "Had any more trouble with your pack rat friend?" He slowed his pace so she'd draw up beside him.

"I've seen it a few times. I'm conducting an experiment to see whether rodents prefer Mrs. Brown's snickerdoodles or her butter cookies."

"I could set a trap, if you'd like."

"No, I've grown attached to the little fellow. He hasn't tried to steal anything else."

"Just tell me you haven't named the vermin." He pushed a branch out of their path and held it as she walked past.

"I won't tell you if you don't want me to." She ducked her head as if to hide a smile. "Mrs. Brown tried to help me block all the nooks and crannies where he might have been getting in, but it doesn't seem to have stopped him."

"That cabin is built like a cracker box."

She glanced at him. "She said she was surprised I was living in that particular abode. Apparently there are several cottages close to her home that are brand-new and unoccupied. Not that I'm complaining."

"I'd been meaning to speak to you about that." Ford swallowed, prickly heat climbing his neck. "I'd been holding those for our seasonal staff, but it looks like we won't need quite so many as I'd thought. If you'd like, we could move you to more . . . suitable accommodations." Especially considering the amount her father had donated toward the new administration building.

Margie turned her face forward, the light catching her profile in a flattering tone. "Thank you, but no. I like my little home. It's quaint and rustic. Like Thoreau's cabin on Walden Pond. Besides, now I have Archibald for company."

"Archibald?"

"Oh, I forgot. You told me not to tell you."

The knots eased out of his shoulders. The newer section of housing was on the far side of Longmire, and there was something comforting about knowing she was close enough for him to reach if there was any trouble. Like more rats. Or troublesome businessmen.

The encounter with Carmichael left a bitter taste in Ford's mouth, and so far he'd not mentioned it to Margie. She'd given the man his walking papers, but he didn't seem to be getting the hint. The idea of that skunk spending the night at the National Park Inn—only a short walk from Margie's cottage—sent a sickly sweat across Ford's skin. Likely as not, Carmichael didn't know which one was hers. Ford intended to keep it that way. "You have two days off coming up. Do you plan to return home to Tacoma? Your father's campaign gala is this weekend, isn't it?"

She wrinkled her nose. "I'd rather enjoy my time here. He'll be too busy to see me."

"Don't you miss your family—your friends?"

"Sometimes. But the summer is all about meaningless garden parties, luncheons, and society teas. With the exception of some rowdy picnics at Point Defiance Park, my social calendar is rather frivolous." She gestured at the trees. "I feel more at home here than I have anywhere in my life." She turned toward him, her brown eyes warm. "My soul is at peace here. Like God has led me to the promised land. I don't suppose you'd understand."

"Since I've never lived anywhere else, I don't suppose I do."

"Have you ever wished to?"

Ford studied the stream as it swept past. "Sure. As a boy, I read books about foreign lands and big cities. Everything sounded more exciting than here. When the Great War broke out, I dreamed of enlisting, but I was too young. By the time I was of age, it was long over."

"Thank goodness." Margie shivered. "My uncle fought. He's never been the same since. It's almost like he left the best pieces of himself over there."

"We have quite a few veterans among the crew. They traded one uniform for another. I guess it seemed natural, since the parks were originally overseen by the army."

"I'm sure nature's touch provides healing for those men, ravaged by the horrors of the battlefield. As John Muir said, 'Thousands of tired, nerve-shaken, over-civilized people are beginning to find out that going to

the mountains is going home.' I assume that applies to shell shock, as well."
She brushed fingers across her forehead, as if clearing a spider's web. "There
I go again. I tend to run to quotations when I don't know what else to say.
It's easier to trust another's words than my own, I suppose."

"I appreciate your words."

A smile toyed at her lips, even as she refused to meet his gaze. "I know
I talk too much. I tend to prattle on when I get nervous."

"Nervous? With me?"

"Of course. You're so much a part of this place. You're like one of these
trees—planted on the side of a mountain and as much a part of the landscape as they are." She shrugged. "I'm just a little bit of fluff, blown in by
the wind."

"I'd say you're far more than that." Ford loosened his tie, determined
not to allow this conversation to derail him like their previous one.

Her eyes grew serious. "I wanted to thank you for agreeing to hire me
for the summer. I know I don't have much to offer. I am indebted to you,
truly."

An uneasy sensation rose in his chest. She didn't know her father's
promised donations had secured her position, did she? Senator Lane could
have put his daughter up all summer in the Paradise Inn for less money.
Should Ford be keeping such a secret from her?

Margie halted abruptly, her eyes widening. "Are we crossing this
river?"

He pushed aside the branches blocking his view, though the thunder-
ing of Kautz Creek was unmistakable. "If you want to go to Indian Henry's Hunting Ground, we must." Spring runoff had swelled the tumbling
stream into a mighty cataract.

"Please tell me there's a suspension bridge. I can't possibly wade
through that."

"You wouldn't last ten seconds in that water. It's straight out of the Kautz Glacier. Not only is it freezing cold, it can roll boulders." He gestured upstream. "There's your bridge. I'm glad it's intact. It's been known to wash away in high water like this."

Margie craned her neck and then grasped his arm. "Ford, that's not a bridge." She dug her fingers into his sleeve. "That's a log."

The man had to be insane. There was no other explanation. To quiet her pounding heart, Margie plopped down on a nearby rock, letting the spray of the river dampen her skin. *I can't cross that. What was I thinking?*

A dimple showed in Ford's cheek, as though he battled against a smile. "You'll do fine. There's a handrail."

The wet surface of the bare log glistened in the afternoon sunshine, a single thin pole apparently serving as a support. A surge of nausea rose in Margie's belly. *I can't. I won't.* Of course Ford wouldn't think twice about walking the log. He probably bathed in glacial meltwater.

"Don't you want to see the alpine meadows?"

"I do." The hairs prickled on the back of her neck beneath her scarf. "But there must be a more suitable crossing."

Ford looked left and right. "It only grows wider—and wilder—downstream."

"And upstream?" Margie swallowed. Certainly there must be a better option than this. A swinging suspension bridge was bad enough, but balancing on a damp log mere inches from the surging water?

Ford gripped his pack's straps, hoisting it higher on his back. "We're hardly outfitted for glacier travel. How much ice climbing have you done?"

Margie covered her face, willing her stomach into compliance.

Travelers must manage this path every day. The guide service took folks up here regularly.

"I'll help you, Margie. You'll be fine. It's not as frightening as it first appears."

She pushed her head upward in preparation to stand. Hopefully her trembling knees wouldn't give way. That wouldn't be much help on the slick surface. "If you say it's safe, then it must be so."

A tiny crease formed between Ford's brows, but it vanished just as quickly. He held out a hand to her, his jaw set. "I do. I promise, I'd never lead you into a dangerous situation."

She studied the ranger's stance, legs apart, sturdy arm outstretched. How could a girl refuse such a robust offer? She didn't doubt the man's confidence in himself—it was his faith in her that seemed far-fetched. She'd never been sure-footed as a child, and she was certainly no mountain goat now. Margie placed her hand in his.

Ford's victorious grin melted the last of her resistance. "Come on. Once we're past this, it's a short climb to Indian Henry's. You'll be ankle-deep in wildflowers in no time."

"Assuming my ankles are still intact." She glanced down at her fingers, clasped in Ford's palm. A shiver raced up her arm.

"Do you trust me?"

She met his gaze, those blue-gray eyes turning her thoughts to mush. "With all my heart."

Ford dropped his hold as if he'd only just realized their connection. "Good." He turned to the stream. "Let's get going."

As he stepped away, a sudden chill swept over her. Margie lifted her chin and forced a breath of air deep into her lungs. If she wanted to be a woman of the mountains, she needed to start acting the part. Even when her heart cowered.

He set out across the large cobbles toward the river with a self-assured stride, the green of his uniform standing out against the slate-gray stones.

She picked her way, her boots doing little to steady her feet on the uneven surfaces. If only she could have held onto him a little longer. Her pulse raced faster the closer they got to the water.

Ford glanced over his shoulder. "Do you want to go first?" His voice barely carried over the clamor of the rapids.

"No. I'll follow." *Eventually.*

He traversed the bridge without bothering to slow his pace or touch the railing. Hopping down on the far side, he turned and beckoned to her before cupping his palms around his mouth. "It's as easy as falling off a log."

Margie kept her voice low, allowing the river to steal her words. "That's a great comfort. Thank you." She closed her fingers around the peeled branch rail, the icy damp soaking through her skin. She climbed onto the trunk, tottering for a dizzying moment. Is this what it had felt like as a babe, taking those first hesitant steps toward her nanny's outstretched arms?

Margie lifted her eyes, focusing on Ford's eager face. At least she felt a strong connection to the person on the other side. Stronger than she should. She slid her boot sole along the slick surface. Perhaps she could just edge her way across.

One corner of Ford's lip curved upward. "I'll come help you."

"No, don't—" Margie waved him off. "I'm not sure it can support the both of us."

"Don't be ridiculous." He grasped the wooden bar, causing it to tremble in her grip.

"Stop, please!" Margie crouched, as if getting closer to the log would keep her from falling. Of course, that only put her closer to the roaring water. She anchored her second arm around the pole, her heart jumping into her throat. "I can do it."

Ford backed up. "All right, all right. I'll stay here."

Margie laid her forehead against the wet rail, her breaths tearing at her chest like icy claws. "Don't be a ninny." She whispered the words even though rushing water gobbled every sound. The wood quivered in time with the swirling cascade hurtling past. One slip and she'd find herself spun downstream like a clipper in a maelstrom. Margie turned from the sight and pushed up to a standing position. Edging ahead, she took one tentative step and then another.

Ford's voice beckoned. "You're doing great. Just eight more feet, and you'll be on solid ground."

Two more shaking steps got her to the midpoint. No return now. She'd done her best to impress her new boss, but this little misadventure had likely confirmed his initial opinion of her. She didn't belong here. Still, as the breeze caressed her face, an odd sense of calm descended. Her heart-beat slowed. She'd come this far. What was to stop her from going the distance? With a deep breath, Margie released her secondary grip on the wobbly rail. It was there for balance, nothing more. She straightened her spine, relaxing the muscles that kept her in a hunched position. *I can do this.*

"Attagirl, Margie. Almost there."

Margie focused her attention on Ford, the sight giving her forward momentum. She placed one boot in front of the other until she reached his outstretched arm.

He pulled her down onto the bank and into a firm embrace. "Not so bad, was it?"

The unexpected warmth of his shoulder against her cheek sent a jolt through her chest. She held her breath, resisting the urge to press further into his arms, yet not wishing to let go either. "I made it in one piece."

He released his hold. "On the way home, you'll be an old pro."

Her throat tightened. She hadn't really considered the return journey. "I'm sure you're right. After all, as Virgil said, 'They can conquer who believe they can.'"

Ford's voice sounded over the splashing water. "Is this Virgil fellow a friend of your father's?"

She opened her mouth to explain, but Ford's teasing smile inspired a bubbling laugh instead. "He's a very, *very* old family friend."

"I knew you were well-connected, but that's impressive indeed." He gestured at the path winding up the opposing ridge. "If you're recovered, perhaps we should get on the trail? It'd be nice to eat our lunch at the top. My stomach is growling already."

Margie adjusted her knapsack. "Yes, I'm ready. I can't wait to see this much-lauded location. I hope it lives up to its reputation."

"Trust me. You'll be thankful you braved the crossing."

TWELVE

*F*ord slowed down, letting Margie lead as they approached Indian Henry's. He wanted the best view possible, but not necessarily of the scenery. He hadn't anticipated her anxiety, but watching her conquer her fear had made the entire journey worthwhile.

Margie's hurried pace eased as they stepped out into the meadow. "Ohhh . . ." Her voice drew out the sound, like a long breath exhaling. "It's—it's magical." She turned in a slow circle.

Warmth spread through Ford's chest. "One of my favorite spots."

She stretched a trembling hand toward the mountain. "It's as if you could reach out and touch it. Look how the slopes glisten in the sunlight."

He forced himself to look away from her face and instead studied the summit. "Fresh snow." With the exception of his encounter with Philip Carmichael in Longmire, this day couldn't get any more perfect. He wouldn't mention the meeting. She'd find out soon enough, and there was no sense in spoiling her day. Or his. He chuckled as Margie darted across the open space, stopping every few feet to admire a different flowering plant, like a bumblebee hard at work.

The patrol cabin stood empty. Rather than claiming a spot on the log cabin's porch, he found a flat rock and sat, opening his pack. Let the woman have her fun. He was famished.

After a while, Margie wandered over and collapsed next to Ford. "I spotted two marmots just over there." She gestured to the west. "What a treat. This place is even lovelier than you'd promised. I can't imagine a better view."

Ford handed her a sandwich. "From the summit, perhaps."

Margie unfolded the brown paper. "You'd just be looking out across ice and snow." She nodded at the plant life splayed at their feet. "You'd miss all this."

Tilting his head, he studied the small clumps and tufts of greenery studding the ground of the subalpine parkland. "How many samples are you taking home?"

"I've seen six or seven already. Most won't be in full bloom for a few more weeks yet. I'll gather some of their early stages and preserve them with my flower press. It might be useful to create a guide on how to recognize plants when they're not flowering."

"Would there be interest in that?"

She frowned. "Among serious botany-focused individuals such as myself, yes."

"There are more like you?"

Margie offered a coy smile. "A few, perhaps."

Still warm from the vigorous hike, Ford shrugged off his jacket. "It's nice to be up here on a day when the hotel doesn't have a tour group. We have the place to ourselves."

"It would be an idyllic camping spot, I'd imagine."

"Too crowded for my tastes. I prefer to find a quiet place deep in the woods. I never understood the desire to camp with a large group of people."

"You must know all the best camping locations." Margie pulled a strawberry from the container and popped it into her mouth.

Ford opened the box of cookies and offered it to her. "A few, but I keep them under my hat. No sense in having them overrun with city folk."

She raised a brow. "Like me?"

If she had been one of the boys, he'd have invited her camping on the spot. He was never one to turn down a night on the trail. He shook his head, trying to rid himself of the foolish thought. No sense in even letting his imagination hike down that twisting path. "Especially not you. You'd want to bring along a whole group of folks and teach them about the 'glories of wilderness living,' or some such thing. The next thing you know, Luke Johansson would be building another lodge, and I'd have to move to the Alaska Territory for some peace and quiet."

She took a sugar cookie and broke it into bite-sized pieces. "That would be a tragedy. If we continue adding roads and lodges and other amenities, it would steal the serenity. We could end up with nickelodeons and carnival attractions instead of alpine meadows and primeval forests."

"I'm glad to hear you say so." Ford picked up a stone and rolled it between his fingers. "Sometimes I feel I'm fighting an uphill battle to prevent development in the park. I know it belongs to the people, but I can't help feeling—in a small way—it belongs to me."

"It belongs to us all, and that's why we must fight to protect it from unscrupulous forces that would simply develop the land for the sake of the almighty dollar."

His heart rose in his chest. "Exactly. Well said."

"I'm glad I meet with your approval, in one area anyway." Her face softened as she gazed toward the peak.

Ford studied her brown eyes, rich as the forest soil, a sudden desire to touch her cheek sweeping over him. He never would have expected to find himself dotty over an outspoken woman like Margie, but could he deny it any longer? Ford busied his fingers reknotting the laces on his knee-high boots. He needed to get his heart under control. The senator's daughter stepping out with a park ranger? No matter his feelings, it was a waste to dream of the impossible.

"Thank you for bringing me here." Her smile added to the graceful beauty of her face. "I love seeing God's creation laid out in front of us. 'The earth is full of thy riches.' How anyone can look at this natural order and not see the Maker's hand, I'll never comprehend."

And there it was again. She was always quick to bring God into everything. Ford took a deep breath, pushing down his irritation. "I hate to disagree, but nature is beautiful because it's random and unpredictable. Why do you think they call it wilderness? There's no order to nature. God has nothing to do with it. The stuff men build is ordered and boring. This—this is the opposite."

Her smile faded. "I—I'm sorry you feel that way."

He felt as if he'd crushed her fragile petals under his boot. "I know it sounds harsh, Margie, but as lovely as it is—the wilderness is a dangerous, unforgiving place. If you don't take it seriously, you won't take steps to protect yourself."

"It's not the mountain's dangers that frighten me." She gathered the leftovers. "I'll collect my samples and then we can be on our way. I'm sure you're eager to return to your reports."

He exhaled. "Take all the time you want."

Margie's feet dragged by the time she and Ford approached her cabin, practically every drop of daylight already wrung from the sky. She gritted her teeth and pushed on, determined not to let him see how each step had become a chore. The pain in her big toe suggested the last layer of skin had surrendered its fight and not even a blister remained.

After a few miles of silent prayer, she'd finally surrendered Ford to God. *I tried, Lord, but it's not up to me, is it? If only You'd whisper in his ear.*

How could she be drawn to a man who held such a different philosophy of life? From here on out, she needed to remain focused on her job, and remember to think of him as only a boss and friend. "I can't thank you enough for today, Ranger Brayden. I'm sorry you were saddled with such a slow hiker."

"We're not back to titles, are we?" Ford's smile was evident, even in the dusky shadows. A woodpecker's hammering carried through the quiet evening air. "I should be thanking you. I'm sorry we saw no bear sign. Maybe the report was a mistake."

The familiar scent of crushed pine needles and damp moss welcomed her, the fragrance speaking of her new home. Margie stopped at her door and turned, her face immediately warming at the sight of Ford's handsome face.

Squashing her feelings might be more difficult than she'd anticipated. They'd talked and laughed so much—more than she'd ever dreamed—but now she couldn't think of how to properly conclude their evening. It was more awkward than returning from a romantic outing. At least she didn't need to worry about a goodnight kiss. "Shall I come to your office in the morning?"

Ford had been studying the ground, but his head lifted at her question. "My office?"

"To type your report?"

"Oh, yes. I'd nearly forgotten." He nodded, running a quick hand over his shirtfront. "Do you need help with the fire?"

Her breath caught at the idea of inviting him inside. He'd been in her cabin before, so why did it feel like such a scandalous thought now? "No, no, I think I can manage. You're a talented instructor. No one will ever know I was a hopeless ignoramus when I first arrived."

"We couldn't have that." He tipped his hat. "I'm nearby if you need me."

"If I find Archibald has invited his friends in for a party?"

Instead of humor, a shadow seemed to deepen around his eyes. "Yes. Or if any . . . anything else bothers you."

"Thank you, Ford. It's been a perfect day. Nothing could ruin it." Almost perfect, anyway.

Ford backed a step and tipped his hat. "I'll see you tomorrow."

She nodded, her throat thickening. What was wrong with her? If only she couldn't start her own fire. Having the man come inside sounded much more pleasant than entering a cold, dark room alone. She swallowed hard. Mustn't get carried away. "Good night."

Margie twisted the doorknob and pushed herself inside before she could embarrass herself further. *He's your supervisor, not your love interest.* When had the distinction become muddied?

Closing the door, she leaned against it in the darkness, the latched shutters blocking what little light was left in the day. She let the pack thump to the floor, the precious books and specimens forgotten in her weariness. Stumbling to the fireplace, she reached for the box of matches. "As Shakespeare says, 'Parting is such sweet sorrow'"—Margie whispered the words to the quiet room—"'that I shall say goodnight till it be morrow.'"

A rustle in the gloom stopped her in her tracks. Archibald? She struck the match and surveyed the cabin by the small glow.

"Quoting *Romeo and Juliet*? I must say, that's an interesting choice." Philip Carmichael sat on her bed, hands folded in his lap.

Ford hurried over to the park headquarters. If Margie was coming first thing, he needed to assess the damage. After climbing the stairs to his loft office, he pressed the light switch. The electric glare illuminated countless unkempt stacks of papers, two unwashed cups, and various other reminders of day-to-day life. He dumped the last dregs of coffee into a long-suffering potted fern perched in the window sill and stashed the mugs on a high shelf. He'd deal with those in the morning. After a second glance, he swept the plant off the sill and stuffed it into a drawer. Knowing the lady's feelings about botany, it might be better to keep its cringing, yellowed fronds out of sight.

As he grabbed a handful of papers, he glanced out the window at the night sky. This summer promised to be one of the more interesting seasons he'd encountered since he'd started working in the park ten years ago. Sure, there'd been a couple of minor flirtations with waitresses at the Inn, but no woman had agreed to keep him company on an all-day hike and then inspired a late-evening cleaning spree. He sank into the chair, lowering the stack of papers to his lap. There was no denying Margie Lane had wormed her way into his heart.

The question was—what would he do about it?

Just because she'd joined him for a hike didn't mean she'd be willing to see him socially. The sweetness in her eyes when she said goodnight had quickened his pulse almost to the point where he'd been unable to step away. How would she have reacted if he'd followed his instincts and pulled her into his arms?

She'd have run home to Seattle. And Ford would be looking for a new job.

Wooing someone at the park would be a challenge, anyway. It's not as if he could take her to the pictures or out dancing, like a normal fellow. And every overture he made would be in full view of his staff. The best he could hope for would be long hikes in the woods, picnics by the creek, dinners at the Inn, maybe stealing a kiss by Narada Falls. A prickling sensation crawled up his arms. Would that be Margie's idea of romance?

He sighed, dumped the old reports into a box, and then pulled a clean stack of typing paper from the drawer. He needed to get control of his feelings before they walked him right over the edge of a crevasse.

Margie gripped the burning match, but the light bounced with the trembling of her hand. "What are you doing here?" Her throat squeezed until it nearly choked off her words.

Philip sat on the mattress's edge, feet on the floor. "I'm here to see you, of course. A Ranger by the name of Carson pointed me to the right shack. It's a shame you kept me waiting so long. I must have dozed off."

Margie tossed the dying match into the fireplace grate and reached into the box for a second one, her stomach churning. It took three strikes to get it to light, her fingers suddenly damp. She touched it to the lamp's wick, creating a small bubble of light in the darkening room. "You shouldn't be in here. What will people think?" She could feel his presence behind her, like the low pressure of an approaching storm front. Crazy she didn't notice him the moment she crossed the threshold. She must have been too distracted by Ford.

Ford. He mustn't know Philip was here. She turned to face her former fiancé, just as he rose to his feet. "You need to go." She lowered the lamp to the desk so he wouldn't notice her shaking.

"What are you concerned about?" His voice curled about her, smooth as silk. "Someone seeing us, or being alone with me? Because it's not as if we haven't been alone before."

"Not in my bedroom, we haven't." She clenched her teeth and backed away as Philip stood, not that there was far to go.

His gaze didn't waver. "Is that what you call this? Surely you'd be more comfortable in the Inn. It's not as if your daddy couldn't afford it. Why are you staying in this hovel?"

Margie swallowed her protest. Arguments were pointless with Philip. She'd learned that years ago.

Philip's eyes traveled the length of her. "Dressing as a lumberjack these days? Your mother would be proud." He stopped a few feet away, laying a hand on the mantel. "So, where have you been?"

A murky chill touched her skin. She rubbed her arms. "I was hiking."

"Alone?"

"Don't be ridiculous. I was with Ranger Brayden. I believe you met the night of the Paradise dinner."

"And I hear he lives right next door. I'm not sure I approve of you living so close to a bachelor." A slight smile played at the corners of Philip's lips. "Did the good ranger tell you of my lunch meeting today? He'll be glad to know it was a rousing success."

Margie's thoughts spun off in different directions. Ford knew Philip was in the park today? "Meeting—what sort of meeting?"

Philip began stacking wood in the fireplace. "With the superintendent and with the manager of the Paradise Inn."

She laid a hand on her hip, fingers digging into her side. "I know you don't approve of me working here, but you have no business going behind my back with the superintendent."

Philip chuckled, a low dry sound. "You give yourself far too much credit, Margaret. You were not the topic of conversation."

"Then what?"

He retrieved a match from his pocket. After a quick strike, he touched it to the crumpled paper and kindling. "It became clear to me on my last visit that the current administration has frittered away its opportunities here." He stood, his gaze locking on her with an intensity that could melt the mountain's snowcap. "My dear, you're looking at the new chairman of the Rainier National Park Company."

Margie backed two steps. "Why would you do such a thing? You have no interest in wilderness. You'd just as soon plow everything under."

His eyes narrowed. "I never lose, Margaret. If this park is to be my rival, I'm going to ensure I'm the one in control of it." He strode to the door and pulled it open. "And if I turn a handsome profit in the process . . . all the better."

THIRTEEN

June 24, 1927

*F*ord pushed open the office door. Morning sunshine glared through the smudged windows. *Not too bad.* He pulled a handkerchief out of his pocket and ran it across the dusty lamp.

Margie hadn't shown up to breakfast, and Carmichael's auto remained parked out front, sending Ford's mind to a dark place. Had she passed up a meal with the crew to meet her former lover? The idea curdled in his stomach with the coffee and half bowl of oatmeal he'd choked down.

He sank into the wooden chair. A stack of crisp, white paper awaited Margie's arrival. Ford ran a finger along the top edge of the typewriter, the suffocating silence stealing away his thoughts. Even the birds had gone quiet this morning, as if aware of an unwelcome stranger in their midst.

At ten minutes past the hour, Ford pulled the reports from the file drawer. He might as well start himself. Perhaps Margie had forgotten her promise. Or she'd met up with Carmichael, and he'd talked her into giving up this folly. He sucked in a deep breath and blew it out hard, hoping to chase away the unpleasant thought.

Ford slipped a piece of paper under the roller and twisted the knob, drawing it up under the bail. He never seemed able to secure a sheet straight in the machine. One of these levers would release the machine's iron-clad grip, but which? He tried each in turn, finally righting the document.

Ford tapped the space bar several times and pecked out the words "Annual Report" before remembering the title should be centered. "Blast." Yanking the paper from the device, he crumpled it into a tight ball. He'd forgotten to use the carbon, anyway.

Pushing up from his seat, he sent the chair skidding across the floor. Perhaps Jennings could give him a hand. He must have learned to type at that college of his. Ford grabbed his coat and hat and hurried down the stairs and outside. He'd spent twenty minutes in the office. That must count for something.

Margie spilled out the door of the National Park Inn, her eyes narrowed like a cornered wolf. "Ford, wait." The flowered dress hugged her slim figure.

The sight sent his heart scudding in his chest. He cleared his throat. "We missed you at breakfast. I was getting concerned."

She stopped, taking a moment to button the pink cardigan to her neck. "You should have told me you saw Philip Carmichael yesterday."

Ford swallowed, regretting having left his office so soon. "I didn't want to ruin your day." He glanced toward the parking area. The garish vehicle was gone.

"Did he tell you he intended to take over the Rainier National Park Company?" Her chest rose and fell as if she struggled to get enough air.

"He spouted some nonsense about trying to buy the mountain for you. I thought he was crazy."

"Don't sell him short. When he sets his mind to something . . ." She bit her lip. "I need to speak to the superintendent. Or the park service director. I've got to stop this."

Ford pulled off his hat. "He'd only be running the hotels. It's not like he'd actually own the place."

Margie clenched her fingers. "You don't know him. He'll ruin everything."

"Perhaps we can change his mind. Convince him it's not a good investment. Where is he now?"

"He's driving back to Paradise for a second meeting with Mr. Johansson and Superintendent Brown. He's going to outline his planned improvements."

"We can take the truck up there. Head him off."

She swung around to face him. "You'd do that?"

A surge of energy pulsed through him. *That and more.* "My job is to protect the park. If you feel Carmichael doesn't have the mountain's interests at heart, then it's my duty to try. Right?"

She hesitated before snapping a quick nod. "Right. Let's go."

Margie was already three steps down the stone walkway before he could offer his arm. Obviously she wasn't going to miss her chance to confront Carmichael in front of Harry and Luke.

Ford hurried to catch up, jamming his hat on his head. If anyone could talk her way through a crisis, it'd be Margie Lane. And he'd do whatever it took to ensure her success. The idea of working shoulder to shoulder with the likes of Philip Carmichael was enough to make his skin crawl.

Margie picked her steps through the slushy parking area in a vain attempt to protect her heels and stockings. Rather than her typical outdoorsy attire, she'd made a calculated decision this morning and dressed in the most feminine outfit she had on hand. She'd hoped the indulgence would encourage Philip to listen to reason. Slogging through Paradise with wet feet hadn't been part of the plan. The fat raindrops pattering on her hat merely added to the insult.

Ford, in his sturdy park-issued boots, maneuvered the parking area with ease. "I imagine Carmichael will be surprised to see us." He reached the Inn first, hurrying to pull the door open for Margie.

A rush of warm air greeted her, as if the building huffed at the intrusion. "Perhaps. But once he sets his mind on something, he's very difficult to derail." She hurried in, brushing the moisture from her coat and stomping the last vestiges of ice from her pumps.

"And if anyone could accomplish such a feat, it would be you."

As her vision adjusted to the dim light in the open room, she spotted Philip, Mr. Johansson, and Superintendent Brown. They stood, clustered around one of the massive oak tables, large rolls of paper spread across its surface. Even Henrik Berge, from the guide service, stood nearby. His well-worn sweater and wool cap making a stark contrast to Philip's fine suit.

Her stomach sank to her knees. Philip had already drawn up plans? He was further along in his scheme than she'd imagined. What kind of horrific ideas would involve actual blueprints?

Ford hesitated, his eyes growing dark as he studied the gathered men. After a moment he touched her wrist and gestured to the group. "What are you waiting for? Go speak your piece."

Lord, help me. Margie took a deep breath and moved to join the group. "Hello, gentlemen."

The men looked up, their conversation fading.

Philip straightened, a hint of a smile pulling at his lips. "Margaret.

What a pleasant surprise." His attention wandered to Ford, squinting as he studied the ranger. "And Ranger . . . Brayden, was it?"

He knows very well it is. Margie ignored the bitter taste in her mouth. Philip never missed an opportunity to put himself in control of a conversation. "Pardon me, Superintendent, Mr. Johansson. I hope you don't mind us barging in on your meeting."

"Not at all, Miss Lane." A wide smile crossed Superintendent Brown's round face, his head bobbing. "I'm delighted you could join us. In fact, I'd appreciate having Ford's opinion on some of these proposals. Of course, I'm pleased your father would take such an active interest in our future that he'd send his young protégé to take on this important role. The National Park Service Director, Stephen Mather, has encouraged us to seek ways to increase visitation in order to rally public support. I must say, Mr. Carmichael has some rather grandiose projects in mind."

"*Grandiose* is the perfect word for Mr. Carmichael." Margie stepped around to the far side of the table, placing the men directly in her sights. "And I don't believe he's here at my father's beckoning."

A shadow seemed to darken Philip's face for a moment. "Margaret, you wound me. Would I come here under false pretense?" He ran his fingers across the papers. "Take a look at these blueprints. I think you'll be as excited as I am, once you've grasped the scope of this project."

Margie studied the drawings. "Is that the Paradise Inn?"

"It's a brand-new lodge, consisting of two hundred guest rooms, outfitted with the finest luxury money can buy. The Paradise Inn won't suffice as is, not with my plans for the area."

Mr. Johansson's brows bunched. "I've been trying to explain to Mr. Carmichael, we simply can't support that many more rooms with our short summer season. We're snowed in from September to May."

Philip waved a dismissive hand. "We'll fix that problem."

Ford leaned against the tabletop. "You'll fix the snowfall? Now that I'd like to see."

Philip folded his arms. "I intend to construct an aerial tramway. We'll bring the visitors in by cable and outfit Paradise as the premier ski resort in North America. After the International Winter Sports Week in Chamonix in '24, people can't get enough. Paradise is the perfect location. We'll install rope hoists and a massive ski jump. With a little effort, we could even host one of the new Winter Games."

The climbing guide nodded. "Bringing in skiers, you'll create more interest in climbing and glacier tours."

Heat and anger flashed through Margie. "Paradise is a sacred retreat, not some alpine playground for the wealthy."

Philip shook his head. "That's where you're wrong, my dear. If parks are to survive, they must be made showpieces for the new American leisure class. And not only winter sports. The meadows will feature a world-class golf course to draw summer visitors. Plus, for those who prefer a more rustic experience—one hundred cabins laid out in a grid. Summer activities could include horseback excursions, rodeos, jazz revues, organized sporting events. Everyone who desires to take in the mountain air can do so in style." His eyes glazed, as if the images already danced before him. "And as more automobiles visit the park, we could sponsor races. Which vehicle can travel from Longmire to Paradise at the fastest speed? Automakers will compete for the honor of being the official model of Mount Rainier."

Margie sputtered. "You're insane. You can't transform Paradise into a sumptuous resort. The purpose of the national park ideal is to protect lands from the exact type of development you're suggesting."

Color rose in Ford's face. "Harry, you can't possibly support this. It'd wreck the place."

The superintendent chewed on a toothpick for a moment before turning to Philip. "Where would you get the funding for this level of development, Mr. Carmichael? I can't imagine the federal government would spring for this sort of lavish facility. I can hardly get them to throw us a few breadcrumbs at a time."

"Leave that to me, gentlemen." Philip gripped the top edge of his vest and lifted his chin. "I'll find the investors to make it happen."

Margie's stomach rolled. Philip seemed to have a knack for making money appear out of nowhere, like a magician pulling coins from behind people's ears.

Mr. Johansson frowned. "I don't like it. Too much, too soon. Where would I find enough staff to run a place like that? And year-round? Do you have a clue how much snow we get every year? We spend all winter just keeping the roofs from caving in. You want to stock the place with high rollers?"

Philip's brow furrowed. "I have an idea about that, too."

"Of course you do." Ford muttered under his breath.

"The key is sound management. I'm bringing in an expert from Switzerland. A resort of this quality deserves the best. Herr Baumgarten is the finest hotel manager money can buy."

Mr. Johansson sank down into a nearby chair. "I see. You're replacing me."

Philip turned to the superintendent. "You can keep your man on, if you like—in a reduced capacity, obviously. There'll be plenty of work to keep everyone busy."

"Philip . . ." A chill claimed Margie, even here near the fireplace. "You can't march in here and expect everyone to kowtow to your demands."

A slow grin spread across the man's face as he dug a pack of cigarettes from his pocket. "Oh, but I can. Don't forget—I'm here at Senator Lane's request."

Her heart stopped for a dizzying minute and then resumed beating at double-speed. "It's not possible."

"You've been off in the woods too long, Margaret. Your daddy and I mended fences." Philip leaned across the table. "I have his full support on this project."

The breath seeped from her chest. *A lie. It must be.* "I've only been here a few weeks. I can't believe my father would have—"

"In fact, Senator Lane and I have a stipulation." He spun around to face the men, drawing their attention from Margie. "Margaret Lane will work for me. And she'll take charge of all programming at the Paradise resort."

The edges of Margie's vision blurred. This couldn't be happening.

"Miss Lane works for the park service." Ford's hands clenched. "And our naturalists have always been responsible for programming."

Philip cocked his head. "Have they? Well, we'll see about that. If Margaret refuses, I'll bring in someone of my own. We're through with dreary little nature talks. We need something with verve to appeal to the upper-class visitors. You can't expect them to sit around and listen to boring old rangers spouting useless facts. Margaret has a sense of showmanship, or should I say show-womanship?" He shrugged. "She and I will run it as a team." He dropped into a plush chair by the fireside. "We'll call the position an engagement gift. What say you, Margaret?"

"You're out of line, Carmichael." A vein pulsed in Ford's temple.

Margie stepped closer to Philip. "Can we have a word in private, please? I think we need to discuss this."

He shrugged. "I've made my decisions, but I always have time for you." Philip led the way across the room, pausing by the massive Bavarian grandfather clock.

She kept her voice low so it wouldn't travel back to the group. "Why would I want to run your programs? I find your plans disgraceful."

"I thought you might wish to maintain some level of control over what happens here." He tipped his head back, as if studying the clock's finials while he spoke. "Of course, if you were to accept my marriage proposal, I'd probably lose interest in these petty investments altogether." Philip turned his attention back to her, his eyes unwavering. "I'd be far too busy planning our nuptials to bother with such a mundane project."

Margie pressed her elbows close to her sides as Philip's intentions became clear. He was giving her a choice—bow to his control or he would decimate the place.

"It's your decision, of course." Philip turned back to the clock, running a hand down its wooden case. "But trust me, it won't be the same park without you."

Ford slammed through the doors, pulling fresh air into his lungs. If he had to endure the businessman's smirk one more moment, he'd have decked the man. Apparently Carmichael wasn't content to spoil everything Ford loved at Rainier; he planned to take Margie with him. A rush of foul-tempered words spilled through his mind, but he managed to bite them back.

Men like Carmichael knew how to snap their fingers and make everyone dance to their tune. Unfortunately, Ford had never been particularly light on his feet.

The door opened a second time, and Margie hurried through, squinting as she buttoned her long coat. "There you are. I was afraid you might have left without me."

"You could have ridden home in style." Ford gestured to Carmichael's long automobile, parked prominently out front.

She sighed. "This is all my fault. If I'd never come here, he wouldn't have gotten a bee in his bonnet to do any of this."

"You didn't answer him."

Margie placed her palms on her cheeks. "I needed time to think."

Don't marry him. The words collected in his throat, but stuck there.

She shivered in the light wind. "What I don't understand—well, one part of it anyway—is why my father would be supporting him. They parted ways years ago. Then I hear that he's managing Papa's campaign. And now this?"

"Maybe he's lying?"

"Perhaps. But he'd be found out easily, and then his whole house of cards would collapse. Philip's not foolish."

But he was foolish enough to try to coerce Margie into marrying him? The idea turned Ford's stomach. He'd thought his feelings for Margie were an innocent, temporary infatuation. When had she wrapped herself around his heart?

"I need to speak to my father." She glanced at the Inn. "Perhaps he can put a halt to this . . . this desecration."

"Can you telephone him?"

"I should meet with him in person. Something Philip said troubles me. I think there's more to this than them 'mending fences.' I don't know what it could be, but I need to find out." Her brows pulled down. "I suppose you can spare me for a few days? I know I'm not exactly integral to operations here, and if I hurry, I might catch my father before the campaign gala."

"Of course." If Margie revisited city life, would she ever wish to return to muddy Longmire and her vermin-infested shack? One thing was certain—he couldn't allow Carmichael more opportunities to convince her. His thoughts raced. "I'll take you myself."

Margie's lips parted, her eyes wide. "All the way to Tacoma? What about your work here?"

She was right. It was the worst time of year to consider leaving the park. But if he stopped in to chat with Harry and Carson, they should be able to cover for him. Jennings was already swamped with work. "The summer staff is all in place, and they're an experienced lot. They can do without me for a day." He moved toward the truck. "Besides, it gives me a good excuse to postpone that report."

She followed a few steps behind. "I don't know what to say. I'm so grateful."

"Think nothing of it. I have selfish motives. I don't want that man taking charge of things here." He opened the truck door. *And I don't want him to have you.*

"Thank you, Ford." Margie laid a hand on his arm before climbing into the vehicle. "We'll do this together."

He closed the door behind her and stared out toward the bank of clouds obscuring his mountain. *Yes. Together.*

FOURTEEN

*A*s the truck passed under the wooden archway marking the park boundary, knots formed in Margie's stomach. At first she'd been overjoyed with Ford's suggestion to accompany her. Now all she could imagine was his reaction when he saw the excess her parents considered normal life. Their house overlooking Commencement Bay had no less than thirty rooms, four servants, and manicured English-style gardens draped over the steep hillsides. And then there was her mother . . .

She cast a discreet glance at Ford while he drove. He'd changed from his park service uniform into a smart suit jacket over a matching vest and trousers. He wouldn't be mistaken for a member of the elite, but even in these simple clothes he cut a fine figure. Mother might not be pleased to see Margie arrive on the arm of a park ranger, but no one could quibble over the man's appearance.

Margie forced her attention back to the road. It's not as if she were bringing him home in search of her mother's approval. Ford had come as moral support, nothing more. He'd said as much.

The forest canopy gave way to familiar lowlands dotted with pastures and farm fields. Margie pressed fingers against her temples, the tension gathering like storm clouds. *Do life's pressures rest heavier at sea level?*

After nearly a month of park life, she'd almost forgotten how it felt to be among her family. She sighed. "I wish we were going the other direction."

"Are you nervous to speak with your father?" Ford glanced over at her.

She shifted on the hard seat. "A little. But mostly, I'm not looking forward to stepping back into my old life."

"You come from a prestigious political family, yet you choose to live in a run-down shack in the middle of the woods." He shook his head slowly. "You truly are one of a kind."

"As Thoreau said, 'I went to the woods because I wished to live deliberately.' I couldn't do that trapped by the expectations of high-society life."

"Which is why you're the one to fight against Carmichael and others like him."

Ford believed she'd come to Rainier for selfless reasons. She'd never told him she hoped this job would serve as a safe haven from Philip's controlling ways. "It's my fault Philip is there in the first place. He'd never have taken interest in the mountain except for me."

"If it weren't him, it'd be someone else."

"I suppose." An ache settled in the back of her throat, and she blinked back tears. How had things gone so wrong?

The conversation veered in other directions, and by the time they pulled into the steep turnaround in front of the Lane estate, the pair had discussed every aspect of park management, from winter snowplowing to stringing telephone cables over secluded ridges and river valleys. Margie reached for her bag, hidden on the floorboards by her feet. "I wish my father could hear you speak of all this detail. He'd see that park work is similar to running a large, complex business."

"Without the payoff, I suppose."

"The payoff comes in a different form."

Margie stayed put and waited for Ford to come open her door. If they'd been at work, she might have hopped out on her own, but she couldn't take the chance that her mother was watching from the window. And likely as not, she was.

Colorful flower beds lined the circular drive, filled with exotic ornamental blooms—as if hybridized plants from Europe or Asia were somehow preferable to the lovely natural sprawl of American foliage. Mother always employed gardeners willing to subdue nature into well-behaved rows, every blossom chosen for its exact size, shade, and smell.

Margie ran a hand over her wrinkled dress. Her mother viewed her in much the same way. A rose strapped to a trellis and trained in the way in which it should grow and bloom. *What a disappointment I must be.*

Ford opened the door and offered his hand. "This is where you grew up?" He glanced up at the house and whistled softly under his breath. "Welcome home."

The building in front of him loomed larger than any house Ford had ever seen. He'd suspected Margie's family had great wealth, but he'd never taken the time to consider what that would look like. No wonder she didn't care about frivolous things like paychecks. She could live on Daddy's money until the day she died.

Margie stared up at her home as if she'd been gone years rather than weeks. Was she comparing it to the rodent-infested shack Ford had placed her in?

Perhaps it had been foolish to accompany her on this trip. He knew nothing about how this type of people viewed life. His world consisted of trees, trails, leaking roofs, and wildlife.

She glanced back at him, her hand brushing his. "Shall we go?"

Tension eased from his muscles. With one subtle motion she'd proven herself the same woman he'd felt drawn to over the past weeks. "I hope your parents don't mind me coming along for the ride. I shouldn't have presumed upon their hospitality."

"Nonsense. You're my guest." She led the way down the stone walkway, the fragrance of jasmine and rose another reminder they'd left the woods far behind.

Ford straightened his tie and hurried after her. He should have worn his uniform. At least then he could present himself in an official capacity, not as some starry-eyed suitor.

He expected a white-tie butler to open the door, but the elegant middle-aged woman who greeted them was no serving staff.

"Margaret, you came! Your father will be delighted." The woman scanned Margie before turning to Ford. "And you've brought a . . . a . . ."

"A friend, Mother. This is Ranger Ford Brayden. He's my superior at the park. We hoped to speak with Father."

Mrs. Lane stepped back from the doorway and waved them inside. "Welcome, Ranger. Margaret, your father is in meetings all afternoon, but you can see him at the gala tonight."

Margie frowned. "I'm not here for the event. We're here on business."

Ford followed Margie into the stately foyer, their shoes clicking over the tile floor. He glanced up at the eight-foot ceiling and the grand staircase leading up to additional floors.

The older woman laughed. "Business? Gracious! Whatever kind of business could you be talking about? You've been traipsing about in the woods for weeks. Now you want to go into your father's business?" She led them to the sitting room. "I'll have Marta run you a bath. It's clear you could use one."

Ford stayed close to Margie. "Perhaps we could catch him between meetings. Does he have an office?"

The woman didn't bother to look Ford's direction. "Senator Lane is a very busy man. He doesn't see visitors without an appointment."

"Not even his daughter?" The words slipped out before Ford could corral them.

She ignored him. "Margie, did you even read the papers the morning after your little display at the mountain? The press had a field day with your antics. 'Lane's Daughter Plays Ranger.' After all the grief my friends gave me, the least you can do is put in a respectable appearance."

Margie sighed. "Mother, we cannot attend the party. We hadn't planned on an overnight stay, and we didn't bring anything suitable to wear. I have a quick question for Father, and then we'll return to the park."

The woman's brows suggested battle lines as they pulled together. "Margaret Lane, I don't care to be dismissed so lightly. Tonight's event is important to your family's future. You have many dresses here—in fact, there is a beautiful new gown waiting in your room." She lifted her chin. "Philip Carmichael is hosting the festivities at the Tacoma Hotel, and I'm certain he'd be delighted to see you again."

"Of course he is." Margie pressed a palm to her forehead. "I should have known." She turned to Ford. "We didn't plan to stay, but this might be the perfect opportunity to speak to both of them."

Ford's stomach dropped. A gala at a swanky hotel? Him? "Of course, if you think it important. But perhaps I should stay behind."

"Yes, that might be for the best." Mrs. Lane brightened, a sweet smile touching her lips for the first time since she'd ushered them inside. "Now, please sit down." She gestured to a floral settee.

"Ford—Ranger Brayden." Margie retreated to formality in her mother's presence. "I'd be honored if you would escort me to this function."

Her mother's smile vanished. "Margaret . . . but, Philip—"

"Please," Margie gripped Ford's arm, her nails pressing against his sleeve. "I'd like for you to be there."

"Certainly, if that's what you prefer." A loud buzzing took up residence in his chest, like he'd stepped on a yellow jacket nest.

Margie turned to her mother, her fingers still resting on Ford's inner arm. "There you are, Mother. We'd be pleased to attend. You can make the arrangements."

The woman's eyes narrowed. "Very well. Your father will be pleased. As I said, there's an evening gown upstairs for you." Her eyes roamed over Ford. "And we'll find *something* for Ranger Brayden."

Ford brushed a quick hand over his jacket, suddenly aware of every flaw in the garment's design. "I apologize for being so much trouble, ma'am. That was never my intention."

"Oh, wasn't it?" She raised one brow as she flounced across the room and out the door.

Ford lowered himself to the seat next to Margie.

Margie sighed. "I'm so sorry. I should have realized this would happen. We could have arrived more prepared."

He wouldn't know where to begin to prepare for such an evening. "It'll be fine. We're here to speak to your father, not to impress anyone."

"I do appreciate you being at my side. I wouldn't want to face Philip alone."

The tiny lines forming around her pinched mouth cut into Ford's heart. Was she actually afraid of the man? Sure, Carmichael was a grandstander, but could he actually be dangerous? "I'm happy to help. I only hope I don't embarrass you."

A warm smile brightened her face, causing the elegant room to fade in comparison. "You could never embarrass me."

FIFTEEN

*F*ord donned the fine black trousers and sighed. What had he gotten himself into? When he'd pulled on his park service green this morning, he'd never dreamed he'd end the day in a tuxedo. Never in his life had he worn such ridiculous garb. He fastened the pants and lifted the starched shirt from its hanger, his skin crawling. A garment this white was destined to get stained. How had Mrs. Lane managed to secure these items so quickly? They obviously didn't belong to the senator. Ford was at least three inches taller than Margie's father.

A light tapping on the door jerked Ford to attention. "Just a moment—"

The door swung wide despite his protest. A sallow-faced man filled the opening, several jackets draped over his arm. "You've begun without me, I see." A vague European accent embellished every syllable of his drawn-out words.

"Without you? I don't know what you mean." Ford shook out the shirt and began jamming his arms into the holes, not wishing to be seen in a state of undress.

"Please, sir. Please. You must respect the fabric." The stranger's jowls sagged with his frown. "I am Senator Lane's valet, Mr. Wilson. I am here to dress you." He hung the jackets on a wooden stand.

"To . . . what?" Ford struggled with the left sleeve. "I've done for myself since I was a child. I don't think I need help now."

Mr. Wilson cleared his throat, the harsh sound cutting through the room. "Nevertheless, I have been charged with the task. Now, please remove the shirt, and we will begin again."

The tips of Ford's ears grew hot as he did as ordered. "Are you here at Mrs. Lane's bidding? Does she think me not capable of putting on a suit?"

Wilson lifted his chin. "It is not a *suit*. It is a tuxedo. And yes, I'm here at my mistress's request. But do not be concerned. I dress Senator Lane multiple times a day, as well. I don't believe Mrs. Lane intended any personal affront." He glanced over Ford's sleeveless union suit, his expression flat.

Ford ran a quick hand over the undergarment, trying to ignore the minor discolorations on the threadbare fabric. He'd never been a stickler for laundry, particularly when the item never saw daylight.

The valet shook out the formal shirt and held it outspread.

Best to get this humiliation over with. Ford turned and slipped his arms into the sleeves. He reached for the buttons only to have Mr. Wilson circle around. "Sir, allow me."

"You really don't have to."

"I understand. But we want this done properly."

As if Ford had never buttoned his own shirt. He shoved down the growing irritation, trying not to squirm like a schoolboy under a mother's ministrations.

The valet carefully fixed the studs down Ford's chest. Would the man spit comb his hair as well?

After being outfitted with cuff links, black tie, a white vest—which

Wilson referred to as a waistcoat—and finally the dinner jacket, the valet tucked a silk square into the breast pocket. Wilson stepped back and surveyed Ford's appearance. "I suppose you'll do."

Do for what? Ford hardly recognized his own reflection in the long mirror. Margie would laugh to see him decked out like a fashion plate. "How am I to eat in this getup? I'm bound to spill something."

Wilson exhaled loudly. "Don't. I'm to return the ensemble in the morning, and I'd rather not spend all night removing stray bits of crab and sauce from the fabric."

Don't eat, or don't spill anything? Ford ran fingers through his hair, fighting the urge to throw off the coat and make a dash for the truck. He was in over his head here. He'd rather face a winter-starved bear than show up downstairs in this costume.

Wilson ran a quick brush over Ford's shoulders. "Will there be anything else, sir?"

"I sure hope not." Ford glanced over to where the valet had carefully hung his old clothes in the closet like royal robes. They'd better still be here when he returned. He wouldn't put it past the man to sneak them out to the burn pile.

"Very good. And Mrs. Lane had a fresh bottle of Brilliantine sent up, since it seemed unlikely you packed your own." The man glanced at Ford's hair, somehow managing to keep his face civil. Perhaps they taught that air of detachment in valet school. "I'll leave you to it." Wilson strode from the room, leaving the door ajar.

Ford sighed and reached for the hair oil. *In for a penny, in for a pound.* If Mrs. Lane wanted to shape him into a facsimile of Philip Carmichael, he might as well go along. For one night, anyway. He worked the greasy substance into his hair and pulled a comb through to complete the slicked back look. Leaning toward the mirror, Ford checked his smile. One good thing—if he wasn't to eat all evening, there'd be no danger of having lettuce stuck in his teeth.

"Ford?" Margie's voice sounded soft like music behind him. "Oh, my. Don't you look handsome!"

He swung about, relieved she hadn't witnessed the disgrace of him being dressed.

The sight of her stole every other thought from his mind. The soft blue gown followed every curve of her body—even curves he'd never quite noticed before. He scrambled for an appropriate response. "You—you look like a mountain bluebird."

Margie's nose scrunched, and she fiddled with the neckline. "I can't imagine why Mother believed I'd want a gown covered in feathers."

"No, I mean . . ." His compliment had missed the mark. Better to keep it simple. "You look pretty."

She touched fingers to her throat, her mouth dropping open. "Oh. Thank you." A red tinge rose in her cheeks. "I just pray a flock of birds didn't give their lives for this silly outfit."

He tugged at one of his sleeves, the cuffs suddenly feeling a bit close. "I'm used to green and gray, not black and white. I must look like a skunk."

"You look wonderful."

Ford followed the path of the long pearl necklace as it cascaded down her front. Forcing himself to look away, he made a show of digging through his old suit jacket for something. "I'm almost ready." He needed to be careful to keep his eyes where they belonged. With Margie dressed like that, every man in the place would be falling over themselves to get to her. A backwoods clod like him never stood a chance. A deep breath helped him shake off the uncomfortable thought. He was here to fight for the park, not for her—even if she had stolen his heart.

Margie clutched Ford's arm as they walked along the rain-splattered curb outside the stately Tacoma Hotel. The massive Tudor-style building rose like a castle against the dark sky, the tall windows glowing with life. Jazz music spilled out through the entrance as the doorman welcomed a line of well-dressed people into the hotel. Rather than parking out front, Ford had chosen a discreet place a few blocks away to stash the old truck.

"Better we make our entrance on foot, don't you think?" Thankfully the rain had let up before they made their dash for the party, otherwise it might have been a soggy entrance, indeed.

As they approached, Ford leaned close to her ear—a considerable effort considering their height difference. "Will there be dancing? I'm afraid I'm a bit out of practice."

"No dancing up on the mountain?" She couldn't resist smiling at his anxious tone.

He shrugged. "One or two at the Inn, but not much beyond that."

She squeezed his arm, enamored with the idea of this mountaineer-turned-gentleman waltzing her around a dance floor. She'd be the envy of every woman in the room, no matter his skill level. "I think we can avoid it. After all, we're here to speak to my father, not for a romantic evening." Margie managed to push the words out without sighing. He'd been a good sport this evening, but a fairy-tale ending was too much to hope for.

"Right." He tugged down on his vest. "Then we'd best get ourselves in there."

He was probably quite relieved not to have to dance with her. The minor letdown was chased away by a maddening itch working its way around her torso. She dug a gloved hand under her wrap, tugging at the

gown's feathered bodice. Assuming she survived this evening, she was returning to the woods never to reemerge. The night had barely begun, and
she'd already had several reminders that she didn't belong in her parents'
highbrow world—particularly her mother's chilly reception at the house.
Would she ever cease to be a disappointment?

The doorman greeted them with a smile. "Welcome, sir. How would
you like the Master of Ceremonies to announce you?"

Margie placed a hand on Ford's sleeve and leaned forward to answer
in his place. "No, thank you. We're hoping to surprise someone."

The doorman's eyes narrowed. "But you *are* on the guest list?"

She pushed a smile to her face. "Of course. I'm Margaret Lane,
daughter of Senator and Mrs. Lane. This is my—my friend, Mr. Ford
Brayden."

His face smoothed. "Miss Lane, of course. Terribly sorry. This way,
please." He led the way inside, pointing the way to the ballroom as if the
jaunty music didn't give away its location.

Ford's steps slowed as he surveyed the gathering. "We're not in Longmire anymore."

The number of influential and affluent businessmen filling the room
suggested Philip's control over the guest list. Standing on tiptoe, which still
brought her head only to Ford's chin, Margie whispered, "It'll be all right.
Just be yourself."

Ford cleared his throat, a pained expression darting across his face.
"Somehow I don't think these people would know what to do with a country boy like me."

"Just remember how enamored Sylvia Chambers was with you at the
dinner we had at the Paradise Inn."

Ford tore his attention from the crowd. "She won't be here, will she?"

Margie stifled a laugh. "I can't make any promises, I'm afraid. But if she attends, her husband will probably be at her side. I think you'll be safe."

"I never understood why someone like her would bother with me."

Margie's mirth evaporated like dew in the hot sun. She could completely understand Mrs. Chamber's attraction. She squeezed Ford's arm. "Don't worry. I'll protect you."

"That's supposed to be my role. Now, where will we find your father?"

"Probably near the bar." She tugged him in the direction of a large group clustered on the far side of the ballroom.

"Bar? You're kidding. So much for Prohibition—or is that only for the working classes?"

She spotted her father, surrounded by a cluster of men near one of the buffet tables. "There's my father. I'm not sure if my mother's already broken the news of our arrival or not. She's probably been busy gossiping with the governor's wife and daughter."

"The sooner we take care of business, the sooner we can escape."

Margie led the way, focusing on her father so as not to lose him in the crowd.

Philip appeared out of the throng, a grin spreading across his face. "Margaret, Ranger Brayden. What a surprise."

Margie's heart dropped. She should have realized he'd spot them the moment they walked through the door. Perhaps before. Philip had senses like a bloodhound.

Ford jostled against her shoulder, moving between them and sticking his hand out to Philip. "I hope you don't mind us crashing your little shindig here, Mr. Carmichael."

Philip returned the ranger's grip. "On the contrary, I am delighted."

His focus bounced across Ford and came to rest on Margie. "And honored you chose to wear my gift, Margaret. I knew the gown would fit you like a glove. When I saw it presented at the fashion luncheon last week, I thought of you right away."

A surge of nausea rose in Margie's stomach. Mother said the dress was new. She hadn't considered it might be from someone else. "I . . . I didn't . . ." She didn't what? Know he was capable of such a pretentious gift? "How thoughtful of you."

He stepped close, touching her long strand of pearls. "It's too bad you didn't wear the necklace I picked out. You deserve diamonds, not these trinkets. Every flapper from here to New York is wearing pearls these days. Never be common, Margaret." His knuckles brushed the tender skin at the base of her throat, his eyes lingering on the feathered trim on the less-than-modest neckline.

Her fluttering stomach grew hard. She knocked his hand away and jerked back, bumping into Ford's arm. "I prefer my own style, thank you. I'll have the gems returned to you, immediately. I don't find myself in need of such finery in my current situation." The sensation of Ford's fingers in the center of her back gave her strength. He might not desire to be a suitor, but at least he was a solid friend.

One side of Philip's mouth twisted up. "Yes, your current *situation*." He cast a quick glance at Ford. "I must say, I'm a tad intrigued about that."

Ford's voice sounded over her head. "We're not here to satisfy your curiosity, Mr. Carmichael. We'd like to speak to Senator Lane, if you'll excuse us?"

Margie slid her hand under Ford's elbow once more, holding on to him as if he were a life preserver in a stormy sea.

SIXTEEN

*F*ord tugged at the tourniquet-like collar as they made their way through the crowd toward Senator Lane. Why had Margie agreed to such tomfoolery? He no more belonged at this party than a penguin in the jungle. Philip Carmichael's comments proved as much. And then the man had the audacity to caress *his* date.

He glanced down at her delicate fingers, nestled against the fine fabric of his dinner jacket as the feathered fringe of her bodice brushed against his arm. A sickly feeling descended over Ford. Not only could Carmichael step in and take over companies, apparently he could choose fashions as well. What skills did Ford have? Felling trees and building campfires? He'd like to light one under that Beau Brummell right now.

At least with Margie at his side, no one questioned his invitation. Otherwise he'd have been tossed out on his ear the moment he stepped foot on the Oriental rug in the lobby. He'd heard stories of the Tacoma Hotel, but had never had the opportunity—or desire, really—to see it for himself. This little lumber town had truly come into its own. Pretty soon it'd rank up there with San Francisco and Chicago.

Senator Lane greeted his daughter with an enthusiastic embrace.

"Margie, my dear, I'm so touched you would come all this way." He set his glass down on a nearby table. "How are you?"

Philip sidled up next to the senator. "Were you aware your daughter was going to honor us with her presence? She said nothing when I presented my ideas to the RNPC committee this morning."

Margie toyed with her pearls. "It was a spur-of-the-moment idea, I'm afraid, Papa. Philip mentioned how you two had reconciled. I had to see this miracle for myself."

He scrubbed his hand over his brow. "Yes, well. It was quite unexpected, I must admit."

Philip slapped a palm onto the senator's shoulder. "We've been like family for so long you couldn't expect a minor disagreement to keep us apart, now could you?"

Ford folded his arms. A minor disagreement? The storm in Margie's eyes suggested otherwise.

Margie's father coughed once before turning to greet Ford. "Ranger Brayden, isn't it? I hardly recognized you out of uniform."

"Yes, sir. I wanted to make sure your daughter made it safely to Tacoma and back."

"Good man." The senator snapped a quick nod in Ford's direction. "Someone has to look after this girl. She sometimes gets strange notions of how the world works."

"Father," Margie touched Senator Lane's arm. "I'd like to speak privately with you, if you don't mind."

"Margaret,"—Philip's pout crumpled his whole face downward—"we're at a party. You can't spirit him away. The senator's much in demand here." He grasped her hand. "You two can talk anytime. Now, dancing with me? That's a rare opportunity one should never miss."

Margie's mouth fell open. "Well, I . . ."

Philip steered her to the dance floor where several other couples were busy foxtrotting up a storm. Several more moved that direction upon spotting Carmichael and Margie.

Ford pushed down the instinct to follow and rip Margie's hand from the man's leech-like grasp. There was no need for a scene, and perhaps that's why Margie hadn't protested.

At least Ford had her father alone. "Sir, I wanted to speak to you, as well."

The man's expression grew serious. "I expected as much. I take it Philip unveiled his grand scheme this morning."

"Yes. Margie is quite concerned, as am I. Does this project actually have your support, as Carmichael insists?"

Senator Lane swept a palm over his brow, as if wiping away perspiration. "I'd like to help you, Ranger Brayden. I truly would. But I'm at a bit of a disadvantage here." He glanced around before leaning close. "I'll try to find a way to explain to Margie when I get home tonight. But I don't think I can be of much assistance. I'm afraid you're on your own."

A weight settled in Ford's stomach. If someone as powerful as Lane couldn't put the brakes on Carmichael's plans, what luck would he have? He unbuttoned his jacket and turned to watch the dancers. The pretty flush on Margie's cheeks as she danced sent a jab through Ford's chest. "I'm sorry to hear that, Senator. But I have no intention of letting that man have his way at my park." *Or anywhere else.*

The pressure of Philip's arm around her waist sent Margie's breath ricocheting through her chest. He'd always been a fluid dancer, and even now she had little time to think where to place her feet. It was like riding a carousel—all you had to do was hold on.

The band didn't pause between numbers, and Philip swept her into the next dance without loosening his grip. "Margaret, it's been too long since we've danced. Remember the Moonlight Merriment Ball at Union Station? We nearly closed the place down that night, you and I."

A lump rose in her throat. "How could I forget?" She'd just turned seventeen and he was packing for university. After a full year of trying to discourage their romance, Father had bought Philip off with the promise of an education.

"You wore a blue gown that night, too. I still have the photograph on my desk—hand tinted." He slid his fingers up her back, toying with the soft fringe on her dress. "But that was a dress for a girl. This one . . ." He drew her closer, the heat from his body obvious through the delicate material. His eyes wandered lower.

She took advantage of the music's syncopated beat to draw back a step. "That was a lifetime ago. Much has changed."

"I'd say improved. I'm not the cipher you befriended as a child. Thanks to your faith in me, I've risen to the top of society." He tipped his head to the growing crowd on the dance floor. "People watch me now. They follow." He squeezed her hand. "That's your doing. You and your father. It's my ambition for us to climb to the highest ranks—together. I'll spend the rest of my life repaying you for that early support. No, not repaying. Rewarding. It's time for you to enjoy the bounty of what you've created."

Margie closed her eyes. *What she'd created, indeed.* "You don't seem to understand, Philip; I'm no longer part of your life."

He laughed, his head tipped back, garnering smiles from nearby couples. He lowered his chin and stared into her eyes. "Margie, you are the one who fails to understand. You don't have a choice."

A chill swept over her, regardless of the exertion and the warm room. Surely Philip couldn't be this delusional.

He lowered his head until his mouth touched her ear. "Your park ranger is watching. He looks like he's about to pop a cork." He nuzzled his cheek against her hair. "You'd think a man who works so closely with nature would have a better understanding of it."

On the next beat, she brought her heel down hard on Philip's oxford. As he jerked, Margie slipped from his grasp. "You know nothing about nature." She wove through the middle of the crowd, desperate to put as many couples between her and Philip as possible.

She needed to speak to her father and then get out of this place. Waltzing down memory lane had never been on the evening's schedule. Margie ducked between dancing couples.

A hand caught hers and she hopped back, her breath catching. There's no way Philip could have followed, especially since every man—and woman—here seemed to want his attention. She glanced up into Ford's face. "You surprised me."

"And you look as if you need a new partner." Ford's low voice carried just above the sound of the band. He tugged her close, her body folding neatly against his.

She wrapped her wrist over his shoulder, the best she could do considering his height. "You said you didn't dance."

"Is that any reason to abandon your date in the first fifteen minutes?" His brows lifted. "And I said I didn't have much experience."

Within a few steps, she could confirm the truth of his statement. His trot was more buffalo than fox. She fought back a smile. "No problem. I can think of no one in this room I'd rather dance with." The sensation of being held in Ford's arms weakened every muscle in her body. She straightened. If she didn't concentrate on keeping her toes out of stepping range, she might need medical attention by the end of the song.

"Not going so well for poor Carmichael?"

"Philip's as persistent as a mustard plaster. He seems to live under the mistaken belief that with a few sweet words, I'll fall into his arms."

Ford looked down at her. "And you disagree?"

"With my whole heart."

"Good. I'd hate to think of you fraternizing with the enemy." He pulled her closer, an unidentifiable expression flitting across his face.

An ever-expanding ache lodged in her chest as she gazed at the ranger's face. Even with his fancy clothes and his hair slicked back, she could see the touch of wilderness about him. She nestled closer to his chest. "I wish we were at Indian Henry's."

His fingers rolled across her back. "I don't think there's one other woman in this room who would feel the same."

"I'm afraid I've always been a bit unusual." Much to her mother's dismay.

Ford stumbled midstride, jostling against her hip, before regaining his footing. He shook his head. "Don't I know it? No one else would be willing to risk her feet to a corn-shredder like me. Come on." He stepped back, maintaining a grip on her hand.

"Where are we going?"

"For a breath of fresh air?" He cocked his head toward the doorway. "Your father said he'd speak to you at the house. He doesn't feel comfortable discussing the matter here."

"We just arrived." Her desire to leave had eased somewhat, probably due to a more interesting dance partner. "And you went to such trouble to dress the part." *And to be the best-looking man in the room.*

"Just for a few minutes." He tugged her a step toward the door. "It's a nice evening, and I hear there's a quiet walkway along the waterfront. I think that might be more my style." His dimple deepened. "And if I know you at all, it's yours, as well."

Her heart hitched upward. A romantic, moonlit walk? She couldn't fight the smile bubbling up from within. "You do understand me, Ford Brayden."

Moonlight streaked the waters of Commencement Bay, as if beckoning Ford to walk straight out into the Puget Sound. The steady lapping of the water against the rocks chased the unpredictable jazz rhythms from his ears, settling his heart back to a familiar beat. Music like that could jar a man into doing something he never intended. Seeing Carmichael dancing with Margie had unhinged his better judgment. As soon as Ford had her in his arms, he could think of little else than what it would be like to kiss her lips. Best to get out into the fresh air before something crazy happened.

Margie nestled her wrist in the crook of his arm and sighed. "Tacoma can be beautiful, especially the waterfront."

They'd been off the mountain for only eight hours and already he felt lost. "I hope you don't mind that I dragged you away. All the noise was making me as nutty as a ground squirrel."

"I know what you mean. I only wanted to speak to my father. I never expected any of this." She dropped his arm and gestured at her dress.

He glanced away. One more look at her dress and all hope of sensible conversation would be gone. "I'm glad I got to see you in your natural environment."

"Don't you understand? I don't belong here. It's in nature that I find my solace."

"No, I see that—I do. I recognized it the moment we entered the hotel." He couldn't resist reaching for her hand. "I just meant that this is where you found your beginning. It shaped you into someone who can truly appreciate the mountain's solitude."

Rather than pulling free, she laced her fingers through his. "And I've appreciated seeing you *out* of your element." A light smile teased at her lips. "You've truly risen to the occasion, Ford. I know you must be uncomfortable with all the fuss. I appreciate it more than you'll ever know."

Her touch launched Ford's remaining shreds of self-control headfirst into the bay. He stared down into her face, losing himself there. "I'm surprised to say this, but I'm actually enjoying myself."

"You are?" Her eyes crinkled at the corners.

"Not the gala. Being here with you."

She bumped her shoulder against his arm. "I feel the same."

"You do?" His breath hitched in his chest. Before she could move away, he slipped an arm around her waist. "Margie . . ."

Margie stepped in closer, her shoulder fitting under his arm like a puzzle piece.

Ford's thoughts scattered like the surf against the rocks. "You look . . . you look beautiful tonight." The expectation in her eyes was like strong drink. He brushed his thumb against her jaw. "I can't believe we're doing this."

She tipped her cheek into his palm. "And what exactly *are* we doing?" A breeze from the water lifted her hair, tickling it against his wrist.

Only a fool would let this moment escape. He bent closer, closing the distance between them, and brushing his lips against her cheekbone. The scent of her skin ratcheted his pulse another few notches.

She turned to face him, meeting his mouth with an eagerness that caused his heart to jump to his throat.

He kissed her with the hunger of one who never thought he'd have the honor. And once she came to her senses, he might never have again.

Her senses. What about mine? Carmichael, Senator Lane . . . work.

Ford gripped her arms and drew back slightly, allowing a wisp of air to pass between them.

Margie gazed up at him for a long moment before reaching for his face, her hand trembling against his jaw. She leaned in and kissed him with feather-soft lips, the sensation nearly dropping him to his knees.

A sound from behind Margie jarred him back to reality. He lifted his head, glancing over her shoulder.

Carmichael stood near the hotel door, his unflinching stare sending a chill over Ford.

"So that's how it is?" The businessman's lips pressed into a thin line.

Margie spun around, stepping out of Ford's arms. "Philip—"

"I should have guessed." He folded both arms across his chest. "Oh, wait. I did."

Ford stepped in front of Margie. "This is none of your concern."

"None of my . . . You're jesting, right?" Carmichael scowled, deep grooves forming around his mouth. "I'm very concerned." He turned to Margie. "Does your father know about this? And about your living situation?" His attention darted back to Ford. "I want her out of that cabin—and away from your influence."

Ford bristled. "I don't think that's your decision."

"Perhaps not yet, but I'm making it anyway." He pointed a finger. "Move her out of there or I will."

Margie gasped. "Philip, stop this."

Carmichael lowered his hand. "We're not done here, but what I have to say will have to wait. I thought Margaret might want to hear her father's big announcement. I was just about to introduce him."

SEVENTEEN

*A*fter Philip departed, Margie allowed herself one last glance over the dark waters of Commencement Bay, her emotions bubbling up like Longmire's Soda Springs. Since their trip to Indian Henry's, she'd attempted to put away her feelings for Ford, but right now she struggled to dredge up her logic on the matter. Logic and moonlight didn't mix.

Perhaps—no matter how unpleasant—Philip's arrival was the splash of cold water she needed.

Ford slipped an arm behind her. "That was unexpected."

The kiss or Philip's interruption? She lowered her head against his side. "It's been a rather surprising evening."

He rubbed her shoulder. "In many ways."

She couldn't resist a smile, though the turmoil in her stomach nearly prevented it. "We should go in. Maybe my father's remarks will help us make sense of everything."

"I'll be right beside you."

The music had hushed by the time they returned, and Philip was already addressing the guests.

They edged close to the crowd, finding a place where she could view the podium but remain inconspicuous.

Philip stood with his arms spread like some sort of iconic figure drawing all eyes to himself. "As you know, we're here to honor Senator Lane and
his years of service to our state and our community. Now as we approach
an election year, it's time to look to the future, right Senator?"

Her father lifted his hand in response as the guests applauded.

Margie fidgeted; Philip's voice set her on edge. Why was she the only
one who saw him for what he was? And now that he knew about Ford,
things would only get worse.

Philip spoke at length of her father's merits and achievements, working his audience into a positive frenzy. After a loud round of applause, he
quieted, as if contemplating his next move. "I'd like to turn our attention
to an issue that concerns all the citizens of this great state. God has blessed
our region with abundant resources—minerals, timber, water—not to
mention scenery. The time has come for us to grasp our potential and become the nation's leading producer of lumber and hydropower."

Margie's chest tightened as it always did when conversations with
Philip or her father turned this direction. Progress was inevitable, but how
much more could they squeeze from the land?

He gripped the microphone with both hands, angling toward a red
velvet curtain hung over some sort of massive placard. "Senator Lane in-
tends to propel us into the next decade on the wings of prosperity. And
who will profit from this? Seattle? Olympia?"

The guests murmured, several men cupping palms to their mouths
and booing the businessman's contentious words. The battle for superior-
ity among Washington's biggest cities was stuff of legend.

"No?" Determination settled into his steely eyes. "How about here in
Tacoma?"

The room erupted in cheers. The ladies clapped their white-gloved hands while well-dressed gentlemen stomped and hooted like lumbermen at a barn dance.

Ford shook his head. "It looks as if he's loaded the room with local men."

Philip raised his arm, evidently taking pleasure in the control he wielded. "Please, gentlemen! Let's conduct ourselves with decorum, shall we? There are ladies present." He cast a glare in Margie's direction.

Margie placed a hand on Ford's arm, needing a reminder that at least the ranger was on her side.

Philip waited for silence before continuing. "Tacoma is the shining gem of this state. Not just because of our fortunate placement as a port city, but as a gateway to the mountains beyond."

Margie held her breath. He wouldn't dare talk about his plans for Paradise—he hadn't received approval yet.

"I entreat you, citizens of Tacoma, look not only to the Puget Sound, but turn your eyes to the glorious peak from which we derived our fine city's name. The federal government named the park after an English naval officer who never set foot on our country's fertile lands." Philip's expression hardened. "I say it's time we took the mountain back."

On Philip's cue, the curtain was torn from the giant placard, a painted depiction of the mountain rising behind the glittering city, the bay spreading out in the foreground. Sprawled across the top in two-foot-high letters, the title read, "Mount Tacoma—Jewel of the Cascades." Carmichael led the clapping this time, stepping down from the podium to stand in front of the massive sign. He lifted his hands, encouraging people to their feet. He shouted above the din, "Why should we call it Rainier? Let's proclaim it to the nation—the rightful name is Tacoma, and we all know this to be true, don't we?"

The crowd's energy pressed in around them like a storm about to break. Margie twisted her necklace. "I can't believe he's doing this."

Ford placed a hand in the center of her back. "Let's see what your father says."

Margie held her breath as her father approached the platform. Mother followed, fingers fluttering to her chest as if overwhelmed with pride.

"Tell him no, Papa." Her whispered voice didn't carry through the raucous gathering.

Ford leaned down and spoke into her ear. "What does it matter? You said yourself that the Indians called the mountain 'Tahoma.' Who cares what they call it?"

"It's not about the name. Philip is laying claim to the mountain. For the city—for himself." Just as he'd laid claim to her.

Margie's father climbed the three steps to the stage and straightened his jacket before taking the microphone. Philip leaned in, whispering into his ear. For men who'd been estranged for years, they appeared rather chummy.

In that moment, Margie knew what was coming. Somehow Philip had snared her father in his trap. Since he couldn't control Margie, he was grabbing hold of every other aspect of her life, painting her into a corner. How long would she be able to hold out?

Father scanned the room and cleared his throat. "Mount Tacoma is a source of pride for this community. A sign of God's blessings and providence." He glanced at Margie, his lips pulling downward for a heartbeat. "I believe it's time for us to invest in the mountain that has brought us such prestige. Its natural beauty brings people to our state from the world over. Do we want them to see the place neglected and wild? Or do we want to build it up into a symbol of what makes the Northwest great?"

He tugged at his collar as if struggling for breath. "I'm asking for your support in this great endeavor. Together we will make Mount Tacoma into a showpiece for the world."

Philip stepped closer, slapping a hand onto her father's shoulder. "I believe it's time for our second unveiling, don't you, Senator?"

"Yes, of course." He gestured to the curtain on the opposite side of the platform. "Be my guest."

Philip beamed. "Because we want the world to be our guest—at the aptly named Paradise, complete with every luxury and service they could desire."

The curtain dropped to reveal two massive color prints of Carmichael's vision for Paradise Valley—one representing summer and one winter. The depictions held only minimal resemblance to the proposal he'd brought to Paradise. Apparently those had been but the precursor to the actual plans.

Margie pressed fingers to her throat. "No."

Guests surged forward to examine the horrific paintings as an excited buzz of conversations filled the room. Above their heads, the monstrosity was still visible, with all it meant for the future. Just below the mountain's peak, the meadows of Paradise were filled with sprawling ski lodges, hundreds of tiny cabins, rope tows, vehicles, and a cabled gondola delivering skiers to Carmichael's idea of Paradise. The summer scene showed a golf course and paddocks filled with trail horses.

Philip lifted his voice above the tumult. "Beyond what you see here, I envision campgrounds, restaurants, petting zoos, dance halls, theaters— and a modern hydroelectric dam on the Paradise River will provide electricity to the whole resort. This is the national park of our future." He spread his arms, voice booming over the gathering. "Welcome to Mount Tacoma!"

An ache had burrowed into Ford's temples by the time he escorted Margie back to the truck. Carmichael's idea of "minor" improvements spelled disaster for the park as he knew it. Civilization was marching its way up the mountain slopes. Suddenly he understood the pressure his father felt to protect Rainier—or "Tacoma." But Ford's training focused on taking care of the land, not battling greedy businessmen.

Margie smacked a palm against her leg, sending a couple of blue feathers wafting to the ground. "He can't. He just can't."

Ford swung open the truck door. "He seems to think he can, and most of that crowd agreed."

She sighed. "I want to get as far from this place as possible."

"I've had enough city life for one night. Maybe even for a month." He waited as she climbed in.

"I can't believe my father is going along with this. I don't understand." She pressed a fist to her eyelids as if to force the tears back.

He stopped and faced her, taking her fingers in his hands. "I spoke to your father, briefly. He said something about being in a tough spot."

"And obviously it involves Philip in some way. What could it be?"

"He didn't say. I'm sure he'll explain in private." He glanced down at her hands, lost in his grip. The chill on her skin sent a quiver through his heart. She seemed to blame herself for this predicament, but Ford saw Carmichael's plans for what they were—a blatant money grab.

"I thought perhaps we could drive back to Longmire tonight, but I guess we need to return to my parents' house." She drew her fingers away, pulling them to her lap.

The gesture wasn't lost on him. Her earlier romantic feelings had cooled in light of the evening's events. He should have expected it. He stepped back, hand on the doorframe. "I wouldn't want to take the truck so far after dark, anyway."

"If we got stuck somewhere, we'd be . . ." Margie bit her lip, not finishing her sentence.

Alone. Overnight. The idea sent a wave of heat through his chest. "Yes."

She managed a mournful smile. "I suppose it's time to face my mother."

He closed her door. A night at the Lane house didn't strike him as a good time, but maybe it'd give him a chance to figure out his next step. Because now that he'd kissed her once, he wanted to ensure it happened again.

EIGHTEEN

*M*argie stood in her childhood bedroom, slipping off the blue gown along with her hopes for the evening. She'd come to Tacoma to speak to her father, but instead she'd stood and watched as Philip whipped the gala crowd into a drooling frenzy. Those businessmen couldn't wait to get their hands on her treasured Paradise and transform it into a circus sideshow.

Somehow Philip had managed to ensnare her father in his vulgar plans. It was up to her to untangle this mess she'd created.

And then there was Ford. Margie sighed. *What a kiss.* But he was her boss—and an unbeliever. Hadn't she always said she wouldn't get entangled with someone who didn't share her faith? Then again, Philip claimed to be a believer but showed little evidence of it. *Lord, what am I supposed to do?* Forgetting that kiss would not be an option.

And all this happened with her dressed like a molting Steller's jay. Margie tossed the detestable garment over a chair. Knowing who'd picked it out, she was certain to never wear it again. Perhaps she should cast it out the window—set it free. She stood in her slip and swiped a handkerchief across her damp eyes. Reaching for the dress she'd worn from Longmire, she pressed it to her chest.

Was Ford changing out of his tuxedo at this moment? Her throat tightened. He'd done so much for her tonight.

A knock sounded at her door.

"Just a moment." She yanked on the simple dress, fastening the buttons as quickly as she could. After pulling a brush through her disheveled locks and blowing her nose, she hurried to the door and opened it.

Ford stood there, dressed in his own suit. "I was going to head downstairs. But this house is so large, I wasn't sure which staircase to take."

Margie stepped back. "Let me finish getting ready, and I'll walk you down."

He hovered in the doorway. "I probably should wait out here."

"I'll just be a moment." She sat down at the dressing table and dug in the drawer for a clip. Anything that would make this mop more presentable to her mother. After clipping her hair back, she pulled on her shoes and grabbed her sweater. "I think I heard my parents come in. It's time we got some answers."

Her mother's voice drew Margie to her father's study. The double doors stood ajar, light spilling out into the living room. "You let Philip do all the talking. What's wrong with you this evening?"

Margie shot a quick glance at Ford. Perhaps they'd chosen a bad time to descend the stairs. And yet she could hardly suggest a return to her room.

"Katherine, you know Philip had me at a disadvantage. What was I supposed to say?"

"He wanted you to announce his and Margie's engagement."

Margie gasped, backing straight into Ford.

"Never." Her father cleared his throat. "I'll not see that man wed my only daughter."

Margie strode forward. "And nothing could convince me to marry Philip. Is that why you're doing this?"

Her father jerked his head up at her intrusion, his cheeks splotched with color. Both of her parents still wore their evening clothes, but her father's tie and collar hung loose about his neck.

Ford appeared at the door, his lanky frame filling the space.

She hated the idea of subjecting him to her family drama, but there was no help for that now.

Her father pinched the bridge of his nose. "Margie, I didn't know you were there."

Margie turned to her mother. "I don't know what Philip has told you, but we are most certainly not engaged."

Father sagged down into his desk chair. "That's a relief."

Mother's lips pursed. "You always liked Philip, Margaret. Why have you turned on him?"

"And you always despised him. When did we swap sides?"

Her mother glanced at Ford. "I'm not sure we should have this discussion in front of company, Margaret. You're putting Ranger Brayden in a most uncomfortable position."

Ford rubbed at the back of his neck. "I'm here to support Margie."

Margie exhaled, the tension of the evening bubbling over. There was no reason to further subject him to her family turmoil. "Perhaps you should give us a moment alone."

He held her gaze for a long moment before nodding. "I'll wait in the living room. If you need anything, I'm nearby."

After he departed, Margie's mother shook her head. "Why did you bring a stranger into this? What's that man doing here, anyway? Please don't tell me you've gotten involved with a park ranger."

Margie bit down an acerbic reply. Her mother's condescending attitude was a problem for another day. "He's here as a friend. The park is Ford's life. He deserves to know Philip's intentions. And Father, I think I deserve an explanation as well. Why did you let Philip say all those things tonight if you don't agree with him?"

He lowered his chin. "Margie, sit down, please. We need to talk."

She sank into one of the plush chairs opposite her father's desk. The dark shadows around his eyes spoke volumes.

He turned to Margie's mother. "Darling, why don't you look in on our guest? I hate to think of him sitting alone."

Mother huffed. "Very well. No one could ever accuse me of not being a good hostess."

Margie waited to speak until the door closed behind her mother. "Papa, please tell me this is all a bad dream."

Her father sighed, scrubbing a fist across his forehead. "I wish I'd run that boy off when he followed you home years ago."

"You know I wouldn't have stood for that."

He grunted. "You always had a soft spot for the downtrodden, and I wanted to encourage that in you. It's the sign of a good leader. Christ modeled compassion for us, and I was delighted to see you embrace your faith."

Margie scooted forward in her seat. "It didn't seem like it at the time. Neither you nor Mother had a kind word for Philip."

"I could see his intelligence and his drive—but he was using you, Margie. From the very first day. There wasn't a stroke of kindness in the lad." Father shook his head. "I thought if I helped him achieve his goals, he'd find his own way and leave you alone. I was setting a backfire in order to preserve what meant the most to me."

"What meant the most . . ." The answer came to her midquestion. Her. She shook her head. "Philip and I were close once, but we parted ways after he left Tacoma for school. When he returned, I could see the coldness in him." Had there ever been warmth, or had she just seen what she wanted? "I told him I wouldn't marry him."

"I'm sure he took that well." Her father rarely resorted to sarcasm.

Margie touched her cheek, still shaken by the memory of Philip's rage. It was so unlike him—or so she'd thought at the time. Now she wondered. "This is all history now. How did he weasel into your campaign? None of these ideas sound like you."

Her father's gaze locked on her. "The ideas aren't bad, in and of themselves. To draw attention to the parks, one must also draw visitors. A careful plan to develop certain areas at Mount Rainier could be good for the park, the state, and the nation."

"How could you say such a thing?" Margie's throat closed. "Have you studied Philip's plans?"

He waved a dismissive hand. "Oh, his plans are excessive, certainly. But you can't deny development is needed. If we do nothing, the increased load of visitors and their automobiles will destroy the natural beauty of the place. Even now, people are parking all over the Paradise meadows, cutting trees for bonfires, leaving their trash in the lakes, trampling the most beautiful places. Is that what you want?"

"No, but—"

"Then you must concede that the park service needs to plan with an eye to the future. Find a way to accommodate more tourists and more vehicles—or close the gates forever. Which would you choose?"

Tears stung at Margie's eyes. He was right. "But Philip's not interested in preserving wilderness. He wants to exploit the park and line his pockets with the proceeds."

"As I said, he doesn't have a spark of kindness in him. He needs a firm guiding hand."

"And that's you?" Hadn't her father stood in defeat as Philip spun a web of deceit over a group of hungry business moguls?

Her father stood, stepping around the desk to her side. "No, my dear. It's you."

Her breath caught in her throat. "What do you mean?"

"He's offered to let you help run the park. You can push for what you think is best."

"In exchange for my freedom? Why are you supporting him at all? Why don't you meet with the park administration yourself? Come up with a plan that works for everyone?"

"Margie . . . I must be honest." Father swept a handkerchief across his nose. "I haven't always been the pillar of the community you believe me to be. I've cut a few corners over the years."

A sour taste rose in Margie's mouth. "What are you saying?"

Her father sighed, lowering himself to sit on the edge of the desk. "Philip has obtained some privileged information. Information that would ruin me—and this family." His head fell forward. "He has every intention of using the situation to his advantage."

She shook her head. "I don't believe it. You couldn't have done anything so terrible that someone could blackmail you. It's not in your nature."

Her father's eyes filled. "Oh, my daughter—I've long protected you and your mother. I desperately wanted to be the virtuous statesman your mother envisioned me to be, so eventually I started to believe it myself. But one doesn't rise to this position on his laurels. I don't want to give you all the sordid secrets, but trust me when I say I will not be elected to another term if Philip leaks what he knows to the papers. And a scandal of this magnitude would kill your mother."

Scandal of any sort would kill her mother. Margie closed her eyes for a brief moment, letting the news wash over her like a sudden rainstorm.

Her father had always been a pillar of the faith—at least in her eyes. Was she really so naive?

Father leaned forward and touched her wrist. "Margie, the Pacific Northwest is a battlefield. Resources against preservation—it's a war that'll tear our state apart. Money has flowed both ways, and I'm afraid quite a bit of it has landed in my pocket."

Margie yanked back. "You accepted bribes? Is that what you're telling me?"

The color washed from his face. "Creative financing. As the chair of the Committee on Expenditures in the Interior Department, I have to look to the interests of my—my constituents."

"Those who slipped you cash, you mean? Timber and mining interests?" Her mouth grew dry. "So you cut funding to the parks?"

"I cut government spending wherever I could—even for federal lands, yes. Whenever possible, I diverted other monies back their way." He pressed a hand against his forehead. "It's all a bit of a hodgepodge, I'm afraid."

Margie took several deep breaths. "I always thought you above graft."

"As did I. But now you need to know the truth. Philip is ready to throw me to the wind. And perhaps I deserve it."

"So what do we do?"

"Your mother believes you should marry Philip. I'd rather not see it come to that."

"Me either." She may have dreamed of marrying him when she was young, but certainly not now. A wave of nausea washed over her.

"I'd sacrifice pretty much anything else to the man, but not my daughter."

She crossed her legs, leaning back in the chair. "I'm glad we're in agreement about that point, anyway. But where does it leave us?"

Her father sighed again, a sound that immediately took her back to the early days when she could see no wrong in Philip. Why hadn't she trusted her father's instincts then? But knowing the truth—could she trust his instincts now?

Father laid his hands on his knees. "I don't know, my dear. I really don't know. As I see it, he's going to use the situation against us both. He'll threaten you with my future. He'll threaten me with his knowledge." Father stretched his arms wide. "Philip holds all the cards."

The image of the playing card she'd found in her journal drifted back into her memory. Philip had planned this out from the beginning. Margie tapped a thumbnail against her lip. "Maybe we could convince his backers it's a bad investment."

"But it's not. Everything Philip touches turns to gold. Look what he's done for the Tacoma Hotel. It was falling apart when he took over. Now it's a showpiece."

Margie stood up and wandered over to the bookcase. Just as it had when she was a little girl, a row of games lined the bottom shelf. She crouched, pushing through backgammon, checkers, and Snakes and Ladders, until she found the familiar goldfinch-design playing cards. "Somehow we have to beat him at his own game."

Ford sipped the black coffee, forcing himself not to bounce his knee in frustration. He'd endured enough for one evening, but sitting here in the silent room across from Margie's mother was asking too much. What were they discussing behind those closed study doors?

Mrs. Lane crossed and uncrossed her legs like a petulant child, frequently glancing toward her husband's study. Obviously she didn't care to be left out of the discussion either. With a sigh, she turned to Ford. "So, what exactly are your intentions here?"

Ford choked on his drink, the scalding liquid burning its way down his throat. "I'm sorry? I'm not sure what you mean."

The woman's brows pulled together, at least as much as was possible in their highly plucked state. "Margaret is obviously fond of you. She's an impressionable young woman. It makes perfect sense that she'd be drawn to someone such as yourself."

"Margie and I work together. We are friends." The words sounded hollow, even to him.

Her eyes narrowed. "How many young women work at your park?"

Ford shifted in his seat. "A handful. Mostly in the hotels and eateries."

"And you're the boss?"

"I oversee the ranger staff, and I coordinate with the concessionaire." Where was this interrogation headed?

"How often do you date the girls who work for you?"

A wave of heat climbed up Ford's neck. He glanced toward the study. "I've never . . . I wouldn't . . ." The words died on his lips. Isn't that exactly what he was trying to do?

A wry smile twisted Mrs. Lane's mouth. "I see. So you're not interested in my daughter?"

He'd faced off with bears, cougars, and the occasional irate visitor, but none compared to this woman. "She's very good at what she does, Mrs. Lane. I believe you'd be proud of her. Margie cares deeply for the park and for nature."

"And it's obvious to me that she cares deeply about her boss." Mrs. Lane leaned back in her seat, gripping her coffee cup with both hands.

"Never mind. It's inconsequential. This lark of hers is nothing but a temporary distraction. She's meant for better things, and Margaret will realize that in time. We didn't send her through Bryn Mawr to have her throw it all away on someone like you."

"You'd rather see her with someone like Carmichael?" The words sprang out before he could bite his tongue.

She tapped her fingernails against the cup, like a woodpecker in search of a meal. "Mr. Carmichael has made something of himself. He came from humble beginnings—not unlike yourself, I'm sure."

Ford pressed himself into the seat. He might be lousy with words, but he should at least try to be polite. "He's seen some success. That's certain."

"Senator Lane has poured his financial resources into seeing that young man succeed. Now Philip is finally in a position to help this family. Who are we to turn him away?"

And her daughter was part of the bargain? "I'm sure you're merely looking out for your daughter's future."

"To be honest, I've never liked the man. I never thought him good enough for her. But Philip has been very loyal, and he could give her everything she needs or desires. What can you provide?" She studied his attire.

Ford's throat tightened. What *could* he provide? He didn't even own a home. He lived in a crumbly little shack, and even that belonged to the park service. What woman would ever care to settle down with a man like him?

The study door swung open and Margie appeared, lines of tension obvious on her face. She crossed the room and stood beside him. "Ford, I think we should go."

He stood. "Now?"

Mrs. Lane jumped to her feet. "You can't leave tonight. I've had rooms made up for you. And Philip is coming to breakfast."

Margie nodded. "Exactly." She turned to Ford, her brown eyes pleading. "We've got what we came for. Let's go home."

A rush of warmth swept over him. They might be rickety little cabins, but to Margie they were home. It didn't matter that it was well past midnight and the roads were dark. He'd drive through a volcanic eruption to get her there.

NINETEEN

*F*ord rubbed bleary eyes as he strode across the clearing to the community kitchen the next morning. He was forty-five minutes late for breakfast, but there were always leftovers. All he needed was a cup of coffee and a piece of dry toast. A man couldn't expect much at this late hour. Especially a man who'd been out all night. He'd never had much regard for staff who frittered away their evening hours and showed up to work too exhausted to be of much value. From now on he'd show more sympathy.

At least at this hour, he'd be unlikely to run into Margie. She probably already had her face buried in plant samples and preparation for tomorrow night's magic lantern show at the Inn. Hopefully she was in better shape than he was. Since she'd slept an hour wedged against his shoulder in the truck, he imagined she was. His arm still ached, but it'd been worth every sore muscle.

Ford tapped on the door before ducking inside. "Mrs. Brown? I just thought I'd grab a cup . . ."

Margie stepped out of the kitchen, her hair tucked up in a yellow scarf. "Good morning."

He pulled the door closed behind him. "I'm running late this morning."

"As am I." She wrapped her arms around her middle and looked down at the floor.

Mrs. Brown bundled past Margie and reached for the empty coffee pot. "Here, let me make you two a fresh batch. It looks as if you could use it." She patted Ford's arm as she walked past. "Late night?"

He cleared his throat, not daring to glance in Margie's direction lest his face give them away. "Yes. Those reports will be the death of me. Be sure to tell your husband."

The corner of her mouth lifted as she smoothed a hand across her stained apron. "That's odd. When Harry retired for the night, he mentioned the park truck was missing. Yet it was right in place when I got up this morning. Obviously, he must have been mistaken." The teasing tone in her voice sent fingers down Ford's spine.

Margie took a biscuit from the table and wrapped it in a paper napkin. "I believe Ranger Brayden had to check on some things last night."

Mrs. Brown laughed as she headed to the kitchen with the empty pot. "I hope he found everything to be to his liking."

Ford sighed as the woman disappeared. "We're going to be a topic of conversation for quite some time."

Margie shrugged. "I'm used to it. I've been a source of gossip most of my life. I'm sorry to have dragged you into it."

Dragged? He'd jumped in with both boots. "My men don't gossip. You make them sound like a passel of old church ladies."

Mrs. Brown leaned through the swinging doors. "What would you know of church ladies? You haven't darkened the church door since your father passed away. He'd be quite annoyed about that, young man."

Leave it to Mrs. Brown to notice such things. "I've been busy. Work never slows down for Sunday morning."

"And yet your father rarely missed." She wrinkled her nose before returning to the kitchen.

"Yes, well." He lowered his voice. "I went to please him. There doesn't seem much point now." He glanced at Margie, but she seemed intent on brushing crumbs from the table.

"Is that what you think of us?" Margie's voice barely stirred the air in the room.

"What?"

Her brown eyes lifted, fastening on him like an owl's eyes in the moonlight. "Old church ladies—gossiping and judging people?"

He swallowed. "You're not old."

She pressed a hand to her chest. "But the rest?"

Ford's head swam as he thought back over his words. What had he said, exactly? "Of course not. It doesn't bother me that you go to church. Just don't try to haul me there." He strode to the kitchen doorway. "How's the coffee coming?"

"It's percolating," Mrs. Brown called back. "Not fast enough for you, I'm afraid."

"I'm actually not very hungry." Margie's voice sounded behind him, cracking as she spoke. "I'll head over to the office. Is everything ready for me?"

Ford spun around. "My office?"

Her eyes narrowed. "To type? Is it all set out?"

The report. "Yes, yes. I tried to make a start, but I just muddled things, I'm afraid."

"I'll sort it out." She was out the door before he had the chance to say another word.

Mrs. Brown tromped back into the dining hall with the pot and a plate of fragrant sweet rolls. "I thought you might need these."

Ford sat at the table and held out his cup like a beggar asking for alms. "No good can come from pre-coffee conversation."

After filling the cup, she sat down next to him. "Conversation has never been your strongest suit."

"I can't argue with you there." He gulped a mouthful of the brew before considering how hot the liquid might be.

"Don't louse this up, Ford. She's a good woman." Mrs. Brown folded her hands in her lap.

He choked, covering his mouth with a fist. The older woman had always seen through him, even when he was a lad stealing cookies from the pantry. "Yes, well, she comes from a different world."

"She's chosen ours. That's worth its weight in gold." She pushed the plate of rolls closer to him. "But it's not your different upbringings or your lack of conversational skills that has me concerned."

He helped himself to one of the sticky rolls, even though the sight turned his stomach. One didn't turn down Mrs. Brown's food or her advice. He might as well take it like a man.

"You need to get yourself right with God. She won't have you until then, and I agree with her."

He twisted his neck to look at the matronly woman. "You two have been talking about whether or not I attend church?"

Her lips pressed together. "Ford Brayden, we haven't discussed you at all. Not in a personal sense, anyway."

"Then how do you know this?"

"She's come to church with Harry and me several times. I know her faith is dear to her." Mrs. Brown pushed to her feet and adjusted her apron. "But it's not about whether you warm a pew at services that matters, Ford.

It's whether you're willing to trust Him, and I know that's going to be a challenge for you considering how grief still owns your heart."

Ford swept his hat off the table and stood. "My feelings about God—or my lack of feelings—are my business. No one else's."

"Perhaps so. But this much is true, Ford. Your soul cracked when your father died in that avalanche. How can you expect to offer someone your heart when you need a basket just to hold all the pieces?"

"I need to get to work. I'm running late."

"You're running, all right." She topped off his coffee mug and handed it to him. "You can't expect that young lady to heal you. It's not fair to her. That's God's job."

"I don't need healing. My father died two years ago, and I haven't missed a day of work since."

"You haven't missed a day doing your father's job. Think about it."

"I'm doing the job Harry asked me to do."

She pinned him with a motherly stare. "I mean it, Ford. Don't pursue her until you've got yourself put back together."

Margie rolled a sheet of paper into the typewriter, determined not to let any more of this day get away from her. Her conversation with Ford had sent her stomach into a sickening downward spiral. She'd wanted to believe he was only steps away from finding God and at the right moment she could nudge him in the appropriate direction. It was time to be realistic. Ford Brayden was an unbeliever and determined to stay as such. Could she live with that?

She clamped the paper guide into place, mentally throwing a similar guard over her heart. She'd been foolish to let her feelings run away with her. Isn't that what she'd done with Philip all those years ago?

A tiny doubt niggled in the back of her mind. While her father had taught her everything she knew about faith, he obviously wasn't the up-standing man she thought him to be. And Philip certainly wasn't. Scrip-ture was clear about not yoking yourself with an unbeliever. The second part of the verse wafted through her mind: *"For what fellowship hath righteousness with unrighteousness?"* And yet, in so many ways, Ford seemed far more righteous than the other men in her life.

So where did that leave her?

His handwritten notes lay on the desk. She slid her fingers along the script, imagining him bent over the work.

The fact remained: their beliefs were completely at odds. She saw God in every loving brushstroke of creation. Ford saw only beautiful chaos—something to be appreciated, but not trusted. There could be no reconcili-ation between these viewpoints. He could laugh off her faith as childish fantasy, but in so doing, he'd never understand who she truly was. He could never really love her.

The idea left her hollow. She couldn't lead him on. It wouldn't be fair.

Margie laid her head against the typewriter, tears stinging at her eyes. Could things get any worse? Philip. Her father. Now Ford.

She took a deep breath and straightened, laying her fingers on the keys. It was time to fix the mess Philip had made of things. And she'd need to do so without the help of Ford or anyone else. In fact, it would be far less distracting without having the mesmeric ranger within an arm's reach at any given moment.

The sound of footsteps on the stairs made her heart jump a second before Ford appeared at the office door. How long before she could main-tain a calm demeanor in the man's presence? Their kiss had thrown her entire equilibrium off-balance. "Will I be in your way?"

Ford leaned against the doorframe, putting her in mind of a mountain lion draped over a tree branch. "No, I'll just sit over there and stay out of your hair." He reached for a chair and dragged it to the opposite side of the tiny office.

"If you have other duties, I can take care of things here." The room suddenly felt very close. How much work could she accomplish with him breathing down her neck?

"I'd like to proofread the report as you finish each page." He lowered himself to the seat and crossed his ankles. Ford drew a stack of papers onto his lap, shuffling through the sheets.

So he didn't trust her in his office alone? The man was as territorial as a wolf. If the typewriter didn't weigh a ton, she'd carry it to her cabin and do the work there. She'd seen some smaller portable machines in the Sears, Roebuck catalog. Perhaps she should order one. Margie focused on the round keys, rubbing her palms discreetly against her skirt to dry them.

She began picking out letters, her attention flicking back and forth from Ford's notes to the keys. After a few minutes, she eased into a rhythm. If only men could be more like this—steady and predictable. You did your part, and they reacted in a predictable manner, producing the wanted results.

But if men were anything like typewriters, she'd never mastered the art of controlling one.

Ford leaned his chair against the office wall, one foot propped up on a lower desk drawer. He tried to study the visitation numbers displayed on the typed pages. No matter his intentions, his eyes kept drifting to Margie perched on the edge of her seat, diligently tapping away at the infernal machine.

Mrs. Brown's words hung on the edges of his thoughts. *"You haven't missed a day—doing your father's job.*" What did she mean by that? How could doing a good job be a bad thing?

Margie's back was straight as a flagpole as she concentrated on the keys with an unwavering focus. Why couldn't he do the same? Perhaps because his mind was consumed with the memory of her lips. A kiss should seal a budding relationship, but he could sense her drawing away. It was as if someone had driven a splitting wedge between them.

The papers blurred in his peripheral vision. He wasn't accomplishing anything by studying the lines of her shoulder blades beneath the light flowered fabric of her dress. He really should issue her a standard park uniform, if only for his own sanity.

The ding of the typewriter's bell jerked him from his reverie, the motion nearly upending the precariously balanced chair. The two legs slammed against the floor.

Margie turned and eyed him over her shoulder. "You really shouldn't lean in chairs like that. Didn't your headmaster ever correct such behavior?"

"I didn't spend much time in school. My teachers were generally relieved to see me in a seat at all."

With a steady hand, she slid the carriage back to the margin. The tapping resumed.

His heartbeat ratcheted up another notch as if matching the cadence of her speedy fingers. This was ridiculous. Whatever Mrs. Brown thought, it was obvious he and Margie were meant for each other. Either fate or nature—or maybe even that God of hers—had brought the two of them together. He'd just moved too fast.

"Are you watching me, by chance?"

Ford lifted the sheets in front of his face. "Of course not."

"Good. Because I get nervous when someone watches me. I'd hate to make stupid mistakes because my fingers got all fiddly."

Fiddly fingers. The room was growing too warm to breathe. Ford jumped from his seat, hurried over to the window, and threw it open. "That's better." He braced himself against the sill. "Have you thought any more about our situation?"

Her brows shot upward and a rosy tinge touched her cheeks. "Our—our what?"

"Carmichael taking over the RNPC."

"Oh." Margie took her hands off the keys and laid them in her lap. "I've thought of little else."

Ford reached for his chair and dragged it close to her side before sitting down. "You know I want to help."

"Because you don't want to face Philip's grandiose ideas?"

"Because I care about you. I don't want to see you forced into something you don't desire."

She lowered her eyes. "I should finish these reports. I'm leading a nature walk at Paradise this afternoon."

Ford stood, fighting the urge to touch her hair. "What about lunch, first? Then I could drive you up the hill."

She focused on the report again. "I'm dining with Luke Johansson at the Paradise Inn. Ranger Jennings said I could ride with him. I'll be staying over at the Inn, as well, since I'm doing the evening magic lantern talk." She rolled the paper forward, as if checking the type. She glanced up at him, her eyes serious. "In fact, I might move to Paradise for the rest of the summer. All this driving back and forth doesn't really make sense."

"We only have the male dormitory up there."

"For the rangers, yes. But there is housing for the female Inn staff. Or

I could get a room at the Inn—at my own expense, of course." She glanced up at him.

"Oh." Ford pushed down the disappointment rising in his gut. Somehow when he'd kissed Margie next to Commencement Bay, he hadn't anticipated life returning to normal so quickly. Could she just put that moment behind her so easily? He cleared his throat. "Well, I should let you finish then. I'll . . . I'll take a walk over to the Community Building."

"I'll leave the report on your desk when I've finished."

"That'll be fine. Thank you." The tapping faded as he made his way down the stairs and outside.

Longmire without Margie? Even with the summer sun beating down on the trees, the forest had never seemed so dismal.

TWENTY

July 1, 1927

*F*ord rolled over in bed, the frame creaking in protest. He rubbed the back of his hand across his eyes, straining to make sense of the odd crackling sounds that had woken him. *Rain hitting the roof, perhaps?* They hadn't seen any in weeks; the forest was dry as three-day-old toast. They could certainly use some moisture. But the racket? It must be one intense storm.

An eerie flickering light danced on the far wall. Ford pushed up on his elbows, his sleep-muddled thoughts clearing. *No.* He launched across the room, barely getting his feet under him before colliding with the door and wrenching it open.

Flames licked the inside of Margie's cabin windows as the small building lit up from within like an oil lamp.

Ford's heart hammered as he stood rooted to the stoop. *Margie.* A harrowing few seconds passed before he could breathe again. She'd been staying at Paradise—what was it—five days, now?

He dashed through the night, pounding on every door he could find before running for the fire hoses. By the time he and Jennings lugged a hose back, the cabin was fully engulfed. The searing heat drove them back. His cabin could be next—and the surrounding forest, besides.

Unless they got this blaze under control, this fire could spell the end of Longmire.

Carson and the other men arrived within moments and aimed a second hose at the surrounding trees and undergrowth.

The scent of smoldering ash filled Ford's nose as he sprayed water at the base of the flames, soaking the cabin from the ground up. Had it only been a month since he'd helped Margie get settled? Thank goodness she hadn't been home. The thought of losing her curdled in his gut.

Smoke rolled from the structure, filling the night air, even as the flames died down. His arms and back ached from gripping the hose, but their work seemed to be effective. The small shack crumbled inward, casting sparks into the night air.

Jennings grunted, hoisting the hose over a few feet. "I think we've got it. Good thing this place was slated for demolition anyway. Right, boss?"

"Yeah. Right." He handed the hose off to one of the other rangers and brushed his hands against his stained pant legs.

Only now, there was no chance of Margie coming home.

He strode around the smoldering ruin, questions racing through his mind. How had the fire started? If Margie had been home, he'd have suspected her lack of fire-tending skills. But the cabin had been empty for several days.

Move her out of there, or I will. Carmichael's voice stole through his memory.

Empty cabins didn't just burst into flame. They had to have help.

Margie offered a cheery wave to the bus passengers heading home from their weekend excursion. The RNPC driver had been kind enough to offer her a lift down the hill to Longmire this morning. She needed to gather the rest of her belongings and have someone help her ferry them up to Paradise before tonight's program. Staying at the Inn was expensive, but convenient. Mr. Johansson had promised her a room in the women's dormitory as soon as they had space.

A little distance from a certain chief ranger had been a good thing, too. Or so she kept telling herself. The more Margie tried not to think about him, the less her heart cooperated.

She already missed living in Longmire. If only she weren't so attached to her little Waldenesque cabin. And having Ford right next door . . . A shiver raced across her skin. She needed to put such thoughts out of her mind.

Margie lifted the knapsack over her shoulder and trotted into Longmire as the red bus departed in a cloud of dust. She sniffed the air; the place smelled of soggy campfire ash. Had there been a problem in the campground? Turning the corner past the National Park Inn, she spotted a crowd lingering near the entrance to the older housing area. She rushed forward.

Ford intercepted her. "Margie, there you are. I telephoned Paradise, but they said you'd already left."

"What's wrong? What happened?" She pushed past him, spotting the charred beams. "My cabin—" *No.* Her throat clenched as grief ripped through her. "Was anyone hurt?"

"Everyone's fine. We managed to keep it to your place and a few nearby trees." He grabbed her arm as she surged toward the smoldering mess. "Don't, Margie. It's still hot."

She couldn't tear her eyes from the smoking rubble, the sickening smell turning her stomach. "How did this happen?"

"We don't know yet. But it started inside."

Margie pushed against Ford's forearm, an icy chill draping over her shoulders. "Inside? How is that possible? No one was in there."

A shadow crossed his face. "Tell me you came back at some point and left a lamp burning. Or hot ash in the fireplace?"

"I was gone for days, Ford. You know that." Tremors spread through Margie's core. How could this have happened?

The stench clung to Ford's clothes. His gray eyes fixed on her. "Then I think the fire was set intentionally."

"Set?" She swallowed, her mind racing. "By whom?"

The look on his face provided her answer. She stepped back, the thought taking a moment to settle into the depths of her being. This was her fault. She'd unleashed Philip on this place, and now he'd see it come down around her ears—risking those she loved in the meantime. She pressed the back of her hand to her lips to prevent the moan that threatened to burst out. After a moment, her breathing steadied. "My books? My things?"

He took her hand, his fingers streaked with soot. "I'm so sorry."

TWENTY-ONE

August 25, 1927 (Thursday)

*M*argie led the last tour group of the day through the meadow, pointing out the late-season lupines and red splashes of Indian paintbrush. The women from the Mountaineers club stopped to admire each of the blooms, murmuring appreciation of every tidbit of information Margie offered them.

In between questions, her mind wandered. The month of July and most of August had passed in a blur, filled with a dizzying number of wildflower tours and fireside talks. Her dreams of opening people's eyes to God's wonders had been answered beyond her imagination, and yet the one person she most longed to reach remained unmoved.

She'd seen Ford only a few times since moving to Paradise. The summer season apparently kept him too busy for casual conversations with the naturalist staff. Unfortunately, every glimpse of him still made her heart leap into her throat. It seemed best to maintain a safe distance. The temptation to fall back into his arms was more than she could bear.

She needed to stay resolute. There was no future for the two of them, and staying away might keep him safe from Philip's wrath. Ranger Jennings had told her that they'd found no evidence of arson at her cabin, but she couldn't shake the sense that Philip was somehow responsible. Either he'd set the blaze himself, or—more likely—he'd paid someone else to do so. Would he target Ford next? How long could she hold out against such tactics?

Moving into the women's dormitory had lifted her spirits. The small group of residents enjoyed a rare camaraderie, giggling late into the night and sharing their secret hopes and dreams, which often involved the men who worked on the mountain. Even though most of them seemed taken with the fellows living at the nearby male dormitory, a couple of the girls had set their sights on the handsome Chief Ranger. Margie had bitten her tongue rather than join in the idle gossip. If anyone found out she'd actually kissed Ford, there'd be no peace.

As the Mountaineers club ladies explored the variety of blossoms, Margie glanced toward the Inn and its parking area packed with automobiles. If Philip built his massive luxury resort, what would happen to this fragile mountain vegetation? Even now, the rangers had to patrol the tent camp to ask campers not to cut the small clumps of subalpine trees for their bonfires.

She'd taken to rising early each morning to walk the meadow trails and pray. God wouldn't let Philip succeed; she was sure of it. Somehow He'd intervene. *Just show me what to do, Lord. Please.*

"These seem so tender and delicate." Mrs. Winters frowned, running her finger along the tiny pink petals of a spreading phlox. "You said this meadow was snow-covered ten months out of the year. How do they manage to survive?"

The question pulled Margie from her musings. "They protect themselves by hugging the ground and thrusting their roots down deep. They cling to the mountain with every ounce of their might and only grow a tiny bit each year. And these lupines"—she gestured toward the purple flowers lifting their heads slightly above the others—"are experts at growing in poor, thin soils, wresting nutrients out of water and air and storing nutrition in their root systems. Sometimes a fragile appearance masks deep strength."

Mrs. Winters laughed with her companions. "Do you hear that, girls? Just like us."

The other women wandered back toward the Inn, but Mrs. Winters touched Margie's arm. "I wanted to thank you for giving us a tour. We've been out with rangers before, but it's a delight to hear from such a knowl-edgeable young woman."

"Thank you." The woman's kind words warmed Margie's spirits. "It's my pleasure, really." And a nice distraction from the situation with Philip.

A smile warmed her lined face. "You should consider joining our club for one of the climbs, Miss Lane."

"I don't think climbing is for me." Margie bent down to study a Sitka valerian's tiny white bloom, almost lost among the showier meadow flowers.

"That's what I thought the first time, too." She laughed. "Now moun-taineering's an obsession of mine."

Margie stood. "Really? You've scaled Mount Rainier?"

"Two years ago." She turned to gaze upon the snowy dome in the distance. "There's nothing to compare. It's as if you can see the whole world." She placed a hand on one hip. "There were three women in our group that year, Miss Lane. Don't think because you're not a man you can't do anything you set your mind to do. You spoke truth—a fragile appearance can mask great strength."

Margie felt anything but strong right now. "Thank you. I'll keep that in mind." Margie lifted her eyes, gazing at the glaciated peak. Would it be worth risking avalanche, rockfall, and crevasses just for a better view? Granted it would be a pretty spectacular vista. But with her fear of heights, it would take more than scenery to get her to rope into one of those climb-ing teams.

Margie strolled the Skyline Trail, the late-afternoon sun warming her shoulders. Ranger Jennings had promised her a ride to the Browns' in time for supper, but for now she relished a little free time to explore unhindered. The flower composition seemed to change on a daily basis as the small plants made the most of the short growing season, popping out their blooms like firecrackers then transforming into seedpods almost as quickly.

Sometimes a fragile appearance masks great strength. Margie had come to the mountain to hide from Philip, fearful of his controlling ways. Now, after everything that had happened, did she really have the strength to fight him? She brushed her fingers over the soft seed head of the pasqueflower, several of the fuzzy seeds falling free into her hand. Like these plants, Margie had sunk roots into this mountain. Now she just needed to hold on.

Strolling back toward the Inn, Margie stopped to pluck a few of the early mountain huckleberries. One of these evenings, she should bring a pail and gather some. Popping the fruit into her mouth, Margie let the tart juice overwhelm her taste buds.

A crashing sound off to her right made her jump. A black bear sat about thirty yards away at the edge of the meadow, rooting through the squat shrubs with its short muzzle. Margie's legs tensed as the lumbering giant swung its head side to side, likely suctioning up the same tiny blue morsels, and reached one curved paw through the branches to guide the fruit into its mouth. Was this one of the bears Margie had seen Carson feeding over at the trash heap, encouraging them to stand and turn for the crowd of onlookers? If only she could bring those people here to see the mighty animal behaving as it should rather than like a silly trained dog.

Why do we need to reduce wilderness into something we can control? Transform the frightening to the ridiculous. If Philip had his way, the park would be revamped into sideshow antics meant only to please the visitors.

The beast lifted its head, the tan-colored snout scrunching as it sniffed the wind.

Margie backed slowly. As much as she appreciated the majesty of the wild creature, she certainly didn't trust it. God had given it claws and teeth for a reason, and she didn't care to view either of those at close range. Competing for the meadow's food sources was not high on her list of desires.

The bear snorted, hunching its shoulders and sniffing the air. The four giant paws shuffled out onto the dirt trail, the main route leading to the Inn.

Retracing the trail system in her mind, Margie moved up the slope. She could loop around the far side of the developed area and avoid troubling the animal any further. She typically walked her groups this way because of the varied flowers, but several paths crisscrossed the vicinity.

The bruin lowered its head, the smell of the huckleberries more enticing than that of a solitary woman. Standing midpath, it snuffled its way through the feast.

Margie started back up the hill, her encounter with the wild buoying her growing sense of accomplishment. She'd already learned so much. Superintendent Brown probably hadn't realized how inept she was when she arrived, luggage in hand, or he'd never have allowed her to stay. Most of the items she'd brought had proven useless. She picked her way along the ridgeline, the bear growing small in the distance. Shrugging the bag higher on her shoulder, Margie wound her way over the hill and down to the next patch of trees.

Twenty minutes later, she'd lost herself in the memory of dancing with Ford when she came upon a fork in the trail. Margie hesitated. She hadn't wandered this far from the Inn alone before. One path dipped down the hill, the other traversing over a short ridge to the east. Which led back? Her stomach sank. She'd left her compass and map back in her room. A quick flower walk didn't require orienteering.

She'd climbed to get to this point, so the downward route made more sense. She quickened her pace. Ranger Jennings would be annoyed if she kept him waiting too long. He had evening plans with one of the housekeepers from the National Park Inn.

Tonight she'd add this most recent sighting to her journal. This summer had been a boon to her life lists—she'd checked off eighteen mammals, fifteen birds, and two amphibians. Margie had already claimed the shaggy creature, since she'd seen it performing for scraps, but this viewing seemed far more legitimate. Perhaps she'd scratch out the former date and change it to this one.

A Clark's nutcracker swooped low overhead, darting into a nearby grove of firs. As she dropped in elevation, the trees reached higher above her head, casting longer shadows in the late-afternoon light. The thick foliage must be blocking her view of the Inn.

The trail swerved to the left just past the trees. Margie slowed, enjoying her last moments of solitude. She cleared the trees and stopped. A shimmering blue lake reflected the deep sapphire sky—exactly where the Paradise Inn was supposed to be.

Margie's breath caught in her chest. If she didn't find her way soon . . . *No. Don't think about it. Just hurry.* The Inn couldn't be far. She checked the angle of the sun. Perhaps slightly more to the west? She'd just misjudged the trail. With a direct route, she could still reach Paradise before Jennings left.

Margie set out over the meadow, cringing each time she crushed one of the fragile plants under her shoe. If the hour weren't so late, she'd retrace her steps along the main path. But she had no desire to be out here after dark.

Ford steered the truck around the final curve on the Paradise road, the mountain looming into view just ahead. At breakfast, Mrs. Brown had dropped the hint that Margie would be joining her for dinner—in case Ford wanted to stop by. The long afternoon spent directing traffic at the Nisqually entrance had given Ford ample time to make plans. He couldn't keep avoiding Margie forever. His heart couldn't take it.

Rather than just stop by at dinner, Ford was determined to do one better. He'd intercept her at Paradise. The drive to Longmire would give them time to talk. Whatever had happened between them, he wanted to set things right. Even if she'd decided not to pursue a romance, it would be nice if they could at least be friends.

Jennings glanced up as Ford burst into the Paradise ranger station. "What are you doing here, boss?"

Ford shut the door behind him. "I wanted to catch Margie before you two headed down the mountain."

The naturalist leaned on the long counter. "She's out on the trail somewhere, but I wanted to leave an hour ago." He pulled a watch out of his pocket. "Gertie will be hot under the collar. I was supposed to meet her for a late picnic by the river."

"Margie probably got sidetracked. You know what she's like when she's looking at plants."

"Doesn't help me with Gert."

Ford folded his arms. "I can drive her. You go on ahead."

A smile spread across Jennings's face. "Thanks, Ford. I didn't want to leave Margie stranded, but . . ." Without even finishing his statement, he shot out the door. At least someone was sure of some romance tonight.

Margie never went far—there were too many flowers to distract her.

What had intrigued her this time? The image of the woman sitting cross-legged on the trail, sketching some minuscule weed, brought a smile to his face.

Ford tipped his hat to a group of visitors as he headed up the steep slope behind the Guide House. The best blooms were usually to the north, along the Alta Vista Trail. She wouldn't have gone as far as Panorama Point. Chances were he'd encounter her heading back. Even though she'd arrived in the park pretty green, he'd discovered over the past two months that she didn't lack for common sense. Still, a trickle of unease spilled through his chest. She knew of Jennings's plans. It wasn't like her to show casual disregard for one of the men.

A sharp whistle rang through the evening sky, the marmot's call echoing through the clusters of stubby subalpine trees. Ford glanced to the left and right as he walked, his mind wandering to places where his heart didn't want to go. If she was preoccupied with her botany, he wouldn't put it past her to misstep and end up injured . . . or worse. He quickened his pace as the fading evening light colored the sky with orange and purple.

Reaching a high point, he scanned the slope below as it spread out like an apron all the way to the Inn and the campground. The jagged Tatoosh range and Pinnacle Peak dominated the horizon. Margie was nowhere to be seen. *This isn't right. Where else would she go? Not as far as Glacier Vista, surely.* Wrapping his fingers around his mouth, he called out her name and listened to the echo carrying his voice far beyond his reach.

More whistles greeted him, as though the tubby mammals continued the call. If only they could give him a hint. Ford pulled off his hat and ran fingers through his hair. Should he return to the ranger station and get up some volunteers for a search? He pressed on, winding farther up the hill.

No matter what he did, this woman always seemed one step away from disaster.

TWENTY-TWO

*M*argie pulled the cardigan snug around her shoulders as she scrambled toward the tree line, hoping for a glimpse of Paradise. She'd been a fool to leave the trail. *Who gets lost in the subalpine? You can see for miles.*

Darkness crept across the forested landscape, and with every footstep, Margie raced it to the higher slopes. She'd packed her knapsack with flower books instead of maps or survival equipment. This was supposed to be a short nature walk with the Mountaineers, not an overnight stay by herself. The thin alpine air tore at her lungs, slowing her pace. Would Ranger Jennings come searching for her? His romantic evening would be ruined. She was just getting on a good footing with the staff, and now she'd be the source of more ridicule.

Margie stopped for a breath and turned to survey the scenery. The mountain above had pulled on a colorful wardrobe of purple and blue in the dim light. As long as the mountain remained in view, she wasn't truly lost, just disoriented. Paradise couldn't be far.

She wrapped her fingers around her elbows, hugging them close to her chest as a chilled breeze swept past. A few hours ago, Margie had been marveling at her own strength and accomplishment. Now she was at the mercy of the elements. No matter how much she loved Rainier's wildness, it didn't harbor the same protectiveness for her. Hadn't Ford warned her of such?

Her hero, John Muir, had spent weeks and months rambling the High Sierra. Margie closed her eyes, the expansive view overwhelming her senses. *Lord, help me find my way. I love Your creation, but I'm not ready to spend the night alone out here.* A gentle breeze lifted the ends of her hair, bringing the lush smell of the heather. She took a deep breath, thankful for her slowing heartbeat. God was present, even out here in the dark. Scripture floated into her mind, and she whispered the familiar words to the wind: "The darkness hideth not from thee; but the night shineth as the day: the darkness and the light are both alike to thee."

Margie pushed on a little farther, but the light was fading too fast to continue. Pulling off her knapsack, she checked its contents—three books, a small canteen, and a wool scarf. She wrapped the scarf around her neck and took a sip of water. If only she could trade the books for a compass. And what sort of outdoorsman goes into the mountains without a jacket and any navigation tools?

Margie sheltered next to a tight cluster of stubby subalpine firs, groaning as she sat down. She pulled her knees close and hugged them. She'd come to Rainier with the fantasy of finding refuge in God's creation, but she knew nothing of survival. Perhaps a night in the outdoor world was just what God had in mind to lead her into the next great adventure. Margie sighed and lifted her eyes to scan the darkening world. That or prove her dream was nothing but foolish girlhood fantasies.

If Ford were here he'd whip together a log shelter, start a fire, and have them toasty warm in less than fifteen minutes. Of course, he wouldn't have been in this situation to begin with. Maybe it was better not to let her mind go down that track. Imagining a night alone with Ford as the only source of warmth would do nothing to protect her already wavering heart. Tears squeezed between her eyelids. *Idiot, idiot, idiot.*

Margie ground her boot heel against the dirt. It was too late to climb back down to the forest for better cover. Trapped here at the edge of the tree line, she'd face a chilly night. Still, it was safer than stumbling along in the dark.

And after all, she had her books to keep her warm.

Ford trotted back into Paradise just as the last glimmers of light dipped below the western horizon. The Inn's lights cast a welcoming glow over the small development. Hopefully Margie was there.

The lobby echoed with the soft sounds of conversations and piano music. He pulled off his hat and strode toward the front desk.

Luke glanced up from the register book with a smile. "Ford, I haven't seen you in weeks. What brings you in?"

Ford dropped his Stetson on the counter. "I'm looking for Margie."

Luke's brows drew together. "She took the Mountaineers club out this afternoon, but they returned on schedule. The spokeswoman even stopped by the front desk to compliment us on Margie's tour."

Ford's heart dropped. He'd hoped Luke would laugh and point him toward the dining room where Margie would be waiting. "Jennings expected her by five o'clock."

The caretaker glanced toward the wall clock. "That was hours ago." He shook his head. "She's a smart girl, Ford. She wouldn't do anything foolish."

"I know, but things happen. Even to the best of us."

A shadow crossed his friend's face. "Of course. Perhaps she got turned around. I could round up some of the busboys and outfit them with lanterns."

Ford took a deep breath, filling his chest. "I've already walked the entire Skyline Trail to Panorama Point. There was no sign of her."

Luke closed the book and set it to the side. "Perhaps she went down to Narada Falls or Deadhorse Creek? Or south along the Lakes Trail?"

"That's the trouble. There are too many choices." *She's fallen somewhere or gotten herself lost.* Ford clamped his fingers along the edge of the desk, refusing to entertain any darker thoughts. "She might show up any minute."

"It would make more sense to wait for daylight."

"Yes. It would. I'll check in with you first thing. If she hasn't shown by then, I'll put together a search." Ford grabbed his hat.

Luke nodded. "I'm sure some of the boys will want to go along. We've got some budding rangers amongst the group this year." He wrinkled his nose. "Unlike the ones Carmichael's brought in."

"Carmichael?" Ford's breath caught. "Already?"

The manager's eyes widened. "Haven't you heard?"

"Heard what, exactly?"

Luke leaned forward across the wooden counter. "Groundbreaking begins tomorrow."

"Not possible. I would have been informed."

Luke shrugged. "That's what the man said. Claimed he had the superintendent's signature, too."

"Even if that's true, why would they break ground now? They can't finish anything before the snow flies. It's August already."

"Don't ask me; I just work here. And I won't even be doing that for long, from the sounds of things."

Ford loosened his tie, the collar suddenly chafing at his neck. Carmichael had been silent too long. He should have realized the man was up to something.

Margie gritted her teeth, the constant shivering making every muscle ache. She pressed her back against the stubby tree, its skirt of stiff limbs pulled over her legs. The temperature had continued to drop through the night, though she was pretty sure it was still above freezing. The dry weather was a godsend. If she'd been soaked through, she might have succumbed to exposure. She pushed the frightening thought away.

The darkness teemed with sounds, and her imagination kept busy attempting to identify them. Was a wolf prowling through the meadow waiting for her to fall asleep? Ford had said there weren't many wolves left in the park, thanks to the predator control program. She'd informed him how much she hated the idea of the rangers shooting the beautiful creatures. Now that she might face one, she was less sure—even if it was only her mind playing tricks. She rubbed her fingers together, then wrapped them in her scarf.

A sound crackled in the gloom just a few feet away, sending her heart pounding. *It's just a creature scampering through the brush. Like Archibald.* She swallowed. *Poor Archibald. Had he escaped the flames?* She buried her head in her arms and recited every small mammal she could remember from her life list. Would it count if she only heard them?

After many hours wrestling with her thoughts, she dozed, still twitching at every sound. She finally woke to the first glimmers of dawn cresting the ridge to the east, spilling over the valley with warming fingers of light. Margie unfolded her knees, stretched her stiffened limbs and crawled out into the open. She pressed her fingers against her mouth and blew warm air across the chilled skin.

Margie's side ached where a limb had pressed itself against her ribs. Maybe she wasn't fit for the wilderness life. At least Thoreau had a cabin in *Walden*. She didn't even have that anymore.

She glanced out over the valley, and her breath caught in her chest. The colors of dawn tinted the valley like an oil painting. A black-tailed doe and her two fawns nibbled at the foliage on the meadow's edge. Margie lowered herself to the ground as her heart overflowed. Her eyes could only take in so much beauty at once and the overload brought an ache to her chest.

A wisp of smoke rose above the ridge to the west, and Margie clambered back to her feet. Could it be the Paradise Inn? Or possibly the campground? She gathered her books and crammed them into her bag.

Her joints limbered as she walked, her steps lighter than they had been for days. Let the men laugh at her. She'd survived a night alone in the wilderness. After a brief scramble up the ridge, she stared down the far slope. The Paradise Valley spread below her—the Inn, the Guide House, the ranger station, and the campground. Margie dropped down to her knees. All this time, she'd been less than a thirty-minute walk away from where she needed to be.

A shrieking mechanical whistle—quite different than the typical marmot calls—pierced the quiet morning. Margie lifted her head, staring down toward the Inn. A large piece of equipment sat near the Guide House sending puffs of steam rising into the air. She jumped up as a fresh wave of chills draped over her. A machine like that had no place in a fragile alpine meadow.

TWENTY-THREE

*T*he sick feeling that had plagued Ford the entire night followed him up the hillside as he pushed ahead of the group. Margie hadn't returned. No one had seen her since yesterday afternoon. If it were one of the rangers, he'd be only mildly concerned. But Margie? His stomach tightened. There could be no good reason for her to be gone overnight. She was lying hurt somewhere. That was the only explanation. She'd fallen, been attacked by a mountain lion, gotten hopelessly lost—or perhaps all three.

Searchers fanned out at first light with groups heading down each of the trails leading away from Paradise. Since he'd already walked the Skyline Trail, he planned to work his way across to the Lakes Trail. He couldn't envision any situation that would drive Margie upward toward the snowfields. If she'd gotten disoriented, she'd head downslope. Wouldn't she?

Seeing the steam shovel waiting in the parking area had nearly sent him over the edge. Carmichael couldn't have received approval already, but apparently reporters were present from three different newspapers to cover the groundbreaking. The man's slick nature seemed capable of greasing wheels Ford never even knew existed.

As soon as he got back, Ford's first task would be to telephone the superintendent. But Margie came first.

Memories of the massive search following his father's death flashed through his mind. The idea of losing someone else to this mountain sat on his chest like a boulder, making every breath difficult. He hadn't slept last night, sitting up in the lobby and silently begging Margie to come trudging through the door.

He looked up from the path in time to see a small figure scrambling over the ridge top and dropping down toward the trail. Ford accelerated to a slow jog, his heart rocketing upward as he confirmed Margie moving toward him.

She hurried along the path, her hat crushed in one hand and her clothes dusty and trail-worn. She'd never looked so beautiful. Her voice met him twelve feet before she did. "What is that thing in my meadow?"

"Your meadow?" He reached out a hand, desperate to touch her and make sure she was in one piece. After he accomplished that, he'd shake her silly for frightening him so. "Where have you been? Half the park is searching for you."

She pointed toward the Inn, eyes wild. "Is that a steam shovel? Tell me that isn't a steam shovel."

"Margie,"—his hands shook as he grabbed her arm—"I'll answer you in a moment. But first tell me you're not hurt."

Her attention shifted from the equipment. "I'm not hurt. Can't you see that?"

"Where have you been?"

She glanced at her dusty boots. "There was this bear . . . and a lake where it shouldn't be . . . then it got dark . . ." She closed her eyes and shook her head, hair flying in odd directions. "Does it really matter now? I made a mistake. Or a whole slew of them."

Their moment alone was quickly evaporating as the rest of the hikers approached. He wrapped an arm around her back, crushing her to his chest. "Don't ever do that to me again."

She laid her head against his shoulder, her breaths coming in short gasps as if the truth of her situation had just hit her. "I-I'm sorry. I feel so foolish. Really, I was just over that ridge. If I'd known I was so close . . ."

Ford rested his chin on top of her head for a brief moment. "We've all done foolish things. I'm just glad you're in one piece."

Margie buried her icy hands in the front of his jacket. "You've never done anything like this. You're all man-o'-the-mountains."

"Wish my dad could hear you say that." The thought sent a jagged spear into his heart. His father would have adored her.

"Are you going to answer my question now?" She spoke the muffled words into his chest.

He hadn't realized he was squeezing her so hard. Releasing his grip, he glanced down the hill. The group had stopped a considerate distance away and appeared to be waiting for instructions.

A billow of steam rose from the grumbling engine lurking in the meadow below.

Ford ran a hand across the back of his neck. "I'm afraid what you're seeing is Philip Carmichael's latest attempt to drive me to an early grave."

Margie flew past the rescue party and on down the hill, her heart ramming against her ribs. If only she could have shut Philip down the first day he stepped foot on park grounds. How dare he come in here and start upending things even before she'd had time to formulate a plan to fight him. There should have been months of meetings and planning, not machinery arriving on their doorstep unannounced. It had been less than two months since the gala. She'd never dreamed he could move so fast.

Philip's laugh carried across the meadow even before she could spot him in the throng. A gathering of men crowded around the steam engine, obscuring her view, but Philip must be standing center stage. His voice echoed over their heads. "I'm delighted to move ahead with this project. It will be a boon to our state; people will flock to see this new resort located here on our glorious mountain."

Forcing a breath into her lungs, she elbowed her way to the front.

Philip rested one hand against a shovel as the men hung on his every word. He flicked the ashes from his cigarette onto the flowers below. "I know I can count on each of you to rally support from your local communities. Getting in on the ground level of this project will ensure your rights to future business in this park and others. You want us to serve your foodstuffs in our restaurants? Feature your products in our shops? Hire your favorite entertainers? Then make your support known now and ride the wave to a prosperous partnership that will benefit us all."

Margie called to him. "Philip, I need to speak with you."

Ford angled through the crowd, his height and uniform making him easily discernible from the businessmen.

Philip turned his focus to Margie, a purposeful silence stretching the moment. A curl of smoke escaped his lips before he reached a hand toward her. "Margaret, how good of you to join us." He turned to his associates. "This is the young woman I spoke of earlier, though I hardly recognize her in this condition. What happened to you, love? I heard some terrible rumor about a fire."

As dozens of eyes turned toward her, a prickle crawled across Margie's skin. There was no way to know what Philip may have told them. "Please, Philip. A moment alone?"

The corner of his mouth lifted as he addressed the audience. "You see?"

Several men chuckled, the sound lifting hairs on the back of Margie's neck.

Philip extended his hand again. "Margaret, join me, and then I promise . . . we'll sneak away for some privacy."

Her stomach twisted. The man's ability to manipulate a gathering with a few subtle gestures bordered on the fantastical. Had he exerted that same control on her at one time? If only she could tell that naive girl to wise up before she delivered everyone she loved into his grasp.

The group jostled her forward until she stood at Philip's side, staring at a sea of eager faces all reflecting the sun's glow—or Philip's.

He took her hand and drew it possessively to his chest. "Miss Margaret Lane will work her magic on our Paradise resort, organizing events, bringing that Lane class and elegance to every function from the fine dining room all the way to the open-air amphitheater. I can't wait for you to witness her skills in action."

Margie tore her fingers from Philip's grasp and stepped clear. "I will not. Your designs on this place are a travesty, and I'm not afraid to say so."

The audible intakes of breath around her sent a tremor through Margie's chest.

Ford halted a few steps away, his arms held stiff at his sides as if ready to leap into the fray at her behest.

She needed to make these people see reason. She looked around the group, studying their faces. "Gentlemen, I know you love this park or you wouldn't be here. This can't all be about dollars and cents. You must see what Philip Carmichael has planned will make a circus of this place. It will ruin everything that makes Mount Rainier unique—the tranquility, the wildness, the breathtaking beauty. Do you truly wish to see it replaced by modern hotel rooms and dance halls?"

One gray-haired man in a blue suit lifted his cleft chin. "You mean Mount *Tacoma*, Miss. And tranquility doesn't pay the bills. We're giving people what they want—better access to the mountain they usually only see from afar. If they're willing to come all the way up here and plunk their money down for rooms and entertainment, I want a piece of that pie."

A round-shouldered fellow with a straw boater elbowed him. "And your pies will go over well at that resort, won't they, Monty?"

"Served alongside your bottled sodas? Sure will."

A wave of exhaustion washed over Margie. She was swimming upstream with this lot. Philip had chosen his supporters well. These men all stood to earn significant profits if his vision was achieved. She glanced toward Ford, standing off to one side, and took strength from his presence. Unfortunately, this was a battle only she could win.

Philip clucked his tongue. "Margaret, we're on the same side. When will you realize that? I'm the best thing to happen to this mountain in years, next to you, of course." He turned to the eager men pressing around them. "Doesn't her beauty rival that of Mount Tacoma, gentlemen—even covered in trail dirt? Now you see why I'm so determined to have her for my own."

The men laughed, a smattering of applause carrying over the rumble of the steam engine.

"I'm not some possession to be garnered, Philip, and neither is this mountain. What can I do to make you stop this madness?"

He lifted one brow. "Haven't I made myself clear on that point? Come work by my side and all of this could be yours."

"I'd climb this mountain before I'd submit to you."

His sharp, barking laugh echoed through the morning air. "I'd like to see that. You wouldn't make it halfway."

As the men joined in with Philip's laughter, a burning heat seared through Margie. "I certainly could—if I wanted to."

"Never." Philip blotted a silk handkerchief against his eyes. "You've lived in the lap of luxury your entire life. You'd get a few hundred feet, slip on the ice, and ask your daddy to come help you." His gaze darkened as he focused on her. "How many times have you run to Daddy, Margaret? Did you even get this job without his help?"

Tension wrapped around her shoulders. "My father gave you your start."

"Yes, he did. And now I'm repaying him. In kind."

She grabbed his sleeve and towed him away from the crowd.

He glanced over his shoulder. "Excuse me, gentlemen. I believe the lady wants a word."

Just out of earshot of the gathering, she turned and faced the infuriating man. "What does any of this have to do with my father?"

"Everything." Philip's face gained a quiet intensity, his eyes as cold as the glacier above them. "He had it all—money, prestige, and power. I was nothing more than a mutt you dragged home." He turned away, as if gathering his senses. "Margaret, your kindness enraptured me. All I ever wanted was to be part of your family, in some small way. I'd have been happy mopping the floors in your mother's kitchen."

His admission opened a tiny crack in her defenses. She unclenched her hands. "Father paid for your education. He gave you a chance."

"Oh, he paid all right. If that's what he wants to believe happened with the money, who am I to argue with the man?"

Her heart jumped. "What do you mean?"

"Margaret, most men are blind fools." He stroked fingers down his lapel. "You dress the part, wave a few well-placed dollars in their faces, they will believe whatever you tell them." Philip tipped his head toward the gaggle of business owners. "Sheep, the lot of them. You give them hope of a windfall, and they'll follow you anywhere. Even here. They drove several hours to watch me dig in the dirt."

This conversation was going nowhere, as usual. "I won't let you do this."

"I gave you a choice."

Her throat twisted until she could scarcely draw breath. *Choice? There is no choice here.* "If I agree to take the job, you'll halt construction right now?"

"It's not quite that simple." He cupped a hand under her forearm and turned her to face the mountain. "You take the job, and you can have a say in what happens here. Let's say, a thirty percent interest. I'll take your suggestions under advisement."

"That's hardly reassuring."

"Make it forty." He tugged her a step closer until she could feel the warmth of his body next to hers. "But if you agree to marry me, I won't touch your precious mountain. Other projects are clamoring for my investment monies, and I'm sure to find something to satisfy this group of vultures." Philip slid his hand around her waist and leaned close to her ear. "Mount Tacoma will be the dominion of Mrs. Philip Carmichael. You will rule it like a queen." His warm breath ruffled her hair, sending a shiver down Margie's neck. "Though you'll have to stop kissing the ranger staff. That would be unseemly, don't you think?"

She swallowed, forcing herself to remain still. "Why would you want to marry me knowing how I'd despise you?"

He spread his fingers across the small of her back. "It's not about love, Margaret. It's never been that. I want what's owed me."

She froze. "Owed you?"

"When Senator Lane invited me into his study that day, so many years ago, he promised me something."

"What's that?"

"That if I worked very hard, I'd earn my way in this world." His chin jutted. "He said one day, I'd have everything my heart desired."

"And that's me?"

"Don't flatter yourself, Margaret." Philip chuckled. "I want everything Thomas Lane ever had. I'm just starting with you."

Revulsion twisted in her gut. "You're insane."

"I'm determined."

Ford closed in. "Margie, I'm going to telephone Harry. But I'm not leaving you alone with him. Come with me."

She stepped out of Philip's grasp. "Superintendent Brown won't let this happen, will he?"

Ford's expression darkened. "We have to find out what type of approval Carmichael's obtained."

A smile twisted Philip's lips. "Your superintendent is eating out of my hand, thanks to a few well-placed calls. Apparently much of our nation's capital is on my side." He folded his arms and smirked. "I get things done. You know that."

The conclave milled about. The man who'd answered Margie earlier cupped a hand to his mouth. "Come on, Carmichael, let's get on with this."

Philip smiled. "My public awaits. Since you're not forthcoming with your decision, I suppose there's no reason to delay."

She grabbed his wrist as he stepped back. "No, wait. There must be something I can do. Something else."

"Looks like the girl isn't interested, Carmichael." One of the other men piped up. "You heard her, she'd rather climb the mountain."

The first man cackled. "I'd like to see that."

Philip smirked. "So would I."

Margie pulled her cardigan close. This was getting out of hand. "I'm stronger than you think."

He rounded on her. "Prove it."

"What do you mean?"

Ford growled under his breath, "Margie, don't."

She held up a hand to prevent Ford from coming closer. At this moment she couldn't handle two men telling her what to do.

He stopped, deep lines scoring his forehead.

Philip strode toward the group. "What do you say, men? Shall we make a little wager?" He turned and focused on Margie, a grin spreading across his face. "Margaret Lane climbs to the top of Mount Tacoma, and I'll put the construction project on hold."

"Now wait a minute," the soda pop dealer lifted his hand. "What if she makes it? We're out a bundle."

Philip strutted toward him, fingers hooked in the buttonholes of his vest. "Johnston, have you forgotten who I am? As the manager of the grandest hotel in Tacoma, I can provide you with an exclusive deal at all our events. Would you be out a bundle then?"

"No-no, sir!" Johnston's eyes widened.

"This is between the lady and myself. None of you will lose a dime. That's a promise."

Margie stepped closer, her heart racing. "And if I make it to the top, you'll shut down this project—right now?"

"I'll stop work, immediately." He laughed. "I tell you what. I'm so confident you won't make it past the snow line, I'll even pay for your guide."

Margie curled her fingers. "I'll make it. Or die trying."

Ford loomed over her shoulder. "Margie, don't do this. He's gambling with your life here, and he's holding all the cards."

Philip chuckled. "I always have, Ranger, despite your little antics in Tacoma."

Ford lifted his chin. "I care about Margie. If you did, you wouldn't be daring her to do something that might kill her."

"Did you hear that, Margie? Your ranger friend here thinks you won't be able to do it."

Margie stiffened. Ford hadn't said that. Had he?

Philip continued. "Well, regardless, this little adventure will draw attention to my cause. Investors will flock to my side." He spread his hands. "Unless of course . . . she makes it. But that's not going to happen."

The men hooted even as a grin spread across Philip's face. This little escapade played right to his showman tendencies, but Margie no longer cared. Anything to stop that steam shovel from carving a path through her meadow.

"You provide a witness who will swear that you set foot on the summit, and I will postpone this building project until next spring. Without it, work will commence in one week." He walked closer to Margie. "Or we could discuss other arrangements."

"One week?" She glanced back at the steam shovel. Philip hadn't said he'd quit the project altogether, but at least it might buy some time. "I'll do it."

Ford stood rooted to the ground; the idea of Margie risking her life to please Carmichael sent his gut spiraling down to his knees. He hadn't even set foot on the mountain's glaciers since his father's accident. How could he let Margie make the ascent? He grasped Margie's arm as she marched past him. "You're not climbing the mountain."

She rounded on him, her eyes flashing. "You're the one person I thought might support me. But you don't believe I can do it either, do you?"

Her anger shattered him. "You shouldn't play Carmichael's games."

"I play to win, and I'll do whatever's necessary to save the park from his schemes." She brushed a trembling hand over her forehead.

And who's going to save you? "What makes you think he'd even honor the agreement?"

"There are at least fifty witnesses here. Philip is meticulous with appearance. He wouldn't be gutsy enough to withdraw an offer made in front of so many people. I intend to make him eat those words."

His throat went dry. "You just returned from a night lost in the backcountry. Most of your belongings burned in the fire. I had to talk you across the Kautz Creek bridge—all after a misstep nearly sent you down a cliff face on your first day. Now you want to climb the mountain itself? How do you expect to do that?"

"I can do all things through Christ who strengthens me."

"Blast it all, woman!" Ford pulled off his hat and smacked the hard brim against his leg. "I don't doubt your fortitude or your strength. You've accomplished far more this summer than I dreamed you capable of. But you don't just pack a bag and start climbing. You need equipment and training. Book learning won't help you."

Her eyes narrowed. "Do you really think me so simple? I'll hire a guide. The best guide money can buy." She lowered her knapsack to the ground with a thump. "Unless you'd like the job."

Guide Margie up the mountain? A cold sweat broke out across his skin. "You're not going."

"Ford, if I reach the top of Rainier, he'll halt construction. My only other options are to work for him—or God forbid—marry him. Is that what you want?"

The words struck him in the gut like a sucker punch. "Why is this all on you? We could take this all the way to the head of the National Park Service."

"We don't have that sort of time. Besides, Stephen Mather said he wants this sort of development in order to increase support for the national parks. Philip's plans, ludicrous as they are, fit his vision. What makes you think Director Mather would fight them?"

"We'll find another way."

Her brows rumpled. "Ford, other women have made the climb. Fay Fuller did it more than thirty years ago, and Alma Wagen worked as a guide during the war. What makes you think I'm not capable?"

Because you're not. The words stuck in his throat. She couldn't set foot up there. What could he say to convince her? "You're completely unprepared, unsuited. You're a . . . a pampered debutante."

Margie's mouth opened as she took two stuttering steps back from him. "How could you—of all people—say such a thing to me?" Tears welled up in her eyes. She clenched her fists. "Ford Brayden, I can't believe I ever thought I was in love with you."

In love. The words rattled his soul. He steeled himself against the avalanche of emotions coursing through him. Even more reason to stop this crazy plan in its tracks. "I'm Chief Ranger here, Margie Lane—your boss. You will not attempt to climb this mountain. I forbid it."

Her brows drew together, peaked like the mountain itself. "You forbid it?" A tiny gasp escaped her mouth, somewhere between a laugh and a strangled choke. "Then hear me now, Chief Ranger." She took three steps, closing the space between them and staring straight up into his eyes. "I quit."

TWENTY-FOUR

*M*argie lifted the lid of the small box of donated items Mrs. Brown had been collecting for her since the fire. Afternoon sunlight drifted through the windows of the Longmire Community Building.

I quit my job. How could I do such a foolish thing?

The hurt in Ford's eyes had snuffed her anger as quickly as it had ignited. He'd turned and walked away, his long strides carrying him out of reach in the moments it took to realize what she'd done.

The stack of books donated by the rangers brought tears to Margie's eyes. The men didn't realize her learning—so precious to her when she arrived—had become little more than dead weight. Knowledge was worthless without experience. Ford had said as much. She flipped open the cover of a pamphlet, *"Features of the Flora of Mount Rainier."* It looked so much like her well-worn copy, she checked the flyleaf. *"From the shelf of Herman Brayden."*

The tears spilled over, running down her cheeks as she added the booklet to the stack. She hadn't meant to tell Ford she loved him. He didn't feel the same. Even if he did, they were far too different. Margie had spent the summer playing ranger but never truly understood what the job entailed. Apparently she'd never understood the chief ranger, either. She retrieved her journal from her knapsack, running her fingers over the cover. The soft leather binding fell open in her hands, revealing pages covered in drawings of flowers and penciled notes that mocked her. Childish dreams. Better it had burned with the others. She strode over to the fireplace and cast the book onto the cold grate. Before she left, she'd touch a match to it and be done.

She folded the three dresses donated by girls at the Inn and clutched them to her chest. The daughter of a senator, wearing castoffs. The idea brought a smile.

Sighing, Margie closed the box. Carson had offered to drive her back up the hill to Paradise. She had plenty of time to join up with a climbing expedition before the week was out. The guide service would have all the equipment she needed. She had never wanted to climb the peak, and she certainly didn't want to do it without Ford at her side. But he'd made his feelings as clear as Reflection Lake.

She sucked in a deep breath, glancing around at the empty room. "Lord, please just get me to the top."

Ford pushed up the hill, the toe of his boot grinding into the dirt with each step. How had he and Margie gotten so far off track? Back in June he was waltzing her around a ballroom and kissing her by the waves of Puget Sound. For those brief moments, life had been perfect.

Now she'd thrown her job in his face like it meant nothing to her. Like he meant nothing.

Blood coursed through his veins, the vigorous walk pushing energy to his muscles and away from his aching heart. Ford needed to put as many miles between himself and Carmichael as he could before he did something he'd regret. Tossing the man into a deep crevasse was the most entertaining option at the moment.

What good was being chief when his words held no sway? He could send men out to patrol trails, staff fire lookouts, and deal with problem bears, but he couldn't stop the scheme Philip Carmichael had set into motion. The National Park Service and the Rainier National Park Company acted independently. His job was to maintain park facilities and provide for the safety of visitors—not to run off investors who held the blessing of the Interior Department.

Ford balled his fists. Margie should know better. Climb the mountain? She had no idea what she was in for. He'd scaled the peak four times and had endured muscles taxed to their limit, wind-burned skin, frostbitten toes, and lungs fighting for enough oxygen in the thin atmosphere. And that was without the obvious dangers of rockslides, falls, and— and . . . A sickening shudder gripped him.

He halted where the rocky trail curved to reveal the crumpled surface of the glacier carving its way through the valley below. Ford fought for a decent breath as memories of his father's accident enveloped him. The victims were still hidden somewhere in the ice, their bodies never recovered.

His father had been a seasoned climber. Margie had no experience.

Ford sank down on a boulder overlooking the glacier valley. He couldn't lose her too.

Pain welled up in his chest. It made no sense how often Margie reminded him of his father. He couldn't imagine two more different people. But when she spoke of faith, it was as if his father's voice echoed through Ford's soul. They both had some unexplainable depth Ford never understood and a peace he could certainly use right now.

He closed his eyes to the view, lowering his head for a moment. Whatever it was they had, he wanted it too.

Margie plunged the alpenstock's metal tip into the icy snowfield above Paradise. She dug the tip of her hobnail boot into the drift as the guide had shown her. *It's not so hard.* Stick, step, rest. Stick, step, rest. Now, how many of those repetitions would it take to climb a mountain?

Too many.

"Good, good, *ja*? Nothing to it."

She glanced at Henrik Berge; the man's jutting cheekbones and protruding chin reminded her of a vulture hunched over its kill. Luke had assured her the quiet Norwegian was the best guide on the mountain, but the man's silent demeanor did little to set her fears at ease. "I only made it twenty feet."

The guide's eyes were hidden behind dark glasses, but he touched his wool cap with two fingers in a mock salute. "You're getting the rhythm. Next we see how you are with knots."

"Knots?" Her stomach tightened. Chalk that up with chopping wood and building campfires.

"We rope the team together on the upper glaciers. If one member falls, the others can catch him." Berge fiddled with the pewter clasps holding his sweater closed above his black gabardine knickers. He hadn't even bothered with a coat. Didn't he feel the cold?

"What if two people fall?" She dug her gloved fingers against the staff.

He shrugged. "Then we all die."

Her heart jumped to her throat. "What?"

"Just joking. You will be fine, as long as you listen to me and do as I say."

She took a few more steps and looked back the way she'd come. Her tracks spread out behind her like some three-legged animal hobbling off to die.

Maybe Ford was right. Perhaps she was too much of a pampered princess. But she never turned away from a challenge, and here she faced the toughest one of her life.

She turned to the guide. "Right. I think I've got walking down pat."

He held out a rope. "Now we see your knots."

She set down the alpenstock and took the line from his hands. "Sure. How hard can it be?"

The tiny smile on Berge's face didn't offer much hope.

Ford splashed water over his face, the nightmare clinging to his sleep-addled mind like frost on pine needles. It'd been months since he last endured the chilling images of hunting for his father on a dark, ice-covered mountainside. Ford sucked in two deep breaths, pushing down the nausea threatening to overwhelm him.

Ford gripped the sides of the washbasin, the damp porcelain grounding him in reality. His father's accident happened in broad daylight, under a blue sky, but for some reason his nightmares never played out that way. Tonight's dream had taken a new turn—he was searching for Margie.

Ford stared down at the drain, water dripping from his chin. If this was love, it certainly wasn't the meadows of wildflowers he'd been promised. He'd spent two years living under the shadow of his father's accident, and this summer he'd just started to feel hope creeping back in. But now . . .

Ford ran his damp fingers through his hair. There was no hope of seeing Margie at breakfast, but a man still needed to eat. Maybe bacon would make this day bearable. He pulled on his uniform and stepped outside. He gazed across the small clearing at the remains of Margie's cottage.

He and Jennings had gone over the ruins with a careful eye, but had found little. He knew from the night it happened that the fire had started inside. Could someone have set the blaze? *Carmichael.* The man wanted Margie out of Longmire, that much was certain. Would he stoop this low?

Thank goodness she hadn't been home that night. The idea sent a cold sweat across his skin.

Ford had given Mrs. Brown a book for the box she was assembling for Margie, but now it seemed like such a paltry offering. Margie had lost so much—was a moldy pamphlet the best he could offer? Perhaps the collection box was still over at the Community Building. Ford stepped back inside and strode over to his bookshelf. One item would mean the world to Margie. He reached to the top and pulled down his dad's Stetson. It had looked so sweet on her the night of the banquet. She deserved to have it. Dad would have approved.

Hurrying across Longmire, Ford let himself into the Community Building. He poked around, but the box was gone. Perhaps Margie had already retrieved it.

He breathed out a long exhale, laying the hat on the long table. What did he expect? A good-bye letter? A charred log sat in the fireplace, cold and lifeless, reminding him of that night when her scream had brought him hurtling across the clearing to her cabin.

Something sat atop the ashes. Ford bent down and grasped the small book. He shook off the soot and flipped open the cover. Page after page of her careful notes and drawings of plants filled the notebook. Her journal? Why would she discard something so precious?

He pulled the item close as if it somehow held a connection with its owner. Flipping through a few more pages, Ford ran his finger along a drawing of a flowering penstemon. He hadn't bothered to learn the flower's name before Margie arrived. Now it was as close as his next breath.

He tucked the book in his pocket. If Margie was determined to climb the mountain, the journal would only weigh her down. Best keep it safe for her.

He took a quick detour to return the hat to his cabin before loping over to the kitchen for breakfast. The men's banter grated on his nerves, but when talk turned to the guide service, his attention zeroed in. "Wait— who were you talking about?"

Carson turned, his brows lifted. "Are you speaking to us now? You haven't said a word since you dragged in here."

Jennings gestured to Ford's coffee. "The chief never speaks until he's downed at least one cup. Ford's ahead of schedule."

Ford set the mug down with a little more force than necessary. "What were you saying about the guides?"

Carson bit off a piece of bacon and chewed before answering. "Henrik said he'd been hired to lead Miss Lane and her group."

The name sent a chill down Ford's spine. "Henrik Berge?"

"Are there other Henriks who work here?" Carson took another swig of coffee.

Jennings frowned. "Is there a problem, Ford?"

"There are several guides working for RNPC. Why did she choose him?" Ford pushed his plate back, the food suddenly unappetizing.

Carson shrugged. "Couldn't be for his looks. The man's like a walking skeleton. They must not have a cook as good as Mrs. Brown up at the Guide House."

Ford stood. "Who cares what they eat? Their job is to keep climbers safe on the mountain, and Berge's track record is spotty."

"Spotty?" Jennings frowned for a moment, and then his brows softened. "Oh, I see."

Carson grunted. "I don't."

Ford grabbed his hat off the rack. He couldn't escape this conversation quickly enough.

Jennings lowered his voice. "Henrik was the only member of his father's climbing party to survive." He pushed to his feet and then hurried to join Ford by the door. "You can't fault the man for that. No one could have seen the slide coming. Not in time, anyway."

Ford ignored him. He pushed out the door, leaving the men to their morning routines.

He veered away from park headquarters, desperate for a minute or two of privacy. Perhaps a quick drive up to Narada Falls? Ford climbed in the park truck and pulled the door shut. As he shifted in the seat, the edge of Margie's journal jammed against his leg. He pulled it from his pocket, rubbing his thumb against the cover. After a long moment, he flipped it open and thumbed through the pages.

A beautiful sketch of the meadow at Indian Henry's Hunting Ground caught his eye. She'd penciled in the words of a Bible verse at the bottom of the page: "For ye shall go out with joy, and be led forth with peace: the mountains and the hills shall break forth before you into singing, and all the trees of the field shall clap their hands."

The breath leaked from his chest. He glanced up to where Rainier's summit rose above Rampart Ridge. Ford knocked the book's cover against the steering wheel before tossing it onto the seat beside him. Mountains don't sing. Why did the woman think everything in nature was beautiful and kind? Didn't she realize that people died out there? Good people.

People like her.

He closed his eyes, burying his face in his hands. Would her God protect her? He hadn't done anything to save Ford's father. *You can't take Margie too. I can't lose someone else to this mountain.* The halfhearted plea echoed in his chest. If he didn't believe in God in the first place, what good did it do to ask for favors?

Picking up the journal a second time, he searched for the verse he'd just read. What did it say about going out with joy? Margie's looping penmanship drew his eye down another page. Nothing about plants or animals, but his own name jumped out. He turned back a page to where the section began. *Dear Heavenly Father . . .* She'd written out a prayer for him? His hand trembled. Ford closed the cover but kept his thumb wedged inside. What was he doing? It wasn't his place to read her private thoughts, even if they were about him. *Especially* if they were about him.

He sat staring at the cover, his feelings at war inside. After several minutes, he jammed the journal into his coat pocket. No need to decide right now. He reached for the gearshift. All that mattered right now was Henrik Berge. There was no way Ford was going to let him lead that climb. Whatever it took, he would make sure someone else was in charge.

TWENTY-FIVE

August 29, 1927

*M*argie clutched the warm mug, letting its heat seep into her raw fingers. She perched on the high stool in the Guide House, her stomach churning. She was hopelessly inadequate for the task. Two rushed days of glacier training hadn't changed that fact. A passable knowledge of botany and zoology did Margie little good in the higher elevations. In the land of crevasses, andesite cliffs, and steep snowfields, she would be dead weight.

Henrik Berge came through the door and hung the coiled rope on a peg with several others. "We'll leave at dawn. Can you be ready by four o'clock?" He unpacked his knapsack, plunking the supplies on the table with force.

The words chilled Margie to the core. "Tomorrow? You saw me out there; I was a wreck."

The man snorted, hanging his wooden-handled ice ax on the wall. "I've got an experienced party scheduled to go to Camp Muir tomorrow. I'll rope you in with them."

Experienced. That sounded good. Maybe they could drag her to the top. "What if I can't keep up?"

He lifted his head, the first time she'd seen his ice-blue eyes without the dark glasses. "You will."

Or else. She heard the implication in his voice, even if he didn't intend it. "Are there any other women on the team?"

"Not this time." He poured himself a cup of hot chocolate from the pan on the stove. "We'll climb up to the base camp tomorrow—at around ten thousand feet. After a little sleep, we will leave in the wee hours to storm the crest."

Storm the crest. Assault the glacier. Conquer the mountain. Did all mountaineers speak in battle terms?

Margie tugged at the oversized flannel shirt the guide service had issued her. "Then perhaps I should head back to the dormitory and turn in early." Luke had been kind to let her stay in the park housing until after the climb. "What are the beds like at the base camp?"

The man nearly choked on his drink. "Beds?"

She put her hand up. "Just kidding. I assume that's what those are for." She gestured at the pile of bedrolls heaped in the corner. Hopefully they were freshly laundered. The idea of sleeping in the same blankets as a smelly man who'd spent yesterday attacking a mountain didn't appeal much to her. Then again, John Muir probably wouldn't have balked at it, so neither would she.

Berge cleared his throat. "I'll have someone assist you packing your supplies. Don't bring anything extra. No books."

She hooked a hand over one hip. "Whom have you been speaking with?"

The corner of his mouth twisted up. "Ranger Jennings."

Her heart sank. She shouldn't have expected Ford to check on her.

Why should he? She'd thrown his advice back in his face, not to mention the job he'd been so kind to humor her with all summer. If only he hadn't been such a Neanderthal about it. *"I forbid it."*

"Fine. No books." She glanced at the painting of the mountain on the far wall, the summit piercing through a thick band of clouds. She could survive two days without reading material. After all, she'd have a large group of men for company. There'd have to be at least one good conversationalist in the bunch.

Ford tugged at the frayed wire where it lay coiled under the eaves. Sunlight filtered through the cracks in the Inn's roof. "Why did you recommend Berge? Why not one of the other guides?"

Luke grunted as he shifted a crate blocking their work area. "Berge is the most experienced man we have on board. He knows the mountain better than anyone, and he's been leading climbs for over a decade."

"He takes chances."

Ford's friend leaned forward, his eyes earnest. "All climbers do. It's in their nature. But every time someone sets foot on the mountain it's a risk, and he's more cautious and meticulous than most—especially since the slide." He shook his head and heaved the crate a second time. "I know you're haunted by what happened, but you can't blame Berge. He's lived under the shadow of the accident ever since, just like you."

"Not like me. I wasn't there. Maybe if I had been—"

"You'd have died with the rest, and I'd be short a good friend. Ford, I thank God you decided to skip that climb."

Ford yanked the wire loose, "I'm not sure God had much to do with it." He inspected the battered insulation.

Luke's brows drew down. "Why is this eating at you so badly? Berge has led dozens of climbs since your dad's, and he's gone up with lots of our staff. Why does it bother you that Margie chose him?" His friend sat back on his heels. "Unless . . ." His smile grew as the truth dawned on him. "You and Margie? Truly?"

"Don't start. It's not like that." Ford dug through his toolbox for better cutters. "Well, not completely."

"I should have realized before now." His eyes widened. "Does her father know?"

"There's nothing for him to know. There might have been at one time, but not now. She made that perfectly clear."

"Oh." Luke's face fell. "I'm sorry. You know, I never figured out—how did she end up at Rainier, anyway? Did her father pull some strings?"

"And some money crossed the superintendent's desk."

Luke paused. "He's paying you to keep an eye on her?"

"No. He donated money toward the new administration building." Ford rubbed a hand over his eyes. "And I don't think she knows about that. Probably best you forget I said anything."

"It's not good to keep secrets, my friend. They have a way of coming back to bite you in the end."

Ford's mind wandered back to Henrik Berge as he twisted the damaged wire between his fingertips, eyeing the shorn edges. "I think you've got a rat's nest up here." *Perhaps more than one.* Hadn't his father expressed doubt in the Norwegian before the accident? The single offhand comment had bothered Ford ever since. His dad hadn't elaborated, and Ford hadn't taken it seriously. At the time.

"We trap more rodents in this building than a cheese factory. I'm surprised they're not abandoning the sinking ship like everyone else."

"Because of Carmichael? I'd think the hotel staff would be excited about his ideas. Plenty of work, nicer facility." Ford gestured up at the ceiling. "And you, my friend, won't have to spend the winters up here alone."

"Ford, we work on this mountain because we love it. We love this building. We love our guests. That's all going to change."

The low notes in Luke's voice matched the gloom riding in Ford's chest. "I'm sorry. I wish there was more I could do. I've rattled Harry's cage more times than I can count, but he thinks Carmichael is God's gift to the park service. New facilities at no price? Promises of prosperity? The park's on a shoestring budget. There's barely enough to pay salaries, much less upgrade the buildings."

"What we need are more rich senators with lovely daughters. But the next one's mine, you hear?"

Ford ignored the foolish remark as he put the wire cutters away. "I'm starting to sound like my dad, constantly going on about park needs. Maybe I'm wrong about this whole issue. Perhaps I should jump on board and go with the changes. Harry might be right."

Luke laid a hand on Ford's shoulder. "He's not. And your father never would have traded the park's integrity for a few dollars."

"It's more than a few."

Luke leaned in, examining the rodent damage. "Margie thinks this little wager she has with Carmichael might solve everything."

"You think she can make it?"

"Don't you?"

Ford cut the wire free. "I'd feel better if she weren't climbing with Berge."

"You're missing the obvious solution here."

Ford glanced up, meeting Luke's intense gaze. "What's that?"

"Go with her."

A chill washed over him. "I can't do that."

Luke twisted the new wire into place and tightened it down. "You've made the climb at least four or five times. I never knew a seasonal ranger so eager to test himself."

"That was before." Ford dropped the tools into the box and stood, the attic suddenly growing close despite the obvious ventilation.

"What are you afraid of, Ford? You're an experienced climber. You could ensure Margie makes it to the top and then come here and stuff that in Carmichael's face." Luke rubbed a hand across the back of his neck. "What is it? Do you think you're going to die up there like your dad?"

A sickening quiver ran through Ford's gut. "I'm not afraid to die."

"Then what?"

Ford closed his eyes, transported back into his nightmare without a moment's warning. "I'm afraid of finding him."

Luke's pliers clattered to the floorboards. "It's a big mountain. Hundreds of people have climbed its flanks since the accident. You're not going to—"

"I know." Ford cut off Luke's words. "I didn't say it made sense. But I wasn't there, Luke. Harry wouldn't let me go on the search. He hauled me off the mountain three times when I tried to join the rescue parties."

"So you think they're still up there."

"Of course they're up there. Where else would they be?"

"Under twenty feet of ice—at least. Ford, you're not going to see him." Luke shrugged. "But that's not all you're afraid of."

Ford choked, swallowing the pathetic laugh trying to burst from his chest. "Isn't that enough?"

"Your dad's accident may have kept you off the mountain for two years, but you're more afraid of losing someone else now."

Margie. Ford sank down in the dim light, crouching on his heels.

Luke knelt beside him. "Look, you don't believe there's a God to protect her. And it's obvious you're unwilling to trust her safety to Henrik Berge." He laid a hand on Ford's shoulder. "As far as I see it, you've only got one other option."

Spots of light from the ceiling danced across the floor as Ford stared out over the dusty space. "Me."

Margie rubbed her eyes as she left the dormitory and walked out into the predawn gloom. Hopefully one didn't need sleep in order to climb a mountain, because she hadn't managed more than a few catnaps all night. Now a crushing ache throbbed in her temples. She never should have agreed to this. Just as Ford had said, she'd played right into Philip's hands.

Picking her steps carefully through the darkness, Margie made her way to the Guide House. The sun wouldn't be up for at least an hour, but she needed to be packed and ready to go well before then. She tightened the belt holding up the khaki trousers, the seat waterproofed with a stiff coating of paraffin. The RNPC had provided everything from her hat to the tall, lace-up boots. She might look ridiculous, but at least she'd be warm and dry.

She tucked her hands in her pockets to keep them warm. No books, no bag, no supplies. If only she had her journal, at least she wouldn't feel so lost and alone. A sketch of the view from the top—wouldn't that be the perfect last entry for the summer? But no, she'd disposed of one of her most treasured possessions during a childish fit. Margie sighed. At least Carson had interrupted her before she remembered to burn it. Maybe she could still retrieve the book after all this was said and done.

But then, if she failed in her summit attempt, she might never want to lay eyes on it again.

She opened the Guide House door and slipped inside the still dark building.

"Good morning, my little alpine flower." Philip's voice cut through the still air. A circle of light spread out from the lamp beside his chair.

Margie pulled her arms close. "Why are you here?" She scanned the room for Henrik, but no one else was about.

"I came to wish you well, of course." He closed the book on his lap. *Alpine Lodges of Austria*. "And to be certain none of your park service friends interfered with our deal. I'd hate to think they'd be so dishonest, but one never knows."

"How did you know I'd be going today?"

"I have my sources. And I'm glad you're up here at Paradise where I can keep my eye on you. I never liked thinking of you living next door to that man, especially after what I witnessed in Tacoma. The fire was fortuitous, if you ask me."

Fortuitous? That she'd lost her belongings and the park was short a cabin?

He stood, placing the book on the table. "Now, tell me you'll be careful. I couldn't bear it if anything happened to you. And I'd hate to see your father lose something so precious to him."

Philip's obsession with her father had gotten out of hand. "I secured the best guide at the service."

"Of course you did. Nothing but the best. Should I help you organize your gear?"

"I'll do that." Another voice rumbled through the darkness. Ford stepped through the door, an ice ax balanced in his right hand.

Her heart jumped. "Ford?"

Philip's eyes narrowed. "What a surprise."

She rushed over and closed the door behind him. "You're coming?"

The knots in her back uncoiled. With Ford at her side, she could do anything. "I can't believe you're here."

"Where else would I be?" A faint smile crossed his face.

"This wasn't part of the deal." Drawn brows hooded Philip's cool gaze.

Ford drew close to Margie, stopping short of touching her. "I don't remember you saying anything about companions."

"And she has one. I saw to it she hired a guide." Philip folded his arms across his chest. "I want her to be safe, after all."

"That's what we all want."

A tickle of unease crawled through Margie's system. "Ford, I've already trained with Henrik. We're going with a large party."

"I know." Ford's lips turned down as he adjusted the rope coiled over one shoulder. "I wasn't planning on guiding the trip, Margie. I'm only lending a hand. Keeping an eye on things."

Keeping an eye on her, he meant. A little of the excitement leaked out of her. For a moment she'd thought this was a vote of confidence. But no, he didn't believe she could do anything without his assistance.

Philip took a cigarette from his pocket and tapped it against his palm. "I suppose it's fine, then. But I hope you'll leave her in the hands of the experts."

Henrik appeared at the stairway. "Don't worry, Mr. Carmichael. I'm well equipped for any emergency."

TWENTY-SIX

*T*rudging up the Muir snowfield, Ford glanced between Margie just in front of him and Berge in the lead. He was glad to be staring at the man's back because Berge hadn't stopped scowling since Ford walked into the Guide House. The guide's barked orders had cast a pall over the excited party.

Ford had been careful to greet everyone—four students from the University of Washington, two bankers from Olympia, a metalsmith from Tacoma, and three rock climbers up from Colorado. He'd checked and rechecked the gear, then tromped outside to study the clear sky, positive a storm would boil up at any moment. Something—anything—to give him reason to call off this adventure.

Margie floundered in the snow, leaning heavily on her alpenstock as the group moved up the steep incline. Her short legs were a distinct disadvantage.

"Doing all right?" Ford stopped behind her, determined to stay where he could catch her if she slipped.

"You've asked me that four times now." She spoke over her shoulder, pushing the words through panting breaths. Margie had been a good sport for the first few miles, but now the elevation and exertion seemed to be dragging her down. Since they weren't even to the base camp, this didn't bode well for tomorrow's climb.

"You're going to be fine. Just keep placing one boot in front of the other."

He couldn't make out her muttered reply. Apparently he wasn't going to win today. Maybe it was best just to let her struggle along in silence. It didn't matter if she enjoyed herself, just that she stayed alive.

Ford brushed away the dismal thought. Conditions couldn't be more optimal. Even with the August sunshine beating down, temperatures were cool enough to keep the ice firm—as long as they didn't dally too long.

No reason except the sour-faced man at the front, his shoulders pulled forward as he led the way up the snowfield. A sliver of remorse cut through Ford. Other than his father's one veiled comment, Ford had no valid reason to blame Berge for the accident. Ford studied the guide's hunched posture. Did Berge still carry guilt from the accident, clinging to his spine like an extra pack? Did every climb remind him of that fateful day?

Ford had climbed multiple times with Berge before the accident. But for the past two years, he'd stayed clear of the Guide House and everything to do with climbing. After taking his father's post, it had become a simple matter to assign other rangers to any necessary work in the higher elevations. Ford could stay in the forest, far from the glaciers that had stolen not only his father, but his confidence.

Berge hadn't had such a luxury. The man looked a mere shadow of his former self, like a tree stunted and gnarled from the harsh life in the alpine.

Margie slouched to a stop.

He caught himself before running into her. "Are you—oh, sorry. I said I wouldn't ask again."

Her shoulders shook. Was she crying? She couldn't be pushed past the point of exhaustion. He'd seen her conquer the trail to Indian Henry's without breaking a sweat. Ford clambered a few steps so he could stand beside her. "It's all right. We'll catch up at base camp." He ducked his head, trying to get a glimpse of her face in the glare.

Margie threw her head back, her laughter pealing across the snow. She gripped her alpenstock in one gloved hand, placing the other across her mouth to stifle the giggles.

Had she lost all of her senses? "What's so funny?"

"I'm climbing a mountain." She lifted the dark glasses to wipe the tears now dotting her red cheeks. "Can you believe this?"

His heart lifted. "And that's funny because . . ."

"Because of how absurd it is. I've never wanted to climb a mountain. I'm a lowlander. I'm afraid of heights. I never even liked standing on our balcony at home because it hung so high above the hillside."

He shook his head, pushing away the thought that the woman had gone over the edge.

She gestured up at the peak. "And I'm almost there."

Ford squinted up the slope. "Not exactly. I'd say we've still almost two thousand vertical feet before we reach Camp Muir. And then another four thousand to the summit. And that's just the elevation gain."

She stabbed the ice with her stick. "Don't burst my bubble, Ford. I'm farther than I thought I would ever go."

"Does that mean we can go home? Because I can go tell Berge—"

"Don't be ridiculous. I'm enjoying this. That's what's so surprising. It's beautiful up here. There's so much . . ." She swung her arms around and halted, staring down the steep slope. "So much . . ." Her voice faded, her skin losing its rosy hue.

"Oh, no you don't." Ford grabbed her and spun her toward the base camp. "Keep your eyes forward. No looking down."

She dropped to her knees, clutching at the snow. "What was I thinking? I can't do this."

He bent over, awkwardly patting her knapsack. "You're going to be fine. Take a few deep breaths." He waited until she complied. "What were you going to say before? So much what?"

"Sky." She choked out the word. "*Father, help me.* We're so high up."

"You're going to be fine. Don't think about it. Just keep walking." How could a woman be so strong one moment and a quivering mess the next? He glanced up the slope, the rest of the party shrinking in the distance. It's a good thing they weren't roped together yet.

"Yes. Walking. That's good. We're walking. I love a blue sky. I'm just not accustomed to being so close to it." She pushed her gloves against the ice and wavered to her feet. "We're just going to Narada Falls. Or Rampart Ridge. Surrounded by trees, beautiful safe trees. That's what I'm going to tell myself."

He grabbed her alpenstock and pressed it into her palm. "Right. Me, too. Let's go to Indian Henry's again, as soon as we get home. Will you do that, Margie?"

She turned and gazed into his eyes, her lashes damp. "Do you still want to? With me?"

"More than anything." Warmth rushed through his chest. He took her free hand. "You haven't seen the late-season flowers there, and August doesn't last forever."

"I'd like that, but I'm not sure it's a good idea." She pulled her fingers free.

"What? Why?" His chest squeezed. Nothing mattered more in this moment than knowing she'd walk beside him into that beautiful meadow. Only next time, he'd make sure he had a ring in his pocket. It was too soon for such thoughts, but he couldn't help it. She'd said that she loved him, after all.

"Oh, Ford. I'd love to imagine a future with you—you can't know how much." Her chin trembled. "But it won't work."

Her words seared into his soul. He turned, facing out toward the valley below—the view that had terrorized Margie a moment before. Now it beckoned to him. The safe trees below where he could hide himself, forever. "Because of our different worlds?"

"I don't care about such things."

"Then what?" He shoved the glasses back over his face, the glare blinding.

She glanced away, as if avoiding his question. "Deep down, we want different things. We believe different things."

He stared at her back as she returned to the climb, increasing the space between them.

Believe.

Ford wasn't even sure what he believed any more. Cracks were forming in the wall he'd built between himself and his father's faith. But likely that wouldn't be enough for her.

No matter his feelings, he still had a job to do up here. Even if Margie didn't want him, he'd vowed to see her to the top. He took a deep breath. A short night at the base camp, and they'd summit in the morning. What happened after, as Margie would say, was in God's hands. For whatever that was worth.

Five hours after leaving Paradise, Margie plodded the final few steps to the stone hut at Camp Muir, her heart heavier than her pack. When Ford had started talking as if they had a future together, her spirits had spiraled upward like a hawk riding a thermal. But it was no use. She loved him, of that she was certain, but they disagreed on their most fundamental beliefs. To build a relationship without a solid foundation would only lead to disaster. The first time they hit problems, everything would crumble. It would be deceitful to allow Ford to think they had a chance at such happiness.

They'd hiked the rest of the way in silence, trudging steadily upward. Margie hadn't bothered to stop and rest again. *Five more steps. Good. Now five more steps.* She lost track of how many times she'd restarted the count. Her legs trembled, and her chest ached from the thin air. Now that they'd arrived at the base camp, she thrust the alpenstock in the snow and let her knapsack crash down next to it.

Ford paced up beside her and stopped, barely winded. "It hasn't changed a bit."

Margie rubbed her neck, the sudden lightness making her feel like she could float up into the air. "Did you expect it to?"

"Everything else has." He went inside the shelter without a backward glance.

Margie surveyed the scenery, one hand braced against the stone building to prevent any dizziness. The mountainside spread out below her, the snowfield glittering in the afternoon sun. The jagged Tatoosh range spiked upward like a palisade fence, a dense carpet of gray-green forests covering the lowlands beyond. In the distance, the icy domes of three more massive mountains—Mount Adams, Mount St. Helens, and Oregon's Mount Hood—rose against the skyline.

The breath caught in her chest. Seeing God's creation from this lofty vantage point would transform how anyone viewed the world. She glanced upward to Gibraltar Rock, Disappointment Cleaver, and the summit beyond—now hidden by a wisp of cloud. How could anyone see all this and not be sure it was from the hand of the greatest Artist ever known? The knowledge was too pure and powerful to take in.

The rest of the party scattered, some resting in snowbanks and others exploring the area. Margie poked her head into the shelter, relieved its sturdy walls would be surrounding them during the night. Several of the men had come prepared to sleep under the stars, but the idea of refuge appealed to Margie. If she were outside, she'd probably dream of rolling off the mountain.

Wooden platforms filled one wall of the stone hut. Her Longmire cabin had looked cozy in comparison, but at least there was a roof and floor. Being the only woman did complicate things. "Where am I to sleep?"

Ford glanced up from his equipment. "Your choice. I don't think you have to worry about anyone bothering you in this crowd."

"That didn't even cross my mind." It was a half truth at best. She glanced around. There was one spot near the wall that looked relatively private. She stepped around him and dropped her belongings on the bunk. "What happens now?"

Ford tied up his pack. "A quick dinner and then to bed. With the weather as warm as it's been, Berge will want to start out well before the sun rises. You don't want to be climbing during the heat of the afternoon."

"Do you really get overheated with all this snow around?"

"That's not the problem. You want the snow to be good and frozen, or the surface gets unstable. Sometimes it's just the ice holding boulders in place. You don't want to be down below when they let loose."

Henrik's silhouette filled the doorway just as Ford mentioned his name. "*Ja*. We'll start early." He looked between Margie and Ford. "There's been some rockfall recently with the warm weather. As the ice softens, things get . . . unpredictable. The mountain is fickle."

Ford sat on the platform, lifting one booted foot and fiddling with the laces. "Very."

Margie spread her bedroll across the wooden surface, trying not to imagine the hazards ahead. Ford's words from Kautz Creek wafted back into her mind. *"I'd never lead you into a dangerous situation."* What sort of dangers was she leading him into?

Henrik stepped all the way inside and folded his arms. "I thought we'd take the Disappointment Cleaver route instead of Gibraltar. Too much scree for my comfort level. I don't want anything coming down on our heads. You agree?"

Ford tucked his pant leg into the boot before glancing up at the guide. "You're the boss here. Why ask my permission?"

The guide jutted his chin forward, deep grooves forming around his mouth.

"I am fine with whatever you decide." Ford stood, his greater height dwarfing the other man. "But I appreciate your concern."

Henrik ran a hand over the blond whiskers dotting his chin. "I just want to make sure there won't be any problems between us."

Margie glanced between the two, the tension in the room multiplying by the moment. "What sort of problems?"

Henrik jerked his thumb toward the window and lifted his pack. "I'm outside tonight." Without acknowledging Margie's question, he headed out the door.

She turned on Ford. "What was he talking about?"

Ford blew out a long breath. "He led the climb that killed my father."

Margie's knees threatened to give way. She sat down hard on the platform, grasping one of the wooden supports for strength. "Henrik did?"

"He was the only survivor. Five men died. Berge walked away."

And yet Ford was here? Why would he put himself through that? "This must bring it all back."

He shook his head, averting his eyes.

"I haven't thanked you for the book, Ford. It meant a lot to me that you gave me something of your father's."

"You'll get more use out of it than I ever would."

They sat in silence for several minutes, Margie searching for some comforting word or gesture that might help. In the end, she just closed her eyes, praying for the man sitting next to her and for the journey ahead.

Berge's lantern bobbed in the distance, but Ford kept his eyes down as he pushed one boot into the snow after another. The quiet rhythm of climbing left far too much time for thinking.

He'd lain awake in the climbing hut for hours fighting sleep as he listened to the other men's snores. He couldn't risk the nightmarish images coming upon him so close to the place where the horror originated. There was no telling what might happen. Eventually his eyes fell closed, and he slept like the dead. Maybe that's what multiple sleepless nights would do to a man. Or perhaps he'd conquered his demons by agreeing to come on this trip.

Margie had shaken him awake in the wee hours, as everyone else was already moving. Opening his eyes and looking into that face . . . What he wouldn't give to wake up to her smile every morning. The impossible thought made his heart ache.

Gripping the ax head with his gloved hand, Ford jammed the pointed shaft into the ice every other step. The others had been issued metal-tipped alpenstocks, but he preferred the shorter tool. It was more effective in stopping a fall, and if any of this group was going down, he was determined to provide a decent anchor.

Berge seemed to be choosing their path with care, using his ax to cut steps in the more difficult sections. Even Margie appeared to be having an easy time of it. Maybe she'd settled into a steady walking pace and forgotten about her fear of heights. Not being able to see very far due to the darkness probably helped, too.

The line halted in front of him, Berge's hand jutting out to the side in a warning just visible in the early gray light of dawn. Ford used the opportunity to stretch his back, stepping off the beaten path to see why they were stopping.

Margie gripped her alpenstock with both hands, placing her forehead against the stout stick. "Finally. I thought we were going to stop every hour."

"It's only been about forty minutes since our last break." Ford took a swig of water from his canteen.

"No. That can't be possible." She glanced up toward the horizon. "Then why are we stopping?"

Berge turned and faced them, cupping his hand around his mouth to holler down the slope. "First crevasse. We've got a ladder in place, so all you have to do is take it slow. One person at a time. Watch your step because if one person falls and the rest of you aren't prepared, he can pull a whole team down."

Margie's eyes widened. "A ladder? It's not steep enough to need a ladder here, is it?"

The first good sliver of sunlight was cresting the horizon, sending its warm glow across the glacier's surface. Ford took hold of the rope linking them together. It might have been better to do this when she couldn't see what she was crossing. "It's like a bridge. Crevasses can be pretty deep."

He edged forward to examine the crack in the ice, the frosty whiteness giving way to shades of blue below the surface. A stout ladder had been secured into the ice, boards laid down as a makeshift surface. Berge bent down to check the stakes holding the device in place.

Margie's mouth dropped open, and she turned to Ford. She kept her voice low, so as not to carry to the rest of the team. "I'm not—there's no way I can cross that."

"You can." Ford kept his voice steady, placing his hand on her arm to draw her eyes toward him rather than the crevasse. "It's so narrow, you could probably jump across it. A few steps and you'll be on the other side."

"You heard what Henrik said. One slip and I could drag us all down."

That's true anywhere on the mountain. Ford swallowed his words. "You're roped in. You'll have Berge and Lewis on one side, me on the other."

"Crossing!" Berge's voice rang out.

Ford pushed down his irritation. The guide hadn't even checked to see if Margie was panicking. Of course, he was used to people who actually wanted to climb the mountain—not young women who'd been bullied into it. The man in front of Margie anchored himself, watching closely as the guide edged his way over the rickety platform.

She covered her mouth with a hand, her knees bending slightly as if to get closer to the snowpack. "I can't watch." But she did, her eyes glued to Berge every step of the way.

The guide stepped off the far side, gesturing to the second man.

Ford dug his ax into the slope, not convinced that Margie could support the much larger climber in front of her were he to slip. Even though it was a simple crossing, one couldn't be too careful. Her two days of training wouldn't turn her into an expert mountaineer.

Margie braced herself, picking up the line. "I've got you," she called to Lewis, voice trembling.

Ford ducked his head to hide his smile. Perhaps focusing on teamwork would encourage Margie to forget her own fears.

The climber glanced back, his raised brows evident under his cap. "Good. I feel much better."

If Margie was aware of his sarcasm, her face didn't show it. She dug the alpenstock into the ice and looped her arm around it.

The climber checked his pack before gripping the flimsy rope acting as a balance line. Four halting steps and he was across.

Ford relaxed his stance. Hopefully now Margie had seen two people do it, she'd be less concerned.

She crept forward and stopped. "It's no different than walking across a floor, right?"

Except for the two-hundred-foot plunge. "Right. And we've got your rope. You're not going anywhere."

"People do this sort of thing for fun?"

Ford anchored himself again. "This isn't about fun. It's about reaching the top."

Margie's pack rose and fell as she took several deep breaths. "Must get to the top." She touched the toe of her boot to the ladder. "The crevasse looks deep."

"Don't look. Focus on your feet, not beyond."

"Right." She stood still, staring into the abyss.

Berge came a little closer on the far side. "Come on, Miss Lane. It's a few steps." His gentle voice cajoled her. "I'm right here. By the end of the trip, you'll be dancing across these."

"There are more?" Her voice quavered.

Ford gritted his teeth. This was going to be a long climb. "One at a time, Margie. Get past this one, and you're several steps closer to beating Carmichael at his twisted game."

She straightened and pushed her boot farther along the wooden plank. After a rasping breath, she lifted her second foot and drew it up onto the ladder.

That's my girl. Ford released the breath he'd been holding. Berge was right; after she had one of these crossings under her belt, she'd have no more difficulties. The first was always the hardest.

A breeze picked up, swirling up some loose ice crystals and sweeping them into the gaping crack. Margie clenched her fingers around the rope support, stopping any minuscule forward momentum she'd gained. "Noooo. Don't do that."

If anyone could order around the wind, it would be Margie. Unfortunately, the breeze had picked up along with the daylight. Ford moistened his lips, already chapped from exposure. "What was that Virgil quotation you told me back at Kautz Creek?"

Margie bent her knees. "It's swaying."

"The quote, Margie. What was it? I can't remember."

"'They can conquer who believe they can.'"

"Yes. That's it. Do you believe you can conquer this crevasse?"

"Not really."

Wrong answer. Ford glanced up at the mountain. The wispy cloud that had shrouded the peak was thickening. They needed to speed things up if they were going to summit today. "Tell me more about John Muir. Didn't he climb the mountain?"

Margie didn't move.

Ford glanced behind them. The second team was approaching. "Margie. John Muir—when did he climb Rainier?"

Her voice trembled. "Eighteen eighty-eight."

"What did he have to say about it?"

"He said . . . he said,"—she took a step—"Muir said he hadn't meant to climb it. He just got excited and the next thing he knew he was at the top." She managed another step, pushing closer to the far side. "At least that's what he told his wife." Two more steps and she was over.

Ford relaxed. She'd done it. The last in the line, Ford fastened his ax onto his pack and made his way across the ladder in a couple of measured strides.

Margie beamed. "I did it. Did you see?"

"I never doubted you for a moment."

She touched his arm. "Thank you for your help."

Warmth rushed up his arm as if he could feel her touch through the thick coat. "You're stronger than you know. You just needed to get your mind off the crevasse."

Berge gripped the head of his ax. "Yes, very good. Only four more." He turned and started up the slope, the line trailing after him.

"Four more." Margie closed her eyes for a long moment. "But none as bad as this, right?"

Ford clapped her on the back. "You're an expert now. By the time we return tonight you could probably do them blindfolded."

"I think that might be easier."

TWENTY-SEVEN

*M*argie ran her wrist across her forehead. Her steps grew haphazard as she struggled to draw in enough air. The wind had picked up, sending the scarf she'd wrapped around her face flapping against her grease-painted cheeks. The glaring sunshine from earlier had faded. Mist now swirled over the summit.

The climb over Disappointment Cleaver had held more tense moments as they scrambled over the rocky terrain, the wind gusts making every attempt to knock them off. At this point in the climb, the vertical ladder on one section was a relief to Margie. The chilly rails seemed a stronger handhold than the craggy volcanic rock.

She'd seen Ford and Henrik talking in hushed tones at their last rest break. They rallied the group after only a few minutes. Ford had helped her to her feet, the pack making the process cumbersome. "Temperatures are dropping. If we sit too long, we're going to get chilled."

"I'm already chilled," she murmured into her muffler. "Are we getting close to the crest?" For hours she'd gauged their progress by staring up at the snowy dome, though it never seemed to get much closer. Now that the clouds had thickened, she could imagine that it was within reach. Somewhere.

"We've less than a thousand vertical feet to go." Ford pulled his wool cap lower over his ears. "But conditions are worsening. We may have to turn back."

"What?" A high-pitched whine sounded in her ears. Was it her blood pressure or the wind? "We're so close. This can't all be for nothing."

"Not yet, but if things don't improve . . ." Ford's voice trailed off.

"I thought you and Henrik were concerned about temperatures being too warm. This is better, right?"

His eyes, hidden behind the dark glasses, revealed nothing, but his silence did little to conceal the truth.

No, no, no. She'd struggled up miles of icy slopes, nearly lost her mind balancing over deep crevasses, and pushed herself beyond the point of exhaustion just to return empty-handed? *We have to summit, Lord. You wouldn't bring us this far for nothing.*

They had rotated positions on the line and now she stared at Ford's backside as he broke the trail up the steep slope. His shoulders hunched under his pack, he trudged forward, head down.

She choked down her misgivings. Ford wouldn't abandon the climb without good reason. Exhaustion tugged at her every muscle. How could she face Philip? His steam shovel waited to shred its way through the subalpine meadow, clearing the ground for hotels, dance halls, ski pulls, and the hideous gondola cables. The thought sickened her, sending fresh energy to her legs.

Ford and Henrik might argue, but she was going forward. They wouldn't forcibly carry her down the mountain. They wouldn't dare.

The line tugged at her waist. She glanced back to see Lewis, the fourth man in their party, lagging far behind, Henrik just above him. Were they talking? Probably discussing their decision. Maybe she should stop and let them catch up. She had the right to make her argument. She ground her staff into the ice and swiveled to face them.

At that moment, Henrik dropped to one knee on the ice, driving his ax into the snow. Lewis slipped and then began cascading downhill at a rapid clip.

Margie gripped the alpenstock. "Ford! He's falling!"

Lewis's momentum dragged Henrik a couple of body lengths. The guide forced his ax into the snow a second time, digging in with the toes of his hobnail boots.

The line jerked her off-balance, and she shrieked as her back crashed against the ice. Landing with one arm hooked around the steady pole, Margie shut her eyes, expecting to be pulled down the mountain at any second.

The moment never came. Opening her eyes, she stared down at the two men, both secured against the slope.

"I got it," Henrik hollered. "Lewis, you all right?"

The man below responded, but the wind whipped his words away before Margie could decipher them.

"Margie?" Ford called, his voice higher pitched than she'd ever heard.

"I'm fine." She kept her arm clamped on the stick, but forced herself up to a seated position so she could see what was going on below.

Lewis, gripping the line with both hands, sat up on his knees. He appeared to be unhurt.

Sounds from above made Margie turn and look up.

Ford was lowering himself along the rope. He stopped beside her and gripped her elbow. "I'm going to go check on the other two. Wait here. Are you secure?"

She nodded, hugging the staff with all her might. Suddenly the idea of returning early didn't seem so objectionable. "I don't know what happened. Henrik knelt down before Lewis fell. Did he know something was going to happen?"

"It's hard to say. Maybe it's just a coincidence."

She glanced up to where Ford had been when the incident began. "What are you hooked to?"

"I set a picket stake and tied into it. Drink some water while we're stopped." Ford continued on down the slope, leaving Margie shivering.

Water sounded heavenly. So did a warm bed, a roaring fire, and a hot cup of coffee. Without lessening her grip, she unscrewed the canteen's cap. The water was slushy with ice, but she managed to swallow a couple of mouthfuls, the basic action distracting her from the panic clawing at her stomach. What if Henrik hadn't halted the slide? Would she have had the strength to hang on? Would Ford have been able to catch them? The thought sent a wave of dizziness through her system.

She gazed out over the view below. A layer of puffy clouds had blown into the lowlands making the peak look like a snowy island floating in the sky. With mist obscuring the crest above, she felt alone in a world of ice and rock. Margie laid her head against the pole as the buffeting wind seeped through her clothes and stiffened her muscles. Margie closed her eyes. They could continue up or head home. She no longer cared.

Ford dug his heel into the ice with each step. The last thing he wanted to do was destabilize the group a second time.

He hadn't witnessed the fall, but Margie's scream had frozen him in place. *God, protect her.* The knee-jerk prayer sneaked past his lips before his training kicked in. Thrusting the ax into the ice, Ford anchored himself, waiting for the line to tighten and drag them all to their deaths. Could he hold four climbers? Doubtful. But knowing Margie was one of them—he'd fight every inch of the way.

Now as he made his way down to Henrik, a hollow ache grew in his stomach. Conditions were worsening, temperatures plunging, and Lewis appeared to have lost his alpenstock in the fall. Ford scanned the area below but could see no sign of the missing pole. Climbing without one—particularly in this wind—would be disastrous.

Further risking Margie's life was out of the question. They might not have a future together, but he had to know she had a future of some sort. He'd never loved anyone the way he loved this poetry-spouting, plant-obsessed woman, and he'd do anything to get her off this mountain in one piece. Philip Carmichael could have Paradise—every bug, spider, and rock of it. All Ford wanted was Margie. And if he couldn't have her, at least he could rest easy knowing she was safe.

Lewis and Berge huddled, voices raised above the blowing snow.

Ford plunged down the last few steps to join them, ducking his head against the wind. "What happened?"

Berge scowled. "The end of this climb, that is certain. We need to turn back. No one's summiting today. All of the other teams have started back down."

"I agree, but Margie will be devastated. We were so close."

The guide scratched at the tip of his nose, reddened by the wind. "No help for it. It'll be a challenge getting Lewis down the mountain without another fall."

The stout man frowned, averting his eyes. "I'm sorry."

"It happens to the best of us." Ford caught the man's shoulder with his gloved hand. Turning to Berge, he gestured toward Margie. "Margie says you crouched before Lewis slipped. What was that about?"

Berge jerked his head around to face him. *"Nei, I"*—he paused, quickly glancing at the other climber—"I was . . . fixing my bootlace."

A prickle raced down the back of Ford's neck. Henrik Berge, the man who taught every other guide how to fasten knots, had failed to secure his own laces? "You probably saved us all."

Berge averted his eyes. "Timing is everything." He cleared his throat. "We should be going. Should I retrieve Miss Lane?"

"I'll do it. I need to take out that pin anyway." Ford stretched, the cold settling into his joints. Margie must be half-frozen. Pushing up the slope, he retraced his steps and arrived at her side in a few moments.

Margie's head rested against her forearms. She didn't even bother to look up as he approached.

"I've got bad news." He shuffled the last few steps. When she didn't respond, he grabbed onto her shoulder and gave it a shake. "Margie?"

She stirred. "Yes?"

He dropped to one knee. "You can't go to sleep up here. It's too cold."

"Mmm." She rested her head against the staff.

"No, you don't." He grasped her wrist and stood, hoisting her up to her feet in the process. "Come on, it's time to go home."

"Wha—no!" She shook off his grip, lost her balance, and landed on her backside.

He helped her up, his arm supporting her weight. "There's no longer any option, Margie. That storm is moving toward us, and we've got to get Lewis safely to base camp. He can't return on his own."

Margie ducked her head. "Of course. I don't mean to be selfish." She glanced up toward the crest as the mist parted a fraction, a sliver of the snowy dome gleaming in the afternoon light. "We're just so close."

His heart sagged. They *were* close. Another hour and they'd have been standing at the top of the world. Most of the difficult climbing was done. Now it was just up and into the crater, then across to Register Rock and Columbia Crest. "I know; it's frustrating." He turned and gazed at the two men waiting below, replaying the fall in his mind. Carmichael's words floated through his thoughts: *"I paid for the guide myself."* The man wouldn't actually endanger Margie over a silly wager. Would he? The memory of the fire still haunted Ford. He had no proof Carmichael was behind that, either.

The pressure of Margie's body leaning against him pushed Ford out of his dark thoughts. The fall might have been an accident, or it could have been staged. Did he dare to place their lives in Berge's hands on the descent?

What if they went on alone? Could they outrun the storm? Ford jostled Margie's shoulder. "Are you still awake?"

"I'm just using you to block the wind." Her voice sounder lighter and more coherent than before. "Why are we just standing here?"

"I'm thinking." He glanced up at the dome, the exposed stretch growing clearer by the moment. Perhaps this was the window they needed. "Do you trust me?"

She placed her palm on his chest. "With all my heart."

That sealed it. It might be the most foolish decision of his life, but something in his gut said it was right. Margie would probably say it was that prayer he'd uttered earlier. Maybe so. "Let's go on up. You and me."

She yanked off the dark glasses. "Can we do that? Is it safe?"

Could God really be leading him now? "It's not safe. It's probably a mistake. But something is telling me to go ahead."

"Something?"

"I don't know—an inner voice, maybe."

Her lips curved just enough to appear over the edge of her scarf. "He's been whispering the same to me. I was just afraid it was my own selfish desires."

His heart hammered against his ribs. Margie had changed him; there was no denying it. Did God actually answer prayers? Ford grabbed her hands and pressed them between his own. "You need to understand: this is beyond foolish. There's a chance—a good chance—we could both die up here."

Margie's brown eyes shone. "I understand. I trust you."

Her confidence drove a sweet ache through his chest. *God, if You're real—help me do the right thing. I don't want to risk her life.* "We'll have to push quickly to beat the storm."

She slid her arms around his waist. "We can do it. Ford, I've never been more sure of anything in my life."

Margie followed Ford step for step up the glacier, forcing a deep breath with each placement of her foot. Henrik's staunch disapproval had not sown any seeds of doubt in either of them, but Margie's stomach churned at disobeying the guide.

The Lord was at work here. How else could one explain Ford's sudden change of heart? She'd almost been able to watch the progression in his eyes as they spoke. And if God was willing to get her to the top of this mountain, maybe He'd do great things in Ford as well. Her spirits rose with each step even as tears sprang to her eyes. *Lord, You are good. Too good to me.*

The wind rushed along the glacier, blasting loose ice particles and roaring in Margie's ears. At this point, even the strenuous exercise was doing little to warm her blood. Her focus pulled inward as shivers racked her body. Hopefully they'd reach the top soon. Chances were they wouldn't dally long.

Margie pushed her scarf over her nose, trying to minimize how much of her skin lay exposed to the icy sandblasting. Either her imagination played tricks on her, or the weather worsened the farther they went.

Ford struggled on, but their pace lagged.

The clouds cloaked them in a veil of white. With her thoughts in disarray, Margie couldn't even compose a good line about this experience for her journal. Wait—she no longer had a journal. Margie let her eyes fall closed, her world constricting into a tiny bubble bordered by roaring wind and cold.

The words to a hymn floated through her head, and the lyrics helped her keep inching forward. *"When darkness veils His lovely face, I rest on His unchanging grace. In every high and stormy gale, my anchor holds within the veil."*

She needed to keep moving. Eventually she'd remember where she was going and why. *Just follow.* Margie opened her eyes, snowflakes clinging to the edges of her dark glasses.

Empty mist swirled in front of her.

Margie took two more steps and stopped, tension clawing at her throat. Had Ford fallen into a crevasse? Had she wandered off course? Isolation closed in, and she sank to her knees. Wandering lost on the mountain had never been part of her plan, but staying stationary was a death sentence. Margie pushed her palms against the ice and clambered up to a squat when the line ahead tightened, jerking her off balance.

She gripped the rope with trembling fingers. Ford was on the other end—he hadn't abandoned her. How had she forgotten that? Struggling to her feet, she lunged forward.

Ford appeared out of the gusting snow, his shadowy form growing large as he trudged back toward her. "Are you all right?"

Margie's ribs ached from panting for air. "Disoriented," she choked out the word.

He gripped her elbows. "We're not in good shape. This moved in too fast."

She couldn't resist pushing into his arms and leaning against his chest, her heartbeat throbbing in her ears. "What do we do?"

"We're near the edge of the crater, I'm sure." He dug into his pocket and retrieved a compass and map. "If we make it, we'll be out of the wind for a moment and can reassess."

Margie nodded, knowing the motion was worthless. Maybe if they just stayed together, everything would be all right.

Ford leaned close to her ear. "Let's get moving. We need shelter. Stay close."

As if she planned on letting him out of her sight again.

She ducked her head against the wind and followed. Eventually they scrambled over a rocky ridge. With her thigh muscles spent, Margie struggled to keep purchase on the unsteady surface. She braced herself with the alpenstock.

Ford shouted over his shoulder, but the flurry whipped the sound away. He swung his arm, gesturing to something in the distance. Turning away, he skidded down the rough terrain.

Margie hurried after, rocks and ice sliding under her boots. *Where are we going? Is this the top?* A dark opening loomed in the ice ahead of them. She froze and grabbed the rope. Was Ford heading for a crevasse?

He stopped just short, picking at the ice with his ax before turning and beckoning her forward.

She scooted closer. "What is it?"

Ford whipped off the dark glasses, squinting at her as a grin appeared over the edge of his scarf. "Our salvation." He yanked off his pack and let it drop to the ground. "It's a steam vent."

Margie's heart jumped to her throat. "Steam?"

Ford evidently didn't hear her, because he sat on the ice and lowered his booted feet into the narrow gap. "Follow me." Turning his shoulders to match the opening, he slithered out of sight.

Margie wrapped both arms around her middle, pressing the staff close to her side. She had no energy to fight the wind buffeting her from all directions. An ice cave couldn't be any more frightening than a whiteout. She dropped to all fours, casting her knapsack to the side. Leaning forward, she peered into the hole. A gentle warmth flooded her face, and her heart jumped in response. "Are you all right down there?"

"Come on in," his voice echoed.

Sitting on her backside, she scooted down into the gap. Dragging herself over the rocks, she wriggled like an earthworm entering its burrow.

Ford gripped one of Margie's ankles, guiding her down the steep slope to where it opened out to a larger cave—big enough for both of them. Untying the rope, he tossed it beside her. "Stay put, I'm going to get our supplies." He scrambled up the slope, stones skittering loose in his wake.

She retreated, glancing around at the dim cave, the curving ice ceiling shaped into an oddly beautiful scalloped surface. Droplets of water pattered down onto the floor of the chamber. A little farther down, the ground dropped off into a lower section disappearing into the gloom. How far down did the tunnel go? The thick, steamy air held just a hint of rotten eggs and something else Margie couldn't identify. She tucked her nose under her damp scarf. Die outside in the cold or in here with poisonous volcanic gases?

Ford reappeared, lowering the packs to Margie. After crawling down, he leaned against one of the boulders, chest heaving. "It feels so good to be out of the weather."

Margie placed her hands over her ears. "It's so quiet." Other than their breathing and the sound of water dripping, the cavern was eerily silent. "Are you sure it's safe in here? Is the air breathable?"

"It's a chance we'll have to take. We wouldn't have lasted out there."

Pulling her knees to her chest, Margie laid her head down and closed her eyes. Even in here, shivers still racked her body. "So we wait out the storm?"

Ford remained quiet for several moments, as if in his weariness he'd drifted off to sleep. Finally, he took a shuddering breath. "Yes. I'm sorry. We shouldn't have left the group. I thought we could beat the weather to the top and be down before things got this dire. It was a bad decision."

Opening her eyes, Margie studied his face in the dim light filtering down from the opening. She wanted to reach out and touch his wind-burned cheek, but was too exhausted to lift herself off the stony ground. "It's as much my fault as yours."

"But I was here to keep you safe. That's the only reason I came."

"What about to irritate Philip?"

A snorting laugh escaped his lips. "That was just a bonus."

She adjusted her position, avoiding the jagged rock pressing into her hip. "Well, we're not dead yet, so I won't be hearing any apologies."

"It doesn't do much good to apologize after." He heaved a sigh and rolled to his side, glancing up at the cave mouth. "I don't think this storm is going to let up in time."

"In time for what?"

"In time to get off the mountain before sunset. That last push took far longer than it should have. We were less than forty minutes from the summit when the group turned back."

"But we walked for hours—or at least it felt that way."

"We did. We're going to stay overnight."

"Here?" A wave of nausea gripped Margie. "Alone?"

He shrugged. "Unless you have another idea."

"Will Henrik come looking for us if we don't return tonight?"

"No." He pulled off his knit cap, his brow furrowed into deep grooves. "The group will return to Paradise and wait. It'll take days to get a party together. I'm afraid we're on our own."

Margie gripped her elbows and rocked in place. A whole night on the mountain. She didn't want to think how dark it might get—and how cold. The steam from the earth below did seem to warm the enclosed space, but it was no Finnish sauna.

Ford touched her wrist. "I'm so sorry."

She pulled off her glove and gripped his damp fingers. "I still think God brought us up here for a reason, Ford. We just have to find out what it is."

od brought us up here for a reason?" Ford's throat squeezed. Just when he was starting to think his father and Margie might be right about this heavenly Being, Ford ran smack against why he didn't trust Him in the first place. He'd thought it might be God whispering to him, but it was just his own foolish desire to impress the woman he loved. *Pride goes before a fall, right?* Only in this case, the fall came first.

Their chances of making it off the mountain were shrinking by the hour. The steam cave was a lucky find, but it only solved the most immediate problem. How long could they spend in this hole before the volcanic fumes killed them? Would one or both of them drift off to sleep, never to awaken? They'd end up two more casualties of Rainier—fools lost to the mountain's whims. Two bodies never to be recovered. At least he didn't have a son who'd spend years haunted by the father who never returned.

None of that mattered. What mattered was Margie. She was too important to be reduced to a footnote in the park's annual report—whoever would write it this time around.

Ford squeezed her fingers, reveling in the fact that she'd even touch him after the situation he'd dragged her into. "I'll get you home." The words almost stuck in his throat; his voice cracked as he spoke.

Her smile was barely visible in the dark shadows. "I believe you."

The shivering vibrating off her arm spurred Ford into action. "You cold?"

She laughed quietly. "I'm trying to imagine I'm sitting in front of the roaring fire in the Paradise Inn lobby, but it's not working."

"Come here." He tugged her hand, drawing her closer.

"Ford—"

"I don't want you dying from exposure." He shifted, scooting closer to her. "We can worry about decorum later. Let's get you thawed out."

She gave in, sliding next to his side and hunkering under his outstretched arm.

Ford wrapped his elbow around her waist and pulled her closer. "You're like a block of ice. Do you have dry clothes in your pack?"

"Yes-s. But I can't imagine they'll stay dry very long in here. How are you still warm?"

"Exertion, probably." Margie was right about the damp air and the dripping roof turning them both soggy. It would make for an unpleasant night, but that wasn't the worst part. When—if—they emerged into the outside world, their wet clothes would be a serious hazard. Then again, if she froze now, it wouldn't matter much. His father always said to take one crisis at a time.

"Put them on, anyway." He reached for her pack, opened it, and drew out a dry shirt and long wool socks. "This will be a good start."

She struggled to her feet and sighed. "It may be dark in here, but I'd still rather you turn your back."

"Of course." Ford pushed up to his knees and turned away, focusing on his knapsack. He had a tin cup attached to the outside, but it took his clumsy fingers several minutes to untie the knots securing it to the frame. They needed drinking water and soon.

While Margie changed, he clambered up the steep tunnel. As he packed the cup with snow, Ford glanced out the entrance hole. Blinding mist still blocked any potential view. There was no way of knowing what time it was or how much longer the storm would rage. Hopefully it would die down by morning. If not . . . *One crisis at a time.*

Inching back down the incline, he cringed at every rock that rattled down the slope. "Is it safe to come down?"

"Yes, I'm just trying to add some layers."

Ford slid into the lower cavern, finding enough space to stand hunched over. He'd noticed a couple of hissing fumaroles along the edge of the grotto and made his way over to them. The vents spewed steam into the air, but thankfully none seemed particularly foul smelling. With his gloved hand, he settled the snow-packed tin cup on top of one of the hottest stones. With any luck, they'd be sipping warm water in no time.

Margie pulled the cardigan over her shoulders, trying to banish the idea that they'd been entombed in ice. How dark would it get when night fell? She shuddered at the thought.

Ford knelt in a far corner of the cave, his bare hands stretched in front of him like he was sitting in front of a campfire.

"What are you doing?" Her words echoed through the dank space, her eardrums still not accustomed to the quiet.

"Come feel this." He glanced over his shoulder.

Her legs ached with each step. Hopefully a night of rest would revitalize the muscles enough to descend the mountain. The three hissing fumaroles reminded Margie of a steam kettle. Margie warmed her fingers and then ran them across her damp cheeks. With this much moisture, her skin ought to be luxuriant by morning. "Are you sure it's not gassing us? I've read that volcanoes vent toxic gases like carbon monoxide and hydrogen sulfide." She covered her mouth and nose. "I wish I'd brought my geology book."

"I smell only a small hint of sulfur, and we don't seem to be having any ill effects." He glanced up. "Are you?"

"I don't think so. I'm just cold and tired."

"Then I think we're safe enough, for now anyway. We can take shifts sleeping, just to be sure."

Having Ford along was much more comforting than a book. She sat next to him and extended her fingers toward the warm air.

Ford slipped on his gloves and reached for a tin cup he'd nestled amongst the rocks. He swirled the steaming liquid around before taking a quick sip. "Perfect." He handed it to her. "Careful, it's hot."

"Aren't you resourceful?" She accepted the cup and drew it to her lips.

"Survival is good incentive. Your survival is even better."

Margie swallowed, the heated water as comforting as a cuddly blanket. Someday she and Ford would laugh about their experience, if they managed to remain friends after this. *Maybe we'll tell the story to our grandchildren someday.*

She shouldn't allow herself to think such things, but the tiring day had weakened the barriers she'd erected around her heart. Why would God push them together if there was no possible future for them? Margie held the cup out to him.

Ford shook his head. "Finish it. I'll take the next one."

Margie sipped the warm liquid. "Are we on the summit, then?"

Ford stood, laying one hand against the ice curving above their heads. "Technically, we're under it."

"But did we make it to the top?"

His face was lost in the darkness, but his sigh told her everything she needed to know. "We're on the south side of the crater. Columbia Crest rises another couple hundred feet on the northwest side."

The weight of his proclamation seemed heavier than the layers of ice above their heads. Philip had no idea what he had sent her up into. Her stomach twisted. "I'm sorry I dragged you into this. I know you had no desire to ever climb again."

Ford sat down beside her, his eyes barely visible in the dim light. "I thought we said there'd be no apologies."

"I know, but if I hadn't—"

"I needed to face my own demons regarding this mountain, and I've done so. I'm grateful to you for giving me the push I needed."

"Being pushy is a strength of mine."

His face twisted up into a smile. "One of your many fine qualities, I'm sure." He took the empty cup from her. "My dad's accident's haunted me far too long. I couldn't let go of the fact that his body was never recovered. I always thought that if I came up here, I'd be forced to face how I'd let him down."

"What do you mean?"

Ford's shoulders pulled forward. "I was supposed to be on that climb. I'd spent the whole summer patrolling the park's east side with Luke. Dad planned the late-season summit trip as a welcome-home surprise. He didn't realize I'd made plans with some friends to go camping at Mowich Lake." Ford's brow creased, the shadows settling into the lines on his face. "He told me to go ahead. We could climb together another time."

Margie bit her lip. The pain in his voice sent an echoing hurt through her as well. She couldn't imagine never seeing her father again, no matter what he'd done. He'd been so broken by his confession to her. Why hadn't she spoken forgiveness to him? *Because I thought there'd be another chance.*

Ford twisted his neck, looking toward the cave ceiling. "It's odd, though. Being up here—in here, even—I feel closer to him."

Margie's heart lifted. "Really?"

"Like he was still waiting to spend that time together." He laughed softly. "It sounds crazy. I know he's not here, not really, but . . ."

"Maybe that's what God wanted you to experience out of this adventure."

His lips pressed together. "My dad was a believer, like you."

"Mrs. Brown told me. She said he used to lead the Sunday meetings in Longmire."

"That he did." Ford's voice lowered to a husky whisper, focusing on the cup in his lap. "He'd be disappointed to see what I've become."

Prickles rose on Margie's arms. "Don't say that. You're a fine ranger and a good man. How could your dad be anything but proud?"

Ford pushed to his feet, his face hidden by the shadows. "I should go refill this. We're going to need plenty of water to survive the night."

Ford spread his bedroll a few feet from Margie's, the steam vents at his feet. Was it just this morning he'd thought how sweet it would be to wake up to her face again? This certainly hadn't been how he envisioned it.

After digging through her knapsack, Margie pulled out packages of crackers. "I assume we should ration these, since there's always the chance that this could be a longer stay than we intended."

"Sounds wise." The light was fading fast. Ford gestured to the blanket; thankful the shadows hid her face from view. "I hope this doesn't make you uncomfortable."

"We don't have much choice." Her voice seemed a higher pitch than earlier.

They shared a meager meal in silence, and more of the hot water, passing the cup back and forth to share the warmth. This was going to be a long night.

After they'd finished, he patted a hand on top of her blankets. "Why don't you take the first sleep shift? I'll keep watch."

"In the dark? What are you going to watch?"

"I'll listen, then. Make sure you're breathing all right."

She sighed, curling up in the blanket. "We've been here for hours. If the mountain was going to asphyxiate us, I think it would have done so by now. Just go to sleep."

Ford pondered her words. He didn't feel any ill effects from the steam, just exhaustion from the climb. "Makes sense." He lay down, the blankets doing little to shield his back from the stony ground. A heaviness settled in his stomach. He rolled to his side, trying to make out the lines of her form in the fading light. "Are you warm enough?"

A long moment passed. "I'm fine."

Would she tell him otherwise? Ford closed his eyes, useless in the blackening cave, anyway. The weight of the day's events pulled at every muscle. Margie's assertion that Berge was already crouched when Lewis slipped troubled him. Perhaps in the panicked flurry of activity, she misinterpreted what she saw. His faulty shoelace excuse rang hollow. Perhaps Berge sensed Lewis's poor footing, but then why wouldn't he say as much? Had it been a stroke of luck—or a devilish trick?

A huge sigh split the dark. As Margie shifted and wriggled in her blankets, every sound was amplified amongst the dripping echoes.

Ford squelched the instinct to ask her if she was warm enough—again. She'd hardly uttered a complaint since the start of this disastrous climb, and it seemed unlikely she'd start now. The sound of her teeth chattering melted his resolve faster than snow in the tin cup.

Reaching out a hand, he fumbled through the darkness until it landed on the damp wool hat covering her soft hair. When she didn't flinch away, Ford shifted closer.

Margie's hand landed in the middle of his chest. "Ford, I'm not sure it's wise."

"You don't trust me?"

"I don't trust myself."

His thoughts spun in dizzying circles as he tried to puzzle out the meaning of her statement. "I don't understand."

She rolled away, taking her warmth along with her. "It's probably best you don't."

The inky blackness had claimed all his senses except for hearing. Had he not been able to sense her breathing, he'd think he was alone in the dripping cave. *I will never climb without a lantern again.*

"Ford, can I ask you something?" Margie's voice sounded in the darkness.

He lifted himself up on one elbow. "Anything."

"Before we left the group, you said you heard God's voice."

Ford held his breath for a moment. "I think I said an 'inner voice.'"

"Do you think it might have been God?" She rustled around, as if sitting up.

The gentle tone in her voice sent a rush of warmth through him. He rubbed his chin with damp fingers. Had that quiet voice prodding him along come from heaven? "I . . . I thought it might have been. But it doesn't make sense. If God wanted us to continue, why didn't He protect us?"

"We're here, aren't we?"

The woman's reasoning seemed a little shaky. "He could have kept the weather clear for another hour and saved us all this misery."

"Maybe you . . . No, it's not my place."

"What?"

She waited a long moment before responding. "Maybe you needed to be in a position of weakness before you could submit to His strength. Ford, you are the epitome of the strong, self-reliant man. Why would someone like you even need a heavenly Father?"

Her pointed words cut him to the bone. "What I needed was my earthly one."

"Of course. I'm sorry." A few more rustles came from her vicinity. "Do you ever sense God's presence here in this wilderness?"

Ford swallowed. God's presence. Is that what he'd been feeling? "Sometimes, yes." His feet were growing uncomfortably warm. Ford sat up and shifted around to move the rest of his body closer to the warmth. By the end of the night, he'd be like a chicken on a spit.

"There's a psalm that says, 'When I consider thy heavens, the work of thy fingers, the moon and the stars, which thou hast ordained; what is man, that thou art mindful of him? And the son of man, that thou visitest him?'"

"So, what am I? To God, that is."

"A precious child. One He loves enough to send His own Son to die for."

The cavern fell silent. Ford listened to her even breathing until it seemed to deepen into sleep. He rolled to his other side. She was right. The mountain hadn't killed them yet. Why should it do so now?

Perhaps because his father hadn't been as lucky.

Ford pressed his hand against the bridge of his nose, a well of emotion seeping through his system, like the steam slowly melting the solid ice around them. His father's face filled Ford's mind. Smiling, laughing, eyes twinkling—no matter how frustrating a day he'd endured, Dad had a light that spilled from within. Sort of like Margie. And the Browns. And everyone else Ford knew who followed Christ. Could he experience that level of joy?

A hollow opened in Ford's chest. He hadn't been able to protect his father. He'd failed to protect Margie. He couldn't even save himself. Finding this steam cave was nothing but a lucky accident. They should have been lost forever, wandering in the storm.

Get us off this mountain, God. Get her off at least. Then we can talk.

TWENTY-NINE

*M*argie stirred, her neck stiff from being propped on her knapsack. How long had it been? The darkness pressed in, like a smothering blanket. Eventually the sun would have to rise. The earth would warm. They'd trek down the mountain to face Philip and all his cronies. She may not have made the highest point of the summit, but sleeping in the crater—that should earn her a delay at least. She couldn't permit a steam shovel to tear through her meadow, even if she had to throw herself in front of the hideous machine. Did Philip have any idea how hard those precious little plants worked to establish themselves?

Philip should know something about harsh environments. As a child, Margie had followed him home once. She'd never forget the forlorn shack next to the railroad tracks, gaping holes in the wooden shingles. It had burned down a few years ago, while Philip was away at school. No one seemed to miss it.

Ford shifted. "Are you sleeping?"

"No." She whispered, as if her voice might disturb the sleeping cave.

"Warm enough?"

She drew the cover up tight over her shoulder. "Yes." Morning couldn't come soon enough.

Ford must have sat up, blocking the draft coming from the cave mouth. "Margie, I think we should discuss what happened in Tacoma."

"Now?" She rubbed the damp skin on her brow. "If you feel it's important."

"I do." His voice cracked.

Her throat tightened. She rolled to face him, not that it mattered in the dark.

"I feel badly about what happened. You were upset that evening, angry with Carmichael and your dad. I took advantage." His sigh cut through the cavern. "I need you to know, that's not who I am. Or rather, it's not the man I want to be."

A half laugh, half sob bubbled up from her chest. "You were not to blame for what happened. I lost my head. I'd been drawn to you since we first met, but never dreamed you would feel the same. When you . . . when we . . ." Her throat squeezed off the words. "It was such a romantic place, and you'd come to my rescue . . . I couldn't stop myself."

"Couldn't . . . Wait, I kissed you."

Her heart thudded against her ribs, thinking back over the moment. "No, I kissed you."

Ford went silent for a moment. "I'm pretty sure about this."

"As am I." A pinprick of irritation settled in her heart. He couldn't take the blame for something she did.

"Well." His quiet laugh filled the darkness. "Then maybe I'm not so sorry after all. Perhaps it was meant to be." He paused again, as if weighing his words. "Maybe we were meant to be. Have you considered that?"

Meant to be? What did that even mean? "I wish that were the case, Ford. I really do." She blinked hard against the tears threatening her eyes. "But there's no future for us. We don't have enough in common."

The darkness grew very still, punctuated only by the sound of water dripping. Regret lodged in her chest.

Ford took a deep breath. "Mrs. Brown said I was still broken from my father's death and I was looking for you to heal me. I didn't think much of it at first, but the idea has dug at me ever since."

The words settled into Margie's heart like the missing piece of a puzzle. Ford's grief did seem to color everything he did. She ached for him, but nothing she said or did would bring healing. Only God could do that.

He continued. "I sensed you had the same deep peace my father always showed. It's what drew me to you, I think—at first, anyway." His half-hearted laugh echoed through the space. "But it's more than that. Climbing up here and facing my fears, dealing with the memories of my father's death head-on . . ." His breathing sped up, catching slightly as if there was something standing in its way. "I didn't expect to meet God up here."

She sat up, her thoughts scattering. "Ford Brayden, are you—"

"I'm not sure yet, Margie. Maybe."

Margie's heart raced. She couldn't stand speaking to the faceless dark any longer. Clambering to her knees, she crawled toward his voice.

"What are you doing?"

She reached out a hand, colliding with his chest. He was sitting up, legs crossed. "Finding you."

He grasped her fingers, pulling her close. "Why?"

"I need to know this is real." She felt around until she found his face, running her fingers over his bristly jaw. "Maybe" wasn't an assurance of faith, but it was certainly a leap in the right direction.

Ford swiveled to the left, his chin sliding away from her palm. "Margie, I really hate to interrupt, but is that light I'm seeing?"

Margie turned. A faint glow had appeared amidst the black.

∽

The bitter cold swept in as Ford clambered to his feet. The glow had grown stronger, filtering down into the cave like a message of hope from the land of the living.

Margie remained on her knees. "We survived our night in the belly of the whale."

"I'm going to take a look." Pulling off his knit cap, he ran fingers through his damp hair. "We might as well have slept in a rainstorm."

Her voice floated in the darkness. "Or a bathtub."

Ford navigated across the loose rocks and eased his way up the steep slope. The light increased as he made his way to the opening, fresh air wafting through the entrance and chilling his clammy skin. Digging his hobnail boot into the ice, he heaved himself up the last few feet to catch a glimpse of the outside world.

After spending a night in complete blackness, the glare off the snow brought stinging tears to his eyes. Ford blinked, shaded his eyes from the bright sunshine, and surveyed the edge of the crater outside their little shelter. A gentle wind whipped along the surface of the crater, but the colors of sunrise stretched through a perfectly clear sky. He turned and called down into the icy throat of the tunnel. "You're not going to believe this, Margie."

Columbia Crest rose in the distance, the ice a rosy pink in the dawn light. After pushing himself out of the hole, he stood up and shuffled toward the crater's edge, sinking into a thin coating of fresh powder on the icy surface. A blanket of clouds, like cotton batting, lay in the valley below.

Ford pressed a shaky hand to his forehead. *We're alive.* He crouched on the rocky edge, the glowing world too beautiful to behold on steady legs. He'd stood on the mountaintop before, but had he ever really appreciated the view? Perhaps a brush with death made everything more magical. Gripping a jagged boulder for balance, the solid rock lent strength to his tired muscles as he gazed out at the sea of clouds below. Heart pounding, he slid his palm along the rugged stone, oblivious to the cold. Magical wasn't the right word. He murmured the words into the brisk air. "'What is man that You are mindful of him?'" He closed his eyes for a moment. "Is this Your doing? All of this? The land down there? Up here?"

A breeze picked up the icy flakes and swirled them around his feet. A surge of emotions filled his chest, like steam welling out of the volcanic vents. The Presence he'd mentioned to Margie was as discernible as the light dancing off the mist. Ford drew in a deep breath, a shiver racing through him. He hadn't really expected God to meet him on the mountaintop. Why would He take interest in someone like Ford? *I'm sorry I don't have more to offer.*

What had Margie called him? *"A precious child. One He loves enough to send His own Son to die for."*

Ford's throat tightened as he opened his eyes, gazing out at the expanse. *I'm sorry it took me so long to understand.* The light brightened with each passing moment. *Dad always said I had a thick skull. I guess he was right. About everything.*

A lump grew in his throat. What would he say to Margie? Would she think this was a ploy to gain her affection? A shiver crossed his skin. He couldn't tell her. Not right away; it was all too fresh. But this event felt too monumental to be ignored.

He dug through the pile of rocks at the edge of the crater and hefted a couple into a small cairn. No one would know what the monument represented, but he would know it was here. *Thank You for not giving up on me.*

A scrabbling sound drew his attention back to the vent opening. Margie's face appeared in the gap, her eyes wide and mouth opened.

Ford shook his head, the wonder only increasing as she joined him in the outside world. "You look like a marmot emerging from its winter den."

"There's a flattering picture." She accepted his hand and struggled out onto her feet. A smile spread across her lips as she surveyed the scenery. "I can't imagine anything more beautiful." The sun crested the edge of the low clouds, the rays spilling out over the rippled surface and bathing her face in its glow.

His throat thickened with emotion. Keeping a grip on her fingers, he pulled her to his side. "Margie, we survived." His voice sounded rough in his own ears.

She wrapped her arm around his waist and squeezed. "Did you doubt we would?"

The weight of her against his side made his head swim. He lowered his chin to the top of her head. *I love you.* Ford bit the words back before they could escape and steal the moment. He didn't need to frighten her away again.

She gestured to the west. "Is that the real summit?"

"Columbia Crest, yes."

Margie turned to him, an obvious question in her brown eyes.

"Margie, we're soaking wet. We need to get down before we freeze."

She gazed across the crater at the mound rising in the distance. "It doesn't look far. And the sun is coming up—the weather will be warming soon."

The very fact that she wanted to attempt it sent a swell of pride through his chest. "If you're sure you're feeling strong enough."

"I want to stand at the top of the world—with you." Margie's cheeks and nose were stained red with windburn, her lower lip cracked from exposure, but her eyes burned with an intensity rivaling the sunrise.

Ford's pulse raced faster than it had on yesterday's climb. She had to be the most gorgeous creature on the face of the earth. "I'll go get our packs."

The ice crunched under Margie's boots as she plowed her way to the mountain's crest, the sunshine spilling over the horizon like sea foam on the beach. The cold air ripped her breath away as fast as she could draw in a new lungful of air, but nothing was going to stop her from finishing this quest.

The sound of Ford's steps just a few feet behind her gave her courage. After leading the way across the snow-filled crater, he'd waved her ahead.

She thought the final ascent would be filled with dreams of beating Philip, but instead her mind whirled with anticipation of seeing God's earth laid out before her. Pushing up that final rise, her throat ached. Tears filled her eyes. She'd never desired to climb the mountain, but God had made it happen.

Her trousers clung to her legs, the wool drying in the brisk wind. Who had she been when she arrived in Longmire months before? The coddled daughter of a United States senator, accustomed to fine meals, crisp linens scented with rose-petal soap, clothes laundered by nameless servants— unworthy of the life she'd been born into and incapable of reaching for the life she wanted.

Margie slowed her pace on the final few steps, wishing to make this moment last for the rest of her life. She peered down into the expanse, her heart jumping in her chest. The clouds below thinned until only a bridal veil of mist wrapped the lowlands, and the golden light of morning embellished the scene with purple and orange hues. *Lord, Your robes fill the temple.*

To the south, ridges upon ridges appeared through the clouds and several other large volcanic cones graced the skyline—St. Helens, Hood, Adams. The sky looked as if it stretched out forever into the distance. It was difficult to believe that heaven could be any more glorious than this, though she knew the earth was a pale shadow of what was to come.

She swept at the tear trickling down her cheek, the rough wool of her glove scraping at her raw skin. Poor, weak, insignificant Margie—standing on top of the mountain.

Ford appeared at her side, his breath ragged. "You made it."

"We made it." Margie reached for his hand. "With God's help."

A smile spread across his face, the two-day growth of red-gold whiskers catching the light of the sun. He pulled her close. "That we did." He stooped down, pressing a kiss to her wind-roughened lips.

The touch stole any breath she had, and Margie leaned into the kiss, burying her fingers behind his neck. The sweetness of the moment overpowered any hesitation, the warmth of his mouth spreading through her body.

Once they parted, he pressed his head down into the nape of her neck for a heartbeat, then clamped his gloves around her hips and hoisted her into the air, pack and all.

She shrieked, clutching at his head and knocking his knit cap loose. "What are you doing? Put me down!"

"Look around, Margie! Look where you are." He grinned up at her as she clung to him like a squirrel in a treetop.

Margie lifted her eyes, her heart drumming a quick rhythm against her sternum. As Ford turned slowly in place, she loosened her grip on his skull, lowering one hand to his shoulder. The earth spread below her like an intricate tapestry woven with a myriad of blues, purples, and greens. Something broke open in her chest, the energy rushing upward like the steam pouring out of the volcanic vents, but arriving as bubbling laughter. Lifting the other arm she stretched her fingers toward the sky.

THIRTY

*F*ord blew out a long breath as gravity hurried him down the trail, Margie at his heels. Paradise Valley had never looked so good. Even the monstrous steam shovel, with its boom jutting into the sky, seemed to welcome them. Soon they'd be rid of the ugly contraption forever—or at least until the next determined entrepreneur weaseled his way into the director's good graces.

Eight hours ago, they'd braved frigid temperatures at the summit, but now the intense sunshine beat down on their heads. He risked a quick glance over his shoulder to check on his climbing partner.

Margie walked with her head down, a tiny smile toying at her lips. *Those lips.*

Ford turned his eyes forward. He didn't regret stealing a kiss this morning. Even though their situation was far from decided, their shared experience would provide a bond that couldn't be severed—no matter what happened. He'd kiss her right here on the trail, if he didn't think it would complicate their homecoming. *Tipsoo Lake, Comet Falls, Yakima Park, Pinnacle Peak.* With each step, he listed the places he'd kiss her in the future, once this madness with Carmichael was over. And if she agreed to marry him, they'd spend their honeymoon backpacking around the

entire mountain so he could show her every corner of the vast park. He
wanted to see her eyes light up when she saw each new view, even if it took
a lifetime.

And it would if he had a say in it.

Margie's shoulders ached under the heavy pack, but that was the least of
her pains. Her feet, her neck, her legs—the inventory would take weeks.
Spotting the Inn ahead lifted her spirits. Soon she'd be out of these clothes
and soaking in a steaming tub. That idea had carried her through miles of
walking in icy clothes, even after the rising temperatures took away the
risk of dying from exposure.

She followed Ford through the doors of the Inn, tears springing to her
eyes. That first day she'd visited the marvelous structure with the handsome ranger, she hadn't anticipated that one day the place would feel like
home.

She yanked off her wool cap, running fingers through her matted
curls, suddenly conscious of how she must look—and smell—after several
days of hard climbing. Ford appeared every bit the rugged mountain man
of her dreams, but her? Probably more like a three-day-dead porcupine left
by the side of the road.

"Ford!" Luke ducked out from behind the counter. "You two are a
welcome sight. We were concerned." He gripped Ford's hand and shook it
in both of his own. He glanced at Margie, his eyes shifting from her head
down to her mud-splattered boots. "Come with me, both of you. We need
to get you out of sight."

"I know I must look terrible." Margie sighed.

Luke shuffled them through to the kitchen. "It's not that. There are reporters in the lobby from *The Tacoma Daily Ledger* and *The Seattle Star*. And there are a few others lurking about."

Ford groaned. "I guess that was to be expected. At least we have good news."

Margie's stomach sank. "I can't face them. But I want to finish this right. Is Philip still here?"

Luke nodded. "Yes, he's in the dining room. And he's with someone else you'll probably want to see." The man turned, beckoning them to follow. "I've paid one of my busboys to make sure the reporters stay in the lobby, at least for the time being. But once they realize you're here, I'm not sure I can hold them back."

Margie slid the pack off her shoulders and hung it over a forearm as she followed the manager, with Ford trailing a few steps behind.

Brilliant late-afternoon sunlight flooded the long hall. Philip stood, tossing his napkin over his half-finished plate. "Well, well." A smile spread across his lips, but his gaze remained hard.

I go missing and that's the best greeting he can muster? At least she didn't need to feel remorse over breaking his heart. By all accounts, he didn't have one.

The woman at his side sprang to her feet, upsetting several glasses. She pivoted in place, clutching the back of her chair with white-knuckled fingers. "Margaret?"

Mother? A wave of dizziness washed over Margie, and she grasped at Ford's arm without thinking. "Mother? Why are you here?"

Ford intercepted Margie's pack before it dropped to the floor. "Mrs. Lane. Good to see you, again."

Her mother ignored Ford and rushed to Margie, her hands fluttering like wounded birds. "Look at you." Her eyes were rimmed in red, lines radiating from the outer corners. "We thought you were dead. The guide, he . . . he said . . ."

Philip patted her mother's arm. "He said there'd been a fall, and you'd gone on alone in abominable conditions." His eyes narrowed, moving from Margie to Ford. "He intimated Ranger Brayden was leading you to your death."

"Margie, Margie," her mother placed trembling palms on Margie's cheeks. "Why did you do this to me?"

Has she ever called me Margie? Hot tears flooded Margie's eyes, an ache growing in her chest. "I didn't mean to worry you."

"We wouldn't have even been aware, if Philip hadn't telephoned." Mother pulled her into a stiff embrace, the sable stole crushed against Margie's cheek. "Your father's in the capital, or else he'd be here, too."

Ford cleared his throat. "It was uncertain for a bit, but we managed to keep each other alive."

Mother drew back, her eyes like flint. "And what does that mean, young man?"

His mouth opened a hair, his lips raw and cracked. "I only meant, you would have been proud of your daughter, ma'am. She has a very level head." He glanced at Margie with a nod, his gray eyes as warm as she'd ever seen them.

"You can't blame Ford for what happened." The pain in her mother's face dug at Margie's heart. "Philip said he'd stop construction if I managed the climb—"

"Now, now." Philip raised a hand to stop her flow of words. "The crowd got a little unruly. I never intended you to risk your life over a little wager."

Margie folded her arms, clenching her fists behind her elbows.

Mother frowned. "Margaret, you've always been far too impulsive."

Philip smoothed the front of his ivory linen suit. "The newspapers were quite excited to cover the story of a senator's daughter setting out to climb the state's highest peak. Your story sold a lot of papers, I'm sure. Sadly, they seemed equally hungry for the story of you being lost on the mountain. Disturbing, really." He clucked his tongue. "It was a grand attempt, Margaret. You should be proud. A shame it failed."

Ford wanted nothing more than to wipe the condescending smile off Carmichael's face. But this was Margie's story to tell. He folded his arms and waited.

"We didn't fail!" The words exploded from her mouth. "We reached the summit this morning." She turned to Ford. "Tell them."

"The lady's right. We summited this morning just after daybreak."

Carmichael's jaw dropped. "Nonsense. You couldn't have."

"Are you calling me a liar?" The redness of Margie's cheeks deepened as if a fire had been kindled somewhere under the skin.

The man scowled. "You were to summit with the guide. Just because you and Daniel Boone, here"—he darted a withering glance at Ford—"traipsed off alone—terrifying us all—you expect us to believe these grandiose claims? For all we know, he planned some sort of tryst."

Ford surged forward, his fist latching onto the man's lapel. "You want to repeat that accusation?"

Carmichael gripped Ford's wrist, his sudden action somehow eliciting a cool smile. "Then tell us where you were last night, Mr. *Ranger*. Wandering through a blizzard, perhaps? Or were you denned up some place like a couple of wolves?"

Suddenly appearing at Ford's elbow, Luke gripped Ford's bicep and tugged. "Ford, let him go."

"Ford, stop." Margie's voice rang out behind him.

Ford granted himself one small shove as he released Carmichael's suit. The man had a way of sucking all the manners right out of him.

Carmichael coughed once, as if Ford had managed to get his hands around his throat instead of his jacket.

Lord, keep me from choking the man. Not the most pious choice for one of his first prayers. Hopefully God would understand.

"We've all read accounts of polar explorations gone wrong. You know how they stayed alive, don't you?" He looked pointedly at Margie, his gaze like burning coals. "Tell me I'm wrong, Margaret. Tell me you didn't spend the night cocooning with this mongrel like two animals in heat."

Ford's vision tunneled. Before he could stop it, his right fist shot through the air, knocking Carmichael off his feet.

Margie pushed forward. "Stop it. Both of you."

Luke jumped in front of Ford, muscling him backward. "Don't! Don't let him do this to you."

Ford wrestled against his friend's hold. If that man got up, he wanted to be ready.

The businessman pushed up on one arm, touching the bleeding corner of his lip with his thumb. He glared at Ford. "You'll regret that."

"Never." Ford spat the word over Luke's head.

Luke shook him. "Margie doesn't want this."

Ford looked at Margie blocking his path back to Carmichael. The sight of her tears melted every bit of fight from his muscles. He slackened his grip on Luke's arms, a hollow opening in his stomach. She didn't still have feelings for the cad, did she? At least she hadn't moved to assist him.

Mrs. Lane turned toward her daughter, her cheeks pale. "Margaret, where were you? Is what Philip says true?"

Color crept up Margie's neck as she looked at the floor. "We did spend the night together."

Her mother stumbled back, her hands covering her ears. "No, I can't be hearing this."

Carmichael clambered to his feet. "I knew it. Now that'll make a sensational story for the papers, won't it?" He jabbed his finger toward Margie. "And you expect us to believe your claims about reaching the crest?"

Ford fought against the venom threatening his voice. "Would you prefer her to have frozen to death? Is that what you wanted?"

The businessman rounded on Ford. "I expected you would have more honor than to drag her into such a dangerous and shameful situation. You should be fired. I plan to make it my personal mission to see that you are."

"No." Margie moved toward Carmichael, her face pained. "Philip, don't. This was my fault. You must see that. I only wanted to convince you this development you're planning is a bad idea."

He jutted his chin. "The bad idea was letting you hope you could stop me from moving forward. Since you didn't summit with the guide, our deal is off."

"You can't do that," Ford snapped. "You said she had to reach the summit, and she did. I'm her witness."

Carmichael laughed. "Like I'd take your word for anything." He snapped his fingers toward Luke. "Johansson, tell the foreman to begin immediately. We've delayed far too long as it is. I want the foundation laid before the snow falls."

Luke hesitated, glancing between Ford and Carmichael as if expecting more sparks to fly. Shoulders lowering, he left the dining room.

Margie balled her fists. "What you're doing will ruin the whole area. You can't just bulldoze the meadows."

"Don't worry, Margaret. Once my lodge is complete, we'll plant some nice petunias out front. It'll look splendid. Ranger Brayden won't mind a bit, since he'll be long gone anyway."

Her face crumbled. "What can I say to convince you to leave this mountain—and Ford—alone?"

Ford's stomach twisted. "Margie—"

"Tell me what it will take, Philip." Margie's voice cracked as she pressed hands over her ruddy cheeks. "I'll do anything."

"Margie, don't do this. Don't play into his whims." Ford grabbed her elbow, turning her toward him. "Let him have the Inn, the valley, the whole park. You're worth more than any of it."

Carmichael sneered, his head cocked to one side. "And he has a pretty good understanding about your worth. Ask him how much your father poured into his building fund. What was it, Brayden—about five thousand? Ten? I'm not the only one getting ready to break ground in this park, am I?"

A cold sweat washed over Ford. *He can't know about that.*

Margie's eyes widened. She took a step back, leaving Ford's hands hanging empty. "What is he talking about?"

Carmichael folded his arms. "It's simple, Margaret. That's how much money he's taking off your daddy in exchange for chaperoning you on your fantasy of working in the wilderness. Somehow I doubt Senator Lane expected the arrangement would include amorous attentions, but I suppose he's getting a decent value for his dollar."

Margie's mother gasped, looking from Margie to Ford.

Tears welled up in Margie's eyes. "Ford?"

"Margie, I-I'm sorry." The words tore at his throat.

"You . . . took money from my father?" Her brow furrowed. "I'm only here because he paid you?"

Her pain slid over him like an avalanche. "Yes, but—no. Not—"

"Oh, look. There are the newspaper men now." Carmichael waved at two men in navy suits standing at the entry to the dining room. "What should we tell them?"

Mrs. Lane grabbed Margie's arm, drawing her around the table to the far side. "Margaret, this scandal will ruin your father. Is that what you want?"

Margie's face sagged. With her curls jutting in every direction and the flannel shirt hanging from her slender frame, she looked more like a war refugee than a member of an influential political family. "Philip, you win. What do you want from me?"

The man pulled up his cuff to peer at a gold watch. "Obviously, my proposal of marriage is off the table—at least for now. Perhaps, if you return with me to Tacoma, your father and I can work out an amicable compromise."

Margie turned away from Ford, her expression hollow and empty. "Then I'm ready to go."

THIRTY-ONE

*F*ord walked into his cabin, shut the door, and let his pack thump to the floor. His stomach growled, but he ignored its protests and sank down on the bed. Leaning forward, he unlaced the tall boots and kicked them off. With a sigh, he stretched out. Just this morning, he'd stood atop Rainier with Margie, dreaming of the future.

He pressed both hands to his forehead, pushing against the throbbing ache lodged behind his temples. At least the pain proved he was alive. There'd been a moment, back at Paradise, when he'd wondered if they'd actually left the summit. Perhaps the volcanic fumes had created some twisted hallucination.

A knock sounded at his door.

Ford left his eyes closed, his tongue too thick to answer. Whoever it was would have to bother him another time. Just because he was chief didn't mean he was at everyone's beck and call.

A second tap echoed through the room, like the insistent rapping of a woodpecker.

"Go away." The words burst from his throat.

The door creaked open. "Ford?" Mrs. Brown stood on the threshold, a towel-wrapped pot cradled in her hands. "I guessed you hadn't eaten."

She cocked her head, a faint smile turning her motherly cheeks a lovely rosy hue. "You look like someone who spent the day on latrine duty. When was the last time you ate?"

He sat up, his head swimming from the sudden motion. Why was this woman always so concerned about his eating habits? "I don't remember."

"I've got beef stew. It's the best thing for exhausted mountaineers. Sticks to the ribs, as they say." She pushed aside a stack of books on the table and set the container down. "Come and eat. Good therapy for a broken heart too."

He lowered his head into his hands. "News spreads fast."

"Luke telephoned. He was concerned."

Ford shuffled over to the table and dropped into the chair. "He should be worried about his job—working for Carmichael."

She wandered over to the small cabinet by the window and rifled through its contents. "Don't you own a bowl?"

"I eat at your place, mostly."

She pulled one from behind a couple of mugs. "I see. This is one of mine."

"Yeah, sorry about that. I meant to—"

"Don't concern yourself. You're not the only fellow to wander off with my dishes." She filled the bowl and set it in front of him, adding a spoon from her apron pocket.

Ford breathed in the rich smell of the broth. "I suppose I should be worrying about my own job. Carmichael will make life difficult for Harry until he fires me." He lifted a spoonful of broth to his mouth, the rich liquid warming its way down his raw throat.

Mrs. Brown sat across from him and heaved a sigh. "Harry's been in this business a long time. He knows how to handle hotheads like Philip Carmichael."

She underestimated the man's power. *So did I.* Hunger hurried his hand as he continued ladling stew into his mouth. He'd consumed most of the bowl before he noticed Mrs. Brown staring. "I'm sorry. Did you want some?"

She laughed. "Oh, goodness, no. But something's different about you, and I can't put my finger on it."

Ford tried to slow his eating. After two days of little food, his stomach wouldn't appreciate being filled too quickly. "Hope it's not the smell."

Mrs. Brown wrinkled her nose. "No, but now that you mention it, I think a bath is in order."

The spoon weighed a ton. If he was too tired to eat, he was certainly too exhausted to bathe. "Later."

She nodded. "Tell me what happened."

Ford leaned back in the chair. Digging for the last bit of his energy, he told Mrs. Brown the story of the climb, the accident, the night in the cave, and the final push to the summit. Once he began talking, it was as if a log-jam broke and the words rushed out with little control or steering. His fears about Margie, his talks with God, the horror of watching her walk away with Carmichael—nothing was left out. When he'd finished, he bent forward as if the tension had been the last thing keeping him upright.

Mrs. Brown had listened without interrupting, but now she slapped a hand down on the table. "Ford Brayden, you walked up that mountain a strong man and returned a Christian."

A coughing laugh escaped his throat. "What?"

The twinkle in her eye deepened as she shook her head slowly. "You are so used to doing everything in your own strength. But how strong do you feel now?"

"I don't." His voice cracked. "I feel like . . . like someone has rubbed my heart across a washboard."

A grin lit her face. "Then you're right where God wants you."

"God wants me broken and miserable?"

She shook her head. "I don't think I'd go that far, Ford, but when we're weak He is strong. It's in His strength that we find victory."

Ford grunted. "I'm not sensing much victory right now."

Mrs. Brown pushed to her feet and went to lay her hands on Ford's shoulders. "Then I know how to be praying. Be sure that you are, too."

Margie leaned against the balcony rail of her family home, the breeze from Commencement Bay fluttering the hem of her skirt against her knees. She'd never appreciated the view before, the steep drop usually sending her heart rate into hysterics. Somehow, after climbing to the top of a fourteen-thousand-foot peak, standing here seemed like child's play.

And much more lonely.

Another tear slid down her raw cheeks. Her father was due to arrive home today. How could she face him? At least Philip had found a way to minimize her story for the papers. The last thing she needed was to be splashed across every scandal sheet in the Northwest. They'd reported about her climb but with none of the salacious details she'd feared might decorate their stories.

It had been three days. She didn't know what sort of humiliation Philip had planned for her, but it couldn't be as wrenching as hearing Ford had been paid to hire her. Her stomach lurched at the thought. She should have realized. Why else would he put up with a know-it-all woman, who actually knew nothing of any value.

Margie gripped the wood railing, gazing out to where the Olympic Mountains decorated the horizon across the bay. The jagged peaks held a mystic beauty, but not the overwhelming stature of Mount Rainier. When she closed her eyes, she could still see her cottage nestled under the mighty cedars and firs, a generous coating of needles covering the shake roof. Only it was gone, nothing but a pile of charred cinders.

A tender ache had settled in the depths of her chest over the past days. What did her future hold? She'd dreamed of nothing but the mountain for years. Now, even if she could return, she wouldn't be able to face Ford. All those things he'd said—how she had a gift of working with the public, how she'd opened his eyes to the intricacies of nature—were they more lies? Sweet compliments paid for in full by her father?

"There's my darling girl." Her father's voice carried out across the balcony as he poked his head out from the upstairs library.

She wiped a quick hand over her eyes before hurrying over to him. "You're home."

He took her into his arms. "And so are you. How we've missed you."

Margie laid her head on his shoulder, tamping down the emotions welling up inside. "I don't know how everything went downhill so fast."

"We all have mountains and valleys in our lives, Margie. This summer was your mountain time. Now you've got to face the lowlands."

"Thanks to Philip."

"My dear, there's always a Philip. The question is, how does one deal with a person like him?"

She lifted her head and met her father's eyes. "Does that mean you have an idea?"

His face held more lines and shadows than she remembered. "One, but I don't think your mother is going to like it." He took Margie's hand and led her inside, closing the French doors. "Philip is holding two things over you."

Margie followed her father to two damask chairs and sat across from him. "The park, for starters."

He leaned forward, bracing against his knees. "Yes. But he's also using me—threatening to smear my campaign with his gossip." Father drew a hand across his scalp, smoothing the few hairs that remained after a lifetime in political office.

"He's added a third item." A weight settled in her heart.

"Oh?"

She lowered her eyes. "Ford. Philip wants him fired."

Her father touched her wrist. "And you've grown fond of the ranger."

"Yes." Margie blinked back tears, squeezing the bridge of her nose. "I wish I'd known he was on your payroll."

He pulled his hand back. "My payroll? Ranger Brayden?"

"Isn't he? Philip said . . ." She thought back through the altercation, her breath catching.

Father chuckled. "And why would you believe anything he says?"

"But Ford didn't deny it."

He shook his head. "I understand the confusion. I promised a donation to the superintendent. It was something I'd planned anyhow, considering my role in their money troubles. I knew there were plans in the works for a new administration building, and I felt I was to blame for the delay." Father shrugged. "Now, I may have mentioned it when I telephoned Superintendent Brown about your interest in working up there . . ."

"Conveniently."

"Yes. Perhaps. But I would have made the donation regardless of his decision—and I told him as much. I wasn't paying for your upkeep, if that's what concerns you."

The squeezing pressure in her chest eased a little. It didn't take away the humiliation, but at least it softened the blow. "Philip said something else that confused me. When I mentioned how you paid for his time at Harvard, he said, 'If that's what he wants to believe hap-

pened with the money, who am I to argue?' You did pay for his education, didn't you?"

"I did." Father drummed fingers on his knees. "Or so I was told."

A knot formed in Margie's stomach. What sort of game was Philip
playing?

Father glanced around the room. "You and Philip spent a lot of time
in here when you were young. Do you remember?"

The library's walls embraced her like an old friend. "Of course. On
rainy days we'd come in here and play checkers, backgammon, or cards.
He taught me a few card games Mother didn't approve of."

"And who won most of those games?"

"He did." The memory sent heat flushing through her body. "Always.
And if I was close to winning, he'd change the rules."

"You used to storm into my office complaining about injustice."

"And you told me to fight my own battles."

Her father nodded, tapping two fingers against his lips. "And how did
that work out?"

Margie took a deep breath, this foray into her childhood memories
taking a toll. They'd had lovely times, too, usually away from home.
Something about spending time inside her house turned Philip nasty. Perhaps it was the reminder of what he was missing in his own home. "He'd
argue his point until I gave up. Quarrels were just another thing for him to
win. I didn't like him much when we were at odds. I'm not sure why I put
up with it for so long."

Her father scooted forward in his seat. "Fighting with Philip Carmichael is like wrestling one of those silly fingertrap toys from Chinatown.
The more you squirm, the tighter his hold."

Margie pondered his words. "Are you saying we should just let him
have his way?"

"I'm saying, we need to stop playing his game entirely."

"And how do we do that?"

"I've already taken the first step." Her father unbuttoned his suit jacket, letting it fall open. "I resigned my Senate seat."

Ford herded the line of boys along the Alta Vista Trail, careful to keep them together. As usual, there were two who wanted to race ahead and others who whined and dragged behind. "Come on, men. We're going to see a glacier. That's pretty exciting, isn't it?"

"What good is a glacier?" The scruffy-haired lad beside him snorted. "They just sit there. I'd rather have ice cream."

"Mr. Ranger?" A youngster in short pants tugged on Ford's jacket. "Are we going to see bears? My dad said to watch out for bears."

"Probably not." Ford laid a hand on the kid's shoulder. "The huckleberries are pretty much spent, so they're off looking for other grub right now. Storing up for winter, you know?"

"Aw, man. I wanted to see a bear." The boy's face screwed up into a classic pout. "My sister said she saw a bear at the campground last year, and it could dance."

The first boy groaned. "We're not going to see anything good."

Where was Margie when he needed her? She'd always been the Pied Piper, leading bands of visitors up and down these trails like they were on some sort of magical adventure even if they saw nothing but rocks and plants. He jostled the loud-mouthed complainer. "You know what that is?" He gestured toward a tiny bloom with four blue-violet petals.

"It's a flower." The child huffed, pulling his cap low over his eyes. "Flowers are for girls."

Hard to argue that one. "Come along. We've got a glacier to see. I'll tell you how climbers cross crevasses safely."

The group fell in behind him, hushed conversations buzzing like a swarm of bees across the meadows. It was difficult to believe almost a week had passed since Margie had left. Every time he stepped out of his cabin, his eyes were drawn to the remains of her charred shack. If she ever returned, he'd make sure she had the finest quarters in Longmire.

If only he had told Margie about her father's donations when he had the chance. Why had he hidden it from her? His throat tightened. *Because you're a fool.*

"You walked up that mountain a strong man and returned a Christian." Mrs. Brown's words rattled in his empty heart. Pride had always stood in his way. It led him to accept his father's post, even when he knew he wasn't ready. It kept him from developing friendships with his crew and almost prevented him from accepting Margie for who she was. Worst of all, pride had stood in his way of understanding God's love.

After entertaining the boys with climbing stories and then returning them to their parents, Ford headed for the Paradise ranger station. Being on the trail without Margie left a gnawing hole in his chest. After a quick lunch, he'd drive back to Longmire and start work on the August reports—if he could bear to face the typewriter.

Superintendent Brown waited at the desk, his face drawn.

Ford's heart kicked into overdrive. "What's happened? An accident?"

Harry pushed his hands into his pockets, rocking on the balls of his feet. "Ford, I need to speak with you."

Ford dropped his hat onto the coat rack and shook off his jacket. "I assumed as much." A heaviness lowered itself into his stomach. Harry's tone left little doubt what lay ahead. Ford had been dreading this moment since Margie left.

"Ford, you know I admire you. You've done fine work here for the park, and your father was one of my best friends." The man cleared his throat, as if the words clung to the insides of his mouth.

Ford remained on the visitors' side of the long counter, a sick feeling descending over him. "Say it, Harry."

The superintendent sighed, laying both hands flat on the wooden surface. "It has come to my attention that you willfully endangered a member of our staff and then proceeded to lead her into a compromising situation."

"Harry, you know that's not—"

"She's a pretty gal, Ford. I should have seen it when I delivered her to your doorstep three months ago. It was a mistake to expect an unmarried woman to work side by side with the ranger crew. It was my mistake."

A rush of heat crawled up Ford's backbone. "You said the park needed the money. Facilities and repairs."

"I should never have agreed to the arrangement. It put you and the other men in an awkward position. We should have anticipated this."

"This what?" Ford thunked his palms down on the counter's edge. "That an educated, imaginative woman would put us all on our toes and make us far better rangers than we'd ever been before? That she'd show us that park work is more than clearing wind-downed trees and busting trails?"

Harry's brow crumpled. "Ford, you know I hate to do this."

"You're going to let Carmichael bully you into decisions about the staff? If that's the case, maybe I should get out of here while I can."

"I have no choice. I have to let you go." His boss's face had taken on a hint of gray.

Harry's voice sounded distant, as if Ford had somehow retreated down a dark tunnel. Fired? Had it really come to this?

"And Ford, you should know"—the superintendent leaned forward, resting all his weight on his elbows—"the petition didn't come from Carmichael."

The breath vanished from Ford's chest. "Then . . . who?"

"Margie."

THIRTY-TWO

*L*ess than a week later, Ford slouched at the end of the long table in the Paradise Inn, the white cloth napkins a stark contrast against the glossy wood. *This is like attending your own funeral.* Staff had arrived from every corner of the park to say good-bye, thanks to Luke's devious scheming. Jennings and Carson sat at the far end, surrounded by friends from White River, Ohanapecosh Hot Springs, and Paradise.

Slinking away under the shelter of night without saying a word to anyone would have been preferable. What could be more uncomfortable than to look each ranger in the eye, searching his face for either sympathy or condemnation? Most of the men had rallied to his cause. Unfortunately, listening to them take potshots at Margie and women like her sucked away any pleasure in their support. *They don't understand anything, Lord. I'm the one at fault.*

Obviously he'd driven her to lash out. Not only did she regret falling for him, now she was determined to ruin him. Who could blame her?

Luke leaned close, trying to be heard over the nearby conversations. "Where are you going to go? You've lived your whole life in park housing, haven't you?"

The truth of his friend's words hung over him like an old coat. He'd never known anything else. "I thought I'd hop the train to Seattle. Then maybe Alaska." It seemed as good a place as any. He could disappear into the woods and never face anyone again.

"Maybe you could get work at that Mount McKinley Park."

"Maybe." Ford stared out the long bank of windows. Hopefully this would be done soon. He'd heard a rumor Carmichael would be at the Inn today. The last thing he wanted was to hear parting jabs from that snake.

A hand touching his shoulder drew his attention back to the party. Henrik Berge stood at his side, his cap pulled low over his eyes. "Ford, can I speak to you?" He glanced down the long table. "In private?"

Anything to get away from this wake. Ford set his napkin atop his plate and leaned toward Luke. "I'll be right back."

"Better hurry or we won't save you any dessert. Huckleberry cobbler."

Pushing up from his seat, he followed Berge out to the lobby. The man aimed for a deserted corner of the long hall. When they arrived, the guide's eyes scanned the open space, taking in every occupied seat and alcove. "I need to tell you something—clear the air."

Ford pressed his hands into his pockets. Was he finally going to hear details of his father's death? On a day like this? "I'm listening."

Berge fiddled with the clasps on his wool sweater. "The guides—we don't work for the National Park Service. I never worked under you. I wish I had."

"What are you talking about?" The man's nervous shuffling was getting irritating.

"When I took you and Miss Lane on that climb, I was working for the RNPC."

"Obviously." Ford snapped out the word, then paused, realization sinking down on him like an early snowfall. "You mean—"

"I answer to Carmichael."

A chill washed over Ford. He took a step closer to the Norwegian, glancing about the room to make sure the subject of the conversation wasn't lurking around somewhere. "And?"

"He wanted to make sure she didn't summit."

I'll kill the man. Both of them. "That's why you faked the fall."

Grooves formed in Berge's forehead. "He said whatever it took. I got the sense he wouldn't have been disappointed if she'd never come back. But I could never do that. *Nei,* I thought . . . one little slip . . . would do it. The weather was going downhill so quickly, anyhow, I never dreamed you'd go on."

"And then you figured we wouldn't be coming home."

Berge closed his eyes, his complexion going gray. "I never meant to put you two in danger."

The blood pounded in Ford's ears. "And my father's climb?"

The guide's eyes flew open. "That was an icefall off the Kautz Glacier. You accuse me of planning that?"

"But you would have left Margie and me up there, just like you left my father?"

"I was mounting a rescue party when you two walked in." Berge backed away, lifting both hands in defense. He nodded toward the door. "Speak of the devil."

Carmichael strode through the doors, aiming toward the front desk like a man on a mission.

"Please, Ford . . . I'm sorry." Berge edged away. "And I can't work for that man anymore."

"Good plan." Ford pulled at his collar, suddenly longing for a breath of fresh air. He needed to cool off before facing Carmichael.

Ducking out the rear door, Ford let the late summer sunshine ease some of the tension from his shoulders. He'd already turned in his uniform, so none of the visitors gave him a second glance. Sauntering over to a log bench, Ford dropped onto the seat, scanning the mountain all the way up to its glittering crest.

Carmichael's flashy auto sat out front, its gleaming hood speaking volumes about a man who cared more about appearance than facts.

A dark vehicle pulled up and slid to a stop next to Carmichael's. The door swung open, and a rotund gentleman stepped out, adjusting the bowler hat atop his round head. He turned and surveyed the mountain and the Inn.

Senator Lane? Ford jumped to his feet.

Two other men appeared from the rear seats as the senator walked around the vehicle and opened the passenger door. Margie stepped out, her pink dress fluttering in the light breeze. She resembled one of her beloved alpine wildflowers.

Ford's chest tightened. He hadn't expected to see her before he left—and certainly not here. He hurried back into the Inn to give himself a minute to think. Did she expect him to be gone already? Likely as not, this was Carmichael's doing. Ford curled his fingers against his palms. He was done letting Carmichael railroad the woman he loved. *You're a fine ranger and a good man.* Margie's words swept back into his thoughts. *Time to act like one.*

Luke hurried across the lobby to meet him. "There you are. We can't have a going-away party without the guest of honor. Everyone's asking about you. Let's go back to the dining room."

He had to get away before Margie saw him. "I can't stay. Can you give me a ride down the hill?"

Luke's brows closed together. "What are you talking about?"

"She's here—Margie. I don't want to upset her any more than I already have, so I need to get out of here. In fact, I'm going to see Harry. I don't care if I have to take it all the way to President Coolidge, but I'm going to find a way to stop Carmichael once and for all. Now, can you help me?" A wave of heat crawled up his neck. Margie and her father were going to walk through the door any second. He grasped Luke's arm and tugged him toward the dining room. "We'll say a quick good-bye to the crew and then sneak out. No fuss."

Luke chuckled, patting Ford's shoulder. "I think you should stay for the whole party. Trust me on this one."

If Luke wouldn't listen, Ford wasn't going to wait around for him. He ducked back into the dining room only to come to an abrupt halt. Harry Brown was talking to Philip Carmichael as the crowd of rangers looked on. Who would he rather face—Carmichael or Margie? A cold sweat broke out across Ford's skin.

"Ranger Brayden?" The senator's voice boomed out behind him.

Ford spun around, all hope of escape vanishing. "Senator."

As Margie stepped out from behind her father, Ford couldn't help but notice that the windburn on her cheeks had faded to a healthy glow. "Ford, I'm so glad you're here. Luke was so kind to arrange everything for us."

"Luke?" Ford's world tilted on end. What had Luke arranged, other than his unwanted good-bye party?

The senator gestured to their two guests. "Ranger Brayden, allow me to introduce Henry Clark of the *Tacoma Daily Ledger* and Frederick Bailey of the Department of the Interior. I'm glad you can be here as well. The more witnesses, the merrier. That's why we had Mr. Johansson assure that as many of the staff were on hand as possible."

"I don't understand what's going on." Ford glanced toward Luke.

His friend grinned, touching two fingers to his forehead in mock salute.

Margie squeezed Ford's arm. "We're changing the rules."

His skin tingled at her touch. "I thought you were angry with me. The money—and the climb. Harry said—"

She stood on tiptoes and whispered in his ear. "I'll explain later. Just trust me."

Her smile sent a jolt of adrenaline through his system. Whatever she had in mind, he was ready.

Margie released Ford's arm; the mere sight of him provided the strength she needed to set this day into motion. If only she'd had time to inform him of her plan. He seemed out-of-place without his uniform, but it was obvious that the staff still rallied around him. The fact that so many of them had come at Luke's invitation spoke of their respect. The dark looks they were shooting her spoke volumes as well.

She'd felt sick the day she'd put in the telephone call to Superintendent Brown. He'd spent twenty minutes defending Ford's actions and arguing against his dismissal. It had taken the threat of involving her father and references to several dubious legislative committees to push him over the edge. She'd considered being completely honest with him, but she couldn't take any chances on the truth getting back to Philip.

Hopefully Ford would forgive her after the dust settled. "Wish me luck. Or better yet, pray for me."

"You got it."

His smile sent a surge of energy through her body. He agreed to pray?

Her father touched her elbow. "We can't wait any longer."

She nodded. "I'm ready." Striding across the floor, she joined the superintendent and Philip by the head of the long table. "Hello, gentlemen."

Philip's eyes widened. "Margaret. I'm surprised to see you here. I thought we were meeting tomorrow at your parent's home to go over my . . . requests."

"About that, Philip." Margie moistened her lips, willing her voice to stay even. "I'm afraid I won't be able to accommodate those requests."

Philip rubbed a thumb down his jaw. "You astonish me, Margaret, and that's not easy to do. I thought you had strong feelings regarding my construction plans here at the park and equally passionate emotions for a certain member of the staff. You'd just toss it all away when pressed for a tiny sacrifice?"

Tiny sacrifice? "You're right, Philip. I care deeply about Ford. But since he is no longer employed by the park service, I don't think that's a problem."

Philip jerked his head upward, digging in his vest pocket. "Really?" He drew out a small silver cigarette case and flipped it open.

Superintendent Brown took off his Stetson. "We're all here for the big good-bye party, aren't we fellas?"

Drawing out a cigarette, Philip shrugged. "No matter. There's still my agreement with Senator Lane. He and I are partners. As his campaign manager—"

"Actually, Carmichael," Margie's father interrupted, "you'll have to find another candidate to back. My camping gear and fishing tackle are all packed. I'm anticipating many quiet afternoons enjoying God's green earth. And then I'm taking my lovely wife on a long-overdue European vacation."

"You're retiring?" The unlit cigarette drooped between Carmichael's lips.

"Already done. I'm trading that other Washington for this one." Margie's father spread his arms wide. "My home."

Margie took her father's arm. "So, Philip. What's left?"

The corner of his mouth twisted upward as he glanced around at the gathering. "I can work around those minor details. I'll still get what I want. But this place?" He stared up toward the rafters. "It's going to make me a wealthy man."

Margie shook her head. "And here we thought you already were. But that's not exactly true, is it?"

Philip reached for a water goblet on the nearby table, the ice clanking against the glass. "You know I hate to brag, my darling. It's not money that matters in this world. It's drive, ambition, and education." He lifted the drink, as if offering a toast.

"I can't argue that you have the first two in spades." Margie's stomach churned. The time had come to call Philip's bluff. But as she knew from the past, he wasn't a man who took kindly to losing. She cast a quick glance at Ford, hoping his presence would lend her strength.

Philip's eyes narrowed. "What are you saying, Margaret?"

She folded her arms. "Where did you say you went to school?"

Philip's skin paled, slightly. He took the cigarette from between his lips and tapped it against his palm. "Why are you doing this? Have you gathered all of these people together because you're so afraid of me?"

Her chest tightened. Philip had spent his life slipping through people's defenses. What made her think she could put him in his place so easily?

Ford strode forward, taking a spot at Margie's side. "Answer the question, Carmichael."

Philip took a long drag, rolling his eyes skyward. "St. John's Preparatory Academy for Boys, and Harvard University where I graduated with honors. All of which you know, Margaret, being that your father paid for every cent of my education."

"Every cent, yes. That's a good way to put it." Margie pulled a notebook from her pocket. "The problem is, I telephoned both schools. Do you want to know what they told me?"

The man's Adam's apple bobbed in his throat. "You what?"

Ford cocked his head. "I think the rest of us would like to know."

"They have no knowledge of you." Margie flipped open the book. "Well, that's not exactly true." She tapped her pencil against the page. "St. John's said you attended for one term. After failing two classes, you withdrew your tuition and disappeared. Harvard has no record of you even applying for admission."

Her father cleared his throat. "I won't ask where my money went, but I believe the Tacoma Hotel and the Rainier National Park Company might be interested to learn that you falsified your paperwork."

The newspaperman flipped the page in his notebook, scribbling down details as quickly as they emerged.

Philip's face flamed red. "What does it matter? I've achieved my goals through resourcefulness and ingenuity."

Margie's chest ached. To see her childhood friend torn down to his bare bones dropped a cloud over anything she achieved here. If only he would have come to her when he'd had difficulties in school instead of showing up years later full of bravados and threats. "What you've achieved has come through chicanery and subterfuge. You've twisted everything I tried to do for you and turned it into something malicious."

"I deserved better." He strode toward her and knocked the book from her hands. "More than your pity, more than your family's charity. I wanted my own life."

She blinked back tears. Sadness would only play into his game, and she refused to abide by his rules anymore. "You wanted my life."

Deep lines formed around his eyes. "Who wouldn't?"

Ford wedged himself between them. "You can't play the victim here,

Carmichael. I'm not buying it. You decided if you couldn't have Margie, you'd get her out of the way, didn't you?"

Margie turned to Ford. "What are you talking about?"

"He paid the guide to sabotage our climb. Carmichael didn't want you to summit—and if you did, you weren't supposed to make it home."

Ford's words came as a blow. *Philip wanted her dead?*

"And I have a few questions to ask about the fire, as well." Ford jutted his chin forward.

Philip pursed his lips. "Like anyone will believe the word of a ranger terminated for fraternizing with one of his employees."

Henrik lifted his voice from the rear of the room. "They might believe me, *ja*? I still have the money you gave me."

Harry Brown stepped forward. "Mr. Carmichael, I'd take joy in escorting you off my mountain. And if you're smart, you'll leave the state as well." He lifted his chin. "Because I intend to pursue the investigation linking you to the arson at Longmire." He pointed to the man from the *Ledger*. "And I reckon by morning, the story of your little confidence game is going to be all over Tacoma, and it's likely to spread from there."

Philip jammed the cigarette into his mouth. "A few too many bloodsucking mosquitos out here for my taste, anyway."

"Here, you might want these." Margie handed him the deck of playing cards. "It's missing a few, but I'm sure you'll find a way to make it work." She watched the two men until they left the dining room, her heart growing numb. When had Philip become such a twisted mess of a soul? *Is there any hope for him, Lord?*

"Margie, you did it." Ford gripped her shoulders, a grin spreading across his face. His jacket hung loose on his frame, so unlike his well-tailored park service uniform.

"Ford, I'm so sorry about your job."

"I imagine Harry can restore my position, if you're willing to withdraw your complaint."

A laugh bubbled up from deep within. "I don't know. What about my job?"

"Does that mean you'd return to the park?" He tightened his grip on her arms. "Please say you're coming back."

She wrapped her arms around his waist. "I don't know. Would I get a hat this time?"

A laugh burst out of him. "For this—you can have mine!" He dug into his pocket. "And I have something else for you, too."

Margie stepped back so she could see.

He pulled out a small book. "I've been saving this for you."

"My journal?" Her spirits soared upward like a falcon coasting above the alpine meadows. "You found it."

He placed it in her hands, a slow smile spreading across his face. "Yes. Before the climb, actually. I tried not to read it, but . . ." He closed his fingers over hers. "But reading your prayers for me—it really helped me understand. I hope you're not upset."

She pulled him close, laying her cheek against his chest. "Ford, do you remember what I said when I first started here?"

"That you wanted to sit at the feet of a master, discover the secrets in the soulful eyes of the black bear? Had any luck there?"

"Of all the things I've said, that's what you remember?" A wave of heat crept up her neck. "One of my goals was to share God's love with at least one person while I was here." She drew back to study his face.

He smiled. "You succeeded."

THIRTY-THREE

October 8, 1927

The thin layer of snow crunched under Ford's boots as he and Margie picked their way up the rocky slope. The river roared below them, echoing through the forest. "It's not far now." He claimed her hand, a rush of little-boy excitement pouring through him. He'd been dying to show her this spot for months, and today was the perfect day.

The upper limbs of the trees swayed in the early fall breeze, the blue sky above allowing sunlight to dapple the ferns at their feet. He'd taken her off trail, winding around the long way to keep their destination a mystery.

"My legs aren't nearly as long as yours." She panted.

He slackened the pace a notch. *No need to hurry. We've got a lifetime.* Was it any surprise he was eager to get started?

She wrapped her mittened fingers around his. "I can't believe it's been a month already. And no word of Philip."

The name scraped against his thoughts. "Let's keep it that way." He squeezed her hand. "Today is just about us."

"Just us." Margie sighed, her breath curling up in a mist of fog. "I must admit, I miss living across the clearing from you."

Ford stopped for a moment and drew her into his arms. "We discussed that. If we're going to make a go of things, we need to be cautious." The sentiment had sounded reasonable at the time, but he regretted every day she didn't live within arm's reach.

Margie relaxed in his embrace, laying her head against his chest. "I know. It doesn't mean I have to like it."

"Paradise isn't so far. And the housing is luxurious compared to the squalor you endured at Longmire."

She squeezed his waist. "I miss my dear little cottage. I hope my pack-rat friend found a new home."

"I think the word *cottage* is a little too charitable for that old shack. Harry wants to tear all of those down and build a dormitory."

Margie jerked her head back. "Don't let him do that. I adore the little Thoreau-style cabins."

Her protest sent a wave of amusement through him. "I'll warn him, but you are quite capable of fighting your own battles."

"I know, but it's nice knowing a man at the top."

The warmth of her body against his lulled him into a comfortable peace. He could stay here and hold her all day. But he had other plans. He leaned down for a quick kiss before moving on.

As his lips met hers, Margie caught the back of his head in her hand, deepening the kiss before he could get away. The sweetness of her mouth sent his heart pounding, the depth of her passion pulling at both his heart and his soul. He grazed his lips up her jawline, nuzzling against the warmth of her ear and trying to remember why he'd been in such a hurry.

She giggled, pulling her head back. "Your nose is cold."

He pressed her into a bear hug. "That's because we're just standing here. If you keep distracting me, we'll never get where we're going. And trust me—you don't want to miss it."

Margie wove her arm through his as they began walking through the undergrowth. "You weren't complaining."

"No, I surely wasn't."

"Where are we going?" A question she'd already asked a dozen times.

He'd had her close her eyes when they left Paradise. Then he drove around for a little while trying to throw her off the track. "Where do you think?"

She turned and surveyed the landscape. "We're still at a pretty high elevation, so not far from Paradise, I'd guess—based on the subalpine firs. And it's obviously glacial outwash, so we're not far from the terminus of one. Smells like Stevens Creek."

"You can't smell that." He sniffed the air. "Can you?"

"Ha! I knew I was right." She tugged on her arm.

"You got me."

She stopped as the meadows opened out before them. "Wait—are we going to the Paradise ice caves?"

He pushed a fir limb aside, holding it in place so she could pass. "You said you hadn't seen them yet."

"No, because the guides and the climbing rangers lead all those tours. I hadn't cajoled one of them into taking me yet."

Ford squeezed her hand. "Hey now, no cajoling the other rangers."

She hid a smile. "I thought they trekked across the snowfields to reach them."

"Only because they like taking the groups nature coasting as part of the trip. People sure love sliding down the hill on the seats of those paraffin-coated pants. There are more folks lining up all the time." He played with one of the curls hanging just under the edge of her red woolen cap. "I was trying to surprise you. If I'd handed you an alpenstock and tin pants, you might have gotten wise to my plan."

"I probably would've wondered if we were heading for the summit again." She tugged on his arm. "I'm sorry I spoiled the surprise."

"I should have known you'd be able to guess."

"I'm glad we came this way. I've had enough glacier travel for one summer."

They walked on for several miles, taking the circuitous route Ford had planned. At least it gave them plenty of time to enjoy the afternoon together.

After the confrontation with Carmichael, Ford had let Harry hold onto his badge for another week. It felt good to make the man sweat a little. And it had given him time to enjoy Margie's company without the pressure of typing those confounded reports.

Even though he'd intended to hire Margie for the crew, Luke got ahead of him, asking her to take over some of the planning work for the RNPC as well as entertaining guests at the Inn with her poetry and nature talks.

Ford clambered up a craggy hillside and held his hand out for Margie. "How are the plans coming along?"

She made a face as she dug the toes of her boots into the steep slope and grasped his hand. "We've gone through the blueprints with a fine-toothed comb. I've explained why some of them are impractical, but there are others Harry's determined to implement."

"I'm afraid to ask."

After reaching the top, she brushed dirt off her knees and stood. "The golf course, of all things. Why would anyone tear out an alpine meadow to build a golf course?"

"Especially since the snowmelt will make it soggy most of the time." Scanning the land ahead, Ford saw the toe of the Stevens Glacier in the distance.

"And the cabins. Rows upon rows of little housekeeping cabins." She sniffed. "I know we need overnight accommodations, but why must they look like military barracks? How about some sweet little A-frames or small groupings of canvas tents down in the forest?" Margie bent down to examine a maidenhair fern sprouting from a crack in the craggy cliff. "No, humans are obsessed with order. They can't see the beauty in the randomness of God's creation. In the little surprises."

Ford touched the outside of his coat, feeling for the telltale lump of a certain item in his pocket. He knew all about surprises. "You'll just have to show them."

She sighed. "One person at a time."

Twenty minutes later, they were picking their way through the rocks to the cave mouth, where the Paradise River gushed into the light of the early fall day.

Margie grinned. "The birthplace of a river."

"Watch your step." Ford ducked into the cavern, the light taking on a blue cast.

She balanced over the loose stones, glancing up at the scalloped ceiling. Once they'd passed a few feet inside, it swept upward to over twelve feet high in places. "I can't believe it. It's like a church."

"Not like any church I've been in."

She placed both hands against her cheeks. "It's the light, like stained glass—except all cerulean. The summit cave wasn't blue."

Ford thrust his hands into his pockets and looked around, trying to see the place through her eyes. "Jennings told me that by the time the ice has moved this far down the mountain, it becomes quite dense and all the air bubbles are squeezed out. It absorbs most of the light, but scatters the blue rays—like the ocean."

"It's like stepping inside a sapphire."

"A sapphire, really?" He picked his way over to her, drawing her into his arms.

She smiled up at him, the dim light casting a sheen across her hair. "A little bit of an exaggeration."

"Poetic license." He pressed a kiss to her forehead. Ever since she'd returned to the park, he couldn't seem to get enough of her touch. Thankfully, the feeling appeared to be mutual.

Margie sighed, melding into his grasp like the glacial ice to the mountainside. "This cave's quite different from the steam vent we visited on the summit—though the other holds some precious memories."

"If I have my way, this one will as well."

She looked up at him. "What did you have in mind?"

Her lips drew Ford's attention, sending his heart beating in a rapid motion. He bent forward until their mouths met, the soft touch lifting the hairs on the back of his neck.

Margie curled her fingers around his collar, responding to his kiss in a way that stole the breath from his lungs.

As he slid his thumb along the silky skin of her throat, his heartbeat accelerated until it nearly matched the nearby stream. *And that's why she can't live across the clearing from me.*

"This would do." Margie tipped her forehead against his. "For a memory, that is."

"It's a start." A tiny thread of tension wormed its way through his shoulders as he dug into his pocket. "But I had something better in mind."

"Better?" Her breath tickled his cheek. "What could be better?"

Ford's fingers closed around the ring, the metal warm against his chilled skin. He stepped back, keeping a grip on her left hand as he lowered himself to one knee on the muddy cave floor.

Margie's eyes widened, and her cheeks reflected the luminous blue glow. "What are you doing?"

He squeezed her fingers, willing his voice to remain steady. "Margie, you know I could never give you the mansions and fine jewelry of your youth, but I can promise you my love. With it comes mountains, lakes, forests, and all the bugs and dirt you can stand. Most girls wouldn't think it terribly romantic, but I hope you say yes, anyway." Ford lifted the ring, squeezing it between his thumb and forefinger so as not to drop it in the dirt. "Will you be my wife?"

The careful words he'd scratched out on a piece of notepaper remained folded in his pocket. He hadn't gotten them exactly right, but the sentiment was there. He hoped it was enough.

Margie's skin flushed cold and then hot, her heart racing. *Did he just say that, or did I only imagine it?*

Ford remained balanced on his knee in the mud, lines forming around his eyes. "Margie?"

"The river is so loud, would you mind saying it again?" A tremor raced down her arm, all the way to her hand, warm in Ford's grip. "I want to be absolutely certain I heard it right."

The crease in his brow softened, a tiny smile playing at the corners of his lips. "Which part?"

"Just the last few words." The fog from her breath curled into the air.

"Will you be my wife?" He shifted his position, grimacing slightly.

"Yes." Margie threw herself down into his arms. "Yes, I'll marry you."

Her sudden motion pushed him off-balance, and they both landed on the wet ground. A grin spread across his face. "Thank goodness. You had me worried there."

She wrapped both arms around his neck. "Ford, I'm so happy."

He loosened her grip and clambered to his feet, pulling her along with him. "Let's get this ring on your finger before you change your mind."

She yanked off her mittens and held out her trembling hand. "I can't believe this. When did you have time?"

"Luke and I slipped away a few days ago. Tacoma and back in seven hours. It might be a new record for that rickety old truck. I also stopped by and asked your father for his blessing." He grinned. "Believe it or not, your mother was the first to agree. I think retirement suits them."

Margie gasped as Ford slid the ring over her finger. Twin pearls sat nestled together in a delicate gold setting.

He bent his head close, holding her hand in both of his, rolling his thumb over the pearls. "They're your pearls, Margie. I found them in the ashes of the cabin, and the jeweler cleaned them for me. The only two to survive, it seemed. And when I saw the pair of them together there—well, it reminded me of us."

Margie's heart swelled. "I love it." She lifted her hand to his cheek. "Just like us—together." She drew his head down for another kiss, her lips lingering on his for a long moment. Afterward, she slid her hands inside his jacket and around his waist, relishing the warmth against her palms.

Ford nibbled a few kisses along her earlobe before drawing back and smiling down at her. He glanced around the cavern. "I'm tempted to yell our news, just to hear it echo all around us. But I also don't want to bring ice down on our heads. Maybe we should step outside?"

"Or maybe," she snuggled in a little closer, "we should just stay here a little bit longer."

THIRTY-FOUR

December 15, 1927
Paradise, Mount Rainier National Park

Ford struggled through another drift, careful to tromp down the path for Margie. She was on the edge of exhaustion already and the foot of fresh December snow wasn't helping matters any. The seven-mile trip from Longmire to Paradise was a glorious hike in summertime, but ascending almost three thousand vertical feet while negotiating snow-drifts taller than a person's height was a challenge even for him. Margie had only used snowshoes twice, and here she was bravely placing one webbed foot after the other. "We're almost there."

She pushed her red knit cap off her forehead, her face rosy with exertion. "You said that two hours ago. I stopped believing you a mile back." Margie's breath came in puffs of fog. "I hope Luke has a pot of coffee on. Or better yet, hot chocolate." She gave him a pointed look. "Did we bring cocoa?"

"There's at least a year's supply at the Inn, don't worry. We're not going to run out of food." He scanned the route ahead, the sunlight creating sparkles on the icy surface. "Some honeymoon, eh?"

Margie puffed her way up next to him and stopped. "The best."

He slid an arm around her waist and pointed at a rise in the field ahead. "We're home."

"What?" She craned her neck. "Where?"

Ford grabbed Margie's hand and started forward, dropping his grip on her in a couple of paces. Snowshoeing didn't lend itself well to romantic walks. "Right there. Don't you see the smoke?"

She looked ahead. "The Inn's completely buried—up to the eaves."

"We'll be able to toboggan off the roof. It'll be dark inside, though. Sort of like being back in the summit cave."

"Except infinitely more comfortable."

It took another fifteen minutes to reach the Inn, where a tunnel pointed the way to the second-floor entrance.

Luke popped outside, a giant grin lighting his face. "I thought I heard voices. I'm glad you survived the trip. I've got the kettle on. Would you like some tea?"

Margie threw her arms around him. "I would love some. I'm so glad to see you."

"I'm sorry I missed the festivities. How dare you get married during the worst snowstorm of the year."

Ford unlatched Margie's snowshoes and helped her step out of them. "You weren't the only one who missed out. It ended up being a rather cozy affair."

She beamed. "It was idyllic. Like Robert Frost's 'Stopping by Woods on a Snowy Evening.'"

Luke led the way inside, steering them toward the apartment just off the huge kitchen. The stove kept the rooms toasty, and the hot drinks were a welcome treat after their long day in the snow.

Margie sighed as she sank down onto the sofa. "I think I'm going to sleep for a week. I am exhausted."

Ford folded his arms. "Then you'd miss Luke's departure."

Their friend grinned. "I can't wait to get out of here. Christmas in Seattle with my aunt and uncle—no snow, just lots of rain. Now that sounds perfect. I've spent the last three winters moldering away up here. I can't believe Harry talked you two into spending the rest of the season here. Are you sure you won't go crazy? Not everyone can stand the isolation."

Ford glanced at Margie, his heart warming. "It was Margie's idea."

"My own Walden experience." She smiled. "And Ford bought me a new journal. I can't wait to fill it with winter observations."

Luke chuckled. "Day one: Snowed. Day two: Snowed some more. Day three: Doesn't it ever stop?"

Ford took a sip from his steaming cup. "I'm sure it'll be much more poetic than that."

Margie folded her legs under her. "Besides, we're not isolated. We have each other."

Ford tipped his head. "Three months alone with my bride? Sounds like Paradise."

A blush tinged Margie's cheeks. "And that's how I talked him into it."

Luke shook his head. "You're a lucky man, Ford."

"Don't I know it?"

A bump and scraping sound made him jump. Something skittered by on the far side of the wall, making enough noise for dozens of tiny claws.

Margie's nose wrinkled. "Oh, no. That's not . . ."

Ford set down his cup. "*Neotoma cinerea* or *Tamias townsendii*. Perhaps even a *Zapus trinotatus*."

"You've been practicing. And don't even joke about jumping mice—I can handle anything except rodents that jump."

Luke shook his head. "No weaseling out now, Margie Brayden. I'm already packed. You two are on your own."

Ford settled onto the sofa next to his wife, sliding one arm around her waist. "Just you and me."

She pulled him close. "And dozens of pesky rodents. Do you suppose there's an Archibald Jr.?"

Luke cleared his throat. "I have some soup heating in the kitchen. I'd better go check on it." He slipped out of the room.

Ford took the opportunity to place a kiss on her lips. "I think we scared him off."

She laid her head against his neck, stifling a yawn. "He's just being polite."

He rubbed his fingers across her shoulders. "And you're sure you can endure three months snowed in with me?"

"I can think of nothing I'd love more. Come spring, Harry will have to drag me out of here."

Ford glanced at the darkened windows. "He's certainly going to have to dig us out."

She nuzzled along the tip of his ear. "I've already made a list in my journal about ways we can stay warm."

"Have you now?" He reached toward her pocket, the small book a bulge against her hip. "I'd like to take a look at that."

She squirmed away, giggling. "Later. We've got all winter."

His pulse jumped a few notches in speed. "Mrs. Brayden, I think this winter honeymoon is your best idea yet."

"I do believe you're right." Margie laid her cheek against his. "And for a few short months, the Lord is blessing us with the mountain all to ourselves."

"He's given me much more than that." Ford smiled. "If I'd known what a treasure Harry was delivering the day you arrived, I'd have been much more of a gentleman."

"And I wouldn't have expected you to be some mystic spiritual guide into the wilderness." She ran a teasing finger along his jaw.

"You were the spiritual guide. You helped open my eyes." He ran a hand around the curve of her hip. "It's strange—now I see Him everywhere. I can't believe I missed it before."

"I didn't actually do anything. It was all Him." She placed a kiss on his lips. "But now we've got the whole season to enjoy His creation together."

"Not just a season." Ford pulled her onto his lap. "We've got a lifetime."

AUTHOR'S NOTE

*D*ear Reader,

I hope you enjoyed this fictional journey through Mount Rainier National Park as much as I did. Years ago, I had the honor of working as a seasonal ranger at Rainier, and taking a peek further back into the park's history was a treat.

In several places, I simplified Rainier's history to help the flow of the story. Paradise, in particular, involved a wide array of buildings at the time including multiple dormitories, a day lodge, campground store, a photo shop, and many other facilities. For the characters to speak of the Paradise Inn, the Paradise Lodge, and the Paradise Camp Lodge might have been confusing. I imagine it probably was for people at the time too!

Most of the characters in this story are fictional, but I did use a few real names.

- In 1890, twenty-year-old teacher and journalist Fay Fuller became the first woman to reach the summit of Mount Rainier.
- Alma Wagen was the first female guide to work at Mount Rainier, hired after many of the male guides left to fight during the First World War. Though she primarily led glacier tours, she did occasionally lead summit ascents and became a popular favorite among climbers.
- In 1918, Helene Wilson was hired to check in vehicles at Rainier's Nisqually entrance. She was one of the first "rangerettes" (as they were called) to work for the NPS.

- I named Ford's father "Herman" in honor of Herman B. Barnett, who served as Chief Ranger during the era of *The Road to Paradise*. I didn't realize when I started writing the book that I shared a last name with the ranger who held Ford's position in 1927. What a fun coincidence! Ranger Barnett's descendants still live in the area and, like the fictional Braydens, the family continued to work at Rainier, actually boasting three generations of rangers. Thankfully, unlike Ford's father, Herman Barnett enjoyed a long life.

- And finally, for those of you who are familiar with the life and writings of Floyd Schmoe (1895–2001), I hope you recognize his spirit within the characters of both Margie and Ford. Hired as Mount Rainier's first naturalist in 1924, he is directly responsible for shaping the interpretive program at this incredible park. I was honored to work on the interpretive staff many years later, and his name was still mentioned on a regular basis. Schmoe's book, *A Year in Paradise,* was the inspiration behind the closing scene of *A Road to Paradise*. A longtime peace activist, Schmoe went on to build Seattle's Peace Park, and he also traveled to Hiroshima, Japan, to build homes for survivors of the atomic bomb. His organization was responsible for housing over one hundred families. May we all leave such a legacy.

I hope this story encourages you to visit our beautiful parks. They are a national treasure that we should never take for granted. Margie would probably remind you of the words of the great naturalist, John Muir: "The mountains are calling and I must go . . ."

Blessings!

Karen

READERS GUIDE

1. *The Road to Paradise,* the first of the Vintage National Park series, takes place at Mount Rainier National Park located in Washington. Have you ever been to Mount Rainier? Which of the national parks have you visited? Do you have a favorite? Is there one you dream of seeing?

2. Archibald the pack rat made a big impression on Margie during their first encounter. Have you ever dealt with unwelcome visitors in your home or while camping? What did you do about it? Which of God's "lesser creatures" (Margie's words) do you find difficult to appreciate? For me, it's spiders!

3. In chapter 4, Margie tells Ford, "The beauty of His creation speaks of the Father's love." Have you ever sensed God's love while experiencing nature?

4. Ford feels differently about nature. After losing his father to an avalanche, this is his opinion of the mountain: "Rainier cared little for those who walked its flanks. It didn't need their help any more than it desired their devotion." My eyes were opened to this truth after I misjudged a trail and ended up sliding ten feet down a rocky slope, stopping just short of a precipitous drop-off. How do you reconcile Margie's belief that creation is God's gift to humans with the inherent dangers found in wilderness?

5. Ford and Margie view nature in very distinct ways at the story's opening. Do you feel like they reached a middle ground by the end? In what ways did they change? Who made the biggest change?

6. When Margie is speaking of the Paradise wildflowers, she says, "Sometimes a fragile appearance masks deep strength." Is there anyone in your life who fits this description?

7. Mrs. Brown is one of my favorite characters, even though she doesn't appear often in the story. At a pivotal moment in Ford's journey, she tells him, "You walked up that mountain a strong man and returned a Christian." What do you think she meant by that? How does being strong sometimes stand in the way of our faith? Has God ever had to take you to a place of brokenness?

8. Margie never desired to climb a mountain, but God led her there. When she stood on the summit, she was overwhelmed by God's power and goodness. Is there a mountain in your life that He is calling you to climb—through His strength?

9. Don't you just love to hate the villains? Philip Carmichael was driven by a desire to control and possess. What caused him to be that way? (And don't say the author!) When you are faced with people who have nicer things and more advantages in life than you, how does it make you feel? How do you deal with jealousy, envy, and other dark feelings? After you discuss this, take a peek at Galatians 6:4–5 for Paul's suggestion.

10. Margie falls in love with her Longmire cabin even though she's
    accustomed to the finer things in life. What type of park accommo-
    dations do you prefer? If you were to visit 1927 Mount Rainier,
    where would you rather stay?

    a. Margie's Waldenesque cabin (with or without Archibald the pack
       rat)
    b. Longmire's National Park Inn (enjoying a rocking chair on the
       front porch)
    c. The Paradise Inn in summer (the finest room, if you please)
    d. The Paradise Inn in winter (with or without a handsome ranger)
    e. A tent in the campground (no dancing bears)
    f. A tent somewhere in the wild backcountry (you choose)
    g. Who needs a tent? (out under the starry sky)
    h. I'd rather just read about it from my own cozy bed.

ACKNOWLEDGMENTS

*W*riting a story set at my beloved mountain has been a dream come true. Thank you to the staff at WaterBrook Multnomah, particularly my editor, Shannon Marchese, for catching my vision and making it all possible. Special thanks to my agent, Rachel Kent of Books & Such Literary. I treasure your calm presence and wise counsel.

Many thanks to my critique partners for sharing both their skill and their encouragement: Heidi Gaul, Marilyn Rhoads, Christina Nelson, Patricia Lee, Tammy Bowers, and Rebecca DeMarino.

I owe many thanks to the staff and volunteers at Mount Rainier National Park, especially Brooke Childrey, Park Curator. I showed up on the doorstep of the archives begging for historical information, and she generously came to my rescue with stacks of documents, photos, and microfiche. What a treasure trove! Thank you to Greg Burtchard, retired Mount Rainier Archaeologist, and Donna Rahier, retired superintendent's secretary, for reading and offering suggestions on early drafts of the manuscript. Your knowledge and experience helped to breathe life into this story.

Thank you also to my supervisor, Jack Morrison, and the many wonderful rangers I served with in my two years working as a seasonal interpretive naturalist at Mount Rainier. Like Margie, I showed up with plenty of enthusiasm and book knowledge, but a definite lack of know-how on anything practical. Their patient teaching and mentoring shows up several times in these pages.

And finally, thank you to my family for enduring years of writing, research trips, deadlines, and overall craziness. I could do none of this without you.

I love connecting with readers, so I hope you will look me up on social media. To hear about future releases and other author news, please sign up for my free newsletter at KarenBarnettBooks.com.